BY THE SAME AUTHOR:

WHITECHAPEL

THE DRESSMAKER CONNECTION

An Edwardian Political Scandal

by

BRYAN LIGHTBODY

A historical thriller set in the shadowy world of Special Branch Protection about political corruption, its use for personal economic gain and its repercussions at the turn of the 20th Century.

authorHOUSE

AuthorHouse™ UK Ltd.
500 Avebury Boulevard
Central Milton Keynes, MK9 2BE
www.authorhouse.co.uk
Phone: 08001974150

©2008 Bryan Lightbody. All rights reserved.

No part of this book may be reproduced, stored in a retrieval system, or transmitted by any means without the written permission of the author.

First published by AuthorHouse 12/8/2008

ISBN: 978-1-4389-3006-0 (sc)

Printed in the United States of America
Bloomington, Indiana

This book is printed on acid-free paper.

Front cover design by Kris Knox-Crichton

For Michael Gyseman

And

William Dinsdale

Acknowledgements

Inspiration for 'The Dressmaker Connection' has come from many quarters. Some readers may recognise a little of themselves within the text. I thank you for fuelling my imagination. I would like take this opportunity to thank Mike and Mary Osborn for their interest in my work and for the use of their house in Spain; my wonderful wife Christine for her tolerance and support; my parents Stuart and Catherine; the late, great Ian Fleming for igniting my interest in writing; my friends and colleagues who have supported me and encouraged me in my writing endeavours; the agents who have inspired me to continue to write despite their best efforts; Glenn Stares for your interest and encouragement; Jay and Kris Knox-Crichton for their work on my website and the book cover; Ian Pratt and Sandra Walker for your proof reading and creative input; Susanna Shadrake, again for taking the time to read the manuscript; Mark Winter for keeping me upright on two wheels (most of the time); Sarah Banham, fellow author, thank you for your mutual support; and finally my very best wishes to Andy 'bloody nice bloke' Whitley.

Chapter One

Robert Ford had been in a deep and restful sleep before he awakened. Nothing had disturbed him; he just came out of a restful slumber of his own accord. He had visualised his time for waking prior to sleep. Seven a.m. He had become quite accustomed to such self-programming. It helped to keep him sharp in the dangerous profession he now indulged in. As he shifted slightly in the soft and generous double bed in his luxurious West London house, he could feel the warmth of another body pressing into the front of his own. It was soft and smooth, and as his eyes became accustomed to the early morning light that filtered through the curtains he remembered how he had come to be here. She was beautiful, possibly one of the most naturally beautiful women he had ever seen since his brief affair with Mary Kelly. Blonde, with a slim but curved figure; as he looked down he could see the generous swell of her breasts and her long lithe legs. Her slightly olive complexion would not have been out of place in the Mediterranean. The thought of her wild sensuality excited him knowing that he had yet again made love to her only hours before. Her back was pressed into Ford's chest with its smooth contours; he looked it up and down and saw the large Celtic tattoo on the small of it; such an unusual feature in a woman of that time but deeply erotic. Its pattern and colours were sensual upon the canvass of her radiant olive skin; it seemed to reinforce the sheer sexual allure that she possessed. In her sleep she must have sensed him waking and moving slightly; she rolled over to look at him, her long blonde hair streaming across her elegant, natural facial features. Her eyes opened and Robert saw again those deep-blue, pool-like eyes that he had first seen many months ago and had drowned so easily within consumed by sheer passion. So much had happened between then and now and he found it hard to believe that he lay next to her, looking into the eyes of the woman whose looks and personality had driven him to distraction seeing them abused so much by someone else. It had been nearly sixteen years since he had felt these kinds of emotions. Suddenly, as they lay there clasped in each other's arms, he realised he was in love and he would do anything not to give this woman up. Who was she? She was the dressmaker.

* * *

Three months previously

Robert Ford had been in close protection for a year having worked within Scotland Yard's Special Branch for the previous three years. It was being moved to a secret protection posting that had brought him to meet the dressmaker when he was assigned to the Minister of War. The Minister had become a target for an apparently lone, disgruntled and disillusioned serviceman for reasons that were as yet unclear to anyone. Ford perceived that the legacy of the so-called evolution of 'civilised' Western Society was the increasing need for high profile individuals to secretly receive armed protection. With an ever growing level of threat from the emotionally disturbed or 'fixated people,' bitter or dissatisfied citizens and the purveyors of domestic terrorism such as the Irish Fenians, allegedly struggling for independence for Ireland against 'British Tyranny', protection was a growth industry.

The longer he worked within the field of public service the more Ford despaired at the erosion of moral values within society and the dire leadership that seemed to vanguard this decline. The Minister of War, as Ford would discover, was a case in point in this matter; he gave the public face of being happily married with an admiring wife and loving children who were in the dark about him and as naïve as the rest of the cabinet and the public as to his true nature. He kept his wife's dressmaker as a mistress with whom he could do as he pleased. Ford himself would fall for her within weeks of first being introduced and once they became lovers he discovered that the Minister had been forcing sex upon her for quite some time. As the personal seamstress to the Minister's wife and being excellent in her role, she had begun tailoring for him too and was forced to travel with them on official engagements; but mostly on occasions just with the Minister at his request. She sadly had fallen into the trap of allowing him to degrade her at his will when he had discovered she was the single mother of a disabled boy. She had struggled since his birth to look after the boy whose father had been killed in army service. Money from the Minister for the sexual gratification she supplied kept the boy cared for in a private nursing home. The long term prognosis for the boy was not good with apparent heart and lung weaknesses and she desperately wanted his painful life to be as comfortable as possible.

Sometimes within him Ford wrestled greatly with a personal conflict of interest; would he really be prepared to face or absorb a threat of death for some of the people who over the years members of Special Branch had been secretly assigned to protect? He frequently found it a difficult question to resolve in his mind and normally answered it by thinking at a tangent of his colleagues; they were part of the team with the same goal of protection and his role was to be there for them in this task to form a cohesive response to attack. That allowed him to safely conduct his duties responsibly and professionally.

He met the dressmaker when he first arrived at the Minister's house in leafy Belgrave Square. He attended to introduce himself as the Minister's new personal protection officer heading the team that included a sergeant and a constable who would be charged with protection duties. She was there with the Minister in a recently made Saville Row suit that he decided he was not satisfied with. It was a dark, heavy, woollen weave double breasted suit that looked fine to Ford as he entered the room. He considered it odd that only the Minister and the dressmaker were in the room and wondered where his wife was; as far as he knew she didn't work. There was a uniform constable outside the front door of the grand Edwardian residence and when he entered the house he met Detective Sergeant Bob Spicer in the hall. He sat there comfortably awaiting any movements by the Minister. Ford had worked with Spicer when they were young constables in Whitechapel. They spoke before Ford entered the room.

"Rob, mate. How are you?" said Spicer standing to shake hands with a man who he had not seen for many years.

"Yeah, very well thanks. Where's the Boss then?" Ford replied amiably.

"He's in there having a bit of tailoring done with young Karen."

"Karen? Unusual name for a tailor?"

"Yes, I know. She began doing his wife's gear, then because she was so good he got her doing stuff for him." Spicer spoke casually and obviously didn't question this arrangement considering it to be the norm. Ford entered the room.

"Good morning, Minister," Ford spoke dutifully. "Detective Inspector Ford, sir." He remained stood just inside the door he had closed quietly behind him.

"Ah, Inspector. Good morning to you. Excuse me being a little tied up, Karen's got me covered in pins." Sir Cecil Patterson spoke in a jovial and friendly fashion. Karen Wood had her back to Ford as he entered the room but he noted her slender shape and flowing blonde hair as she crouched in front of Sir Cecil. She turned round as she stood to face him. He was staggered by her natural beauty.

* * *

North West Frontier, Afghanistan 1898.

Captain William Holden shivered with the penetrating bitter cold of the relentless Afghan winter, never before having observed his own breath almost appearing to freeze as he exhaled heavily; a result of his efforts in climbing the steep mountain path. He looked around to see his small party of men following him in single file with a mixture of steely determination and fear of the perishing cold on their frost encrusted faces. These hand picked men forming the experimental 'Special Raiding Party' were now undertaking their first mission in line with its remit established by the Minister of War.

The late 19th century had seen the invention of the internal combustion engine by German inventors Daimler and Benz. These engines were initially powered by coal based derivatives, but with the discovery of oil and the creation of kerosene and it's by product of petrol, it was discovered that petrol was a natural fuel for them. The problem in the latter part of the 19th century was finding oil in convenient and sufficient quantities. Early pioneers who had entered Afghanistan, a country that as yet had never been successfully conquered, spoke of vast underground lakes of shimmering 'black gold' that sat serenely beneath the Kuh e Baba mountain range. None of those pioneers had any idea as to what the substance was and its economic potential. The stories of what it was, now assumed to be oil, did not go unnoticed in governmental circles; it was deemed as being in the Empire's interest to confirm the nature of the substance in these great lakes and capitalise on it for industrial purposes. Sir Cecil Patterson for one, a shrewd and successful business man with interests in the burgeoning petrol-chemical fuel industries, was keen to monopolise this natural resource.

The Special Raiding Party was a small, secretive experimental unit established by Captain William Holden following an idea proposed to him by an old major he had served under, who was a veteran of the Boer War of 1880 to 1881. The major had seen the advantages of creating small and specialist raiding parties that could strike behind enemy lines suddenly and sporadically and then disappear. A unit that could also conduct forward reconnaissance stealthily without detection when required to avoid the unnecessary slaughter of greater numbers of troops. Holden approached men who he had served with personally during his army service to form an initial unit for active operations. He chose men with a combination of specialities and soldiering skills or experiences that he knew he could trust or be of value. He was a respected officer who had served much time in the light infantry and was therefore an experienced skirmisher. None of the six men he approached turned him down.

His second in command was Sergeant Major Nigel Green. He had served most of his years in the Guards regiments and had been on active deployment in Africa in the late 19th century fighting against native insurgency. He had just short of twenty years army experience and was thirty-eight years old having served with Holden when the officer was a young lieutenant in the Guards. Although at the time he was an experienced non-commissioned officer and Holden a relatively 'green' new officer, he could see the man's natural leadership qualities which proved themselves in the overseas deployments very early in Holden's career. Holden chose him as he was tough, resourceful, commanded respect and was a natural born soldier with the rare quality of being able to kill without remorse but when with good reason.

William or 'Will' Bayley was a full corporal in the light infantry with ten years military service around the empire in many different theatres of conflict. It was in this unit that he met Holden when he had been promoted to captain and had come to Bayley's unit as the new adjutant. Bayley was twenty-seven years old, had the typical lean build that came with the territory of being a skirmisher, but walked with a limp as a result of a spear wound to his right thigh. He was a Yorkshire man with archetypal belligerent working class views which he was never shy to express; this foible was most likely why he had remained a corporal for so long.

Then there were the four privates that completed the SRP. Holden chose the rank of 'trooper' over any other army subordinate title, influenced by time during his service with the Cavalry. He felt it befitted the work these men had achieved in passing his training for the unit and elevated them from the run of the mill infantry. They were all aged in their early twenties; Scots guardsman Jock Sutherland, 'sapper' John Waldron from the engineers, Welsh fusilier Cledwyn Jones and from the Durham light infantry private Pete Burwell.

These men along with the two NCOs had passed the training and selection course devised by Holden. They had successfully completed the tasks of a twenty mile route march in full light infantry marching kit across the Black Mountains of South Wales in six and a half hours, two shorter endurance marches of nine miles completed in an hour and three quarters followed by shooting on a one-hundred yard range in which they had to score ninety-five percent. Holden had created a special obstacle or assault course which had to be completed in six minutes over a half mile distance which included rope swings, elevated log walks, a ten foot wall and tunnels. Each had to complete a two hundred yard man-carry along with two rifles in ninety seconds, achieve an intermediate level sabre fighting qualification and competence in basic horse riding skills. This gave him men who were tough, resourceful, skilful soldiers and flexible; all of them proud to have completed such pioneering training and form this unique military unit.

All of them were in some way thinking about their selection and training process as they struggled against the thinning atmosphere in the frozen and desolate Afghan mountain range. The Black Mountains in Wales could be cold and treacherous as each of them had experienced, but it was nothing compared to the plummeting temperatures and lack of oxygen they were now enduring. It felt that with every step up, they took two back as they all occasionally slipped on the snow covered path or trod on some loose surface rocks which would send them off balance and subsequently back a few feet along the narrow and steep path they were desperately trying to follow. All were dressed in a local manner so as not to draw unnecessary attention, at least at a distance, with a practical but non-conventional British military field uniform underneath. It had initially proved a good barrier to the elements but now they reached the upper altitudes of the mountains the cold savagely bit into all of them. The visibility was down to only a few feet and Holden leading the party could no longer tell how close they were to reaching the summit of the ridgeline they were tackling, that would eventually drop down towards the Khyber Pass and the gateway to Afghanistan. This treacherous route had been chosen deliberately to try to avoid detection as they covertly infiltrated; the Afghans had never been successfully conquered and jealously protected their sovereignty, their homeland and its resources.

Finally with exhaustion about to strike, Holden gained some visibility and could see as well as feel under foot that they had reached a plateau at the top of the ridge and the descent ahead appeared less arduous. He called the good news that was echoed in turn down the line.

"Gentleman, we have reached the top and have easier going ahead. Well done chaps keep it going. We'll drop down away out of the weather and have a brew up." Looking around at the men he could see the visible relief on the faces of all of them as they received the news and then grouped around him on the plateau and viewed the descent.

They all carried a substantial amount of weaponry and equipment for their mission; each had a back pack covered in sheepskins that contained some tinned food, two water bottles a large thick blanket, dry clothing, wash kit and additional ammunition. They had belt kit too that consisted mainly of ammunition pouches, a holstered pistol sidearm and another water bottle. They each had what was entitled the 'survival pouch' that had a compass, some basic first aid equipment, a flare and flints with wadding to make fire. Each of them also carried a bandolier of ammunition, a cutlass or sabre and a bayonet. Their choice of rifle was the Lee Enfield; a direct 'descendant' of the Martini-Henry rifle made famous by the British army action at Rourke's Drift in Africa. It was massively reliable, had a bolt action with a ten round magazine allowing twenty to thirty rounds to be fired in a minute and had considerable stopping power.

They began the descent and scrabbled their way down the steep path for nearly a quarter of an hour during which time they came down several hundred feet and out of the freezing, snowy weather and into relatively calm, dull sunshine. Holden also spied a shallow cave alongside the path cut by flowing water which he decided made an ideal location for a fire and traditional British army 'brew'. The cave was deep enough for everyone to gain shelter inside, all of them removing their heavy personal kit and piling it across the cave mouth to create some additional draught exclusion. Bayley got a fire going from wood that the group of troopers collected from outside taken from the fledgling trees that grew coarsely upon the hillside. They sat round the fire warming themselves as it grew stronger and brighter fuelled by Bayley on a gradual basis. Sutherland unpacked an iron kettle from his back pack as Jones readied the tea, a strainer and some sugar. No milk, they would drink it black but sweet to try to maintain their energy levels. Burwell took a slab of Kendal's Mint Cake from his kit and broke it up passing everyone a generous portion; made up in the Lake District of Northern England it was produced with the sole purpose of giving hill walkers an instant energy boost.

They all intently and silently watched the kettle slowly come to the boil; Green was forced through the need to lift the mood to break the silence.

"Come on, Will, how long is this going to bloody take? You never could build a decent fire!" Will Bayley knew that Green was out to begin some morale lifting banter and was equal to the task.

"Beg your pardon, sergeant major. I'm not fucking Moses with a burning bush. That is how conventional fire works. Sir." Instantly the troopers either broke into a smile or a full blown laugh at this response. Holden felt compelled to join in.

"Pity you aren't Jesus. We could carry fewer rations because you'd be able to turn it to more to feed us all!" This worked to lighten the mood further and it kick started responses amongst the troopers.

The Dressmaker Connection

"You just want to hope that Jonesey's tea isn't that usual shit he makes up in barracks. I suppose at least here you can't keep using the same leaves making your usual maiden's water," said Burwell.

"Cheeky fucker, just you make sure you don't short change me for mint cake, you see."

"Do you know, hearing your accent just makes me imagine what it must have been like at Rourke's Drift," piped in Waldron.

"Listen, you'd sooner be surrounded by taffies than Zulus, mate," replied Jones.

"Not if I was a fucking sheep, mate!"

The group around the campfire erupted at the quick-witted reply as Bayley stood to make the tea with the kettle having finally boiled. Very simply to avoid using too many pots and pans, he put the leaves straight into the kettle and readied the strainer as he left it for a few minutes to draw. The entire group had got their enamel mugs out ready for the welcomed warm energy boost. All of them had long since finished their mint cake and began to feel quite revitalised. They each settled into a steaming cup of sweet black tea chatting and bantering in an increasingly good humoured and positive nature as they began to feel more ebullient. The SRP rested up for around fifty minutes before Holden stood and chivvied up his men again.

"All right chaps, lets get loaded up and get going. We want to make The Pass before nightfall and camp in the low ground."

He led the party again continuing down hill all now smiling and talking as they descended by paying attention to the world around them rifles in hand; they all knew that as they got lower the chances increased in meeting local tribesmen, shepherds or muhajadeen fighters, those that had always defended their country's independence. Holden kept himself on a high state of alert as the lead man, his usual position leading from the front, scanning the low ground ahead. He could get by in the local tongue as could the two NCOs as they had all received some intensive coaching before embarking on the mission. His continued vigilance paid dividends; about a quarter of a mile ahead as the ground levelled off he could see what appeared to be a small nomads travelling encampment. He was keen to get the locals support rather than opposing them so if they could win their confidence they may well assist them, perhaps for a price, in their quest. He had been instructed to offer local leaders, tribal elders or whatever authority he encountered arms in exchange for help. The Minister had foreseen as a result of previous forays that chieftains craved power and advantage over their rivals; new small arms technology always stood to offer that chance.

Holden stopped and called the men to huddle around him to be able to clearly hear his intentions. Green maintained a watch as Holden spoke.

"Right, gentlemen, there looks to be a nomad caravan ahead. They may well be able to point us in the right direction in our quest for a fair exchange. Follow any directions that myself or Mr Green give you." The party of soldiers nodded in acknowledgement as Holden turned and walked forward with the group following on. They all felt a degree of trepidation towards their first encounter with Afghans who had a fierce reputation. Parts of the Minister's briefing ran through Holden's mind as he approached.

Sir Cecil Patterson had promised Holden that if they were not heard from after four weeks a second party of conventional troops would be sent in on a rescue mission. If they encountered any violent opposition and could not escape due to weather conditions or being hunted, the SRP were to go to ground and wait for this rescue force. Holden began to feel a little ill at ease the closer they got to the camp and stopped again. He was sure that as yet they had not been seen but didn't want to take anything for granted. He huddled the men together again this time keeping low to the ground out of a line of sight thanks to the greenery of the lowlands.

"Men, just as precaution, I suggest that I go forward just with Will." He generally kept things fairly informal within the SRP, although through respect for his soldiering abilities the men still never used his Christian name. "If anything goes wrong and we don't call you all forward then Nigel will take charge and lead you men out, or if feasible, on a rescue. Do you all understand?" The men looked at each other and nodded again in acknowledgment, all staying in cover from view as Holden and Bayley continued forward.

"We don't want to appear aggressive in our approach, Will, so let's sling our weapons. You can always draw your Webley if needs be," said Holden quietly. Bayley nodded in response and they both slung their weapons across their shoulders.

The Dressmaker Connection

They had approached to fifty yards in before a young boy around the camp noticed them. The youth who was tending three goats ran into one of the tents silently and seconds later emerged with a large, thick-set, traditionally dressed nomad carrying an ancient looking rifle. The nomad kept it down by his side seemingly not wishing to bear any ill will which made Holden feel a little more relaxed. Holden and Bayley continued forward confidently to show no fear or trepidation to this man which in itself may signal ill intent. They came face to face at the edge of the camp. Holden spoke in Afghan dialect and placed his hands together in prayer like fashion and bowed his head.

"Greetings, may the peace of Allah be with you and your house."

"May peace be with you too, foreign stranger," replied the nomad. Holden knew that once at conversational range of people it would be obvious they were outsiders despite prominent facial growth and tanned weathered complexions.

"We are British visitors here to explore your land in peace and looking for assistance." The nomad then replied in fluent English, much to the astonishment of both the SRP soldiers.

"You are welcome in my camp. Come, I am Mahmood Baryalai, a tribal elder here. Is there only the two of you?" This was a major judgement call for Holden. Should he immediately show his strength here? If not he would be insulting them by later disclosing their number; they would find it a matter of deep distrust and threat. This man was also highly educated; he needed to keep him on his side.

"I am William Holden and this is Will Bayley, both of us from the Royal Geological Survey. No, I have other men still making their way down from the ridge line. I will send my friend here back to bring them here if I may."

"You are all welcome in my humble dwelling. It is the first chance to practice my English for many years, come inside."

He beckoned them into the tent from which he had emerged. Holden entered alone sending Bayley to bring the rest of the party forward. Inside the tent was laid out in very comfortable fashion. There was a fire pit in the centre, though not currently lit, which was surrounded by a circle of comfortable looking piles of cushions laid over with various types of animal skins. Scattered around the edges of the tent were items of wooden furniture, a couple of heavy folding chairs but mainly chests the size of which could have held anything from jewels to weapons. The young boy was still inside but there were no other occupants. As yet Holden had seen no one else around the camp.

"Surely, Mahmood, it is not just you and the boy here in such a generous camp?" Holden had noticed a total of four tents all of a similar size. There were also plenty of pack animals and camels tethered around too; Holden deduced that there must be a substantial number of members to this caravan.

"There is myself, young Ahmed here and my two wives, they are in another tent of their own along with some serving girls and my three daughters. There are also six of my personal fighters who are out hunting, my new English friend. Which is just as well as it seems we have many more mouths to feed tonight!" He gave out a bellowing laugh and slapped Holden on the shoulder as if he were a long lost friend. Then a quizzical look came over his face.

"William, I must ask, you are well armed for surveyors, yes?" Holden had already considered that this would be a question and was equal to it.

"Mahmood, we both know that the North West Frontier is a dangerous place. We of course need to defend ourselves from bandits."

Baryalai rubbed his bearded chin and nodded his head in accepting acknowledgement of the answer. It was of course true that it was a dangerous place for any unarmed people.

"Come, take off your pack and sit, rest as we wait for your men." Baryalai turned to the boy and gave him an instruction in a dialect or language that Holden could not quite understand. It sounded like instructions regarding hospitality, or at least he hoped so. Holden took off his rifle, his pack and his belt kit and then removed his outer garments down to his non-descript uniform. It was very much in the style of a heavy weight safari suit so it seemed to arouse no suspicion from his host. He wore a shoulder holster under the tunic with another Webley service revolver under his left arm and additional ammunition in pouches under his right. It was safely out of sight but provided him with comforting security.

As he seated himself there was a commotion at the door. It was the rest of the SRP entering in their weathered, grubby condition. Baryalai got up to greet them as Holden made himself comfortable amongst the skins.

"All right there are you then, Boss?" asked Jones, as he unceremoniously dumped his belt kit just inside the tent doorway. The rest of the men were following suit and seeing that Holden had also dispensed with his local outer clothing they too stripped down to their non-descript uniforms.

"Gentleman, welcome to my humble caravan, please, my home is yours. Make yourselves comfortable. Tea will shortly be served," said an amiable Baryalai beckoning them to sit around the circle with a friendly open arm gesture. The men wearily but gratefully accepted his hospitality and most of them simply slumped onto the skin-covered cushions sighing heavily as they did so. Their host remained standing and once they were all seated he went around in turn introducing himself to each of them giving them a firm sincere handshake.

As he finished this action with Nigel Green being the last for him to greet, the boy Ahmed returned with two of the serving girls that Baryalai had spoken of. They each carried a tray, the girls with steaming metal cups and the boy with dried fruits piled high in two wooden bowls. The girls were dressed in traditional long robes but were unveiled; their looks took the breath away of most of the men present who hadn't seen a woman for weeks. They had flawless olive complexions, striking green eyes, high cheekbones and full lips. Baryalai was no fool and he could see the natural male reactions amongst his guests.

"My friends, these two are sisters I saved from unlawful slavery in Kabul. They have taken a vow of allegiance to my household so you will find them immune to any of your charms. But please, admire their beauty and show them the courtesy they deserve." The SRP men looked at each other and nodded acceptingly, wishing not to offend their host. They each took a steaming cup and tucked into the fruit that the boy offered around. "It is mint tea, very natural and very refreshing. Let us toast our new found friendship and again I welcome you to my land."

"Mahmood, I know I speak for the men here of the Royal Geological Survey, thank you for making some weary and vulnerable strangers most welcome. We hope, either now or later, to repay your generosity."

They all sat in silence for just a minute or two as the gathered group enjoyed their refreshment. The SRP whispered amongst themselves as to how good the tea was, and joked that it was considerably better than their last brew. The girls and Ahmed waited to one side of the tent watching the men all now sat contently. With a hand signal from Baryalai one of the girls disappeared from the tent. Baryalai turned back to Holden to speak.

"So, William, what brings you to Afghanistan? What purpose does her Britannic Majesty Queen Victoria have for you here, hmm?" It was quite obvious to Holden and the rest of the SRP men that their host was no fool. His education had most likely taken place at least in Europe, if not Britain, and he would probably be very au-fait with the West, its ways and trends.

"Well, I will be frank. Have you heard of the invention of the internal combustion engine and its use towards building horseless carriages, Mahmood?" Holden spoke honestly and earnestly.

"Yes, I have. I have no doubt that in the developed and decadent West it may one day have a purpose. But for us, a country with no roads, it will never have any practical relevance," replied the wily Afghan.

"Indeed I believe you are very wise in this assumption, but nonetheless it will one day have a world impact. Not least of all in the need to have the appropriate fuel to drive these horseless carriages which is a commodity that brings those that have the natural resources potential riches." Baryalai sat back and rubbed his chin in a thoughtful manner as he considered Holden's answer. He knew what the Englishman was driving at; sadly he could see the natural human folly of greed would influence Afghans and could lead to the rape of his country for short-term gain.

"William. I appreciate your candour and what you speak of is very interesting. I assume you know or suspect that we may be rich in this natural resource?"

"Yes, rumour has it that under the Kuh e Baba mountain range inside caves are vast lakes of what has been termed 'black gold'. We suspect this to be oil, the product needed to produce lighting fuels such as kerosene, but as importantly a substance called petrol which is the fuel for the engines of these horseless carriages. Do you know of such lakes?"

At that point the serving girl returned with a tray but this time holding a smouldering pot of tea for the purpose of replenishing the men's cups. Although all intently listening to the conversation between Baryalai and Holden, each happily accepted her offer of more tea.

"You are right, William, such underground lakes do exist but they have brought many who enter bad luck. There are stories of men and boys entering with lamps or torches and instantly turning to fire themselves. And would you propose to harvest this 'oil' as you call it? You are a long way from Europe." Baryalai was now less welcoming but not, at least, aggressive or belligerent over the matter.

"That is an excellent point. It is something that us as mere geologists do not have to worry about. Our task is purely to confirm or deny its existence." Holden was careful not to use the term 'mission' for want of not sounding too military.

"I can confirm that it exists, William. So now that you know, what more must you do? Does that render your expedition complete, my friend?"

"Sadly, no. Despite the dangers you have highlighted we need to go to these lakes and draw samples from them to confirm that is the case. Scientists back in London need to test the substance to confirm its suitability for the refinement and production of petrol. So you see, we as a group must still see the 'black gold' at first hand. We would be grateful if you could offer us just overnight rest with you as the hour is now late and then perhaps tomorrow you could point us in the right direction. For that I would be indebted to you, Mahmood." The Afghan considered his words before he replied. It was a pause long enough to cause discomfort amongst the Englishmen.

"So be it. I would be failing in my duty to help a stranger who is now a friend to find his way. Tonight you shall eat with me and my family, then tomorrow at dawn my two best warriors, Hamza and Omar will go with you as guides to the Kuh e Baba region. I shall instruct them on your safe passage and return, William." Baryalai spoke with genuine hospitality.

"Thank you greatly, on behalf of ourselves and her Majesty. On our safe return you shall have all of our rifles and ammunition, Mahmood. I appreciate that life is as dangerous for you here as it is for us on occasions and they will serve you well. At that time we shall no longer have use for them. It is the only gift I can offer." Extending his hand to Holden, Baryalai replied as they shook hands firmly.

"It is generous and thoughtful. They will be gratefully received."

Then, at that moment, everyone's attention was drawn to the sound of men arriving on horseback outside. The hunters, Mahmood's warrior fighting men had returned.

Chapter Two

Only two men entered the tent. They came through the doorway flap throwing it harshly aside as they did so; both were covered in dust and sand with their faces caked with the combination of dirt, sweat and blood from their hunting activities. Both were fearsome looking men in their late twenties, appearing well built underneath their traditional Afghan garb, with leathery complexions and full beards. They were the antithesis of warriors so feared in the North West Frontier region and the type who ruled the Khyber Pass with ruthless efficiency. The Englishmen turned to look at them as they entered and could quite clearly hear a number of men outside sounding as if they were engaged in the post hunting activities; preparing the lifeless carcasses they unloaded one at a time from their beasts of burden used to transport them.

Baryalai stood to greet the men who paused just inside the doorway with stern and unwelcoming expressions on their faces. They were clearly not pleased to see foreign strangers in their camp.

"Hamza! Omar! Please, do not be so stern. These are friends from England, here to conduct a survey for Queen Victoria's Geographical Survey. Be welcoming to our guests my adoptive sons!" He spoke with passion to these uncompromising looking men and approached them embracing each in turn. They appeared to relax a little and came and took seated positions next to Baryalai either side of him back where he had come from amongst the circle of cushions and skins.

"Gentlemen," began Baryalai, "these are my adoptive sons as you guessed no doubt, Omar and Hamza. They are my best and most loyal warriors and having only been blessed with a son late in life, they will inherit my caravan initially once I am gone before handing it on to Ahmed. Each of them is promised to two of my daughters who you may meet later." The last remark prompted a reply from Hamza; taller than Omar he was distinctive from a large scar running across his right cheek and partially over the bridge of his nose.

"Father, it is not seeming to introduce these strangers to your daughters in these circumstances. They are not Muslims and therefore have a different value system and a lack of respect." Like Baryalai, he spoke with impeccable English. Holden suspected that these two men had been indulged as boys by their surrogate father in an education. Baryalai was, despite his nomadic appearance and lifestyle, a man of influence and wealth. Holden and his men would need to be cautious of Hamza and Omar not guarding their family position too jealously. In the wake of the last comments Holden quickly interjected before anyone else could speak, wanting to allay any fears the two young Afghans may have.

"Hamza and Omar," he began and then gave an Arabic respectful greeting sign, "may the peace of the almighty be upon you and thank you in advance for welcoming us into your house. I am William Holden of the Royal Geographic Survey. Please let me explain as a sign of respect to your great father why we are here." The apparent brothers looked at each other, nodded and then Omar spoke and gestured to Holden.

"That is kind Mr Holden, please speak freely, and may the peace of Allah be upon you and your party too. Hamza and I would be pleased to hear."

Holden stood to speak and once upright coughed to clear his throat before beginning. All in the tent looked to him as he began to speak.

"Myself and my men here," indicating to the gathered group of Englishmen, "have been sent here to discover the truth behind the legend of the 'black gold' in Kuh e Baba. It may be instrumental in the latest invention in the Europe, that of the horseless carriage. If it is, it stands to bring great potential wealth to the people of Afghanistan as the lakes of it, if they exist, will be easily accessible." Hamza eyed him with suspicion.

"You are very well armed for scientists, Mr Holden?"

The Dressmaker Connection

"As I explained to your father and as you know of the reputation of the area, the weapons are purely for self protection. I have offered all of our rifles on the successful return here from the mountains to your caravan as, once we depart, we shall no longer need them. I hope that you find that a sign of good faith equally as your father does." Holden spoke with conviction.

The brothers stayed silent for a few moments, looked at each other and then both began speaking with Baryalai in a dialect that Holden and none of the other Arab speakers could understand. The Englishmen sat uncomfortably for a few minutes as the Afghans had a hushed discussion. Holden remained on his feet. After a conversation between the three of them that seemed to remain calm, Baryalai spoke to the Englishmen with the same warm, welcoming tone and still with a smile on his face.

"Friends. Hamza and Omar have agreed to take you to the lakes of the 'black gold'. They are naturally concerned about our country being exploited but I have assured them that this expedition is purely to ascertain the nature of the lakes. With that they are satisfied but command full consultation from the British government over any matters beyond that." Holden nodded in agreement and responded to the news.

"That is kind and helpful. I shall ensure that diplomacy is used in any further interest." Holden couldn't help but think that perhaps these people were more than nomads wishing to be consulted on such a national issue. Were they local warlords, or chieftains? If so there would be more that six warriors in this caravan.

"So friends," began Baryalai anew, "feast with us tonight and enjoy the comforts of our humble camp. Then tomorrow you will set off with Hamza and Omar and some others on camels to get to the lakes under the mountains. I shall see you on your return." The serving girls appeared with more mint tea as he spoke and began offering it around. Holden responded graciously as he made roving eye contact with all as he spoke.

"We are most grateful after an arduous climb and descent to arrive. I thank you on behalf of all of us." The men of the SRP looked on to Baryalai and nodded respectfully to acknowledge his hospitality.

* * *

Dawn. With no cloud cover on the desolate plains on which the caravan was camped, the morning brought a heavy frost to all those who were party to the early hour. The camels had been prepared for the expedition with each man of the SRP, still masquerading as the Royal Geographic Survey, being allocated one each along with both Hamza and Omar and one other of the warriors. Holden, despite his suspicions, could still not see any other warrior types around, a matter which troubled him. Such an influential family must surely be a target to rivals for power and without a visible deterrent would appear vulnerable. He had not had a chance to brief his men on this concern and would have to find an opportunity during the day out of ear shot of their guides. The SRP men were back in their full travelling garb appearing very native with their equipment including their Lee Enfield's and sabres now lashed to each of their camels. They all kept their Webley service pistols with them as well as their bayonets. Each with horse riding experience, they would be quickly able to master the art of riding the camels; it was mounting and initial 'take off' as the camels got to their feet that seemed to present teething troubles.

Being the first one to observe mounting the camel and getting it to its feet, Holden had, by luck, managed it completely trouble free and gave the appearance of having done it before. Nigel Green was not so lucky. As he got on the camel, it turned its head and spat at him catching him off guard. Almost seeming to sense this success, the wretched creature quickly got to its feet whilst he was unbalanced. He immediately fell off the back of it landing heavily on the sand, which at least softened his impact. It nonetheless knocked the wind out of him as the rest of the SRP laughed at his expense. He was seething with the stinking animal as it refused to sit.

"Let's see the rest of you wankers do any better then, eh?" he barked at his subordinates. The camel now sat down again looking, if possible, smug.

"You fucker," Green hissed into its ear, "you won't do that again."

Cledwyn Jones had an equal lack of success. He mounted his beast which as he did so began to stand immediately. As he hadn't been central on the animal this slid him sideways so once it was fully standing he was hanging off of the left hand side of the beast trapped by his left foot in the stirrup as it slowly walked around the camp dragging his

The Dressmaker Connection

head through the sand. Everyone to a man including all the Afghans roared with laughter at the spectacle of the camel/man sand plough. He spat sand from his mouth as he tried to speak.

"Well don't just bloody stand there you bastards! Stop the bugger and get me off!" The boy Ahmed ran up to the camel and took hold of its bridal and coaxed it to the floor. The camel almost sat on top of Jones who screamed and at the last minute swung himself to one side to avoid a stinking suffocation underneath the flea bitten animal. Most of the SRP men had tears of laughter running down their faces by the time he was free of the animal. "You shagging bastards! Just you wait 'till it's your turn, you see. I'll just laugh my bollocks off too."

Eventually everyone was mounted and Baryalai approached Holden and spoke to him as Hamza and Omar looked on from the perches atop their camels. He extended his hand to shake Holden's and spoke.

"My friend, good luck. All things being well I will expect to see you back here within a fortnight. Then we shall feast once more before you return to England. Take care. My sons will look after you." They shook hands firmly as he spoke.

"Thank you for everything, Mahmood. I am in debt to you, a debt I shall repay. God willing we shall see you in two weeks as you say."

They unclasped hands and the camel train was led away from the camp by Omar, followed by Hamza and then the SRP with the remaining warrior bringing up the rear. Mahmood and Ahmed stood side by side watching them until they disappeared over the horizon.

Looking back, it seemed to only take half an hour on the desolate barren landscape before Holden or any of the men could no longer see the camp. They were well and truly on their way and certainly greatly in the hands of their guides as maps of Afghanistan in 1898 were virtually useless. Despite having compasses if they knew not where to go because of the lack of detail on the maps they would have to call upon all their survival skills to escape. Holden had had the foresight to call upon the experiences of many of the contemporary explorers to come and give lectures to his group and offer practical advice on the harshness and survivability of various types of terrain. Most of the SRP had some sort of background in survival field-craft from their years of service around the Empire. Explorers such as Captain Robert Falcon Scott, a serving naval officer, were willing to give up their time to impart their knowledge and experience to these pioneering soldiers.

They rode for three hours before Omar spoke to his brother and they decided to take a break. They were in the midst of a barren plain with only the occasional outcrops of scrubby vegetation that seemed to defy the odds to survive. There was no-where to take shelter, so the camels were sat in a rough circle nose to tail to create a central area where the group could all huddle from the wind. Jones and Burwell got a fire going to boil some water as the three Afghans looked on fascinated by their methods. They kept themselves very distant from the Englishmen; a matter that Holden felt uncomfortable about and decided he needed to try forging at least a civil working relationship between them. He moved from his position next to his camel giving the reigns to control it to Nigel Green and walked over to Omar and Hamza who were sheltering silently together by their own beasts. They looked up at him as he stood in front of them and then he sat down cross legged with them removing the scarf from his face that had been pulled round his head, as everyone had done, to protect his face from the persistent wind blast of the plains.

"Look, I appreciate we don't have to like each other, but we come genuinely only to explore. I don't wish to offend or exploit you only to confirm the existence of the 'black gold' lakes." Holden spoke openly. The two brothers looked at each other as they considered his words. Hamza removed his scarf and spoke in reply to the SRP captain.

"Englishman, we have never been conquered and will never be conquered. As tribes we hate each other but are always prepared to come together and fight a common enemy. If you are an enemy then prepare to shed much blood over this 'black gold.' We will not give it up willingly if it will bring wealth to our impoverished country. With fair trade and genuine agreement we may allow its use, but never try anything underhand." He spoke with cold sinister eyes that made steely contact. Holden sat silently for a few seconds considering these words before replying.

"I can only give you my word about the intentions of my men and myself. I can say nothing of the future so please at least consider that we travel in peace with a quest for knowledge and understanding of you and the people of this land." Hamza continued to stare at him, then speaking unexpectedly as he broke the gaze. He extended his hand.

"All right, Englishman, we will help you find it and you may examine it. Then you will leave. Do not come back or allow anyone else to come back other than with a fair trade." Holden took his hand reciprocally.

"That is fair. I will not let you down." They shook hands firmly. "Now join me and my men in some English tea and mint cake."

"What is mint cake?" asked Omar.

"Something that will boost your energy for the journey ahead." Holden took a slab from his belt kit and broke it into three and offered it to his now friendlier partners. They took some and began to curiously try it. Very quickly they bit into it feverishly indeed enjoying the energy boost. The third Afghan looked on with contempt under his scarf and settled into his own dried meat and water.

* * *

After days travelling across the rocky plains that stretched between Jalabad and Kabul they reached the base of the high ground of the Kuh e Baba range. The land had been gradually rising since the area of Jalabad but it had been the camels that bore the energy sapping effort that the journey had required. It was late in the day when they decided to make camp just outside the entrance to one of the legendary caves' systems that purported to lead to the lakes of 'black gold'. The atmosphere between the SRP men and the brothers had become cordial but the unnamed warrior continued to distance himself.

"William," began Hamza, "the light is fading and it is dangerous to enter the caves with burning torches. We must settle for the evening in camp and wait to enter in the morning." Holden and his men had a solution to be able to safely explore the caves at any time; they each were carrying a Davy lamp.

The famous Davy lamp had been invented for use in mining in 1815 by Humphrey Davy to allow deep seams to be safely mined despite the presence of dangerous combustible methane or other flammable gases or vapours. Davy had discovered that for a gas to explode it must be heated to its ignition temperature, so this had to be avoided at all costs to prevent disaster. He concluded that if the flame in the lamp is surrounded by metal gauze to distribute the heat generated over a large area then the maximum temperature of this screen should stay below that of the ignition temperature of the gas. The lamp was first trialled successfully at Hebburn Colliery in January 1816. Scientists had assured Holden that he and his men would be able to safely explore the caves with the use of these lamps.

"Hamza, we have a special lamp that we can use to safely explore the caves day or night that is best described as fire-proof. It is our intention just to enter briefly this evening and then fully explore tomorrow," said Holden. Hamza, now joined by Omar, looked at him with suspicion.

"How does such trickery work, Englishman?" asked the less friendly yet still benign Omar. Holden pulled the lamp from his kit lashed to the side of the camel and proceeded to explain its technology to the fascinated Afghans. As he did so the other men began to set camp; small tents, cooking equipment and then gathering together food from various packs on the camels. They all sat nonchalantly on the ground chewing bits of stubby vegetation and spitting at each other from time to time. No one noticed that the nameless Afghan warrior had slipped away from the camp.

"So be it, Englishman, if you and any of your colleagues wish to then enter the caves briefly tonight, we will remain outside as local superstition suggests only entering in daylight." Holden nodded in agreement and walked to the others of the SRP to explain to them his intentions.

"Listen up chaps. Nigel, I want you to stay out here with Pete and Will. The rest of you get out your Davy lamps we're going in for half an hour or so for a look round. Nigel, you and your lads out here with you get some food going. Omar and Hamza will be out here too so please continue the cordiality with them." Holden looked around the group and then beyond trying to spot the third Afghan. "Anyone seen the other fellow? He seems to have disappeared." They all looked around themselves and beyond the camp into the fading light. No one could see any trace of him. Jock Sutherland spoke shrugging his shoulders.

"Maybe he's gone hunting to get something just for the three of them?"

"Maybe he couldn't stand the thought of eating more of Will's shitty food," said Cled Jones specifically to illicit a reply. Bayley was forced to reply of course to this antagonism.

"Or maybe he couldn't stand the shit that comes out of your taffy gob."

"Could have taken the Welsh bastard with him to save an arrow. If he wants sheep he could have got him to scare them to death!" Burwell spoke mockingly but with venom.

"Oi. Pack it in all of you. He'll be back, just all of you get on with what you're told you wasters," Nigel Green interjected.

The caving party unpacked their lamps, slung their rifles across their backs and formed up to prepare to enter the cave with Holden. Omar and Hamza were unpacking their camp when Holden spoke to them.

"Where's your third man gone then?" The brothers looked at each other pausing before answering. Holden was uncomfortable with the delay.

"I believe," said Hamza looking at Omar seemingly for support "that he's gone to try to catch some fresh meat." It was plausible given the circumstances. Holden nodded in acknowledgement and then walked over to Green before leaving.

"Look, watch your backs. I feel uncomfortable with this man having gone missing. They seemed too reluctant to talk to me," Holden nodded towards the brothers as he spoke. "They just took too long to answer convincingly. I know things have become friendly but be careful." Green acknowledged his concerns cautiously and subtlety as the Afghans looked on.

Holden returned to the cave party; John Waldron, Cled, and Jock. He walked straight past them signalling with his right hand as he did so for them to follow on. It was only a matter of fifty yards to the cave entrance where they stopped outside. Holden took a deep breath and then systematically smelled the air several times. He couldn't detect any foreign odours at the cave mouth. He opened up the door of his Davy lamp and pulled out a box of matches from a pocket under his local robes; taking a long safety match he struck it and fed it into the lamp he had already primed, and lit it. A small flame took hold so he closed the door, fastened it and passed the match to others. Each in turn lit their own lamps and then looked at him for direction.

"Right. Remember that if we hit some real pockets of gas in there the lamp will burn much higher and with a blue tinge. If that's the gas, we need to get out and as a precaution turn the lamps down." The three troopers nodded in acknowledgement. He turned away from them and walked into the cave.

The entrance was about seven feet high and around four feet wide and as they had approached it had a sinister and foreboding look as if it was a crack in the earth that would lead them directly to hell. The three troopers paused and looked on as Holden entered and they could see his lamp lighting up the jagged edges of the cave sides as he made his way briskly along it. The further he went in the image of him disappearing gave the optical illusion of the cave getting smaller in front of him. They didn't notice him changing his posture so they reasoned that it couldn't be the case. Cled Jones followed him in followed close behind by Jock Sutherland and Waldron. They caught up quickly with Holden but then spaced out to keep about ten feet between each man as a margin for safety to ensure that number two wouldn't befall the same fate as number one if anything happened. Very quickly as they got around one hundred feet into the depths of the cave they all began to pick up a strange aroma in their nostrils. It was the scent of the 'black gold'.

Chapter Three

Outside the cave in the camp Green looked at the terrain around them as Bayley and Burwell got on with cooking the evening meal. He could see the Afghans toiling over their own fire and felt that he needed to maintain the cordiality as instructed with mind to Holden's concerns and the disappearance of the third warrior. He spoke to his subordinates.

"Look, I'm going over there for a chat and see if they want to join us. Make sure you keep your heads up to what's going on while I'm over there as well as doing the cooking. All right?" They nodded in acknowledgement and Nigel Green went over to the brothers.

"Look, in the interest of camp spirits, why don't you join us for dinner while you wait for your man to come back?" Green made good eye contact with the two of them as he spoke. Omar spoke for them.

"Well that is most generous. However, our religious beliefs mean our meat must be killed in a very specific way. Do you cut a live animal's throat and allow all the blood to drain before you eat it Mr Green?"

"Err..." Green was taken aback by this factor, "no I didn't realise. Sorry. We don't do that. Got some vegetables cooking though."

"Have you cooked meat not killed in this way before in the pots you use?" asked Omar, Green felt almost a little patronisingly.

"All right. Sorry, just trying to be friendly that's all."

"That is very kind, Mr Green." He turned to go but was stopped by a question from Hamza.

"Englishman," Green hated this address, it was the only one Hamza ever used. "If you and your friends are geologists, then why have they entered the caves, where no animal dares to live, with their rifles?" Green was immediately stumped by the question.

"Err... force of habit I suppose."

"Really, you enter all caves with the latest in British rifle technology then?" He had a superior and probing tone to his voice. There was only one answer that Green could retaliate with without tying himself up.

"Yes." He turned to go back to his compatriots.

As he did so and he neared them he became aware of a distant rumbling that was growing closer. He stopped in his tracks. He could see that his men had also stopped what they were doing also distracted by the sound. It grew louder. All of them, experienced soldiers, knew what it was; it was the sound of a large scale charge of horses. Then in the almost faded light, he could see the horde coming towards the camp from the east. There were about twenty-five Afghan warriors on horse back. The three SRP men distracted by this main group were not aware of the foot born warriors who stealthily crept up on the camp. Green was attacked and restrained from behind by two men. He was pushed heavily to the ground and pinned down whilst a third came up and then tied up his hands and feet together behind his back. About to shout to the others, he could see they were being simultaneously taken too. Burwell had nothing to hand and Green could see he was being trussed up in the same way that he was. Bayley, pushed to the floor too, grabbed one of the large SRP cooking knives and rolled clear of his assailants. He then lashed out with the knife contacting the thigh of one man and immediately putting him to the floor. He clutched his upper leg in agony, screaming with the pain of a deep slashing wound. Bayley got to his feet and ran a few feet to his camel that was getting up and about to begin a stampede. The easiest weapon he could grab was his sabre and he pulled it quickly from its sheath.

Two warriors with their rifles slung were forced back as he lunged forward with it and then swung it out to slash at them. He caught one across the chest opening up a fatal wound exposing his chest cavity. He fell to the floor writhing and screaming.

"Look out Will, behind you!" The cry from Green whose head was then struck with a punch from the side came just too late for Will Bayley to react. A mounted Afghan rode up quickly behind him with a scimitar drawn and swung out quickly and viciously at his head. In a surreal sight, despite many battle experiences, in a vision that Green had never before seen, Bayley's head was taken clean from his shoulders. In the split second it happened, but all in slow motion in Green's mind, he saw a look of complete shock and disbelief on Bayley's face as his head rolled from his neck and onto the floor in front of his body. His headless corpse, still gripping his sabre, seemed to stay upright for several seconds before collapsing almost perfectly horizontally to the floor in a lifeless heap.

Green's own head was pushed into the scrubby rough floor and he felt the side of his face grazing. Then he felt something land next to the back of his head. He turned to find himself nose to nose with Will Bayley's head.

* * *

Holden, Jones, Waldron and Sutherland had now ventured deep inside the cave and were totally unaware of what was going on outside; however, a party of warriors was preparing to follow them in and they too would soon be heavily involved in violent conflict. The Davy lamps provided the only form of lighting as the three progressed along the narrow naturally hewn passageway, and Holden paid casual but regular attention to the colour of his lamp to see if they were getting any closer to the lakes of oil that the cave system held. The flame appeared for now to remain burning at its normal level and had not shown any signs of a blue tinge. They soon realised that the further they travelled along the caves the warmer it seemed to be getting. Their outer robes were making them too hot and all could feel the perspiration running down their backs and along the sides of their faces. In an ideal world they would have abandoned them. Holden could tell that the cave seemed to be progressively declining and it naturally speeded up the pace at which they walked; every now and again they would brush the cave sides with the rifle butts or barrel ends of their slung weapons. Sutherland peered down at his own lamp as they continued down the decline and was the first to notice the change of flame and colour; they all were hit at the same time with the strange odour that the cave system began to emit.

"Boss, we must be getting near. Check your lamp." Sutherland spoke in a hushed tone for no apparent reason.

"You're right. Well spotted, Jock," replied Holden. Jones started laughing. "What are you laughing at, Cled?"

"Sorry, Sir. I don't now why that Scottish mug is bloody whispering. It's not like there's anyone here to disturb. Loud voices won't ignite something that's flammable." He carried on chuckling at his own observation. Sutherland had to concede.

"All right, fair point. Just seems to be the natural thing in a black confined space." They continued forward all watching their fronts and their lamps keenly.

Suddenly they came to a huge opening. The light projecting from their lamps had not indicated it as they approached, they just seemed to emerge into it without warning and the surprise of the opening stopped them dead in their tracks. It was just as well as they were only a few steps away from the edge of one of the legendary lakes of 'black gold'. Initially they didn't see it; Holden held up his lamp to inspect the flame and saw it was now almost raging and a deep blue. He was drawn to look beyond it by a distant shimmering. He held is breath as he did so and they all looked wondrously on, stood side by side, at the shining mill pond lake of oil. The smell was quite overpowering and somehow very industrial. Holden walked to the shore of the lake, bent down and just dipped a finger in holding the lamp well to his rear. It was warm and thick like treacle and as he pulled his finger free he could see it drip slowly from the end of it, its viscosity much denser than most liquids he had ever experienced. The realisation to all of them of the find was staggering and they breathed a sigh of relief that they had seemed to have safely achieved their goal. None of them knew what was occurring outside and the monstrous barbarity that they would soon witness.

* * *

"Fuck, fuck, FUCK!" Green was astonished to be in such a horrifyingly surreal position, with the awful realisation that it was not the product of an active imagination. Bayley's eyes stared wide and lifelessly at him and he could feel himself about to vomit. As the burning sensation grew of his stomach contents travelling violently up his gullet, he was pulled to his feet. This exaggerated the vomit effect with it projecting some feet forward of him. His hands were now tied behind his back and he and Burwell were harshly dragged together to face Hamza now stood with the missing Afghan warrior in front of them. He had been tasked following the brothers' orders to disappear and return with the reinforcements to overpower the Englishmen. Hamza looked the two SRP men up and down with arrogance as they were at his mercy. Over his shoulders they could see Bayley's headless body; a grim sign that they were probably to meet a violent death. Hamza spoke.

"You infidels! You come to our land to exploit our natural resources believing that you can get away with it? Geologists? I don't think so, you are trained fighting men. That is obvious which is why I chose such numbers to overpower you." Green stood straight and stared Hamza in the face with contempt. He had faced death on many other occasions and feared nothing. He would speak with honesty as there was little to lose.

"For a filthy Arab you are quite bright. You are right. We are soldiers sent as an expeditionary force as we explained but with the ability to fight our way out if necessary. You may kill me and him," nodding to Burwell next to him, "but the others will give you a run for your money. The only thing that will stop them from killing you all will be a lack of ammunition you fucker." As he expected he sowed a seed of contempt in Hamza.

"You savage English dog!" He struck Green across the face for his insults. "For your futile impertinence you will watch him die first and then you will suffer like you cannot imagine. Take him," Hamza pointed to Burwell, "and let the horses deal with him."

"No, don't fucking kill me! Please, Please! Sergeant Major, help me!" Burwell was harshly bundled away falling to the floor and refusing to stand. He was dragged over to some men sat on horses.

"Shut your mouth, Burwell. Don't show these fucking Arabic animals any fear!" Green was furious with Burwell's cries. The young trooper just continued sobbing. The warriors ensured his hands were bound tightly and then did the same to his feet. Another rope was passed around each of these fastenings and then each was handed up to the men riding the horses. On their saddles were mounted substantial wooden pommels and these ropes leading from Burwell were tied firmly to them. Green could see the ropes were quite long, around twenty feet. He knew what they going to do having heard stories from men who had served on the Khyber Pass talking about it. There was a specific name for this blunt butchery that he could not recall but that hardly seemed to matter. He would show them no emotion as they put this young trooper to death. He did ponder what they were going to do to him that would be worse. Burwell was sobbing and writhing on the floor but in his hugely anxious state he didn't really see what they were preparing to do, which might have been a blessing for him.

Each of the horsemen backed up a little so they were very close to Burwell at each end of his body. This meant that the ropes as they got to their fullest extent would generate a huge amount of tensional force and achieve the ends that the Afghans wanted without pulling the men from their steeds.

"Keep watching, Englishman," said Hamza as Green tried to avert his gaze from the horror. Hamza, drawing his own scimitar, forced Green to turn his head and watch as he jabbed it into his cheek. There was a crack of a whip between the horses that struck Burwell harshly across his back causing him to cry out with pain. The crack of the whip and his scream set each of the horses off to bolt at speed. Within a split second the ropes reached their maximum extent and snapped harshly into action. There was a hideous blood curdling cry of agony as Burwell's body was torn effectively in two at his hips. His legs were pulled from the hip joint sockets and torn away by one horse as the other dragged his screaming torso off in the opposite direction.

He was still alive and screaming in a sickening fashion. Green hoped the massive blood loss he could see in the sand as the young man was dragged around would lead to a quick death. It would, but not quickly enough as the body was brought back around and stopped in front of him. Green could feel his hands untied but with two rifle barrels then shoved into his back. They were at least going to let him comfort the dying man. Burwell looked into his eyes as Green crouched and took him in his arms.

"Sir, my fucking legs feel cold. How am I going to get back?" The pain was making him quite delirious. There were tears in the RSM's eyes and he could hardly speak. Burwell could see that Green was distressed despite his own condition. "Sir, is it bad? What's the matter eh?" Before he could reply to the young trooper, Burwell's eyes glazed over and became locked in a stare skywards. Green could tell his breathing had stopped and he pulled him into his chest and sobbed as the young soldier had just died in his arms.

Green was pulled harshly to his feet by two Afghan warriors and had his arms pinned back as he was presented to Hamza again. Before Hamza could speak to him he spat directly into the sneering tribal man's face.

"You will regret that Englishman. Your suffering will be slow and painful." Hamza then barked some orders at his subordinates who dragged Green off to the centre of the now ravaged camp about ten feet away from the fire that he and his men had begun. It was stoked and further built up by some of the other warriors and he could see that they were creating a small but intense fire. Another three Afghans came to assist their comrades and he was pushed harshly to the ground, but so that he was face up. Two held onto his arms and two held onto his legs as the fifth tied individual rope bindings around his wrists and his ankles. Having completed this task, from a battered leather shoulder bag the fifth man pulled out four wooden ground pegs and a wooden mallet. The pegs were large and were of the type used to secure a tent to the ground. Green watched nervously as each of his limbs was pegged out by the rope bindings until he was pinned down to the camp floor very tautly and totally immobilised. He could still move his head and saw Omar draw his large scimitar and then place the blade deep into the fire. Everyone withdrew from his immediate area to the other side of the fire where they sat down cross legged and spoke in hushed tones. Frustratingly he hadn't understood any of the dialect he had heard spoken. The Afghans casually chatted and began to eat as he lay helpless and silent.

* * *

"Right. We know it's real, we'll come back in tomorrow morning and take samples and then head off later in the day." As Holden finished speaking everyone was silent. For a moment he was a little unsure as to why but then his own hearing became aware of what the others must have been listening to. They could hear a group of men approaching along the cave that they had just followed.

"That's a bit fucking strange, boss," said Cled Jones, "didn't think anyone was going to be following us in."

"Neither did I. Be careful lads, we don't know who it is and the flames are getting very blue and high on these lamps. If there is a problem, use your sabres." The men all nodded in acknowledgement and drew their edged weapons. They had an advantage as they were in open ground and the passageway would not allow the entry into the natural large cavern of more than one man at a time. Their would-be enemies seemed to have made no allowance for this. Holden using hand signals positioned his men for greatest tactical advantage. He stood a few feet back directly in line with the cave's passageway entrance to draw their adversaries in. Either side of the entrance and out of sight to those emerging were, on one side, Cled Jones and the other side Jock Sutherland. John Waldron stood a few steps away again to act as a back up to Holden if too many actually did break through. Holden could then see the distinctive shine of a Davy lamp coming towards him. He spoke to confirm his suspicions.

"Green, is that you or one of those other wankers with you?" There was silence. If it had been any of the SRP men they would have replied to the banter. As the lamp emerged he could see that it was illuminating very distinctive Arabic robes which did not belong to any of his party and he could see a drawn scimitar glinting. Suddenly the robed figure rushed out of the gloom. It caught Sutherland and Jones off guard but they would certainly be ready for the next. Holden was more than capable of dealing with this first attacker; he was even able to say so before he engaged him.

"Don't worry, boys this first one is my privilege." The unskilled Afghan drew the scimitar above his head with one hand and held a lamp in the other and continued charging. Holden simply sidestepped him and accurately lunged with the sabre straight through the man's ribcage from his left side and instantly pierced his heart. He dropped lifelessly to his knees and then straight onto the floor. Holden gasped as he saw the lamp fall from his assailant's hand to the floor but fortunately it didn't smash or leak. His cave sentries were just hacking into the next man and then another, luckily neither of whom were carrying lamps.

"Watch them if they've got lamps, if they smash we're toast boys, there's strong fumes in here. Kill all of them that come through as they must have done our boys outside!"

The three SRP troopers acted instantly on his words with Waldron coming forward to try to intercept the danger created by any falling lamp. The other two were ready to strike at the next to enter to create an ever increasing pile of bodies. In addition to Holden's attacker, in the next ninety seconds they killed another four with Waldron recovering another lamp.

"Bloody hell, Boss," shouted Waldron, "They must have done our boys outside good and proper. That's two lamps now." Holden could see the third along the entrance cave and it was retreating. Suddenly a major concern entered his mind.

"Boys, we need to get out of here, and now! Just follow me." Holden entered the passageway and could see the lamp moving off in front of them at speed as they made towards it. Suddenly he felt something whistle past his head and he heard it impact behind him. He turned quickly to see Jock Sutherland stood silent and raising his hands to his throat. He had received an arrow which had struck him square on in his wind pipe and was sticking out of the back of his neck; he was gasping for air.

"Back, back! Now!" Holden barked the order to the men as he took hold of Sutherland and managed to drag him through the cave to the area of the lake. "We've got to find another way out because their next move has to be sending a flaming torch in here, but right now we've got to see what we can do for Jock." More arrows whizzed past them as the entered the opening and took cover to one side. Jones kept watch on the passageway with his sabre still drawn. Holden sat Sutherland down with his back supported by the cave's wall. He and Waldron looked at him together. He couldn't speak and looked at them with fear in his eyes.

"All right, Jock. I'm going to break the head off of the arrow and then draw it back through from the front," explained Holden. He nodded his head very slightly.

Holden bent him forward and had Waldron hold him as he snapped the arrow head off from behind him. He sat him back against the wall but as he did so Jock lost consciousness. Within seconds he stopped breathing. Holden withdrew the arrow and laid him down flat to begin to give him manual heart massage, a method of revival that a survivalist had taught them. As he did so Waldron picked up the arrow and cautiously sniffed it.

"Wouldn't bother, Boss. He's gone. Sniff this; they've poisoned it." He held the arrow under Holden's nose and he could instantly detect the scent of cyanide.

"The bastards!" Holden was livid. "We're going to kill every last one of these savages! Right, follow me. To the entrance and then lamps out and we'll charge through. Get your rifles ready and fire from the hip. If I go down remember we should get far enough out so that if the firing action of the rifle ignites the vapours we should still be able to escape."

His plan was a good one but unfortunately their adversaries were about to get the upper hand. The SRP men, not knowing the cave system, were outflanked. Just as they were about to move Jones was hit in both legs by arrows. He screamed in agony and fell to the floor knowing he was doomed. He looked up at his comrades and spoke.

"Get going now or we're all fucked. I'll take this lot with me! Now go!"

Holden and Waldron didn't need telling twice knowing Jones too was poisoned. They ran into the passageway as they heard him cock his rifle. He had his adversaries in sight that seemed to have their own safety lamps and he managed to let off four rounds in quick succession before the entire natural atrium ignited. Holden and Waldron heard him scream and could sense flames now chasing them along the cave. It dangerously highlighted their outlines as it pursued them along the passage. Holden was firing from the hip towards figures he could see at the end of the cave that, receiving the fire from him and seeing the flames, ran away themselves. Neither of them could bear to think about their selfless comrade burning to death in agony engulfed by the flaming vapours from the 'black gold'. They reached the cave mouth to begin to hear a hideous screaming that they recognised instantly as that of Sergeant Major Green.

The defenders of the cave entrance had taken cover some distance away as Waldron and Holden emerged. Their rifles were inferior to those of the SRP men by lack of accuracy, poor ammunition and not having the advanced bolt action and magazine of the Mark 1 Lee Enfield .303. As they emerged into the moonlit world outside the cave, they could see some of the Afghan warriors standing up from behind rocks to shoot with their weapon's single action. Their marksmanship was no match for either of the Englishmen's skills, both of whom took aim with full magazines and picked off six warriors between them in less that twenty seconds, as they failed to get back into cover quickly enough having fired or were turning to run. Holden and Waldron then engaged in a classic 'cover and movement' action between them as Holden ran forward first to the cover of rocks just short of the camp then shouting 'covering!' to Waldron who lowered his rifle and ran to join him shouting 'moving!' as he advanced.

It was from this position of cover that they visually located the screaming Nigel Green illuminated by the now roaring camp fire. They could have no comprehension of what the barbaric brothers had submitted him to until they saw Hamza wielding a glowing red scimitar. Omar was shouting to his sword wielding brother.

"Finish the disablement! Finish him!" Whatever the 'disablement' was neither of the Englishmen were going to allow that to happen. They both raised their rifles and fired upon Hamza riddling his body with five shots between them putting him to the floor lifeless. Suddenly Waldron cried out and dropped his weapon; he had received a round in his lower back and they found themselves attacked from behind.

They both turned to engage the enemy but with Waldron forced to stay seated with his back to the rocks as he reloaded his rifle whilst Holden finished the last two rounds of his own magazine. Holden's shots were true and he struck two of four warriors who were all busy reloading with no grasp of disciplined military tactics. 'Reloading!' Holden shouted to the grimacing Waldron who was now back up into the aim but looking as if he was in a great deal of pain. His shots were also true and he finished off the last two of their flanking attackers. Then they both heard another chilling scream from the already wailing Green whose prone figure they hadn't quite made out in the fire light. Waldron couldn't move but Holden turned and ran from cover towards the noise with no regard for himself but to help his obviously suffering colleague. He was aghast at what he saw.

He advanced to see Omar finishing the hideous task he and his now dead brother had started; that of de-limbing RSM Green. With the glowing, hot scimitar he had just swung it downwards and cut off Green's left arm just above the elbow, the last of his limbs to be removed. There was unbelievable cunning in their cruelty; the red hot scimitar instantly cauterised the wound it created, thereby stemming any massive blood flow before it could start leaving the victim to suffer the great pain of the wounds but, other that if shock immediately took hold, not die quickly. Holden had read of such barbarity before they had left England.

Holden raised his rifle and took a shot at Omar hitting him in his right arm making him instantly drop the scimitar. He was about to take a second shot as he heard the crack of a whip and a split second later he felt the whip wrap around his rifle and it was wrenched from his grasp. He turned to see a large giant of an Afghan with the whip to his right. He pulled out his Webley and shot the man twice, one round hitting him square in the chest the other piercing his neck; the giant instantly fell. He ran to retrieve his rifle, then grabbing it and turning to engage his next threat. He could see Omar running away clutching his right arm. About to take a shot he heard a familiar voice crying out to him using his Christian name in a desperate plea for help.

"William, help me, please, help me!" It was Nigel Green in unspeakable agony. He lowered the rifle and ran to his side. As he did so the remainder of the Afghans were making good their escape but as they did so making Holden's situation still ever more desperate; they rounded up all the camels and took them with them as well as their own horses. He heard a shout from the injured Waldron.

"Boss, they're all fucking legging it and Omar's getting away too!" He looked up to see Omar being pulled up on the back of one of the fleeing horses. He had to let them go as his great friend and co-founder of the SRP needed his help and compassion. He knelt beside him horrified by what he saw as he took him in his arms.

Green had had both his arms cut off just above his elbow joints leaving flailing stumps; he had had both of his legs cut off just above the knee in the same act of cruelty, again leaving useless stumps. There was the rancid smell of burning flesh from the wounds which as planned had been cunningly cauterised by the action to stop him bleeding to death. The burns were now making his nerve endings deaden and his pain was beginning to subside.

Holden cradled him in his arms and began to weep. What had he done to these fine men by bringing them here? And for what? He just hoped that now as he sat with one of his closest friends hideously crippled, the Minister would be good to his word.

"Nigel, Nigel, I'm so sorry. I'm so, so sorry, old friend. I'll get you home." Green looked up at him sorrowfully and half managed a painful smile. His soldier's humour was about to kick in through the shock.

"Well, William," he never referred to Holden by his Christian name, "don't think I'll be following you around anymore, Sir. Or carrying your bags. But don't worry there will be a place for me in Chelsea if you get me there." Holden continued to weep as Green tried to comfort him with his huge emotional trauma of the loss of his men and the crippling wounds on others. Holden couldn't speak. The both of them could hear the sound of something being dragged across the ground.

They looked up to see John Waldron dragging himself along the floor by his arms, his legs apparently useless. Holden was even more dismayed as Waldron spoke.

"Beggin' your pardon, Sir. But a slight problem. That shot I got in my lower back? I can't feel my fucking legs."

Holden, normally calm and resourceful, was now for the one and only time in his life completely overwhelmed; he was stuck in the middle of Afghanistan with four men killed and two men life-changingly crippled with no horses, no camels and, so it seemed, no immediate way of all of them surviving. Waldron lay out flat on the floor through sheer exhaustion. Holden clung on to Green and around the camp there was silence.

Chapter Four

Belgrave Square, July 30th 1904

    Karen Wood, twenty-eight years old, slim but shapely with a wonderful hourglass type figure, voluptuous with blond hair and a flawless olive complexion. She was wearing a beaded black capelet over a red tight fitting bodice with a traditional black skirt, and by her posture some heeled boots or shoes. Ford really was genuinely quite speechless when she stood and turned to face him and his reaction to her was noticeable. Quickly he composed himself and stepped forward to greet the Minister and then her in turn. He felt a shiver run down his spine and his blood run a little cold as he shook hands with Sir Cecil who proffered him a very obvious Masonic handshake. With the events of 1888 in Whitechapel and the complicity in covering up the murders that the Freemasons had, he felt reservations in meeting another one so highly placed. For similar reasons to his lifelong mentor retired Chief Inspector Frederick Abberline, he had a deep seated dislike for this organisation and its secretive members.

    "Good to have you on board Inspector Ford. May I dispense with formalities and call you by your first name?" Ford didn't want to forge a friendship with this man but for professional expedience it would be simpler to agree to his request.

    "Certainly, Sir Cecil. Robert will work fine." They relaxed and undid the handshake between them.

    "And this is Karen Wood, my 'tailoress' as it were. She started off as Lady Patterson's dressmaker, but she did such a bloody good job on a couple of little jobs for me that I can't be without her now. Goes everywhere with me when I'm away as I'm such a clutz with damaging my suits." She stepped forward away from the Minister and gently shook Roberts's hand. Taking her delicate hand in his, it felt warm and soft and as they touched he made direct eye contact with her. Was it just him or did he sense a connection? She spoke with a soft East Anglian accent. He deduced most likely originating from the North Essex and Suffolk border.

"Good morning, Inspector. May I call you Robert too?" She inclined her head slightly as she spoke so as having to look up to him in a flirtatious way. Unusually for the time she wore her hair long and loose and it partially flopped across her face; it made her glance appear both innocent and mischievous.

"Please feel free, Karen. For a natural working environment within Sir Cecil's household I think it simplest." They let go hands.

"Thank you, Robert." She returned to her work on the Minister's suit.

"You understand why you are here, Robert?" inquired the Minister.

"Yes, Sir I do. It follows the disappearance and murder of one of your immediate staff I assume, and the fear that you may be a target, Sir."

"Ah good, I'm glad you've been kept up to speed."

* * *

A Fortnight Earlier

Charles Wilmot walked out onto a dark Whitehall heading towards Trafalgar Square. It was 11.p.m on a Monday night. He was private secretary to the Minister of War; Sir Cecil Patterson. As a result and because he was also a well paid high ranking civil servant he was also a major shareholder in Empire Petroleum, a now thriving petrochemical company. It flourished under the directorship of Sir Cecil as not only was it able to capitalise on the growing demand for fuels such as paraffin but also the supply of petrol and diesel for the burgeoning motor vehicle industry. However, these two factors tonight were about to prove his downfall.

As he passed Horse Guards he was aware of an enclosed black carriage pulling up alongside him and then travelling at a walking pace beside him. There were no sentries at this time of night at Horse Guards and as he went beyond it there was a particularly poorly lit length of street between there and Trafalgar Square as a couple of the gas streetlights had gone out. After several uncomfortable seconds he stopped abruptly and was about to speak to the impassive coachman. Before he could do so the carriage door was flung open and a figure dressed totally in black robes jumped out and grabbed him. His assailant was also masked in an almost Arabic fashion. Wilmot would not be able to concentrate on him long enough to a get a fuller perspective; a chloroform soaked cloth was harshly placed across his face and within seconds he was unconscious. The Arabic robed figure hauled him with little effort into the carriage as the coachman continued to look ahead. When he heard the carriage door close he whipped his riding crop around the horse's head and the carriage gently trundled on into Trafalgar Square and then headed off in the direction of the River Thames along Northumberland Avenue.

* * *

Wilmot found himself waking feeling very uncomfortable. He was cold, his body ached, his hands and feet felt uncomfortable and as he regained his composure he realised why. He was in what appeared to be a torch lit underground cavern that had the appearance of being either an old flint or lime mine, and he had been bound by his hands and feet and somehow attached to a wall. He got used to the light as he came fully to; he looked at his outstretched arms and could see that the ropes had been secured to the cave walls by large metal masonry pins. He also sensed that his feet felt particularly cold and he could detect a fuel type odour. He looked down on his feet to see that he was stood in a shallow vat of some sort of petrochemical fluid. A rasping voice spoke to him.

"Charles Wilmot. Lackey of that Machiavellian bastard Cecil Patterson. If only you knew what you and him and all your military-industrial kind put us through. Well all of you are going to experience some of it bit by bit. Brave men lost their lives in a hideous fashion and you never even sent anyone to look for us and save us." The robed figure then emerged from the shadows. Wilmot with his physical predicament and with these threatening, hoarsely spoken words felt a great sense of dread. Rightly he suddenly feared for his own mortality and struggled to speak for fear.

"I...I don't know what you mean? What are you talking about? I am an investor nothing else. I don't know what he or some company man has done to you." The robed figure sensed this man's palpable fear.

"It really is of little consequence, your guilt or want of guilt. You are a political and commercial ally of his and those that are will suffer as the men he sent for his own selfish profit suffered, and he will be the last."

Wilmot watched as the robed figure seemed to produce from nowhere a bow and arrow. He saw the polished head of the arrow glint in the fire lit cavern and it also appeared to be dripping some sort of liquid.

"No! No! Wait, what you are doing! I'm an innocent man! An investor! Don't kill me!" Wilmot had closed his eyes as he protested his innocence so had not seen the bow drawn and the arrow fired. He felt the bone shattering thump as it entered his right thigh and embedded into his femur. It created an agonising pain and he looked down after initially grimacing to see the arrow lodged deeply in his upper leg. The pain was excruciating, but he began to sense a strange numbness within his body; before he could comprehend that sensation fully he saw a flaming torch tossed towards him and land in the vat in which he stood.

The flames instantly engulfed him as the fluid violently ignited and roared up his body. The pain was immense as he felt his clothes burn and then his flesh. The fire began to exhaust air for him to breathe. As that happened, he lost consciousness as the cyanide that had tipped the arrow head took hold and killed him. The robed figure looked on satisfied that the first of his victims had paid in a way that was fitting to how he had seen a very brave man suffer. He left the dead man burning as he made his way out of Chislehurst Caves at just after 2.a.m into Old Hill and his waiting carriage. The caves had many hours before closed to the curious Edwardian public and the robed figure had forced his way in to finish his mission following Wilmot's abduction. They were not due to re-open until Wednesday morning; he calculated that Wilmot would be declared missing for a day before his charred remains would be found. It would be another couple of days before he could be identified and then hopefully Cecil Patterson would start to be concerned about his own safety, especially if he understood the symbolism.

* * *

One Week Later

Chislehurst mortuary 10.30.a.m. Sir Cecil Patterson stood in the examination room speaking with the local coroner Dr Rees Jones. Also present were the deputy secretary of the Department of War, Mr Ramsey Phillips and local Police Inspector John Bradfield. They were positioned around an examination table that contained a body underneath a white cotton sheet; its bare charred feet were exposed at one end of the sheet. There was a very distinct smell to the atmosphere of a mortuary not unlike that of a busy and well stocked butchers shop, although this time with the distinct addition of the aroma of burnt flesh.

"So, Inspector, it's definitely him then?" asked Patterson.

"Yes, sir, I'm afraid it is. We identified him by his teeth. Being a man of class and means Dr Jones came on the idea of seeing if anyone had any matching dental records," replied Inspector Bradfield. "His cause of death is quite obviously homicide as he had been deliberately bound up in the cave and then had a vat of some oil type substance at his feet that was used to burn him to death. He also had some sort of metal object imbedded in his right thigh which I can't determine what it is. It has been subject to melting so I can't tell whether it is some sort of shot, blade, arrow head or what conclusively." Bradfield was quite matter of fact as he spoke. As he had stated, he could not identify the metal object conclusively as the fire had distorted its shape and burnt away the arrow's stem and flights.

"Do you know any reason why some one would want to kill Mr Wilmot, Sir?" Bradfield spoke quizzically with his police notebook poised to record any significant notes.

"No, Inspector, I don't know why any one would want to kill him. Personally it seems like a random attack by a mad man." Ramsey Phillips, who was struggling to deal with the smell of the mortuary and was holding a handkerchief to his nose and mouth, spoke in a muffled tone.

"Minister, work of a mad man or not, it is very unusual for a man like Charles to be abducted and brutally attacked especially from somewhere like Whitehall. I think you should speak to the people at the Metropolitan Police Special Branch and arrange for them to offer you some sort of protection for now. It is a measure that they have been secretly practising and employing from time to time for politicians and the Royals and I think it prudent you use it as a resource for now." They all looked at Phillips as he spoke; only the Minister was aware of this Metropolitan Police Special Branch resource. Dr Jones and Inspector Bradfield looked on very surprised.

"Yes, I think perhaps you are right, Ramsey. Please speak with Scotland Yard this afternoon to get such a protective measure set in place."

"Did you want to view the body, Sir?" asked Dr Rees Jones. Patterson looked back at the charred and blackened feet burnt virtually to charcoaled bone as he considered this suggestion. He looked along the body towards the head covered by the sheet imagining the horror.

"No, thank you. We have concluded it is him and I have no wish to see Charles in this hideous condition thank you, Doctor." Sir Cecil Patterson and Ramsey Phillips turned and left the mortuary.

* * *

Belgrave Square, Patterson Residence July 30th

Ford had noted a recent edition of 'The London Times' lying on a coffee table with its unusually sensational headline:

'MYSTERY DEEPENS OVER RITUALISTIC MURDER OF LEADING CIVIL SERVANT

A William Bates exclusive'

The journalistic nemesis who had plagued the Whitechapel investigation sixteen years before as a headline seeking hack was now the leading reporter for the normally respectable Times. William Bates had

The Dressmaker Connection

climbed the greasy pole of Edwardian journalism and finally achieved a position of respectability. He would come to plague Robert Ford in the same way that he plagued Chief Inspector Frederick Abberline.

"Robert, are you aware of the staff within my 'inner sanctum' as it were?" Karen Wood had finished her alterations and had left the room leaving only Ford and Patterson. The Minister was getting changed back into another suit to prepare for his day's engagements. Ford snapped back into the present, his thoughts having drifted momentarily back to 1888.

"Not fully. Perhaps you could enlighten me to give me a greater grasp of the job in hand and know who is permissible at all times." Patterson looked at the detective inspector quizzically at his reply, adjusting his tie.

"Quite. Well, Karen Wood of course." 'Why did he mention the dressmaker first?' thought Ford as the Minister continued. "Ramsey, who is now the immediate secretary to my department, Steven Pick who is the under secretary, Fiona Shaw the administrative assistant and James Landan my researcher. That all right? Does that give you an idea of the 'permissible' with the job in hand, Robert?" There was cynicism in his voice.

"Sir Cecil, first of all I now know that I am happy for those people to have immediate access to you if there is a safety concern; and secondly if there is threat I shall warn them all to be on their guard against attack too."

"Them? Targets?" Patterson spoke with indignation as if to question how these people could possibly be targets. "It was a one off lunatic attack. The rest of your mob need to just catch the evil bastard that killed my dear Charles so he may rest in peace." Ford stood his ground on the issue. Accepting this man's arrogance, deepening the instant dislike he had taken to this pompous Freemason.

"Even if that is the case, I have a job to do and I shall do it to the best of my abilities and with the best interests to everyone's safety in mind." There was silence between them as they made and held eye contact as Ford spoke. He was not prepared to break the deadlock and with the resolve borne out of a difficult early career, he won out as Patterson broke off from his gaze and uncomfortably made to get on with some pointless tasks to cover up his sense of failure. He spoke off hand to Ford whilst he busied himself.

"Good. Whatever you say, Inspector. We will be leaving here at eleven to go to Parliament for Prime Minster's question time." There was an uneasy silence before Robert spoke once more before leaving the room.

"Is there an opportunity for me to meet your staff this morning?" He was now making the point of trying not to sound subservient and was deliberately refusing to address Patterson.

"Yes they'll all be around my private offices at the House when we get there. I'll see you at the door when we leave, Inspector. Thank you." Patterson stood and stared at Ford to encourage him to leave. He willingly did so. Patterson decided to not address this difficult policeman informally by name again.

Outside the room still was Bob Spicer who would form part of the protection team that Ford was establishing. He spoke to his old acquaintance as he saw him re-enter the hall.

"Well? Go all right did it?"

"As well as it could do. Look, Bob, It's going to work like this; you and I will do close protection throughout the day, either together or on a relieving basis, and at night we'll have uniform boys static here."

"Right. What about the overseas schedule in the next six weeks?" Ford was unaware of such commitments and had only considered the domestic situation.

"Ah. Right. When we go abroad it's you and me and we'll have to have one other detective. We'll do days and have a chap to do the corridor of wherever he is staying at night. Do you know anyone junior in the Branch we can use?" Spicer thought for a moment.

"Yes. There's a young DC called Mark Vincent. He's ex-military and a good lad. I'll get him on board. Do you want to know his programme for the next six weeks?" Ford had a simple way of life outside of the busy Special Branch, so the Minister's programme would have little impact on his personal life. His few indulgences were fencing, fine wines and keeping his smart town house in Eton Square tidy with the continued help of his house keeper Mrs Adkins. In truth she maintained the fastidious state in which he liked the house to be. He gained great satisfaction from the time and trouble she took in tidying the soft furnishings; relaxing into a tidy comfortable sofa always reduced his tensions with a correctly chilled glass of dry white wine or rose in his hand.

"Yes please, mate. Might as well know what I need to pack." Spicer pulled out a leather-bound pocket diary from his inside suit pocket.

"Right, where are we. July 30th today, so next week 5th August we're off to Paris for a conference with the French Interior Ministry, then ten days after that he's off to Rome for a week for a mix of business and pleasure. A week after that he's in Prague and then back to Derbyshire a week after that for some shooting with friends as I recall, haven't got in here why. Each of the overseas trips has an element of business to do with his company too I think." Ford was writing the information down in his own diary. That would be 'Empire Petroleum' business he presumed.

"Good. Places I haven't seen. All rail travel I assume?"

"Yes. He loves it. Occasional carriages I guess, and if he gets the chance he champions the new horseless carriage so he'll use those too. In fact you know that's what we've got to go down to the Palace of Westminster."

"Right. I can't get excited about them. Is that Karen still around or Lady Patterson?"

"Lady Patterson is out in Knightsbridge shopping and Karen is about to leave. She's getting her stuff together in the pantry."

"Right, I'll go through and see her. Does Lady Patterson need or want any protection?" Ford asked before he left the hall.

"No, she refuses it. She's not fond of the police, my friend, so be careful around her." Ford nodded and went off to find Karen Wood.

He found her having packed away the alterations to be done into a leather suitcase and pulling on a light jacket to go out into the warm July late morning sunshine. He startled her as he entered the room.

"I'm sorry Miss Wood; I didn't mean to scare you." 'God' he thought 'she is so beautiful.' She faced him square on. They stood about five feet apart with her leaning back against a work top. She smiled sweetly at him and shyly made eye contact.

"Don't worry. I'll forgive a dashing inspector like you. I guess you'll be around for quite a while now will you?" He ignored her question.

"You're not a London girl. How come you've ended up here?"

"No, I come from just outside Colchester. My husband to-be brought me to London six years ago before he went missing somewhere overseas. I don't know where. We lived in Whitechapel and I got a job dressmaking to make ends meet and it just took off from there as I got recommendations."

"Missing? Didn't they tell you what happened to him? Can't the Minister help?" Ford was puzzled.

"I can't ask a man like him. No one will tell me anything about him. I just ended here on my own with a disabled son and the work pays to look after him." Ford had discovered yet another beautiful but tragic woman.

"Do you still live in Whitechapel?" Memories of the events of 1888 came flooding back to him with the name of the area having been brought up. He hoped she had been able to move on from such a deprived district.

"No. The Minister set me up with a little flat round the corner in Wilton Crescent. I'm very grateful. My lad is at a special nursery just off the Brompton Road. With all that has happened, apart from being a single mum, and who wants one of those with a sickly child? I'm lucky really."

Ford was instantly suspicious as to why the Minister would look after a mere dressmaker in such a generous way. It was not appropriate to ask.

"At least you don't have far to go Miss Wood-" She interrupted him.

"Call me Karen, you agreed to in there."

"Yes of course. Sorry." He had gone 'to jelly' just like when he was first getting to know Mary Kelly and had become very formal as a result. He told himself he needed to relax around a woman he found himself attracted to. They stood silent for some seconds before she broke the pregnant pause.

"Take care, Robert. I must go. I shall see you soon."

"Er...yes. Thank you. Good bye, Karen." She seemed to glide past him as she moved with her case and he caught the scent of expensive perfume; it was quite delightful. It had been so long since he had experienced these types of emotions. He stood lost in his thoughts and didn't hear Bob Spicer silently come in which then got his thoughts back on track.

"You all right, Guv'nor?"

"Yeah. Call me Rob will you, cut that hierarchy bollocks." Ford followed him out to see the 'horseless' carriage outside in Belgrave Square. Spicer had observed the exchange between Ford and Karen Wood and detected the unspoken human interest between them.

"Rob, a word of advice, especially with Sir Cecil in mind. Be careful what you wish for."

Chapter Five

Afghanistan 1898

Adapting much of the equipment scattered around the carnage of the ambushed camp, and having composed himself following a rare moment of emotional collapse, Holden was prepared to extricate himself, Waldron and Nigel Green from Afghanistan. He knew it would be a long and arduous struggle but he had the resolve to get the remainder of the SRP out. If he could just make it close to the Khyber Pass he suspected that the promised rescue mission would find the three of them. He didn't know that it was forlorn hope; Patterson had no intention of sending a rescue party. If the first expedition looking for oil failed he would simply send another. The SRP had been the perfect expendable tool to use as a first attempt, and Patterson assumed that if such a small force were attacked it was unlikely anyone would survive to be a burden to him in any way.

Holden had taken the time to bury the dead SRP men who had fallen outside of the caves. He could not risk re-entering the oil-laden caverns to try to find the other two bodies for fear of fires still burning, and even if that were not the case, the potential residual heat from the earlier inferno made it too hazardous an undertaking. Laying them to rest that night meant that the camp seemed more peaceful as he and Waldron took it in turns to maintain a guard through the course of the night. Although Waldron seemed paralysed from the waist down he was nonetheless lucid and able to handle a firearm. Green, considering the horrific extent of his injuries, seemed to be in hardly any pain but as the realisation of his disfigurement had hit him through the night had become silent and withdrawn. He secretly wished Holden would leave him there with a weapon, but he had no way of being able to use one to take his own life.

Holden had unsurprisingly rested uneasily during his hours of sleep pondering how things could have been different. Had it been a mistake to split the team? Or did it mean that he and the cave party had effectively become the rescue force to those captured outside. No one would ever be able to determine if a different course of action would have been more beneficial for the SRP men's long-term survival. Once first light had come Holden had set to in constructing a method of transporting his two maimed subordinates; using a saddle that had fallen from a stampeding camel he had carved the edges on each side of its base into flat sled type skids. Attached to it using two large branches with the canvas from two rucksacks tied and stitched was a makeshift stretcher to drag along behind it. Thinking of Captain Scott's technique he had developed for polar exploration he would attempt to 'man-haul' Waldron sat astride the saddle and Green laying in the stretcher across the vast plains to the Khyber Pass. He ensured that they carried as many supplies as they possibly could in the form of weapons as well as food, so that they could trade for camels or horses should they come across some nomads or any one else non-hostile. He furnished some straps from the two cannibalised rucksacks to attach between the makeshift sled and himself, as well as wearing his own rucksack and carrying his Lee-Enfield rifle ready to defend the group. Waldron was also able to have a rifle at the ready too. With all his preparations it was late afternoon before he could begin hauling himself and his companions to safety. The temperature was cooling so it was a good time to commence his mammoth task.

To give himself extra purchase on the ground to assist with his pulling efforts he had also made himself two walking poles to dig into the ground in front of him. He braced himself for the first effort. Both the disabled men were silent; Waldron watching him with admiration for his inventiveness and courage and Green laying silently on the stretcher staring blankly up at the sky. Green was actually fortunate to have been rescued despite his condition. It had been Omar and Hamza's intention to complete his suffering by whipping him to death once he had been de-limbed and be entertained by watching a crippled man trying to escape on his stumps. They had heard of a tribe elsewhere in Afghanistan submitting a rival to just such an ordeal. It would have been a slow, massively painful and terrifying way to die. As he lay there watching the sky, he could hear Holden's superhuman efforts as the sled started to move. He found it agonizing to hear his friend's efforts to drag him and Waldron to safety and be able to do nothing to help. Within only three of four agonising steps Holden was sweating profusely with the veins almost popping out from the side of his head and neck. His leg muscles were burning with the effort and his shoulders and back aching with the load. He shut his mind to the pain and mentally 'dug himself in' to the task at hand. Once he had broken the inertia with the stony and dusty ground he was able to keep moving. There was little choice for any of them; they were short on water and food and needed to escape back into the environs of the British Empire. This was their only chance. As the sun set spectacularly over the Kuh e Baba mountains they were leaving behind them, Holden trudged off into the fading light with Waldron and Green watching this awe inspiring sight with the scene etched firmly in their psyche.

* * *

Paris, 6th August 1904

Patterson had arrived with his entourage the day before: Ford, Spicer and Mark Vincent his protection team, Ramsey Phillips now his private secretary and Steven Pick the under secretary. Ford found it odd, but her presence confirmed his suspicions that Karen Ford was Patterson's mistress as there was no Lady Patterson. He was disappointed that he found his suspicions of the Minister having a liaison with Karen were indeed accurate. The group were all staying at the Ritz Hotel, Paris situated in the Place Vendome. It was late evening and the official side of the Minister's visit had concluded and he now had two days of leisure around the city. It was around 9.p.m. and Vincent was taking over corridor duty, as the Minster was due to imminently settle in his room for the evening. Ford had already sent Spicer off duty and his old working colleague had gone for a walk to the Place de la Concorde a short distance away. Ford was sat to one side of the bar area of the hotel keeping a watchful eye on Patterson who was enjoying large glasses of brandy with Phillips and Pick. Both of these men appeared to behave in a sickeningly sycophantic way towards their employer. Ford found it hard to watch such a false display.

Suddenly he felt a presence behind him. Before he turned he heard a familiar voice close to his ear.

"I know for a fact that the Minister will not be requiring my service tonight. When he finally goes to bed would you take me for some fresh air? After all, isn't everyone potentially at risk?" He didn't need to turn to know that it was Karen Wood; her accent gave it away. But more so the smell of her quality perfume that he had noted the first day they met; it was a scent he could pick up from a dozen feet away and a fragrance he would never forget. He felt a welcome shiver of excitement run down his spine at her presence and at her proposal. He didn't turn to reply maintaining observation on his wards. He spoke in a hushed tone to keep the conversation to themselves.

"You are quite right. Everyone is at risk, including me so I do believe that safety in numbers is appropriate. I'd love to take the air with you once he has retired and we could see a little of the City if you wish."

"That sounds very safe and very inviting. I shall be watching from nearby too to see when you are free. I will meet you outside by the base of the Victory Column when you finish." Ford nodded in acknowledgment and she drifted away. He turned quickly but she was gone. He was hoping that the Minister would retire soon.

Ford had to sit watching the three men getting progressively drunk for the next forty minutes before they decided to retire. Patterson got up unsteadily from the table and bade his subordinates a good night. He staggered towards Ford who stood ready to escort him to his room as was his remit. Patterson was the principal and the other two would have to make their own way up or fend for themselves if they were choosing to do anything else. Ford was quite grateful for Patterson's condition as if his suspicions about Karen were true, which it seemed obvious to him they were, he would at least not be in any condition to impose himself upon her this evening. He alone would enjoy her company and get to know her a little better. He walked just behind Patterson as they made their way past reception and towards the building's lifts, constantly ready to take hold of the Minister should he become unsteady on his feet. He was also aware of those around them and anyone that may be paying them too much attention. Ford pushed the call button for the lift which rang a bell instantly and the lift doors opened; the lift's car was already on the ground floor waiting. Patterson moved himself into the lift and then leant heavily against the side to support himself and his spinning mind. It was in this confined environment that Ford gained a grasp of how drunk Patterson was, he reeked of alcohol and was taking deep breaths in the warm confined lift with the doors having closed; he was feeling the sensation of needing to vomit due to alcoholic over indulgence. Ford hoped he wasn't going to be sick in the lift. They only travelled three floors before alighting, but in the short space of time the Minister now needed additional support to get to his room.

Ford, with his arm around Patterson as if supporting a wounded casualty rescued from a battlefield, walked along the corridor to get to the Minister's room. Waiting outside of it was Mark Vincent. He was staggered at Patterson's condition.

"Crikey Moses, Boss, what happened to him?"

"Too much good cheer at the taxpayers' expense, Mark. Get the door open so I can dump him in there." Vincent did as he as told and Ford led the Minister in. He got him over to the bed, backed him up to it and Patterson slumped down onto it falling backwards to end up laying out flat on his back breathing heavily. Ford took his shoes off him.

"Right, Mark, we don't want him choking on his own puke so help me get him on his front. Then we'll pull one leg up towards his chest and make sure one arm is by his side and the other bent up and supporting his head." They placed him in what is now known as the recovery position, a technique that Ford had discovered worked well to stop drunks choking in their sleep when in his custody when he worked as a uniform police sergeant.

"That's clever stuff, Boss. Who taught you that then?"

"No one, trial and error and pot luck over the years." They the both vacated the room to leave the Minister to sleep off his excesses. Outside in the corridor Ford gave his subordinate one last piece of direction.

"Check on him every half an hour to make sure he's not dead. I'm popping out to get some air for a while. See you in the morning." Ford walked along the corridor and took the stairs down to the ground floor to meet and walk out with Karen Wood.

* * *

Ford walked out of the front of the hotel to find Karen was exactly where she said that she would be; at the base of Napoleon's victory column. The Parisian architecture in the Place Vendome looked stunning and gave a very romantic air in the gas lit streets. The air had cooled now that the sun had long set making it a very pleasant temperature to walk out in. She stood right by the base of the ornate column decorated with a frieze of Napoleon's many campaign victories. She was artificially lit by the gas lamps in the famous square creating the perfect shading to highlight the fine bone structure of her face. Her hair rested easily upon her shoulders and as always her clothing contoured her figure. Ford felt butterflies in his stomach as he approached her. Not having shared company with a woman for many years, other than for sheer sexual gratification, it made him look forward to the late evening together; it was just gone 10.p.m. Equally she studied him intently as he moved towards her. She could see under his smart Edwardian suit that he was lean and moved with the air of a large predatory cat, calmly but purposefully, and as he neared she noticed a scar on his forehead just upon the hairline on his right side. Although not detracting from his rugged good looks, it was nonetheless significant and she wondered how he had received it; that was too personal issue to address so early on in their meeting each other.

They stood together now at the base of the 'Column of the Great Army' and made strong eye contact with each other then breaking into a smile.

"Do you know much about Paris, Karen?"

"Nothing. But like London I guess it would look at it's best by night."

"Of that I'm sure there is no doubt. I have studied a little on the City before I came and have a map. How long do you have?"

"As long as you wish, Inspector. Show me the sights and be my guide."

"Certainly." He offered her his arm that she readily took and they began to walk down towards Place Concorde. As they walked away from the column he explained its history to her as they made for the Rue de Rivoli that would lead them directly to the Concorde. As they entered the Rue de Rivoli he explained a little geography.

"If you turn left here it would take you up to the famous 'Louvre' and the 'Ile de Cite' where Notre Dame Cathedral can be found. Ahead of us are the 'Tuileries Gardens' and now having turned right we are heading for Place de la Concorde. The Champs Elysee runs from there right the way up to the Arc de Triomphe or we could cross the Alexandre Fourth Bridge and head for where Napoleon is interred at 'Les Invalides'." As they headed west along Rue de Rivoli they chatted effortlessly until they entered Place Concorde. Ford was about to continue speaking about its history when he completely clammed up. His mind went into turmoil and he could say nothing. An overwhelming sense of grief washed over him and he felt nauseous and light-headed the shock was so intense.

"What's the matter, Robert?" asked a very concerned Karen Wood. He tried to answer but the words just couldn't come out.

He had had a sudden and massive reflective image of Mary Kelly strolling the Parisian Streets over sixteen years ago before they had met with the evil Dr Tumblety. He hadn't realised a city could seem so romantic and so peaceful and here he was, almost fulfilling a fantasy by being in the beautiful city Mary had described, with a woman equal in beauty to that of his lost love. His mind was in such turmoil he almost lost his balance and Karen had to struggle to keep him on his feet with this momentary lapse. She led him over to a bench and sat him down. She realised that the problem was significant as he sat in silence before turning with tears in his eyes and telling her the sorry story of the events of 1888 in Whitechapel.

* * *

Afghanistan, 1898

It had taken Holden a week of primitive 'man hauling' across the Afghan plains before they had met some Bedouins to trade with. In exchange for three Lee-Enfield rifles and ammunition they had got two camels. Waldron rode having mounted with Holden's help whilst Holden rode with Green strapped to his back. He had withdrawn completely, not speaking to either of his comrades. They had calculated correctly that after another weeks riding on top of what they had achieved prior to gaining the camels, they were almost on top of Baryalai's camp and possible salvation.

Every night Waldron had kept a journal that he had begun over the first few nights, composing a full account of the SRP action so far. If nothing else, should they die or fail then it would be a record of what happened to them if it was found by their rescuers. With the length of time that they had been away, Holden felt that the rescue party must be close to going over the Khyber Pass and entering the north of the country as they had. Holden had lost a significant proportion of body weight as they had had to stretch the rations out that they carried during that first week of hauling. Additionally he was normally too tired to be able to hunt for any food when they stopped for the day. Fortunately they had always come across a supply of water so dehydration had never been an issue. Although their second week had been easier they were all still weakening from malnutrition.

They were now all travelling through a sand storm which was taking its toll on all of them; finding a dry wadi they decided to take cover in it. They sheltered with their beasts silently for several hours waiting for the storm to subside which by late afternoon it had. Holden peered over the edge of the wadi now that the winds had dropped and in the dusky light of the fading day in the distance he could see a camp. It was undoubtedly that of Baryalai with Holden recognising the layout by the distinctive colours of the tents. There was no one in sight outside the tents. He suspected that the treacherous Omar would have fled back there claiming that the 'infidels' had attacked him and his brother and slaughtered many of their men before they were able to kill the Englishmen in revenge and by calling on sheer weight of numbers of other local tribesmen. With this in mind he had to approach with caution. He waited half an hour for the light to fade to near darkness before he decided to go forwards. He told the others of his intentions as he ensured his rifle and pistol were fully loaded and he had his sabre in its scabbard on his belt. He ditched the robes to give himself greater freedom of movement.

"Lads. I'm going in on a recce to see who's there. Wally, you wait here with Nigel and don't be tempted to drag yourself up to the camp, you need to be able to defend him." Waldron nodded his head in acknowledgement whilst Green remained impassive. Holden slipped out of the wadi and crawled on his belly right up to the edge of the camp.

In what he recognised as Baryalai's tent he could see now that there was a fire burning inside and there were many figures sat around. All the other tents were in darkness so the whole of the caravan had to be for the time being in one tent, or the junior members of the group were asleep. He crawled up to the edge of it to see if he could make out any conversation inside. Shockingly he could; he could hear the voice very recognisably of Baryalai but also that of an Englishman. He noted that there were few camels and horses around, much like the first time they had visited. Surely Omar had made it back? Or was he out on the hunt? His rifle was already loaded and cocked with a round in the chamber ready to be fired; he crawled around the outside of the tent so his silhouette could not be seen until the last moment and once he reached the door he stood up and entered.

Silence fell amongst the gathering as he did so. His congenial host Mahmood Baryalai was entertaining a very different crowd. Patterson himself was in the tent along with six light infantrymen and their officer, Baryalai's family and Omar. The rest of the warriors must be out fighting or hunting. All seemed equally stunned as each other with what they saw. Holden, tired, drawn, weathered and heavily dishevelled spoke first.

"Well what a charming little gathering. Who shall I kill first, you bunch of treacherous bastards." He had noted instantly that none of them seemed to have a weapon to hand, although he was cautious that the light infantry men may well be carrying pistols as he did.

"Now, Captain, these people say you and your men turned on them, let's not be rash. Put the gun down," Patterson attempted to be persuasive.

"What? Are you fucking joking?" Holden never swore. "You believe these savages over what I might say? Do you know what they did?"

"Put the gun down and we'll hear your side."

"No way. You bastard. You'll do anything for your company won't you, eh? Bloody Empire Petroleum. I've been to this camp before don't forget, and know how they feel about their natural resources. You're taking sides for your own profit margins." In a split second he had to decide who to kill first; he had an order. Omar, then Patterson and then anyone pointing a gun at him, British or otherwise.

From the hip he fired as he began to raise the weapon and got Omar in the chest. With the speed gained of much pressure based training, he got off a second shot with the bolt action rifle and secured Omar's death with a head shot. Patterson was going to be next but two of the light infantry men had drawn pistols on him. Begrudgingly, as he did not wish in truth to kill fellow British soldiers, he took care of one with a chest shot and then the second with a shot in the shoulder. The second one had managed to get a round off that had sailed dangerously close to his head. Now it was time to get out; there were still four light infantry men and Patterson, who had rolled out of sight behind cushions and skins at the edge of the tent and might well be armed too. He turned and ran into the darkness. He could hear people exiting the tent close behind him to give chase; there were still four British soldiers, Patterson and Baryalai. He doubted that the last two would take the chance of being shot and killed giving chase to him. In that he was right, as they remained cowering in the tent.

Having ditched his robes he could move easier and he blended into the dark desert background more easily making him a difficult target, even so reaching fifty yards from the edge of the camp he could hear and feel .303 rounds coming his way. Holden dropped the empty magazine from the rifle as he ran and slapped another into place in a fast autonomous fashion from his pouches as he moved. He was heading for the cover of the wadi and the assistance of covering fire from Waldron which seemed strangely lacking. He called out to his crippled comrade.

"Wally, covering fire, mate!" Initially he saw no movement from behind the wadi following his call but as he neared he could see frantic activity. Omar's men must have ambushed Waldron and Green. At that moment he heard a piercing scream from Green and shouting from Waldron. Almost on top of the wadi now, he could see Waldron lying on the floor fighting off a scimitar attack from an Afghan warrior with his bayoneted rifle. Just beyond he saw Green's fate with horror.

Two warriors were holding what was left of his stumpy arms whilst a third was repeatedly stabbing him with a large bladed dagger. On the run Holden raised his rifle and then planted himself still to get the best and sudden aim. He let off a shot that found its spot at the back of the dagger man's skull sending a shower of blood, tissue matter and bone all over his comrades. Neither had a firearm but they deserved no pity. Before either of them could break into a run they were felled by brisk marksmanship from Holden. Waldron's opponent distracted by the gunfire allowed his concentration whilst engaged in hand to hand combat to lapse and was stabbed full on in the stomach by the English soldier. In line with training Waldron not only drove it in deep but twisted it for good measure to maximise damage, hoping he had inflicted a fatal wound. The warrior fell backwards after a few seconds lifeless. There was a group still advancing on horseback beyond, so the first four must have been the silent attempted ambush attack, as they had left no steeds in sight. Holden loosed off rounds at the group as Waldron sat up and began to do the same; with a few swift volleys they were able to drive them away as Holden took cover next to Waldron in the wadi to concentrate on the Light Infantry men. Waldron watched the rear as Holden looked forwards with confusion. The British soldiers had retreated to the camp; there had to be method in this. Holden now considered that they were a small number from a larger party that may be holed up in a base in the mountains from where he had himself come. He and Waldron had to disappear into the night to ensure survival and fortunately at least one of their camels had remained idly chewing on some scrubby greenery during the military engagement. Then Holden heard a soft groaning and a weakened voice calling to him.

"William.....William"; it was Green.

In the heat of the brief fire fight and with survival forefront in his mind, he had momentarily forgotten about his tortured friend and SRP sergeant major. He crawled over to him and sat next to him. He pulled Green into his arms and was shocked by what he saw and heard. Green's torso was bleeding profusely from three gaping stab wounds and his breathing was shallow and rasping like that of an asthmatic. He was undeniably at the grim reaper's door. Holden looked down at his friend with tears welling in his eyes.

"William. Don't be sad. I have died on campaign with my friends. In the circumstances I can't ask for more. Please when you get back to England just tell my fiancée, what happened."

"I will, Nigel. Where can I find her?"

"Whitechapel. Last place she lived and worked as a dressmaker in Fashion Street. Karen......" Green died in Holden's arms before he could finish her name. His eyes stared lifeless into the sky; Holden gently rolled his hand over his friend's face and closed them to allow him to rest peacefully. Then he heard activity from the area of the camp. It sounded as if the remaining warriors had arrived there and were now mobilising with the light infantry men, it was time for Holden and Waldron to escape. Holden dragged his friend over to the camel, climbed on board himself and then pulled Waldron on with him. He gave an Arabic command to the beast and pulled on its reigns firmly and it stood up sharply from the ground. With another swift movement of the reigns Holden and Waldron disappeared into the night.

Ten minutes later Patterson and his men were at the wadi. A light sand storm had begun and any tracks that Holden had left were already gone. Under lamplight Patterson scoured the area the SRP men had hidden in. He was the first to see Green's body, or what was left of it and was shocked by its condition. He advised the officer commanding the four remaining light infantry men not to look at it and to leave it to the vultures.

"Captain, look at the remains of a body at your own risk. We will do an extended search for these rogue soldiers in the morning." The Light Infantry captain acknowledged his command and the party withdrew to the light and safety of the camp.

Unable to detect where Holden had gone, but knowing that he would possess limited supplies, Patterson, his men and the remaining Afghan warriors went back to the camp as Patterson had directed. Baryalai was waiting for them outside his tent with his young son by his side.

"Will you join me in refreshment to calm our nerves, Cecil?" Asked Baryalai genuinely.

"No thank you, Mahmood. I am tired and need to retire having come so close to death. I will leave my men to help tend the wounded and the dead here and at the wadi. I am truly sorry about Omar."

"Thank you, he was not my true son," he hugged the young boy at his leg, "this little warrior is my true son and heir. Sleep well and may the peace of Allah be with you."

"Yes, and with you, Mahmood." Patterson retired to one of the other tents, the use of which his host had given him. The men would join him in there later. He made himself comfortable amongst cushions and skins, having stripped off his boots and outer garments, then pulled a blanket from his pack over himself and settled down in the lamplight.

* * *

Dawn, the next day

Holden and Waldron had disappeared into the desert and eventually in the moonlight came by another wadi to take rest, cover and refreshment from its water. Both men were dry from the dust and sand they had tasted in combat and in escape and evasion, and from the dehydrating effect of the rush of adrenalin for such a prolonged period of time. Under dawn's early light having managed a ration of pemmican, mint cake and black tea, Waldron completed the last entry in his journal. Holden stared into space with deep inner thoughts of emotional distress with his good friend having been murdered following hideous torture. His bitter vengeful mind began to plot a campaign of violence and fear to wage against Patterson when the chance presented itself. Patterson would never again send good men to well known and certain death.

Waldron completed his entry. He placed the journal into the satchel that he habitually wore to keep the document safe. It was his intention that when recognition of the mission came, his friends would be commemorated and honoured accordingly. What he hadn't noticed as he lay on the rough stone scrubby ground of the wadi, was that one of the buckles holding the strap to the satchel had come undone. He looked up at Holden who suddenly became alert. He was twisting his head around like a canine trying to detect the direction of a sound. Holden stood up to look south in the direction from which they had arrived at the wadi. He could see a moving dust cloud in the distance.

"Wally, we've got go, now!" He flung together the last of their food supplies into a kind of rough Arabic saddlebag and hung it over the camel. He dragged Waldron over to the beast and they both mounted. In the process of being dragged, the satchel simply slipped from Waldron's shoulders and became abandoned in the dust like another of their fallen comrades. Neither of them realised until they were making their escape, just managing to disappear out of sight below the horizon, so their hunters were unsure of their direction as a sand storm began to whip up.

Waldron suddenly realised the bag was missing from his shoulders. "Boss, the bag and the journal, they're gone!"

"Can't go back, matey, I'm sorry." Holden knew that their adversaries would be ready to match any aggressive attack he could perform by countering it now with sheer weight of numbers. Waldron was devastated and fell silent for several hours.

Arriving at the wadi with a mix of British soldiers and Afghan Warriors, Patterson dismounted and began to survey where his nemesis had briefly taken sanctuary. He was fuming inside that Holden had escaped his clutches, but looking up into the distance felt his chances of survival were most likely slim in the harsh Afghan wilderness with limited supplies and, at times, a hostile indigenous population. He then saw the satchel's outline in the sand and picked it up. He shook off the sand and opened it to see what was inside. Within it amongst a few scant personal possessions was a leather bound journal book which he began to flick through and was instantly intrigued by what he saw. He decided he would read it back at the camp where he and his remaining men would spend the night with Baryalai and his faultless hospitality once more before leaving to return back to India via the Khyber Pass once more. Sadly, this upstanding Bedouin man would never know the true fate of the men he had known as the 'surveyors', to whom he had first extended a welcome. His latest guest was a man that he did not realise in truth bore him ill will. Patterson flicked through a variety of pages in the book. It seemed that it was a fascinating story. Holden undoubtedly was a resilient man. Perhaps too much so.

Chapter Six

Early the next morning Patterson took the light infantry officer aside away from the earshot of his men and of their hosts. Having read the detailed account of what had happened to the SRP men and the hostility they had encountered, any attempt to glean natural resources from Afghanistan at present would have to be pursued aggressively. Patterson decided that Empire Petroleum would have to pursue their interests elsewhere as far as anyone else was concerned; he was not about to communicate the truth to a humble infantry commander about a privately funded invasion.

"Captain, we are leaving today to head back over the mountains to the Khyber Pass. It seems that there is nothing to be found here and that the lakes of 'black gold' or oil are a myth. We will thank our hosts having taken breakfast with them and head off." The captain looked at him curiously.

"But, Minister, Baryalai said that they existed last night. How do you know that they don't?" Patterson objected to his mild protest.

"Captain, I am the Minister of War. Do not question me unless you wish to be permanently assigned to the Indian sub-continent until you retire as lieutenant. I have found a journal by a member of the SRP party that states that they found nothing."

"The SRP? That's Captain Holden's brainchild, I've never seen him but he's a legend. Is that who we were fighting off last night?" Patterson was now truly found out by his subordinate.

"This information is subject to the statutes of sedition should you utter anything further from this conversation. Do I make myself clear,

Captain? You are to say nothing and I will tell you nothing more. Now get your men together and we'll soon be on our way. If you value your career then you will do as I say." The captain said nothing and held a contemptible gaze with Patterson for some seconds before silently turning away from him and returning to his remaining men. Patterson would have to be cautious of this man from now on.

After a traditional Bedouin breakfast the light infantry men had prepared all the horses they had arrived with, fastening the bodies of the fallen to their mounts now being used as pack horses to get them all home. Whilst this preparation took place Patterson confronted Baryalai outside the main tent one last time to say his farewell.

"Mahmood, you have been most kind, I have discovered a diary written by one of those alleged surveyors. As you could see they were nothing more than mercenary soldiers of fortune and not representative of Her Majesty's government. The report, however, was not encouraging so for now I will not be pursuing the matter further. Rest assured we shall be back one day." They shook hands firmly as Patterson spoke.

"Thank you, Cecil. Those words and explanation make me feel better about that renegade called Holden. Tell me, what should I do if I see him again?"

"Kill him. Kill him before he kills you. He is an enemy of your world and mine." Patterson spoke without hesitation. Baryalai eyed him cautiously following this reply. This man Holden had actually seemed far more reasonable than the fellow in front of him, there was something deeply untrustworthy about Patterson.

"Tell me, Cecil, what do you do again?" asked Baryalai.

"I am a Minister in Her Majesty's government."

"I see, thank you." It explained a lot in Baryalai's mind; this man was what was called a 'politician' and therefore untrustworthy with only his own self interest in mind.

"May the peace of Allah be upon your house, Mahmood," Patterson tried to curry favour until the very end.

"Thank you." It was a blunt cold reply from his host. To a genuine person he would normally have reciprocated the wish but he did not like or trust this politician. He turned his back on him and walked into the tent. Patterson, a little bemused by this sudden cold turn of events, mounted his horse being held by one of the infantry men and began to ride off towards the mountains followed by the group of soldiers. In his mind he was still concerned with the mindset of the officer within his party.

It took several hours until the group reached, in unusually fair weather, a significant altitude upon the perilous mountains of the North West Frontier. The group had become quite strung out as the climb up the mountains aboard horses had intensified; the infantry officer was now leading the way closely followed by Patterson with the nearest of the regular infantry men some hundred yards or so behind them. Ahead Patterson could see that the path was becoming ever narrower with a vast drop off to one side into what appeared to be a bottomless abyss. With the distance between himself and the officer to the nearest of those lagging behind in mind, none of them would be any the wiser to a tragic 'accident' taking place as they were not close enough to tell otherwise. As the path narrowed Patterson ensured that he had closed the distance between himself and the officer so that he was within touching distance with a stretch to the lead horse's hindquarters. Inside his jacket pocket he carried a fountain pen with a fine, sharp silver nib. It was the ideal weapon to initiate his plan.

To their left the drop was absolutely cavernous, so deep he wished not to look over it himself. Patterson had to just lead his horse to overlap the mount ahead just very slightly so that he could reach. As he achieved his objective he plunged the silver pen into the rear left upper leg of the horse with some considerable force, but ensuring he was able to retrieve it instantly. His plan worked perfectly; the horse reared up in fear and pain from the sharp stabbing it felt, completely unexpectedly to the unsuspecting infantry officer. He tried to control the animal but to no avail in the limited time he had to react and in the limited space that was available to him. The horse unseated him and threw him from its back and into the chasm of the mountainside to their left. There was a piercing scream from the infantry officer as he remained conscious all the way down a sheer drop of two thousand feet. The sound of his chilling screaming did die away as he fell but no one heard the thud of his landing upon some rocks below smashing most of the bones in his body and killing him instantly. There was consternation from behind as the men sped up slightly to see what had happened, although it was far too late for them to be able to do anything.

The remaining soldiers arrived only in time to see the horse bolting off into the distance, at such a speed and demeanour that it seemed unlikely that any of them would see it again. Patterson was inwardly grinning like a Cheshire cat; it would seem that all of his loose ends were tied up, after all Holden was never going to make it back to civilisation.

"What the fuck happened, Sir?" asked a bemused soldier dismounting his horse and walking forward to speak to the Minister.

"Oh, a tragic accident, the horse just shied for no reason, young man." There was genuine contempt in his voice. The simple soldier looked over the drop in disbelief, inwardly now concerned with 'would anyone make it back?' Patterson knowingly and patronisingly smiled and said to the concerned looking soldier, "just follow me and you will be all right."

He was quite correct in his bold affirmation. Within a week they were back in India. The soldiers returned to the remainder of their unit and buried their dead, other than the ill fated officer. Patterson was a skilled horseman from a brief military fling some fifteen years previously. He had learnt his craft within the cavalry but had no wish to stay in the army's employ; better to pull the strings of command he felt rather than being the blunt tool at the end of them. It was the life skills that he picked up during this earlier period of his life that had helped to secure his exit from the harsh North West Frontier with the remaining scared and naïve 'squaddies'.

He ensured that that the journal written by John Waldron travelled safely with him in his immediate hand luggage when he boarded the train from Jodphur to Bombay, and a sailing back to London aboard a very comfortable mail steamer in, of course, first class.

* * *

Paris, August 1904

Karen Wood wept as she sat with Robert Ford on the bench in the Place de la Concorde. It was near midnight now that he had finished his story of the tragedies of sixteen years earlier within the district where she had lived for many years. During that time she had heard what almost amounted to folk tales of the ghostlike elusive 'Jack the Ripper'. He had composed himself during his cathartic retelling of his part in the events and its direct nature; a rare opportunity that had done him good. In the intervening years he had never spoken to anyone of what had happened, although he deliberately did not speak of his trip to Missouri, U.S.A to take complete and final revenge on Dr Tumblety.

As he stared along the Champs Elysee stretched out in front of them he became very aware of the warmth of a woman close to him; he looked down into his lap to see that she was holding both of his hands in her own gently, caressing them. He looked up into her eyes making clear contact with her. The weakness he had felt earlier had died away and he felt strong and clear minded again, but also felt a wave of affection for this woman he knew little about and had known such a short time. He moved his face towards her and she didn't resist or move, although he could feel the grip of her hands upon his tighten slightly. Ford gently kissed Karen on her lips holding the sensation, feeling and contact for just a few seconds. Then he lightly broke away and stood up taking her by the hand encouraging her to stand up with him.

"Right. We came out for a walking tour of this beautiful city so let's go."

Responding to this, Karen took the arm he offered her and smiled, blushing just a little. They walked off arm in arm along the Champs Elysee towards the illuminated 'Arc de Triomphe' in the distance. They chatted easily about lighter matters now and often about the history of Paris as they passed iconic structures on their way west such as the 'Grand' and 'Petit Palais' and beyond them the Bridge of Alexander III. Carriages of all types clattered past them upon the cobbles as they enjoyed the fresh air of the midnight hour. Elsewhere for others within the Minister's party events were about to take a violent turn.

* * *

Steven Pick, the new under-secretary to the Minister, had decided that he would spend his evening in the lively 'Pigalle' district. An evening at the 'Moulin Rouge' had proved too much of a temptation and he came out from the notorious burlesque venue both drunk and almost devoid of ready cash. He would have to walk back to the hotel once he had established his bearings which even in his drunken state he realised would help sober him up, after all it was a walk of about an hour. He stood on the pavement outside the Moulin Rouge trying to steady his mind and gain his balance to walk as the cooler exterior air mixed with his intoxicated state of mind. He could feel his head spinning and he struggled to read the dial upon his fob watch. As he tried to read the time he was aware of a diminutive bearded man wearing glasses and a top hat walking by him accompanied by two striking Parisian women.

"What's that four eyed little sod got then," he mumbled under his breath as they passed him by; the two women smelt divine with their scent of expensive perfume. By their physiology he suspected they were dancers from the venue. He tried to focus on his watch again when an English voice spoke to him from behind and placed a hand on his shoulder.

"My friend it is nearly one o'clock and that is Monsieur Toulouse Lautrec. He is a renowned artist and a famous resident of the district. He has money, charisma, a healthy sexual appetite and apparently a large penis. Some say it only appears so as he is closer to the ground." Pick then heard the striking of a match and could smell its phosphorus burn as the voice from behind him lit a match. He looked around to see no one at eye level; but in an instant he could see a man sat in a wheel chair on his own behind him. He was dressed in black with a black top hat, glasses with dark coloured lenses, a generous moustache but with quite weathered hands and complexion, with what he could see of it. "Forgive me, I am a friendly Englishman abroad and did not wish to startle you. May I be of assistance?" Steven Pick was a little taken aback by this wheelchair bound new acquaintance and had to think for a minute. He had never before spoken to a cripple and was surprised by this man's convention. At home they seemed silent and he thought they often lost their faculties with their limbs or at least the use of them. He took a typical prejudicial view of those that were different to him in any way; but he wasn't sure of the first part of his walk back.

"Well, chap. I'd like to get back to the Place Vendome but don't know the way." In his drunken state he failed to realise he still looked down at this wheelchair bound individual with his normal type of contempt.

The Dressmaker Connection

"Are you going by foot or wheeled transport?" He drew on his cigarette seemingly enjoying its nicotine feed as its tip glowed brightly.

"Walking. I don't have the money for wheeled transport."

"Neither do I but I still would be going by wheels as you see." Someone less contemptible or prejudicial without Pick's arrogance would have seen the funny side of someone's self mocking – or at least another soldier would.

"Let me do you a favour," said the paraplegic, "I need to head partly that way. So if you push me I can get you on track then you can go your own way on your own." His eyes masked by the glasses Pick could not gauge this man's intentions. He was drunk, however, and wanted to get back to the hotel.

"All right. I suppose you need pushing. Which way?" He went behind the wheelchair and took hold of the pushing handles. Facing out towards the street the cripple pointed to the left.

"That way, past near where they're building the new church of the Sacred Heart. You get a nice view from there." He carried on puffing on his cigarette the smoke of which annoyingly to Pick kept drifting into his face.

They made their way east along the Boulevard de Clichy past women selling themselves on street corners, noisy bars and artists' private studios all closed for the night. As they past the 'Elysee de Monmatre' the cripple spoke. Pick was feeling light headed from the extra exertion and sweating with the gradual effects of dehydration creeping up on him following his alcoholic excesses.

"Look, if you fancy a good view of the city, then lets go up there, mate."

"Mate?" Pick said catching his breath "I'm not your mate. There's a bloody hill going up there. Bugger that." He let go of the wheel chair and bent over to take a few deep breaths.

"Come on. I'm an old ex-soldier. I got little money and little pleasure in life. C'mon, take me up there and earn your place as a 'Good Samaritan'."

Pick looked up the building line from Clichy past the famous L'Elysee of Monmatre and up to the sight of the partially complete basilica. He tried to look at his watch again. The cripple spoke before he could focus.

"It's only twenty past fucking one. Come on, you'll enjoy it too."

"Don't swear at me, cripple."

"DON'T FUCKING SPEAK TO ME LIKE THAT NEITHER!" Shouted the outraged paraplegic. "I gave up my legs for the likes of you and your boss. It's the least you can fucking do to take me up there." The weak willed Pick actually felt quite intimidated by this outburst as well as a little shamed. He let out a large sigh and began pushing the chair up the hill towards the unfinished cathedral completely missing the hateful inclusion of a reference to Patterson.

It took him nearly half an hour to get himself and the cripple up to the top of the hill and he sweated profusely from the effort. His mouth was dry and he felt very dizzy. He placed the wheelchair at an angle looking out over the spectacular view of the city and then sat on a bench.

"Don't leave me in the middle of the fucking gardens. Let me sit with you so I can talk you through things." Pick was too fatigued to argue with the objectionable cripple any more. He stood up and wheeled him over so the chair was next to his bench and sat back down.

"That's better. Like a couple of old Chelsea pensioners now ain't we?" Pick couldn't be bothered to reply; he looked out over the sky line which was actually worth the effort of the climb.

"See that great big metal monstrosity over there, boy?"

"Yes. The Eiffel Tower. And don't call me boy."

"That was finished nine years before I lost the use of my legs. You'd fucking know all about that though wouldn't you?" This confused Pick.

"Er, why? Some crippled old soldier? Why would I know about you in particular? There are hundreds out there." Suddenly Pick felt a sharp stabbing pain in his left thigh. At that instant he was grabbed from behind and his arms pinioned so he couldn't struggle or resist. The cripple then pulled some rope out of his pocket and tied it around Pick's left thigh and pulled it tight then tying it off.

"What the hell is going on? Get off of me! What have you stabbed me with?" He was crying out as panic and fear set in with the thought of the murder of Charles Wilmot. The voice of the person restraining him spoke, coming from behind. It was a very calm and calculated voice, the owner of which eventually appeared in the form of a drawn but athletic looking man in front of him.

"Let me introduce us to you Mr Pick. I am Captain Holden and this is my last surviving subordinate Trooper John Waldron. Have you ever heard of the SRP?" Pick shook his head and looked back at him fearfully. "No, didn't think you would have. Well we did a job for your boss in Afghanistan six years ago and those of us that survived were left for dead. In fact, that process was intentionally sped up, but as you can see it failed. As for your leg and you? Well, Johnny here stabbed you with a large needled syringe and injected you with a water based solution of cyanide salts. That's because one of my men was poisoned with cyanide before he had the chance to defend himself. At the moment the makeshift tourniquet is preventing the poison from entering your body quickly and killing you almost instantly, but it's nonetheless in you and it will kill you. If you leave it as it is you will feel its gradual, uncomfortable poisoning effects and die slowly and painfully, becoming slowly more faint and drowsy and you will probably be overcome by a sense of anxiety. You will start to feel nauseous, dizzy and may start to sweat profusely. If you release the tourniquet immediately the poison will take effect swiftly and you will have a quick and relatively, in comparison, painless death." Holden was very cold and calculating whilst the cripple said nothing.

"Why me?" asked Pick feeling weak and beginning to feel nauseous.

"I want your employer to feel the fear I felt as my men were gradually slaughtered before me knowing that death is now catching up with him. I want him to eventually be grateful for death when it comes hoping that it will take him briskly and not leave him agonising as all around him suffer; as all of my men suffered. What happened to my men and to me haunts my every waking hour. When he realises what's coming then so will he feel haunted."

The fight to survive that Holden had encountered when he and Waldron had evaded death so often had left him cold and callous and ripe to seek revenge. As the memories of Afghanistan returned to him he made Pick's decision for him. He gagged him and then tied his arms back to the bench preventing him from being able to move. He then took hold of Waldron's wheelchair and the two disappeared behind the doomed Minister of War's under Secretary Steven Pick. He attempted muffled cries for mercy but to no avail when his killers first left. He died painfully from cyanide poisoning over the next hour, alone, cold and terrified exactly as Holden had intended.

Chapter Seven

Six a.m. Ford had been back at the hotel barely an hour when the commotion began. He and Karen had strolled up as planned to the 'Place D'Etoile' from where they had taken a carriage to see the Eiffel Tower, and then travelled back east to the Ile de Cite and Notre Dame Cathedral. The driver had then dropped them at the 'Place de L'Opera' from where they had walked the short distance back to the hotel; it had been a life changing experience for both of them and they had discussed how to try to secretly spend some time together. They knew that a liaison between them could be quite perilous; the Minister's mistress and his personal protection officer. Ford was not about to let that get in the way of him finding happiness perhaps once more.

It was Bob Spicer that hammered furiously on his door to bring him around from his short lived slumber; it woke him with a start as he had fallen deeply asleep quite briskly.

"Rob! Get up there's been another murder!" Spicer continued hammering on the door to be let in and explain the facts to him. "Let me in quick! Come on!" Ford jumped out of bed and staggered in his tired state over to the door. He opened it up and Spicer burst in and began babbling at him about what had happened. "It's the under secretary, Pick. He's been found by the local old bill up on the hill at a place called Monmartre seemingly poisoned." Ford tried to focus his thoughts. He rubbed his eyes and made for the bathroom as he spoke with the intention to freshen up briskly. He spoke as he moved.

"What? How do they know? How long ago was he discovered? Is he still there?" Ford considered the need to get to the scene of the crime quickly. He splashed some water over his face and head at the hand basin as he spoke. He towelled himself off, brushed his hair and began to get dressed as Spicer replied.

"He's been found with a tourniquet around his leg and his skin has gone an awful pink colour indicating a high level of cyanide in his blood. Apparently his mouth smells of almonds too. They found him about an hour ago. He might still be in situ I just don't know."

"Right, go out and call a carriage for me. You stay here with Vincent and look after the Minister. Someone is out to get him or to scare him greatly." Spicer left the room and went to ensure that there was a carriage for Ford at the front of the Hotel waiting in the Place Vendome.

Within half an hour of being woken Ford found himself amongst a group of French detectives looking at the lifeless body of Steven Pick still sat as he had been left by Holden and discovered by a passing policeman. Inspector Reno was the officer in charge at the murder scene and fortunately for Robert Ford he had a good command of English.

"Well, Inspector, why do you think that someone would kill a member of staff of your principal in such a specific way?" asked Reno who was smoking a cigarette, typically with panache as Ford had observed many middle and upper class Parisians seemed to.

"I just don't know. It's the second member of staff that has been murdered. But the methodology is completely different. I can't fathom as to why his office is being targeted but not him it seems." Ford scratched his nose as he spoke and bent forward to take a closer look at the lifeless Steven Pick. He sniffed cautiously near the dead man's mouth and indeed there was a bizarre scent of almonds.

"Cyanide poisoning, Mr Ford. Very specific in its delivery. The doctor says that he's had a large needle put into his left thigh and had the poison pumped into him that way. But observe the tourniquet, it's still done up tight to give a slow and painful delivery with him bound and having no way to mercifully speed up the process for himself. You have a very callous killer out there, Mr Ford." Indeed Reno was right, someone who intended to inflict maximum suffering and create the ultimate state of fear for his main target.

"Thank you, Inspector Reno, perhaps you could have the body taken to a mortuary and the embassy will arrange repatriation to the

U.K. I shall have a talk to Sir Cecil now this has happened and see what he has to say, see who he may have upset in the past. If you discover anything else, please let me know."

"Well there is one thing. Across the grass over there," Reno pointed to the area behind them and the bench, "there are wheel tracks as if from a wheelchair. They are fresh Monsieur. Very odd, n'est pas?" Ford nodded his head in response and walked over to have a look for himself. In the meantime with a nod from Inspector Reno the undertakers stepped up and began work to remove the body to allow it some dignity at last.

* * *

Unknown to Ford while he was at the scene of the murder, Patterson was conducting a very private and secretive meeting in his suite at the hotel. Dressed in his full burgundy cardinal's robes, Victoire de Vicompte, the Cardinal of the Parisian Grande diocese was taking coffee with Patterson overlooking the Place Vendome. No one else was permitted to be present in the room whilst they met. The Cardinal's transport and aides remained outside discreetly at the rear of the premises. The men spoke politely but frankly; they both had something that the other wanted.

"So, Sir Cecil, you say that in exchange for a short term loan, you can promise me a three hundred percent return on the money and you will assist the church with access to tame the natives of Afghanistan, bringing Christianity to them?" Patterson gulped back a cup of dark, strong black coffee before he spoke. He was still sobering up from the night before and he was very aware of the smell of stale alcohol on his breath. He did his best to keep a distance from de Vicompte. Patterson naively didn't realise that the Cardinal was as partial to alcoholic excesses as he was.

"Yes, your Grace. We, Empire Petroleum, have a plan to assist them to exploit their natural resources. With financial prosperity comes the need for moral guidance. To have the church present can only be of benefit to the populace and to the spiritual wellbeing of our workers." Patterson had no intention of explaining the martial nature of the commercial excursion he was planning. His intention was to gain finance that he could easily repay generously but to nowhere near the extent that his vast profits would be compromised. The project was still being finalised.

"All right. My church will lend you one half million English pounds. We expect our return in no less than twelve months." As he finished the cardinal stood and offered his hand to Patterson. The corrupt Minister grasped it in a reciprocal fashion to seal the deal. The Cardinal felt a chill of objection run through his body identifying the Masonic grasp in which Patterson took his hand to shake it. Still, business was business and Vicompte could look forward to a handsome return for himself and the church. The risks seemed minimal from the confidence of this ungodly freemason and he was prepared to accept an unorthodox union for the capital gain. He silently left the room. Minutes later there was a knock on the door. Patterson opened it to find a priest stood at the door who handed him a leather brief case. The padre turned and left. Patterson shut the door and walked over to a table and opened the case. He smiled broadly at the contents inside.

* * *

An hour later having rushed back to the Ritz, bolted some breakfast and waited for the Minister to return to his suite from breakfast, Ford began to informally interview Sir Cecil over the two murders. Ramsey Phillips had broken the news to the Minister in the dining room and had then informed the rest of the Ministerial staff of the murder. Amongst them there was now a growing air of concern.

"Inspector, I have no idea about why someone would be killing my staff. Perhaps the whole thing is just an unfortunate coincidence. Wilmot was unlucky in London and now Pick is equally unlucky in Paris. They are both big cities and murders happen. I am a successful industrialist and politician. Yes, I've had to make unpopular decisions but never anything that I would have imagined would fuel someone to murder." Sir Cecil had become unusually animated over the matter and now walked to the window of his suite that overlooked the Grand Column of the Army. In the back of his mind he could see that it was Napoleon's plagiarism of Trajan's victory column in Rome and by his own nature he enjoyed the arrogance with which the French General had copied the style of one of the greatest Roman emperors.

"Minister, are you sure that in your past, especially perhaps in the cut throat world of industry, that there may not be someone who wishes to do you harm?" Patterson continued to gaze out of the window listening to his personal protection officers words. He knew potentially that the answer could be 'yes' but dismissed the possibility straight away in his own mind. Neither of those left could have returned from Afghanistan, the savagery of the attacks detailed in Waldron's journal ensured that eventual escape would have been impossible for one able bodied man with a cripple.

"Inspector, what kind of industrialist, or for that matter, man do you think I am? Surely my actions would have to be as despicable as those of the killer in these matters. I find that inference quite offensive. Now, you may have a day resting whilst I continue my official business with Sergeant Spicer in my party for the day."

"Minister, it's normal to have both the personal protection officer and the close protection officer on hand, not just for you but for the PPO's assistance." The Minister turned from the window and faced Ford with obvious fury in his face for the inspector's persistence.

"Right. Whatever is your standard operating procedure; do it. Just stay away from me for today please." He stood just staring at Ford expecting to get his message across. Ford maintained a belligerent stand and said nothing just returning the stare. "Good day, Inspector." Ford knew that this was the cue for him to leave the room.

Outside he met Bob Spicer and passed on the Minister's directions to him. He felt no disgrace or loss of credibility; after twenty years police service he was used to being treated as a cheap commodity. The principle he had found that had always applied to his career was 'shit travels downstream.'

* * *

Ford waited at the main door of the Ritz overlooking the Place Vendome enjoying the warm Parisian summer sun on his face; the sense of warmth and wellbeing it engendered within him reminded him of hot lazy days as a child on the foreshore of the Thames at low tide. He would venture down to the riverside gaining access from the slipways with his friends from the neighbourhood around Cable Street, Stepney where they would paddle in the murky cool water to try to reduce the effects of the blazing lunchtime sun, and occasionally engage in 'toshing'. This was the practice of sieving or searching by hand the mud of the foreshore for any misplaced valuables. They rarely found anything. His mind really began to drift back to the vivid recollections of his childhood.

* * *

Ford was born in 1863 to William and Ann Ford who lived in Cable Street from the start of their married life up to their tragic demise. Young Robert enjoyed, for the East End, a loving childhood due to the fact that his parents had been unable to conceive any further offspring. It had meant that the family of three never went short of food, clothes or the rent money with his father working hard as a 'carman' or porter at Smithfield's meat market. It was unusual for a household to only have three mouths to feed. He was doted on by his mother as an infant for fear that she might lose the only child she had been able to bear for her beloved William. William was philosophical about only having Robert, being one of life's eternal fatalists when it came to any such matters. They were able to ensure that the lad ate well and gained a good basic education with no one else to indulge in. It paid dividends for Robert. He grew up well nourished with a good bone structure and a healthy muscularity as he helped his father on a Friday through to Sunday morning heaving meat around as he reached his early teens.

As a child he was fascinated with the infamous 'Jamrach's Emporium' in Ratcliff Highway where one could gain access to all manners of exotic creatures. Visiting and returning sailors brought Jamrach all manners of animals for a reasonable payment in return. At one time the establishment could supply patrons with a range that ran from elephants, to lions and tigers, monkeys and exotic birds.

Robert's parents allowed him to have a small dog; it was a Staffordshire bull terrier crossed with a Parson Jack Russell. The eight year old Robert found it amusing to simply call the pup 'Jack'. As it matured, Robert found that it had an exceptional talent for killing vermin; rats, mice, squirrels and pigeons after it had successfully stalked them. It allowed Robert, two years later, to earn money from local people by visiting their squalid yards or communal courts and having the feisty and efficient Jack enjoy himself despatching quickly and ruthlessly whatever emerged into the open areas. So noted did the dog become in a small period of time that the eleven year old Robert was asked to enter Jack in a 'ratting pit' competition at a pub in Bethnal Green.

This involved placing the dog in a 'turnspit' with rats, an ever increasing number, whilst bets were placed as to how quickly and how many of the large vicious sewer rats the dog could kill. When he saw the rats Robert was reluctant to take part and his accompanying father also noticed his apprehension. The crowd surrounding the turnspit in the 'Marquis of Granby' public house in Bethnal Green Road resented the boy's decision to perhaps not take part. Robert held onto the dog now becoming agitated in his arms as his father cleared a path for them to leave. An over-aggressive short man, barely taller than Robert, swung a punch from the crowd striking William Ford square in his sternum and knocking him to the floor gasping for air. Alarmed and aggressively infuriated, clutching Jack under his left arm, Robert stepped forward in a lightning movement and lashed out with a punch from a tightly clenched right fist that neither the crowd nor the short aggressor saw coming or expected from what appeared to be not even a callow youth.

It struck its target perfectly; square upon the short man's jaw and he fell to the floor knocked-out cold. The crowd fell silent and almost seemed to clear a space around the lad. Even the barking and snapping terrier under Robert's arm had fallen silent.

"You fucking people let us go, or me and the dog will fight our way out together! And he's got a better bite than my punch," screamed the shaking Robert Ford as he then grabbed his father's left arm and helped pull him to his feet. He was praying that such a display of bravado would help them escape. The crowd stayed silent. Then a lad maybe a year or two older than Robert stepped forward and squared up to him. He was a good couple of inches taller, and by his misshapen nose, was a regular fighter.

"Who's toughest then, you or your fucking dog?" he hissed, mistakenly, right into Robert's face. Keeping his arms static, quick as a flash Robert reacted with a vicious head-butt, exploding the filthy aggressive youth's nose all over his face. He fell to the floor clutching it in agony.

"Both of us, wanker."

He took his father's arm and they strolled out of the pub unmolested. It was after that incident that Ford envisaged that he might be able to make money in a similar way to Jack. A massive tragedy would force him to do so.

* * *

Suddenly Ford had to snap back into the world of reality; Patterson was walking past him and addressed him in a condescending fashion.

"I have some private financial E.P business to deal with and I don't need you around, Inspector. Sergeant Spicer will suffice and I will not discuss the matter." He walked on not even prepared in his arrogance to discuss the matter. The ministerial party of Patterson, Phillips and Spicer boarded a carriage and rode off. Despite the thought of time with Karen, Ford's curiosity was inflamed. 'E.P business only?' He boarded a carriage himself and with a mix of broken French and sign language got the driver to follow the Minister's ride.

They travelled quite sometime and distance through the Parisian Streets before they arrived upon the Ile de Cite. Entering the 'Palais de Justice', the ministerial party certainly had not become aware of Ford's surveillance. The carriage pulled clear of the door but waited outside. Ford paid and dismissed his driver and watched from the cover of the crowds who frequented the island to visit the Notre Dame Cathedral.

Another enclosed carriage arrived ten minutes later. Ford watched with enraged curiosity as to whom else Patterson was meeting. He was stunned by who alighted; it was two high-ranking Catholic Cardinals and two apparent 'bag-carrying' junior priests. Whatever was a leading Masonic, industrialist, British politician doing meeting high ranking French churchmen? If it was for the purpose of industrial investment then Ford really should have no concern. Perhaps it might be for charity. But two members of Patterson's staff had been murdered. He would endeavour to discover what this was about; probably most simplistically back in Britain. It might help him understand the threat to his principal a little better.

Ford remained vigilant at his location to see who else came or went. He never dreamed that it would take up to late in the evening. He was feeling tired, dreadfully tired. It was that sensation that he knew he hated. He would be especially cautious now; he could not afford to

The Dressmaker Connection

allow his fatigue to lead to mistakes as he rubbed his slightly watering and stinging eyes in the warm French summer air.

* * *

11.p.m. Ford finally sat down in the bar area having had a thoroughly dull but curious day. It was most odd that Spicer had not been insistent on having, as was statutory practice, a close protection officer whose role and responsibility was to support the needs or requests of the personal protection officer. It hadn't been a difficult day. Very boring as Patterson had spent most of his day in this very bizarre meeting with a high-ranking churchman; Ford's cynicism drove him to believe it could not be for charitable purposes. Now the Minister was back in his room with Mark Vincent 'on the door', Spicer had gone to bed with hardly a word to Ford who now settled into the Chesterfield type two seat sofa in the bar with a large Calvados in his hand. There was a constant throng of people in the Ritz bar and the atmosphere held the buzz of dozens of conversations in as many languages in this internationally renowned Paris destination. He hadn't seen Karen all day or at any time in the evening for that matter and remembered the delight of the walk the night before. She had probably wisely taken the opportunity of sleeping through the morning, an opportunity not available to him. He felt very tired as the calvados warmed the pit of his stomach. He had managed to fight off most of its effects up to now. Over the years of differing types of policing he had come to loath the sensation of blunted senses that fatigue brought with it as it arrived. The symptoms were all there; sore, watery feeling eyes, occasional muscle spasms in his left forearm, a dry mouth and slowness of thought. He placed the glass on the table in front of him and sat back dropping his head right the way back to stretch his neck off and closed his weary and increasingly sore eyes.

Sitting head-back with his eyes shut was very relaxing and he now realised the urgency with which he had to get to bed. In his relaxed and vulnerable state he then felt a body sit down closely next to him. Whoever it was then placed a hand on his thigh. He opened his eyes and as if to fulfil a dream it was Karen Wood.

"You look exhausted, Robert," she said gently rubbing her hand in a caring and affectionate manner along his left thigh.

"I am knackered to put it bluntly." He noticed that her cheeks looked peculiarly reddened. It didn't appear to be through being too hot or through any form of emotional stimulus. They looked as if someone had slapped her in the face. It gave him a cause for concern. "Are you all right?" She looked away from him embarrassed and seemingly not wanting to answer. He had his suspicions. "Has someone hit you, Karen?" Defiance in her voiced was trying to disguise emotion.

"I'm fine. I feel a little flushed that's all." There was an uncomfortable silence as they sat there. She grabbed his calvados and gulped the remainder of the glass back herself. She grabbed his thigh firmly near to his crotch. "Robert. Take me to your room. I want you now."

The words came as a shocking 'bolt out of the blue' as Ford would have termed it himself, but they stimulated his sense of sexual predatory. In the last year since dispatching the evil Dr Tumblety, he had strayed into a handful of casual sexual liaisons with some high-class West London women from the social circles within which he infrequently mixed. None of these forays had any meaning to him except a sense of sexual gratification. One had enjoyed 'firm' treatment in particular, which satisfied the subliminal interest many sexually active men had in the fantasy of rape. Karen Wood was different though; he had come to accept that she was the most sexually alluring woman he had ever known. She oozed sensuality from every pore; in her look; in the graceful feline way in which she walked. Despite his exhaustion he could think of no experience that he would sooner indulge in.

He had to consider exercising caution, however, the sudden proposition had switched his mind back into full alert, a mental condition that allowed him to think beyond the normal and obvious parameters in society; it kept him alive in an uncertain world.

"I'm in room 212. Go and take the lift and I shall take the stairs and the door will be ajar for you when you get there." These were Ford's parting words as he left the bar and seconds later Karen did the same.

Indeed he was right. As she reached 212 the door was ajar and she walked straight in closing it behind her. She turned to see him stood in the room just in front of the bed having taken off his shoes, jacket, waistcoat and tie and having undone the first three buttons of his shirt. She walked over to him and took his head in her hands and began to kiss him passionately; she tore open his shirt sending buttons across the room and then ran her hands over his muscular chest and shoulders. As she did so, he reached around the back of her outfit and began to undo the metal clips and hooks that fastened the tight bodice top that accentuated her figure. She then broke away from kissing him and turned her back to him to allow him quicker access and giving him the opportunity to gently kiss and nuzzle her neck as he continued to undo the dress. As he unfastened the last of the hooks she shrugged off the bodice and stepped out of the matching skirt dress then turned to face him in a black corset, silk drawers and heeled mid-calf Edwardian boots. With the shirt buttons gone, she pulled the shirt out from his trousers and over his head. She continued to run her hands over his bare chest and lower torso. He was in good shape for a man of his age still quite lean from his early years of being a teenage pugilist and trying to respect his health as he aged. The vigorous fencing sessions twice a week helped to keep him toned along with the strength and warm up exercises that went with every meet with his coach, Andre Moreau formally of Dieppe.

Ford fenced well; he had chosen it as a discipline for many reasons. It allowed him to keep fit with sharp reactions; it allowed him to mix in a gentlemanly social circle in the Victoria postal district in which he lived. It also gave him the satisfaction of single combat that his career as a teenage pugilist had given him in Whitechapel and Spitalfields. He had mastered the foil and the epee but was yet to gain a full grasp of the sabre. Ford knew from his indulgences in West End society that he also made love well.

She removed the rest of his clothes as he pulled down her drawers and then pushed him gently onto the bed and straddled him. She bent forward and kissed him lustfully which signalled the commencement of a long night of passion between them. The night was theirs and the emotion and carnal pleasures in Ford's hotel room was, for now, the only world that existed for them.

* * *

Elsewhere in Paris Holden and his crippled former subordinate Waldron were enjoying the show at the 'Follies Bergere' in the Rue Richer. Despite his weathered complexion from the months fighting to survive during the escape from Afghanistan and then journey penniless through Pakistan and India, Holden was still a handsome man. However, the attention that he courted on occasions when he was out with Waldron was a source of envy that only deepened the cripple's depressed view of life and society in general. There seemed no doubt in his mind that if you strayed from the accepted norm in any way then you were either ignored or treated with distain. He didn't consider himself an ugly man, indeed in the early days of the SRP socialising together he was never short of female company; the loss of the use of his legs and the permanent company of a wheelchair had changed all of that. Although at times he felt resentment towards his able bodied former commander, it was generally always short lived as the man had saved his life getting him out of the Indian subcontinent at a great deal of potential risk to himself. He looked on at the show on the stage with the wonderfully sensuous dancers in their minimal showgirl outfits as Holden sat with one of these stunning young ladies on his left knee. He was jealous of the way that his friend was able to chat so freely to this gorgeous looking individual, who shifted erotically on his thigh and played with her hair in a display of obvious sexual interest.

He tried to stay focused on the music and the show and ignore his friend's sexual success as Holden was led off hand in hand by the woman, who he saw walked in an alluring way. She seemed to move loose limbed like a predatory animal stalking her prey; in truth this was an interesting comparison. She was taking Holden off to one of the luxurious sets of female washrooms in the V.I.P lounge where they were to have carnal pleasure together. Waldron hated the thought; he hadn't had any sexual relations since before he was in Afghanistan and it frustrated him. As Holden left, Waldron downed the last of the red wine in his glass and then poured himself another full glass. An alcoholic haze would help dull the pain.

Holden cautiously entered the ladies washroom with Nicole. She was exquisitely beautiful with the most lithe body he had ever come across despite in his younger years having the pick of many debutantes. Holden's moral value system had been completely eroded since the events of 1898. He now only considered three things; living for today; having what you want; and trusting no one but yourself. This woman wanted him and he would simply respond to his own desire to have her too. They entered a cubical in the spotlessly clean and fragranced ladies washrooms. He sat upon the toilet seat as she straddled his lap. Consenting adults, neither were they strangers to such cold hearted love as he undid his trousers and she pulled her short skirt up, almost an academic act with how minimal it was, and pulled her dancer's briefs to one side. He entered her and she moaned with pleasure as she fully lowered herself onto him which promoted a satisfied grunting from Holden.

How different two sexual acts were taking place across the city; Holden's for pure self-gratification on the part of both parties, and Karen Wood's and Ford's because they were falling in love.

* * *

Whitehall, August 12th

"Rob, why do you persist with this ridiculous nonsense about the Boss having some enemies that are out to get him," said Bob Spicer he sat down in one of the two seat Chesterfields outside the Minister's briefing room. He threw a copy of The London Times onto the sofa beside him that Ford had handed him to read. There were more bold and sensational headlines from William Bates:

'SECOND MEMBER OF THE PATTERSON OFFICE SLAIN – THIS TIME IN PARIS.

> A second member of staff of the Minister of War, Sir Cecil Patterson, has been found dead in bizarre circumstances. Murdered outside a Paris church, Steven Pick was poisoned to death by person or persons unknown. Is it a coincidence? Are they out to get the Minister.....? '

The story rambled on in a scare-mongering fashion as was normal for Will Bates and neither policeman read any further with this in mind.

"Oh, come on. Two bloody murders in a very deliberate fashion of his staff. You believe his assertion that he is innocent. Wake up and smell the coffee, Bob. If you'd been involved in the Whitechapel job as I was then you'd think like me."

"I was fucking there, mate."

"Yeah, but you were green and impressionable spending your time getting pissed with wankers like Taffy Evans. I ended up in the thick of it if you remember."

"Yes I do remember and your mate fucking died because of you."

The comment tipped Ford over the edge. Fortunately for both of them the waiting area was empty as Ford grabbed Spicer by the lapels and pinned him up to one of the walls. He lifted his grip high so that his colleague's throat was restricted and he wheezed heavily.

"Don't ever mention something like that again, you little bastard. I live with that fact every day. I lost a lot in 1888 so don't fucking forget it. Now if I think he's got a skeleton or two in his cupboard I'm going to find them. You worry about your side of the protection and I'll do both." The frightened Spicer nodded his head. He coughed as Ford released his grip and left the waiting area. He knew retaliation was futile because of the tough reputation Ford had always had. It had been insensitive of him to open up such an old wound. He sat down rubbing his slightly bruised throat.

Ford entered the Minister's staff office. He was in luck; there was only Fiona Shaw sat at her desk on her own. The researcher, young James Landon, was out and Ramsey Phillips was in the meeting with Patterson. A new under secretary would arrive later in the day.

"Fi. Look, I need your absolute confidence in a matter," said Ford as he planted himself on the edge of her desk. The forty year old spinster who was the administrative assistant looked up at Ford with absolute trust.

"Yes, Mr Ford. You know that I'm happy to have you chaps around so anything I can do to help I'd gladly do."

"Right. How long have you worked for the Minister?"

"Since about August 1902, so two years now."

"Good. Do you know of anything in the last two years where he's had conflict with an individual or group through his ministerial or industrial interests?" She looked out of the window for a moment as she considered the question long and hard.

"No. Not that I can recollect, Mr Ford."

"What about before that? Do you know of any of his dealings?"

"Well, with Empire Petroleum he went on an abortive mission to the North West Frontier and into Afghanistan to look for this 'oil' stuff. They never found anything by all accounts despite intelligence initially to the contrary, but while they were there he and the soldiers he was with were involved in a skirmish and a couple of them got killed. Then on the way back the officer was thrown from his horse over a precipice, no chance of ever getting the body back. So by all accounts not a very successful trip. Can't see the soldiers wanting to try to kill him or his staff, after all its part of their job." Ford was intrigued by the story; it could be the start of trying to unravel the mystery. It was at least a loose end he would need to clarify.

"Can you find out what army mob it was that went with him on the trip? I'd really like to talk to them if I can."

"Sure. I'll get an answer for you once everyone's back from Rome."

"Thanks, Fi. That'll be great." Ford left the office and returned to the waiting area where Spicer was still sitting sheepishly. He hadn't found anyone as yet he felt he could trust enough to quiz discreetly about the meeting with the church officials. He might have to visit the Minister's office out of hours.

"Look. I'm sorry I should never have said it. Please, I'm truly sorry." As Spicer finished speaking he offered his hand to Ford in a gesture of reconciliation. Ford took it in his hand and shook it firmly.

"All right. Thank you. Lets not let that sort of water flow under the bridge again."

* * *

Karen Wood left the Brompton Road nursery to make her way back to her flat in Wilton Crescent. Young Nigel was not well with the hot weather taking its toll on his breathing. He was barely six years old but with his lack of usual growth despite good diet and care he was often mistaken for a child approaching their fourth birthday. His medical condition had no known label in 1904; he suffered from stunted growth, sinus infections and breathing difficulties that seemed to indicate some form of permanent failing with his lungs. He had seemed to reach a point where his health was in serial decline and he frequently was in discomfort. The poor lad had never even known his father who had gone missing almost immediately after the boy's conception. Karen loved him dearly and wished she could spend more time with him, but with the ever increasing sexual demands of her employer, that if not satisfied would lead to Nigel's perhaps premature decline, she had to go overseas with the Minister every time he went. At least when Patterson was in London she could see Nigel everyday.

The first time she slept with Robert Ford she felt that somebody loved her, as indeed she had started to feel for him. She was, however, fearful of telling Ford the truth. She didn't want him to take any hasty or rash action; she knew that he wasn't stupid and when the Minister had slapped her face twice in the previous week in a show of dominance following one of his favoured sexual acts, she could tell Ford knew she had been struck. She guessed he knew that she was the Minister's mistress anyway with her 'crucial' need to travel everywhere. What she couldn't work out was the position of Lady Patterson. Karen could only surmise that she accepted the situation to avoid the scandal that exposure would bring and to keep her in the manner to which she was accustomed. Karen wouldn't have been surprised if the lady of the household took lovers from among the household staff when it suited her anyway.

She walked up the low step of the entrance to the 'mansions' in Wilton Crescent that housed her flat. It was a lovely, warm, sunny day and she longed to be away somewhere less inhibiting than central London; she wanted to be somewhere where she could feel the sun on her bare skin and it's warming and tanning effect. With her life in the country near a river as a child she had a liberal view to the outdoors from a childhood of freedom, swimming with her brother and their friends. There was so much etiquette to adhere to in modern London Edwardian society. Her penchant for the sun and for being the proud owner of a Celtic tattoo, that her missing common law husband had encouraged her to have, did not fit well in this environment. It was considered fashionable to be pale, so she had to keep both her complexion and her 'ink' under wraps with the traditional fashions of the day covering much of her skin and a little bit of powder to lighten the naturally olive complexion she possessed.

She went to the window of her living room and surveyed the view outside. It was a quiet urban street scene with few carriages or pedestrians passing by. It was a lovely, comfortable flat but lacked the view of greenery such as the Minister's residence in Belgrave Square had to offer. He had promised to sign the place entirely over to her one day in the same way he promised that his love making would always be gentle. Except with his abrupt, callous and self satisfying nature she considered it a forlorn hope.

She picked up her sullen mood with the reminder to herself that Ford was going to come for tea this evening once Mark Vincent took over from him and Spicer. He had told her that he would be using the rear access of the building to not court attention; despite such things as ministerial affairs being taboo, many in the block knew exactly what was going on. They might not tell of the Minister's indiscretion but they would certainly ensure that the Minister got to know of his mistress taking in male callers. It was typical of the hypocrisy of the male chauvinism that dominated British society. She busied herself in the kitchen and looked forward to the company of a man who offered her warmth, care and affection and seemed to be interested in her for being her.

Chapter Eight

Rome, August 16th

Rome in August was not a place that English gentlemen wanted to walk around in sporting their more usual woollen weave suits. With that in mind from Ford's normal meticulous research and preparation at least he, Spicer and Vincent were able to still look smart but sporting linen suits to create the effect. On this trip Patterson was joined by Ramsey Phillips, as always, but this time also with James Landan his young researcher, Karen Wood as normal was present, but much to Patterson's annoyance was Lady Patterson. She had been insistent that she should not be left out of a visit to the 'eternal city'. As with all good protection work in this burgeoning field within the police service, Ford had researched the City's main attractions, transport network, the hotel in advance, the Italian Minister of War's office and where the City's main hospital was located. He had also obtained the co-operation this time of a local police captain who would be on hand throughout the visit to assist the English party. It was a great source of amusement to Ford that the Minister's wife was there as he knew that it should give Karen a break from his enforced company. It would be on this trip that he would discover his employer's callous cruelty.

As they made their way to the centre of Rome from the main railway station by open carriages, one carrying The Pattersons, Spicer and Robert Ford with the other holding Karen, Mark Vincent, Ramsey Phillips and James Landan, it also amused Ford to the see Patterson sweating heavily in his heavy, woven, serge blue woollen suit. He looked at his protection officers with annoyance and envy in their light coloured linen suits. Looking around it frustrated him further to see that he appeared to be the only one in the party to have dressed in such a manner; both Karen Wood and his wife were in white cotton outfits and Ramsey Phillips and Landan were also in linen suits.

"Did nobody think to share information about the climate with me then?" said a terse Patterson as he wiped his forehead with the only item of lightweight cotton he had; his handkerchief.

"Sir, I thought you knew," replied Landan weakly.

"Of course I bloody well didn't that's why I'm sweating like a cat in a fishmonger's you fool!" The rest of the party tried to avoid laughter.

It wasn't long before they were heading along the 'Via Dei Fori Imperiale', or Avenue of the Imperial Forum. At the far end was the Colosseum which looked spectacular from the Piazza Venezia whilst travelling towards it. The view from this point afforded the most complete side of the ancient arena, the North facia; the fact that 67% of the original structure was missing only became apparent as one neared or drove around it, plundered for the construction of other buildings in Rome over the subsequent thousand years from around 453.A.D. They circled the Colosseum and then begun the brief journey north to their hotel the 'Internazionale' at 79 Via Sistina and the four star accommodation it offered. Built in 1870, it was located very near the famously romantic 'Spanish Steps' and the fashionable Via Veneto. It also afforded excellent rooftop views of the city.

An hour later and everyone was ensconced in their rooms. The Pattersons had a suite on the top floor whilst all the rest of the entourage had rooms on the third floor. Robert Ford's fortuitously right next to Karen's single occupancy double room. She had every intention of making use of this room that night with a man she believed from their so far very warm, secret courtship had deep feelings for her. Karen certainly harboured those feelings for him. She knew, however, that Ford wouldn't be free until after the Minister had dined and officially retired for the evening.

Ford changed ready for dinner while Mark Vincent did the corridor security outside the Patterson's suite. Ford had come to an agreement with Spicer that he be the first point of call for Vincent should he need assistance in anyway. Ford also equally had the intention of spending the night with Karen Wood on a discreet basis. He knew by engaging in his own relationship with the Minister's mistress that he was putting himself in a dangerously compromising situation. He could sense that once again, after over fifteen years, he was being potentially blinded by love; but there was more to it than that. He had never felt so emotionally fulfilled as he had when with Karen. She was going to become his and not Patterson's any longer.

The evening's dinner was set to be a semi-formal affair with the Italian Minister of War attending the hotel to dine with the official party; at the table would also be Ramsey Phillips and Landan to help with any detail that Patterson maybe quizzed about by the host nation, and an Italian interpreter that Ford had ensured had been vetted by his police captain contact Franco Bennetti. Bennetti, as it transpired, spoke excellent English too. Ford was just finishing tying his bow tie when he heard a knock on his room door.

"It's open, come on in." The door opened and a tall, tanned, dark haired Italian entered in an evening suit. He introduced himself to Ford.

"Thank, you. I am Franco Bennetti. I am very pleased to meet you." He approached Ford extending his hand and clasped Ford's firmly giving it a very positive and friendly shake. "You must be Robert. Welcome to Roma." Ford returned the greeting and smiled at the captain's affability and disregard of rank; he was quite obviously a sensible professional who respected role and ability over mere rank.

"Thank you very much, Franco. I am grateful for your help so far. Are you sitting at dinner too?"

"No doubt like you I will be sitting at a separate table to one side; eating well but having to tolerate politicians' drunken behaviour whilst remaining completely sober. Sometimes getting drunk too would make it so much easier to get on with some of these people don't you think?" Ford was now putting on his dinner jacket as they spoke and chuckled at his counterpart's frank observation.

"Yes, I do know what you mean. However, I think I'd sooner be sober in our company or my own for that matter as opposed to socialising with the buggers."

Ford and Bennetti were quite grateful once they sat down to dinner in the sumptuously furnished restaurant of the Hotel Internazionale;

they found themselves sharing a table with Karen Wood and another very attractive Italian woman that Bennetti seemed deeply familiar with. She was above average height, with a curvaceous but slim figure; her skin had a rich olive, perhaps archetypically roman, complexion, with long, straight almost black hair, deep brown eyes and wonderfully pouting lips. Bennetti kissed her firmly and passionately on her lips before they sat down.

"Robert, please meet Sophia, my wife." Bennetti then took Karen's right hand and pulled it up to his lips and gently kissed the back of it. Bennetti despite possessing a beautiful wife, found Karen very attractive too. "And is this Mrs Ford?" For a split second Karen and Ford looked at each other to see who would speak first and something in each of their eyes seemed to wish they could answer yes. Ford managed to be able to get the reply out first.

"No. This is Karen Wood the Pattersons' personal dressmaker. We've only recently met but hope to have a closer relationship." He looked directly at Karen as she spoke. His look and the sentiment of his words made her blush in company and her neck went visibly red with the emotion; she didn't begrudge the feeling that it generated within her. Their table wasn't within earshot of the main party, but certainly was in secure visual range for Ford and Bennetti. This ideal distance meant that their conversation could be quite frank and not curtailed because of unwanted listeners in the form of the staff that attended each of the ministers.

The room was finely decorated with renaissance and baroque styling on its walls that were richly decorated with vibrant coloured detailed friezes depicting elements of Italian life and religious scenes. The furniture was handcrafted by some of the finest Genovese craftsmen with intricately carved table and chair legs in a rich mahogany wood, with the chairs topped off with sumptuous red velvet upholstery. The group of four settled down to casual and friendly dining together with Ford and Bennetti keeping a mindful eye on the ministerial party and those coming and going around them.

The official dinner party consisted of Patterson and his wife, Ramsey Phillips and James Landan, The Italian minister of the interior and his wife, a couple of high ranking Italian military officers in lavish evening uniforms and their wives, and a small, wiry, bespectacled

Italian intellectual who was the translator. As the evening drunkenly progressed Ford noticed that he certainly had his work cut out for him.

It was some hours later with Bennetti and Ford having observed the degenerating behaviour from start to finish, with Karen Wood and Sophia Bennetti having retired, that Landan came over to their table to deliver news of a change of plan to their itinerary. He spoke with slurred speech.

"Chaps. Just to let you know the General has invited the Pattersons to Venice for tomorrow night. They'll be going by train first thing to visit him in his house that fronts the Grand Canal, apparently, near St Mark's or somewhere." Ford spoke to Bennetti as Landan hiccupped drunkenly and tried to catch his breath again. 'Why the change of plan?' was now the nagging thought immediately within Ford's mind.

"Do you know Venice, Franco?"

"Yes. Sophia and I spent a week there on honeymoon and I very much like art, so I know it well. No problem, Roberto."

"Good," said Landan, "you'll be ready in the morning then and this Italian fellow will be our guide." Landan spoke unaware of his empirical condescension. Bennetti ignored it as Landan wandered back to his table.

"It will be romantic for you and Karen, yes?" Bennetti spoke smiling.

"Yes, very if I get five minutes peace, my friend." The two of them watched the drunken party break up and go their separate ways with Patterson retiring to his room allowing Ford to let Mark Vincent resume his corridor duty. He said goodbye to Bennetti until the morning and then went to his room.

The door was unlocked as he tried the handle; this came, he hoped, as no surprise. The moonlight streamed through the voile that hung up at the window, the view of which looked out upon the gardens of the Villa Borghese to the North. He looked across the bed to where Karen was asleep under a crisp, white cotton sheet that seemed to contour the lines of her slim physique as she lay peacefully on her left side on the left of the 'sled' style wooden baroque bed. He undressed and slipped naked into the bed next to her on the right and cuddled up close to her warm, smooth, sensuous body putting his right arm around her. She huddled up to him in an autonomous silent response and gave a contented sigh in her sleep. Ford looked at her back with loving satisfaction and with wondrous affection until he fell soundly asleep.

* * *

2.a.m. Holden was asleep in his modest hotel room some distance away from the Minister's in the Via Portico, close to the Theatre of Marcello. Waldron was asleep in a separate room nearer to the ground floor of the hotel to assist his infirmity. Holden lay sweating as he thought of the barbarous events of Afghanistan six years before and the continual nights of sleep deprivation it brought him. Only on nights when he calmed his thoughts with carnal pleasures or dulled the pain of his command overseas with excessive alcohol could he sleep. He hoped that when his course of revenge was complete he might sleep soundly with regularity again. The nagging cough that had begun a day or two before annoyed him, especially as his body convulsed slightly as he was forced to respond to the irritation in his lungs.

The moon streamed in from the open hotel window with him having left the curtains open. It illuminated the floor leading up to the door. Holden rolled onto his side and let out a large sigh as he did so, completely frustrated with his lack of ability to simply fall asleep; surely the most simplistic human action to complete when fatigued he thought. As he rolled over again he gained a view of the base of the door to the room from the corridor. He stared at it listlessly and then saw a piece of paper pushed underneath it; immediately Holden got on the defensive and pulled his Webley pistol from underneath his pillow. He slipped lightly off the bed and crawled around to one side of the door. He assumed the worst at all times as it generally seemed to keep him alive; an assailant with a firearm could be just the other side of the door watching for the note to be pulled clear from their side, a sign of when to open fire if their intention was assassination.

He pulled the note initially straight until it was clear of the door so the potential killer on the other side would assume that their victim was right in front of them. There were no shots. He held his breath for a moment to listen intently for movement or even breathing; there was nothing. He pulled the note towards him and unfolded it and read the words of the familiar writing upon it:

'Patterson set to go to Venice in the morning; breaking completely with his proposed schedule. This could be a good place, however, your choice. Returning to Rome the day after by train.'

'Damn,' thought Holden. He couldn't take the moody cripple there with him discreetly on the same train. He would go and watch Patterson and his cronies and leave the maudlin Waldron here for the day. He respected his former subordinate but had begun to tire of his mood swings; he'd saved the bugger's life for Christ's sake. On their return to England Holden would cut Waldron free of any obligation he felt towards him and finish the 'crusade' against Patterson and those around him on his own.

He knelt up and opened the door to see that the corridor was empty. The delivery of the note unexpectedly had put him on edge. It was no good he had to have a drink as there was no way he'd easily find sex now to relax his tension. He put on a shirt and linen trousers and went down to the reception and bought a bottle of Amaretto from the hotel bar. Back in his room its taste was sweet and in truth for him too sickly, but it was at least intoxicating. He stared for sometime out of the window towards the Tiber and the south of the 'eternal city' and enjoyed the calmness the alcohol began to bring.

* * *

London August 17th

William Bates arrived at the War Office in Whitehall at the junction with Horse Guards Avenue for an unannounced appointment with Sir Cecil Patterson's office. It was a deliberate tactic to try and throw whoever he saw off guard so that he might possibly illicit some information about the two murders for him to form a substantial link. His plan was to generate maximum copy and a political scandal with its upper class nature was the perfect front cover story for The London Times, albeit for a third occasion. He strolled confidently into the reception for the main building and was prepared to lie heavily to get past this first hurdle and get straight to Patterson's secretary. He knew full well that the Minister himself was overseas. He approached the reception desk staffed by a thin, drawn, elderly male civil servant with thinning, grey hair and a pasty complexion.

"Morning, squire, I have an appointment with Sir Cecil's secretary, Miss..." he clicked his fingers pretending to try to remember her name. It was a fact that he had no idea of, but his brash approach worked as planned. The timid looking clerk stumbled over his words but supplied the answer more through bewilderment than any other factor.

"Er... Miss Shaw?" Bates smiled innocently.

"Yes, that's it. Miss Shaw. She's expecting me, so all right if I go straight up?"

"Oh. Er...yes. You better go right up. Room 3.12, Mr..?"

"William Bates, of The London Times, of course." He strolled on to the stairway and started immediately upwards as the confused clerk looked on squinting through his glasses made for short-sightedness.

Fiona Shaw was completing entries in the Minister's diary as Bates quietly walked into the room. The reception area was comfortable and quite ornate in its décor, wood panelling, and parquet flooring, good quality oak furniture and healthily lit from the presence of a generous light-giving window. Initially she didn't realise that anyone had entered until she heard a slight cough. She looked up to see Bates stood in front of her rocking slightly on his toes and sporting a beaming smile. She eyed him suspiciously and spoke with a bored and tired tone wishing to express disinterest to this individual who she quite clearly sensed was a journalist. She had been a private secretary too long and could almost smell them.

"Can I help you, Mr..?"

"Bates, of The..."

"Times. How unsuited you are to such a quality newspaper. If only you had stayed at The Star."

"Well, there's no need for that, Miss Shaw."

"How do you know my name, you common little hack?"

"That's the power of the press you see. Now, may I ask you a few questions about Sir Cecil?" Bates tried to smile sweetly as he spoke.

"I am not at liberty to disclose any information to you. We work within the strictest confidence." Fiona Shaw sat back and folded her arms.

The Dressmaker Connection

"Look, you could save an awful lot of speculation. What dealings has your boss had that would drive someone to want him dead?"

"How do you know that is the case? Two unrelated and dissimilar murders in two different cities? The only tenuous link is that the victims worked here. And why does that indicate that someone wants Sir Cecil dead then?" Bates answered with confidence.

"Well. If for example you wanted to scare him before killing him, then bumping off people close to him one by one must be quite effective. I mean don't you now worry that you could quite innocently be a target of some mad man? Hmm?" This point did appeal to her vivid imagination. She sat quietly for a time before replying.

"Empire Petroleum," she spoke out of the blue as if plucking the name from thin air. It caught Bates by surprise. "There is nothing here, no secrets. But he sits on the board of E.P. That is where I believe that you should look. Good day to you Mr Bates." She returned to the diary.

"Sorry? E.P?" She ignored his request of confirmation and carried on working without looking up. "Miss Shaw, did you say E.P?" Again she ignored him. He looked at her and then around the reception area gently beginning to nod his head.

Bates turned and left the office. He had his next line of enquiry. Their headquarters was in the City of London so it would be easy enough to get there. He decided, however, that his approach and quest for information might have to be with an element of subterfuge; the direct approach that he had just succeeded with would not always work.

He walked back past the ageing reception clerk and out into the very warm and slightly stifling summer air of Central London. He looked towards the east and Trafalgar Square and could see Lord Nelson dutifully as always looking along The Mall to his line of ships that adorned the lamp posts. He then began cautiously to cross Whitehall to catch a cab eastwards towards Fleet Street and the offices of The London Times. Looking west he could see clearly down to Parliament Square which afforded him a good view of the oncoming traffic and his search for a cab. The busy thoroughfare was filled with the sound of horses and carriages rattling over its cobbled surface and the smell of equine defecation. The Household Cavalry stood guard as was traditional with two troopers upon their mounts either side of the arched entrance to Horse Guards parade ground, sometimes referred to as 'Tilt Yard'. This was a tradition with a recent heritage. When the monarch was to pass through Tilt Yard, a cavalry guard detail was supposed to be on duty at the arch to ensure their safe passage and offer a salute as the monarch passed through to Horse Guards parade ground. Only some years before during Queen Victoria's reign, she had passed through Tilt Yard and no guard was present. Outraged, Victoria then decreed that for the next one hundred years a daytime guard would be permanently maintained.

* * *

That same day the Patterson party, having caught the train first thing in the morning from the Stazione Centrale Roma Termini, arrived in Venice for early afternoon feeling quite fresh still from the relaxed first class train journey. No one, Ford and Patterson included, had noticed the respectable looking gentleman who keenly observed the party from the far end of the first class carriage in which they travelled. Holden no longer sported the moustache that he had when he first met Patterson. His skin complexion had become weathered and permanently lightly tanned from the prolonged period of time on the Indian subcontinent. He was also much leaner than he used to be and his hair was significantly greyer; Ford had never met him and the callous Patterson would not recognise him. After all, Patterson was the kind of man who gave most only disdainful glances and only took interest in those from who he could receive a personal gain; 'a typical political industrialist' thought Holden. He watched them all leave the train and stroll off along the platform to catch a 'motoscarfo,' a sleek, steam-driven, large motorboat that would easily accommodate all of the joint Anglo/Italian group. Holden followed at a distance dressed in his linen suit, Panama hat that shielded his face along with some Edwardian sunglasses, for practicality and to provide additional facial obscurity.

His keen observation, coupled with his varied military experience, made it easy to recognise the men who he knew were tasked with Patterson's protection; that was no obstacle, in fact it provided him with further victims to bring an even greater sense of dread 'to the bastard'.

Ford and Spicer were distinctive in their subtly casual observation of the world around them and their proximity on an ever changing basis between them to Patterson quite obviously to provide protection in the event of an attack. He sized them up as they climbed aboard the boat; both men around late thirties to early forties, they looked lean yet powerful and both appeared to be professional by the subtle yet deliberate manner of their actions and by the way they moved. He observed that one appeared to be in charge by some of his occasional mannerisms. This man he noted had a significant scar on his forehead; he appeared to have potentially seen action already. Holden was more right than he could know. He observed the others in the party; Patterson himself, his wife and another very attractive female, two British civil servants that he referred to as 'bureaucratic leeches', the sort that interfered in affairs in which they had no expertise; the Italian general, his wife, translator and a smart handsome Italian man who he rightly assumed was a local protection officer.

The canal side in front of the Stazione Ferrovie dello stato Sainta Lucia that sat upon the Grand Canal was called the Fondamenta Sainta Lucia. It was a bustling port area and therefore easy for Holden to pick up a water taxi to follow the now embarked party to see where they were staying; he suspected that before they visited their accommodation there would be a ride around Venice and particularly along the Grand Canal. Holden deduced that the party's luggage must be going on separately to their hotel or invited-to accommodation as they moved away from their birth before any was loaded. He watched the Patterson party's motoscarfo gracefully begin to glide east along the Grand Canal in the direction of St Marks Square and ultimately the southern area of the Lagoon as he jumped aboard one of the fine wooden water taxis.

"Parla Inglese?" asked Holden of the smiling, tanned driver of the boat.

"Ci. A little." The Venetian spoke with genuine friendliness.

"Buono. That boat," said Holden pointing at the Patterson's launch, "follow carefully, per favour." Holden gestured with his hands indicating to keep their distance to the driver. He nodded his head in comprehension as he manoeuvred from his own berth.

There was a wonderful coolness to the air of Venice in comparison to that of Rome; it was fuelled by the breeze that blew gently west to east, the movement of the air from the forward motion of the boat and the water itself. The water also provided that instinctively calming sound that humans seemed to enjoy as it lapped the sides of the canal and the boat. Holden considered this linked to the theories of Charles Darwin. If we crawled out from the water to evolve then we must through a form of genetic memory feel calm and at home when near water. He put his own travelling bag down in the rear of the boat and keenly observed the activity aboard the front boat.

Holden could see the two protection officers were watching either bank of the canal and the passing traffic, as well as paying casual attention to the people onboard and their interaction with each other. At this time Holden did not know that there was a third protection officer who had remained in Rome. Both Bennetti and Ford, following liaison with the general's personal staff, felt they didn't need a 'corridor' officer, as they were frequently referred to, in a secure private residence. The party would be entertained and stop in the General's home, the wonderful baroque palace the 'Ca' Pesaro' that fronted the Grande Canal on the west bank in the Santa Croce district. This was a building they passed quite early on in their journey and Holden observed a flurry of activity as all onboard took an interest in the palace with much finger pointing and discussion taking place. He noted the attractive blond seemed to sit apart from much of the main party with the protection officer with the scarred forehead paying her more than casual attention.

He eyed the building with deep interest himself; if this was where they were staying then he would continue with his plan to kill again in Rome as it appeared difficult to gain easy access to. Besides, he had come to feel quite relaxed in the wondrous 'water city' and considered it might be quite nice to keep an eye on his prey but enjoy the surroundings.

Aboard the motoscarfo or launch, Ford had touched Karen on the shoulder while everyone else's backs were turned and she responded by placing her hand on top of his. She felt warm and relaxed in his presence and felt it was time to tell him how badly her employer often treated her; it would help clear her mind of the fear of withholding any secrets, but she knew that there was nothing Ford would be able to do. Ford, like Holden, also took an interest in the baroque palace as they passed. He engaged Bennetti in conversation about it having released his hand from Karen's shoulder.

"Do you know anything of the General's security here, Franco?"

"Yes. He has a detachment of four soldiers here when he is in residence. They maintain static watch from key vantage points. I think you and I may have a night off, my friend." Ford relished the thought. It would be nice to have a drink with Franco perhaps, but in his mind an evening in Venice with a woman he was falling in love with was essential now they were here.

"I will take you, Bob and Karen to the Café Florian for the finest coffee later, if I may?" Ford considered his answer. He didn't see that as a problem in reality as he had spent most of the night out in Paris previously so a couple of hours with Franco initially would only be fair to his very obliging counterpart.

"That would be a privilege, my friend."

They were soon passing under the Rialto Bridge with its bustling adjacent market on both sides of the canal as they passed with its very distinctive smell of fresh fish, a staple of its trade. Everyone looked in wonderment at the romantic bridge with its arched colonnade and set back from it an ornate balustrade; it was completed in 1591 and was the only means of crossing the Grande Canal until 1854 when the Academia Bridge was constructed. The imposing white domed church of Santa Maria della Salute was then readily in sight, which indicated that were almost on top of St Marks Square with its high Campanile clock tower casting a shadow over the famous Doges Palace. It had been decided on route to have a proper walking tour of the area of the square as the Minister wanted to visit the palace and the basilica of St Mark with its famous four gilded bronze horses over the entranceway.

Holden observed the disembarkation keenly and noted that the two British protection officers were out first watching the quayside as they moved and then waited for their 'ward'. The party then moved off inland with these two discreetly mingling amongst the group but within a short reactionary distance of Patterson. They certainly seemed to know their tactics, mused Holden. He could easily test them from a distance in the vicinity of the square.

Ford noted the café that Franco had mentioned off to his left as they moved towards the basilica. Florian's was one of the world's oldest coffee houses having been opened in December 1720 by Floriano Francesconi. It sat within the arches of the Procuratie Nuove in St

Mark's Square. Its outdoor seating offered a refined atmosphere with its string quartet playing in period costume along with a splendid view of the basilica. Ford didn't particularly note the well dressed man in a Panama hat take a seat in the sun on the café's terrace or realise that he was scrutinising the General and Minister's entourage. At that moment Ford simply had thoughts of Bennetti's earlier proposal regarding the café, and considered that it would be very sociable.

The group stopped outside of the basilica and the English members admired the horses, all except Ford and Spicer who in turn gave them a casual glance but watched the world around them as a priority. Ford considered that whoever was on this apparent campaign against the Minister and his staff would have to be really dedicated to have followed them here; how right he was. Holden was offered a menu, took it and ordered a large black coffee as he continued to watch Patterson in particular within the group. He recalled the last time he saw him in the Afghan desert and that recollection re-iterated his own thoughts of how much he wanted this man dead but also to suffer along the way. He watched the protection officer with the scar on his forehead as these thoughts passed through his mind; they seemed to briefly make eye contact and Holden felt forced to slowly look away to avoid this man's suspicion. He didn't want to either hold it or break it too quickly and potentially court attention either way.

Ford noted this lean and well dressed man in the Panama hat sitting outside Florian's amongst the crowd of other tourists for a second time. He thought little of him at that moment other than being a curious English 'Grand Tourist' and turned to follow the ministerial party into the Cathedral as they finished admiring its façade. Holden looked on again once Ford's back faced him and the group disappeared.

Chapter Nine

The party spent an hour touring the Cathedral in its entirety from the crypt all the way up to the elevated internal galleries that sat behind its magnificent frontage. From there they left and entered the Doges Palace that sat between St Marks and the waterfront with Holden still sat on the terrace of the noted coffee house. He suspected, quite rightly, that the party would probably then stop at the café for refreshment. He allowed half an hour and then paid his bill and left. He entered the cathedral himself and went straight up to the exterior balcony by the famous gilded horses to overlook the square and the café.

Sure enough, just over an hour after the ministerial party had entered the palace they were pulling up chairs on the terrace of Florian's as Holden looked on from his elevated position in the cathedral. He again noted the dedication to their craft that the two protection officers displayed. When the time came they would be healthy adversaries to deal with close to. He would have to test them before that to decide if a sniper's rifle was the only way to finish the vendetta. He hoped not; it lacked the immediate sense of fear of imminent death that a one to one confrontation would allow. Holden looked across the dock front by St Marks. He could see that the motoscarfo launch was still there. Wisely he had paid his own boatman to wait so he had immediate access to transport.

Holden came from a wealthy background that allowed him to pursue his quest for revenge without financial restriction. He had been born into a family with a long tradition of military service prior to taking up directorship positions with the family co-founded bank;

Holden and Glynn's. The board of directors normally consisted of an even amount of members from the two named families. He would have been due to take up one of these positions in two years time but he decided to shun the tradition. Mainly because he felt like a man apart from society following his long and savage experiences on and around the North West Frontier, but also because of tragedy that had struck whilst he battled for survival.

* * *

It had not been unheard of for sons and daughters from either banking dynasty to marry and sometimes for both parties to sit on the board, though few females decided on this course of action, more from not wishing to defy convention in the staid Edwardian society. However, Genevieve Glynn with whom Holden had grown up had proved to be of those strong and independent women who wished to defy convention. His childhood with her began at weekends when he would be home from his strict, sports competitive school in the heart of rural Essex; Walden Hall Abbey.

It was at Walden H.A, as it was known to its attendees, that Holden had first developed his outstanding physical prowess and his skill at any sport that he turned his hand to. The school building was first constructed in 1676 on the site of the Abbey that was a victim of Henry VIII dissolution of the monasteries. Built by Sir Thomas Audley its initial purpose was as a Royal Palace, a role that the fine Jacobean house amply fulfilled. The main house with its own minor courtyard sat with the village of Saffron Walden in the distance behind it to the east and with the larger enclosed courtyard to the west of the main house adjoining it on its north and south wings. The schooling took place in the main house for the select group of boys that were privileged enough to attend whilst their quarters in the form of dormitories were housed in the wings that surrounded the great courtyard. An unofficial test of skill, speed and guile was to run a lap of the inside main courtyard and then around the exterior of the entire building naked and in under three minutes. This was complicated by the other boys being allowed to hammer their enamel cups upon their window ledges as soon as the challenger left the confines of the main courtyard for the outer lap. He then had to avoid being caught in the act by the night duty house master, who if a younger member of staff, would be out of his own bed quickly enough to catch the challenger.

It was typically adolescent high jinks and to the present day Holden's record of two minutes and thirty-four seconds was unbroken coupled with outrunning the sports master, a recent national one hundred yard dash champion. The unwritten rule for the staff was if the challenger reached the safety of their quarters without hands having been laid on them, then they could go unpunished.

Genevieve's schooling suffered from no such high jinks and often concentrated on the skills that fine young ladies would be required to display in civilised high society. As time went on she found it tedious as she entered her late teens and lived for the weekends when she would go out for a day's spirited riding with 'Billy' Holden. He was equal to her in age and she was equal to him in equestrian skill, a source of great frustration to the dashing young seventeen year old lad. At a time when both of them were undergoing hormonal earthquakes, he found it sexually exciting to see this beautiful, voluptuous society girl taking a horse to task and riding equally with most men. Secretly she lusted after him, especially observing him in his beige jodhpurs worn with traditional brown-topped, black riding boots. One day, after they had both turned eighteen, Billy was set at the end of that summer to go to the Royal Military Academy at Sandhurst to commence his officer training with his commission in the Household Cavalry having been secured, they rode off from the family jointly owned stables into the Hertfordshire countryside. They had both become familiar with a barn within the grounds of a farm at Hertingfordbury that the Glynn family owned and rented out. It was usually comfortably full with hay bales that offered protection from view and a scurrilously adolescent romantic place for them to make love to each other.

Holden had been as prepared as ever, a factor that would eventually keep him alive on many occasions; he had studied a copy of the infamous and banned Indian 'Karma Sutra' sexual techniques book so that their first sexual encounter would be a good one and not full of 'sticky boyish fumbling'. Arrogantly, also he wanted to impress the girl that he had lusted over for many weeks and prove his manhood. The expertise he hoped he would show also gave rise to a sense of dominance that gave the whole penetrative act the intoxicating sense of control bordering on rape; at least on the first occasion they made love. They spent hours in the isolated barn with the second and third forays wiping such a deluded thought from his mind. However, it was a sense that would return to him many years later when everything precious to him had gone. He had been cautious about his climax on each occasion not wanting to disgrace this addictive example of womanhood that he would one day marry.

Those halcyon days were a distant memory to the increasingly bitter Holden whose sole motivations for life were revenge and satisfying wanton lusts for sexual gratification, alcohol and fear. He was overseas for nearly two years without word from anyone as he fought to keep himself and his comrades alive. It was on his return that his heart was broken and the emotions of love, sentimentality and affection were buried forever as he discovered Genevieve had also been. She had been killed during a fox hunt when competing with men in the hunt to lead the chase. Having got to the front she had become obsessed with staying there and on unfamiliar ground she set her favourite mount, 'Flashman' a notoriously difficult stallion, to jump a hedgerow into a small copse. Neither of them were to know that some recent felling had taken place and she had chosen a spot in the hedgerow where on the exit side was a large two foot high tree stump yet to be poisoned and dug out. Flashman's front right hoof landed square on the stump folding over and breaking the fine beast's leg with a sickening crack that could be heard at the back of the hunt. Oddly at that moment with its sound, the hounds fell silent. The horse then pitched to the right and threw Genevieve from her saddle. As she rolled into a reverse kind of rolling break fall and was on her neck, the great stallion landed on her. Her neck was instantly broken and her spinal column was snapped into two. She was dead before the horse rolled off her. The hounds eerily gave up the hunt as the rest of the gathered equestrians stopped, sickened at the awfulness of what happened. The poor beast, Flashman, writhed in agony and was dispatched quickly and, in the circumstances, appropriately with a game keeper's shotgun. Never had a hunt witnessed such a nauseating tragedy.

* * *

Holden was lost in these distant thoughts as he stared out from the upper gallery of the cathedral, his gaze fixed behind his sunglasses towards the far end of St Marks Square. He was unaware of the unhealthy interest now being paid to him by the scarred protection officer. Ford was settled at a table on the terrace of Florian's along with Spicer and Bennetti and looked around him and his environment with the predatory efficiency of a hunting falcon. His colleagues were engaged in conversation with each other as he spotted the Panama hat again, this time on the elevated outer tier of the cathedral. Was this a matter of concern or a tourist who now had gone from rest back to sightseeing? The problem that Ford had in the future identity of this individual was that his face was totally obscured by the hat and glasses. His self protective sixth sense that had keenly developed on the streets of the harsh and unforgiving East End of Victorian London kicked in and he decided to act. The man in the Panama at that moment broke away from what appeared to have been a fixed gaze and looked down towards Ford. For a second time their ocular senses locked; Ford was going to win. He noted his adversary suddenly move briskly away from the gallery and disappear from sight.

Ford sprung from his chair with an efficiency and speed of movement that to those watching resembled a hunting animal's strike.

"Rob, where are you going?" called Spicer from his seat. His enquiry was futile as Ford's single goal was to confront this individual who seemed to have shadowed their movements in the area beyond sheer coincidence. But Ford realised the need for a reply and other protocols to be correctly observed. Without turning he spoke giving clearly projected instructions.

"Stay here there with the ministerial party. I'll be back quickly."

Ford did not know the layout of the Cathedral as intricately as Holden, his unknown faceless opponent. Holden rightly assumed that the policeman would now be converging on him. The fact that Holden knew a second escape from the cathedral from a visit nearly two decades earlier when the family was engaged in the famous 'grand tour' was immaterial. Little fazed Holden; he removed his hat, glasses and tie once he was out of sight away from the gallery edge. He merged with many other men sensibly and fashionably wearing light coloured linen suits and plain white shirts.

It was in the main atrium of the cathedral that he brushed the right shoulder of Ford as he confidently and easily passed him and exited into the sunlight that reflected from the light coloured marble and stone floor of the square, exaggerating the contrast between the coolness of the cathedral interior and the heat of the square. He melted unseen by the protection officers into the surrounding almost medieval streets of the St Marks district. Having passed his adversary so closely and watched the alert efficiency with which he operated he could not discount the need to use a sniper's rifle when the time came. Still, Holden drew satisfaction from continuing to strike fear into Patterson by the gradual attrition of his inner circle.

Ford searched the magnificent ecclesiastical building for fifteen minutes before admitting defeat to himself. As he returned to the main party they were preparing to leave the café, return to the motoscarfo and retire for the rest of the day and evening at the Ca' Pesaro. Ford looked forward to time off it would give him; he would socialise with Bennetti and Spicer and then spend the night making love to Karen Wood. He was beginning to feel overprotective towards her and he began to consider how he could break her away from the clutches of Patterson.

The motoscarfo pulled up on the banks of the Grand Canal immediately adjacent to the wonderful, stately, baroque Ca' Pesaro. The disembarkation was watched closely from a distance by Holden aboard a gondola. In the few hours that he observed the scarred protection officer and had passed him so closely in the cathedral, he was developing a respect for his apparent efficiency and devotion to his craft.

Staying at the 'Hotel Danielli' just along from St Marks on the sea front of the main island of the Lagoon, Holden had found a beautiful high class 'escort' to accompany him on the gondola so as not to arouse suspicion. He would also take great delight in sexual satisfaction from her back in his room, or he felt that if he could not wait, he would bribe the gondolier and have her in a quiet side canal. What he couldn't know was that Ford, Spicer, Bennetti and Karen Wood were all to be resident in the same hotel.

Patterson was smart. Venice was a lower key venue for a mysterious business meeting and the general having set up the meeting with the Vatican cardinals at his house on the Grand Canal was a touch of brilliance. The troublesome Inspector Ford would be out of the way and therefore not being his usual curious self. But timing is everything; the motoscarfo pulled away from its mooring outside the Ca' Pesaro and turned to head back towards St Marks and the Danielli. Ford was taking his usual high degree of interest in the world around him as they passed the Santa Maria della Salute on their right. A boat emerged from the canal alongside the magnificent domed, renaissance church that caught Ford's keen eye. Aboard were purple-robed high ranking churchmen. 'They must be cardinals' was his immediate internal observation. He grabbed Bennetti's arm to get his attention and spoke to him.

"Franco, who are those men? They look very important?" Bennetti whirled to look at the quite garish looking launch upon which they travelled. A devout catholic and regular Roman attendee of service at St Peter's Basilica he knew exactly who they were.

"My goodness, Roberto. They are very important Vaticano churchmen. Two cardinals and a bishop."

"Franco, who are they and what would they be doing here?"

"Cardinals Lorenzo and Ponti and Bishop Caravaggio. I do not know what would bring them here." Ford needed to satisfy his now ardent curiosity. He spoke quickly to Bennetti with directions.

"Franco, get the boat turned around, I need to know where they are going." Bennetti was a little shocked by his English colleague's interest but instructed the motoscarfo pilot to turn around, back to where they had come.

Sure enough, Ford's worst realisations were satisfied. The almost papal launch moored outside the grand baroque palace and the Cardinals and the Bishop were warmly greeted by Patterson and the general. Ford's curiosity went into overdrive; the pilot guided the boat back towards the south of Venice; Bennetti observed Ford puzzled; Karen Wood noted that Spicer didn't seem to want to speak to anyone and stared into space.

In a side canal Holden began to unbutton the blouse of the beautiful Venetian prostitute as she put her hand inside his trousers. His carnal pleasures were to save him from a face to face contact with Ford in the lobby of the Danielli.

* * *

London, August 19th 9.a.m

Bates disguised himself as a City of London postman to trick his way past the reception of Empire Petroleum and find his way to Patterson's locked office. The receptionist had happily waved the postman past his desk and thought nothing of him taking the stairs. The post room was on the second floor of the noted building that stood in Trinity Square overlooking the Tower of London. Its Greco-Roman pillared façade gave an empowering look to visitors; it fitted with the company's wish to eventually dominate the burgeoning petrol-chemical industry. Apart from its grand view of the Royal fortress and palace of the Tower, its steps led down towards Trinity Gardens, the scene of hundreds of the Tower's famous bloody executions, including Charles I.

"Hello, postie. How are you mate? Where's the regular bloke then?" said the friendly, elderly mail room clerk. Bates guile was always equal to such trite confrontations, and more.

"Oh, gone bleeding sick this morning, so you got me. Never mind he'll be back soon. Anyway, I've got a load of stuff for some bloke called Patterson. He must be an important bloke." Bates hoped this lure would work as planned. He had fabricated a load of false blank mail to get the clerk's attention.

"Yeah, he is. One of the directors. Arrogant bleeder though. Typical of a moneyed politician really." Bates felt sure he would elicit the crucial last piece of information.

"Cripes. He must have a bugger of a grand office then?"

"You're right there. Great big fancy oak panelled fucker on the top floor. He shares the floor with only one other director. Patterson's is the one at the front of the building. He likes the view, rich bastard."

Perfect. His ploy had worked a treat. He dumped the mail so as not to arouse the old clerk's suspicion and made off from the post room to find a stealthy route upstairs. His actions would eventually catch him out, however. He had six, what he assumed were all, blank letter envelopes. One amongst the envelopes in the middle of the wad had been muddled with the others and bore a small crest relating to The London Times on the reverse side. Bates in his haste had failed to see this when preparing his fake post.

Using a set of emergency stairs that ran at the side of the building he got to the top floor undetected. He expected that there would be a

The Dressmaker Connection

reception area for the two plush offices staffed by a secretary. He was right, but he noticed that it seemed unattended and that no one had yet been in; the secretary's chair was still neatly pushed up to and under the table and there were no outer garments on the coat stand. It was August, however, and no additional outer garments may have been brought in. He had come too far to not try to find any material that might explain what had been provoking the murder campaign against the ruthless industrialist. He strolled through the oak panelled reception area with its comfortable carpet underfoot and into Patterson's unlocked office. He was amazed by the opulence that greeted him.

When the post room clerk had talked of fine oak panelling he must have been referring to the reception area and not Patterson's own gaudy inner sanctum. Initially the colour that hit Bates was red, closely followed by white and then gold. Each wall was finished in the same basic way; a six inch Victorian skirting board above which sat a plain white painted plaster section of wall extending up to around a quarter of the walls' height ending in an ornate scrolled edge dado rail. Above this was deep crimson red Jacobean flocked wallpaper patterned with thistle crests and holly leaves. This red section extended upwards for another half of the walls' height up to a plain picture rail. Above this up to a plain tiered coving was a white plaster heraldic frieze. To top off this entire garish look was a white ceiling embossed with more plaster mouldings that included nearly foot long bulbous, ridged, decorative stalactites. The gold effect came from the painted white plaster fireplace above the plain marble fire surround on which the protruding patterns were highlighted with gold paint, and also from the framed works of many old masters that hung on every wall of the office. Unknown to the art illiterate Bates were works by Canaletto, including his view of St Marks Square, Venice with a wonderful rendition of the Doges Palace and the Campanile, as well as several landscapes by Van Goyen. The furniture was equally period with white and gold bookcases, white upholstered chairs with fleur-de-lis patterns and brass quilting studs and a large, ornate, light oak desk with brass mouldings, sculptured legs and a crested leather 'blotter.' Opulent was a way to describe Patterson's own arrogant power hungry indulgences. Bates continued to look around the office with its large window that he could see looked out towards the magnificent Tower Bridge. There must be a filing cabinet of sorts somewhere? Sure enough he picked out the reproduction piece of furniture that must be used as such. Set against the wall to the left hand side of Patterson's desk was what looked like a drinks cabinet and a matching bureau. The bureau was in fact the filling cabinet, he discovered, as he went to pull down the desk section. It simply came horizontally forwards to reveal a mass of documents. It was unlocked? The documents looked very mundane; he suspected the information he would be looking for would not be in there. There were two further drawers below it which again were both unlocked.

It seemed too cliché but he examined the drawers of Patterson's desk – the usual place for a dishonest business man to hide incriminating documents. They were indeed locked and he was going to have to force them to get them open. He wondered if he could pick the locks with a metal implement from the drinks cabinet, a bottle opener, knife or some small picks for picking up lemon slices. He returned to the drinks cabinet to rifle through it. He pulled forward some of the bottles to see what he could find. He was amazed by what he did. Normally such an expensive piece of furniture had the main section finished at its back with a mirror, to create the image of a wealth of alcohol filled bottles. This contained no mirror but a poorly fitted false wooden panel in the rear that fell forward when Bates disturbed a dusty bottle of Laphroaig single malt. The bottle was simply used to hold this subterfuge in situ, unlikely to normally be disturbed as there was another bottle of the same malt further forward. Concealed behind was a lone, battered leather bound book or journal of some kind.

He pulled it free; the leather was aged and cracked and the whole item heavily weathered around its edges. He pulled free the new looking strap that must have been a makeshift recent addition and opened the volume up. There were a few grains of sand embedded on the inside of the leather cover and the pages were yellowed, perforated slightly around the edges and all appeared to be hand written. He read what appeared to be the well written, hand scripted title page and knew that this must be what he was looking for:

The Dressmaker Connection

Trooper John Waldron, 247616,
Special Raiding Party
Captain Holden's Inaugural Undertaking
September 20th Onwards, 1898
North West Frontier into Afghanistan

Bates knew to read any further would be dangerous. He reset the drinks cabinet interior as best as he could remember, no longer holding a secret, and left the office as quickly as he could. This, he believed, would reveal a scandalous story behind the murders and make him a journalistic household name. He escaped the building undetected and made for the security of his own home, not the company of jealous fellow hacks in Fleet Street.

* * *

Rome, 19th August 9.p.m

James Landan decided to take a walk along the Via Fori Dei Imperiale as the sun set and the air cooled. It allowed him to gaze upon the magnificent Colosseum as the sun fell behind it. The grand avenue still bustled with local traffic of varying kinds in the fast accelerating and developing twentieth century society. Many pedestrians, a mix of foreign tourists, local entrepreneurs and thieves lightly dusted the footways with human activity. Landan had never been to Rome before and with a first in Classics from Oxford seeing the sights brought a sense of fulfilment. By the time he reached the former 'Flavian Amphitheatre' and stood admiring its most complete north façade with it's travertine blocks, the setting sun illuminated the sky an ironic blood red behind what was in truth a historical theatre of death. Orange-red light shone through many of the arches of the grand tiers each divided by either Doric, ionic or Corinthian columns dependent on the level in question; those that faced the sunset directly and emitted this light gave it the appearance of hideous, multi-eyed, death mask. He walked around its enormous, outer circumference delighting in this ancient miracle of architecture and engineering. He stopped on the opposite side of the structure with the site of the ancient and yet undiscovered 'Ludus Magnus', or gladiator school, located between the Via Labicana and Via di San Giovanni directly behind him.

As he basked in the reflected glory of this first encounter with the Colosseum, he was unaware of the wheelchair-bound individual who had silently rolled up behind him. The first Landan detected it was the simultaneous scent of tobacco smoke and an English voice addressing him.

"Quite magnificent really, isn't it?" Landan turned to see a swarthy but smartly dressed paraplegic smoking a coarse smelling, self rolled cigarette. He was startled by this man's sudden appearance.

"Er... Yes. Quite marvellous indeed, Mr ?"

"John Waldron, formally of Her Majesty's army, or His as it now is. You are?" The crippled ex-soldier drew hard on the cigarette as he finished.

"James. Landan, James Landan. How do you do." He extended a hand of friendship that Waldron readily accepted.

"Very well. Judging by your reaction to seeing this place synonymous with death, bet you'd like a nice, quiet, private look around. Eh?"

"Well how would that work?" asked a puzzled Landan. "I mean it's shut now and how would you sway that anyway?" He was of course patently interested and if the old soldier could arrange such a private viewing he would seize the opportunity. Seeing it in the company of so many other tourists would be most disagreeable.

"I've knocked around Rome a fair bit see. I know the bloke on security tonight so we could wander over, I tap on the gate and make some noise, he comes out and we go in. Easy."

Landan with his degree in classics saw this as too good an opportunity to pass up. It would be quite something to brag about at breakfast the next day.

"All right, Mr Waldron, I shall take you up on your offer. It's most kind. You must let me arrange some recompense once we've finished."

"Oh you won't need to worry about that. I ask just one thing; push me over there and around inside. My arms ain't what they used to be, especially when it's this late."

Within the grounds of the Colosseum Holden was preparing various apparatus for use on his next victim. In 1904, despite the warren of underground chambers, the majority of the floor of the Colosseum was completely solid with most of its chambers and corridors still under many feet of earth and sand. Only part of the eastern end of the ellipse had been excavated, although the project had been suspended since 1866 due to flooding. At one end of the arena's ellipse was a cross to commemorate the Christian victims of Roman empirically indulgent violence and murder. The famous theatre of death was about to claim one more victim. The security guard had been bribed to allow Waldron entry with another and then to leave the building until dawn. This allowed Holden to light what he planned to be a low smoking fire within one of the sub ground level antechambers or 'direction rooms' that led off of the main ground floor interior concourse, to heat up the cavalry sabre he had with him. He also had what was effectively a man size wooden cross, but not as tradition perceives. This was in the shape of an 'X', the style of crucifix often used by the Romans to crucify victims upside down. This evening its purpose was purely for immobilising someone flat on the ground. Holden had rope to tie the person to the cross and, somewhat humanly by his recent course of action, some strong military surgical anaesthetic. As he watched the sabre slowly beginning to heat up he heard a clanking metal sound. Landan had taken the bait and was now entering the Colosseum with Waldron.

At what was the one of the 'imperial' gates on the southern axis, the other being on the north axis, Waldron had rattled the chain locking the iron gate as well as the gate itself to gain the night watchman's attention. An aging, slightly hunched, weathered Italian man shuffled up to the gate. He acknowledged Waldron and opened the gates to allow the two individuals stood in front of him to enter. He was being paid handsomely to 'look the other way' tonight and return in the mid-early morning hours and took no interest in their intent. He simply asked of the well groomed Englishman that he had already allowed to gain access to lock up behind them when they were done. He shuffled away from Landan and Waldron and disappeared slowly south into the dimly lit side streets.

"Oh. Is he not hanging around to let us back out again then?" Landan asked Waldron with some puzzlement.

"No. He's an old acquaintance from my more mobile days and several previous visits here. He trusts me and it gives him a night off." Waldron lied convincingly through his teeth with the efficiency of a cheap watch to the less than street wise post-graduate Landan. With his enthusiasm in gaining a private viewing of the famous landmark he fell totally for Waldron's ploy.

The ground was less than smooth in places as Landan strode away from the now closed gate through the archway that he could see led directly to the mildly illuminated main arena. He had longed since early history lessons as a boy to stand in the centre and look out and around to the remains of the tiered sections of the spectators areas. He could see ahead of him that much of the floor of the arena was sand as it would have been nearly 1900 years earlier during its inaugural games. It was then, he recalled, that in 80.A.D 'naumachias' could be staged, the Roman name for naval battles. Not long after the end of the first century A.D. and leading into the second that the famous subterranean caverns were constructed to house gladiators, wild beasts and scenery all of which could be briskly dispatched to the main ellipse for the baying crowds entertainment via lifts, pulleys or complex tunnels. The purpose built Colosseum could truly be considered the founding home of 'snuff' theatre considered Landan as he had his goal in sight.

"Oi. How about a bit of assistance then, eh? I got you a special visit haven't I?" shouted a disgruntled and stranded Waldron from behind. The floor was rutted, blocked with rubble chicanes and generally impossible for a wheelchair. Landan was startled back to reality by the shout.

"Sorry. I got carried away." Landan returned for his strange companion.

"How did you end up as an invalid then?" He innocently asked as he began pushing the wheelchair. Invalid was not a term that the increasingly short tempered Waldron liked to hear.

"I'M NOT A FUCKING INVALID, YOU TOSSER!" His reply was shouted venomously knowing that this man associated with the politician who had cost him his mobility. "I prefer disabled. Invalid makes me sound like a fucking mental defective too." He added more calmly. "I am just less able than you, matey boy." Landan found his reference common and derogatory. He was not a friend of this difficult man. He would pander to him to complete his visit.

They entered the main arena and Landan pushed the wheelchair into the centre and stopped overwhelmed by the site that surrounded him. There was little actual evidence of the original spectator seating. Much of the Colosseum had been used in the construction of St Peter's Basilica leaving less that forty per cent of the original structure. It was a huge irony that the place where many Christians met their death had been de-constructed piece by piece by them to build a structure to celebrate their religion. Despite this, the site of the interior of the Colosseum for a first time was even more awe inspiring than the site of the exterior. It was from this perspective that the sheer magnitude of the building was truly appreciated as you looked at it in a panoramic fashion.

"It fucking impresses you then, matey?" That same inappropriate endearment riled Landan again and snapped him out of the world he had disappeared to as he pictured the arena in its hey-day.

"Please. Call me James, Mr Waldron. I'm really not used to such colloquialisms. We aren't true friends either." He was condescending in his tone, foolishly. Waldron was more restrained in his response but somehow, despite his disability, very menacing.

"Listen, Mr Landan. I've fought on all the continents of our Empire and had hordes of fucking savage natives outnumbering me and charging me only yards away. I've done those things for the likes of you and your boss, so you show an old soldier who, if I get hold of you, will punch your snooty, Oxford educated lights out, a bit of respect. All right?" Fortunately for Landan he was currently out of arms reach, although he was growing tired of the crippled soldier's rants.

"Look, whatever I say to you I seem to rub you up the wrong way, so why don't you let me have a quiet wander around and I'll meet you back over at the gate. In say thirty minutes?" He thought that this would be less stressful for both of them. The embittered and increasingly difficult ex-soldier spat into the sand, away from either of them before contemptibly replying. The exchange was being observed by Holden from behind a pillar in the interior concourse of the ancient stadium on its west side.

"Right, toff. Have it your way. I'll see you later." Using supreme effort Waldron turned himself around in the soft sand and made in the direction from which they had come, slowly and in a very short time, wearily.

'Thank goodness he's gone,' thought Landan to himself. Holden watched from the shadows. It was only a short distance from there to his makeshift torture chamber, a place that Landan would come never to forget. The Oxford post graduate decided to take a walk around the circumference of the arena, as much as the partial excavations would allow, and visualize it's various elements; the varying types of entrances to it to allow the access of beasts or men, both to the slaughter; the high wall that would have been topped off with long missing convex rounded stones to prevent escape from the combat or hunt; the location on the north and south axis's of the Imperial or 'Royal boxes', the term he used from visiting the Albert Hall, the architecture of which was modelled on the Colosseum, picturing the Emperor attempting to appease the masses or 'mob'. On many occasions, he recalled from the ancient writings of the likes of Suetonius, the Emperor not always achieving this aim.

As he passed along the west side of the arena Holden emerged silently from the shadows behind him with a large hypodermic syringe in his right hand. With no particular skill or methodology he stabbed Landan firmly in the neck and immediately pushed the plunger and filled the young graduate with, what he had intended as being, a massive dose of general anaesthetic. Landan grabbed the wound in his neck as he felt the intrusive item that had stabbed him removed as quickly as it had struck. He didn't even have time to turn and observe his assailant as the near dangerous level of specialised medication took an instant effect. Holden grabbed the limp body under the arms and dragged him into the concourse. From there, he stood the body up against the wall then carried him bent over his right shoulder to his near subterranean personal torture chamber. Holden considered that term in his mind. 'How could it be torture truly if the victim was unconscious?' Waldron was already in there intent on enjoying every minute of one of Patterson's 'spineless subordinates' suffering. He had left his wheelchair in the concourse and dragged himself by his powerful arms and shoulders down the hard travertine stairs. His lifeless knees and feet had felt nothing as they struck the edge of the stone steps on the way down. He spoke to Holden as the former captain deposited the unconscious Landan onto the cross.

"I done a good job preparing that cross, Boss." He was proud of the dovetailed joint of the two seven foot long, diagonally crossing, six by four inch planks of mahogany wood. He had also placed with screws six inch long and half inch deep metal plates on each of the arms of the cross just above where the elbow joints would approximately be and just above the knee joints. Holden was on a crusade of cold bloodied and terrifying revenge during which he intended to strike total fear into Patterson. He knew that to leave a living victim, for now, would most likely be a critical point in his vendetta. The cold hearted and avarice ridden political industrialist would hopefully now sit up and take note of what was going on, perhaps even secretly dispatch someone to try to find Holden; though probably not one of the usually incorruptible Special Branch policemen.

Holden took no delight in what he was doing other than the thought of each being an objective on the way to ultimate revenge. Waldron, on the other hand, as time went on seemed to take a callous and evil delight in an ever growing and sickeningly wanton manner. It was beginning to disturb Holden and he considered that the crippled soldier was perhaps now becoming a liability.

"Yes, Wally, you have indeed done a fine job. Do you really want to witness this whole ghastly procedure?" Holden was himself beginning to feel uncomfortable about maiming this young man, his sense of life and death made him consider that he would sooner be dead than left in such a condition. Waldron's sweating and almost nauseous delight was bothering him.

"You having a laugh, Boss? With what happened to our mates? I don't give a fuck. They're all responsible in some way so let's just get on with it. Or do you want an old cripple to do the work if you've lost your bottle?" Holden had never experienced such dissent from one of the men in his ranks, ever; it riled him greatly and he would only take that kind of insubordination once even from Waldron, no matter what his physical condition. It forced Holden to speak coldly and with irritating and disturbing malevolence. Annoyingly his chest irritated him before he spoke and he had to cough to clear his throat.

"Now you listen to me, cripple, you owe your life to me, no matter what sort of life it may be. We are on a mission that does not require such great delight in its elements, but clear military thought and discipline. You question me again and you'll wish that I'd left you in Afghanistan." Holden stared into Waldron's eyes in the fire lit ante-chamber and for the first time the cold gaze struck more fear into Waldron than he had ever experienced. He swallowed hard and stayed silent. He was about to regret an earlier and as yet undetected act of sabotage.

The room had taken on the look of a fiery workshop of a disciple of Satan himself. The fire coloured the stone walls an orangey-red which continually flickered and changed the shadows cast of those present. Coupled with Holden's words, Waldron suddenly felt fearful as he watched the captain tie Landan to the cross at his wrists and his ankles tightly. He dragged himself to a corner of the room near the steps with his back firmly against the wall. Despite the heat of the fire and the August night time air he felt cold and shivery. Watching the fire lit activity in such an enclosed space he thought he was on the cusp of hell himself. This fear was exaggerated as Holden then picked up the glowing cavalry sabre from the fire with it's only piece of conventionally glinting metal being the hand guard than ran from the pommel to it's hilt.

Holden's entire being was illuminated by a devilish glow as he stood facing the fire on one side of the incapacitated and immobile Landan. Waldron was now watching Landan's face intently; he had diluted the anaesthetic mix earlier in the day, after Holden prepared it, during one of his vengeful, melancholy depressions. It was done with the deliberate intent of making Landan's suffering greater, but with no thought to Holden or his reaction. He sat fearfully in the corner of the room as the situation began to unfold in front of him. He could tell Holden's patience with him was wearing thin; in his need to see Landan suffer he had given no consideration to a negative reaction by his commanding officer.

Holden now stood parallel with Landan's left leg; he looked down upon it to take aim as he lifted the sabre high above his head. Holden paused in the position for quite some seconds as he considered his actions. Then he thought of how needlessly his men had suffered and died for Patterson and his lackeys, whoever they were. It gave him a clear head to carry on with his actions. He swung the sabre down briskly and accurately severing Landan's leg just above his knee. As with this method he had seen so clearly demonstrated in Afghanistan there was no blood as the wound was instantly cauterised – on both sides. A nauseating smell of burning flesh began to permeate the atmosphere of the small room very quickly. The smell was truly sickening in its origin and spurred Holden on to get the job done more quickly and get out.

Holden didn't notice the flickering of Landan's eyes as he struck him with the sabre and its devastating consequences. Waldron had, and he started shivering and cowering in the corner. Holden looked at him as he prepared to sever the other leg and was mystified by his sudden fearful condition considering the fight that he had had within him only minutes ago.

"What's wrong with you?" asked a suspicious Holden. Waldron could not make eye contact and continued staring ahead at Landan. 'Fuck!' He thought, 'his eyes are wide open!' Holden looked away from him shaking his head and looked down on the right leg. Having removed the first limb it now seemed to become easier; a little like the first time you killed a man, he considered. 'After the first one the rest just get easier'.

He lifted the glowing sabre above his head once more and brought it down quickly and efficiently again severing the leg above the knee; the wound instantly smouldered and there was again no blood. For a second time the metal plates Waldron had fitted did their job and stopped the sabre breaking the wooden cross. The smell didn't get any worse. Holden had been stunned by a reaction from what he thought was a well anesthetised body. Landan's back had arched violently with the wound. Holden looked instantly up to Landan's face; he could see his eyes were wide open filled with both terror and agony. He was stunned. He was certain he had used too much anaesthetic as opposed to too little. Landan was silent but undeniably conscious. He appeared to be able to move nothing else nor make any sound. The arching of the back must have been a huge reflex action. Holden turned to the now shaking uncontrollably and helpless looking cripple in the corner of the room. Lit by the fire and huddled up tightly to himself he looked like a pathetic, minor demon that was powerless yet callous.

"You evil, crippled fucker! When did you tamper with the anaesthetic then, eh?" Holden was furious and walked towards him brandishing the sabre. It was beginning to lose its glow a little; that was of no consequence to Waldron as he feared just a simple coup de gras, a quick and ignominious end from it all. He was finding it hard to speak.

"You speak to me, Waldron, or I'll take your arms off and not his!" Holden lifted the sword and having closed with Waldron held it just slightly below his chin. Despite it losing its glow he could still feel its heat by his neck.

"I don't know what came over me; I did it earlier, in a weak moment, Boss. I'm sorry, really sorry......Boss?" Holden was just coldly staring at him, a kind of fixed purposeful stare that Waldron imagined a lone wolf having cornered its prey would display before the kill. Holden said nothing for quite some time holding the sabre in place watching Waldron sweat, beads of perspiration running from his temples around his face and dropping off his chin.

"When we get back to England you and I are finished. You disappear back into your paltry civilian life in the depressing North of England and don't cross my path again. I'll finish what I have started and I don't need your hindrance to do it. Speak nothing of this to anyone or your life won't be worth living. You understand?" Waldron was shivering with palpable fear. He found the strength to answer.

"Yes, Sir. I'm sorry I have disgraced you. Do you want me to go now?" Holden lowered the sabre, walked back to the fire and rested it back in there. He turned back to Waldron to answer his question.

"No, we stay in Rome and leave together. Wait there while I finish this. Where is the rest of the anaesthetic?"

Holden watched Waldron reach inside his jacket pocket. He knew it would not be for a firearm. Waldron pulled free a phial containing a transparent liquid. He held it up as if for Holden to come and take.

"Is that it?" demanded Holden. Waldron nodded his head. "Right." Holden strolled over to him and took the phial from his hand. He removed its cork stopper and found the syringe within his own top coat and placed the needle inside the liquid. He with drew as much as he could and discarded the almost empty phial. Holden walked over to Landan whose eyes still stared widely with sheer terror; so sorrowful

The Dressmaker Connection

and pitiful. Holden began to consider if he could see things through. He now had the added burden of Waldron, however, and if he failed to act his former subordinate might see it as weakness and not be fearful of speaking out against him; after all the establishment for all intents and purposes thought no one had returned from Afghanistan. He changed his mind about leaving a living victim to speak of the horrors, after all Nigel Green had died on campaign anyway.

Holden jabbed the syringe directly into Landan's jugular vein and watched it take its effect. The eyes closed. Holden watched for a little longer before taking any action. He was grateful for the second injections effect. Landan stopped breathing and his pulse came to a complete rest. Holden grabbed the now glowing hot sabre again and finished the grisly task he had set himself by removing the lifeless Landan's arms. To be consistent with Nigel Green's suffering, he then stabbed his torso three times. Waldron looked on still fearful of Holden and the possibility that he may have made himself a target. Holden put the fire out and then dragged the cross holding the de-limbed Landan up the stairs, through the concourse and out into the dimly lit arena. Waldron dragged himself up the stairs slowly behind him and then regained a seat in his wheelchair.

Holden took the crucifix and stood it up for all to see first thing in the morning against the cross of the existing Christian memorial. He retrieved the sabre and joined Waldron by their entry point.

Where did the old man go?" asked Holden of Waldron.

"I saw him disappear over that way," Waldron pointed towards the warren of side streets. Holden had left a small leather shoulder bag by the gate. He pulled from it a quality bottle of Italian liquor and unscrewed the top. He took a generous mouthful. He then took a smaller bottle out and popped its cork cap. It was marked 'strychnine' and Holden emptied it into the liquor.

"You said our man likes a drink; that should keep him quiet." Waldron simply nodded his head in subservient agreement. Holden closed up the gates and they both left heading back towards the Theatre of Marcello and their hotel.

* * *

It was about 7.a.m that the full horror was discovered. The day staff had arrived to prepare for the day's visitors when they found, initially, the aged night watchman dead, apparently poisoned in the concourse with a bottle of only partially drunk liquor. Minutes later they discovered Landan's maimed yet cauterised and stabbed corpse in the arena area of the ancient stadium, its first victim of crucifixion, it appeared, for nearly 1800 years. The police and the carabinierie were immediately called to the scene and were shocked by the ritualistic nature of the maiming of the body. Had it happened prior to death or after, and what was its significance? Only two people would know; Patterson immediately, and Bates once he had finished reading the journal. The authorities were also mystified by the strange parallel minor wheel tracks in the sand that seemed to belong to a disabled chair. The Ministerial party at that hour were all still sound asleep in their beds without concerns.

Chapter Ten

Holden had decided to head back to the hotel via a route that would take him along the banks of the famous River Tiber, the only constant in the evolution of the 'Eternal City'. He was tiring of Waldron's company and particularly his increasingly unpredictable nature. The years of service between them were still of value but he was concerned that he might compromise the entire operation with the events of the latest killing. The crippled soldier's general humour was poor and Holden considered that he needed to 'discharge' him of any further obligation. He knew that there was only one safe way to do this. 'That bastard Patterson has put me in this position' he mused. 'A proud soldier whose physiological state has begun to cloud his clarity of thought, there is only one way I can resolve this.' In truth, Holden's own judgement was without doubt now becoming prone to unpredictable and flawed decision making. His quest for revenge was overtaking any logical regard for those around him; it had turned his thoughts purely towards survival instincts and Waldron now presented a long term threat in his mind. To top it all, the nagging cough that had begun over the last few weeks seemed to be getting more prevalent.

"Boss, are you sure that we aren't going out of our way here?" asked a curious Waldron as he was wheeled along the pleasant balustrade that ran along the banks of the river. Holden had given him a bottle of Absinthe mildly laced with laudanum to try to relax the cripple's mood. His intention was clear; get him slowly drunk, take the wheelchair to the riverside and tip him almost unconscious into the water under the cover of darkness. It would be assumed that he was a foolish drunk when he was found and raise no suspicion. He would ensure that the contents of the bottle were empty so no analysis of the drink could be made, just an empty bottle, so there would be no thought towards poisoning. What he would not have planned for was the potential for a link being made between the wheelchair and the murder of Landan at the Colosseum.

Having passed by the Castello of St Angelo, they came upon the island in the river or 'Isola Tibernia'. It was 3.30.a.m and there was not a soul around as Holden pushed the wheelchair gently and, with its clever rubber tyres that Waldron had wished for to move quietly, silently in the centre of Rome.

"Wally, have you ever seen the sun come up over the Palatine Hill, old friend? It's quite a sight you know." Waldron was becoming quite intoxicated and his speech began to slur slightly as he replied. It was just the condition that Holden wished for. He knew that it would not take to long to achieve as the depressive old soldier found great solace in alcohol.

"No, Boss, I never have. I take it that it's pretty spectacular. Is it as good as was the sunset or sunrise over the Khyber Pass?"

'Damn it! The crippled old soldier was getting sentimental.' Holden didn't want fond memories of distant places where men formed a close bond through combat and the need to survive to cloud his judgement over his 'pragmatic' course of action. He tried to divert the conversation away from such matters briskly.

"Yes, better in some ways, as the early morning light breaks over the ruins of a mighty empire. It's particularly good to see it looking up from the Circus Maximus, the site of the chariot racing course."

"Chariot racing? I bet those Roman sods had nothing on the horsemen of Kafiristan. Those bastards could ride horses that's for sure. Don't you remember?" Holden carried on quietly and steadily pushing the wheelchair along with his eyes beginning to well up with the memories of better times with his men, his friends out in the field. He was now beginning to question everything he had so far done, and what he was about to embark on further. More blood was to be shed before the whole business was finished. He pushed Waldron up to the water's edge and applied the brakes on the rear wheels.

"Yes," Holden spoke with his voice breaking a little and had to cough to continue to try to disguise it, "you are quite right they were amazing times, old friend. Take another drink so we can reminisce some more." Waldron stared out to the smooth flowing Tiber and took a generous mouthful of the Absinthe. Its strong aniseed taste and its alcoholic kick made him grimace as he swallowed down the cloudy green liquid. Silence descended over the two of them for sometime as tears rolled down Holden's cheeks. He was losing the fortitude to end his pitiful friend's life. He stood behind Waldron out of sight, an action that eventually prompted the crippled soldier to speak with drunken curiosity.

"Come on, Boss have a drink with me, will ya?" Holden, if he dared drink any, could only afford to have a little so as not to allow the mind altering effect of the laudanum and the highly distilled alcohol to cloud his actions.

The bottle was offered to him in Waldron's right hand. He stepped forward and took it and then sat cross legged on the hard, warm, dry stone floor on the river bank and stared as sightlessly as Waldron into the water. The tears rolled down his cheeks and he began to sob. He put the bottle to one side in anticipation of his actions. Waldron, although very drunk, was lucid enough to realise his former commanding officer was having an emotional crisis.

"Boss, what's wrong? Why the major waterworks?" He was unaware of Holden slipping off the brakes of the wheelchair and grabbing the arm on its right side. He tightened his grip on the arm and was on the cusp of yanking it forward sending the clearly, heavily drunk Waldron into the river. He couldn't answer his friend and couldn't look at his face. He was shaking with the violence of his sobbing.

Suddenly he acted; with a supreme effort he kept hold of the arm of the wheelchair and yanked himself onto his feet. He got behind Waldron, threw the bottle into the river and took hold of both the arms ready to push it forward. He took a pace back and violently flung the wheelchair a hundred and eighty degrees about turn. He began to stride purposefully towards the Circus Maximus.

"Right, you bastard donkey-walloper; we're off to see this famous sunrise, so sober up or you won't appreciate it!" Holden wiped the last of the tears from his face as they got going.

"Fucking hell, Boss! Wondered why you chucked the bottle away. Whatever you say goes. Oddly enough I'm in your hands."

Holden strolled purposefully forward with a refreshed and logical perspective, although all too aware that emotion was beginning to cloud his judgement. He would have faith in his friend and not allow his alcoholic and emotional depressions to influence him. He'd tell him to 'get a grip' like all soldiers on campaign needed too. And most importantly how could he assist in any quest for total silence that Patterson would be embarking on by killing one of the last two men who carried his dark secret.

* * *

The Colosseum, August 20th, 8.a.m

The local authorities had not yet removed Landan's body on the cross in order for the carnage of the scene to be observed in its entire, horrifying reality by Patterson and his two personal protection policemen. Along with Ford and Spicer, they were the only people to attend from the U.K governmental party. Bennetti had accompanied them to act as a translator. The ghastliness of the scene in its cruelty was almost overwhelming as they stood in the centre of the arena and looked upon the lifeless, limbless corpse that also as a final insult had been stabbed with a sword type weapon. It would be the post mortem examination back in London that would establish that these wounds had been struck after death by the nature of the blood loss from the wounds. What no one could bare to think about was the nature of the removal of all of the limbs from above their central joints. All noted the cauterising of the wounds with no blood loss.

Spicer and Ford had never witnessed such cruelty before, but Patterson staying silent knew only too well where it originated from and now began to have concerns over who had perpetrated this act. He kept this to himself; this was not a matter to discuss with policemen. Having turned their eyes from Landan and the nauseating nature of his cruel demise, Ford noted without prompting by the Italian authorities the parallel tracks made in the sand. 'Damn it! Why hadn't he measured the width of the tracks at the Sacred Heart in Paris?' He would have to cable Inspector Reno and see if any one had; but what a bizarre coincidence. He was about to discuss it with Spicer and Patterson when an emotional scream came up from the concourse. Bennetti translated the excited news about the latest sickening discovery. A young policeman had found the limbs, the remainder of Landan, in an antechamber.

"No, Franco, we don't want to see them. Can you have them take the poor fellow down and arrange transportation of the body to London with us please?" Ford asked of his Italian liaison officer. Bennetti, in an archetypically Latin way with very quickly spoken and exaggerated conversation, directed the local uniform police officers to do as Ford had requested.

"Franco, Bob, will you excuse the Minister and I please?" said Ford. The two nodded their heads and walked away leaving Patterson and Ford to speak away from anyone's earshot in the centre of the arena. As they talked the body was removed.

"All right, Sir Cecil, are you going to come clean about something then?" Ford maintained savage eye contact as he spoke. Patterson looked down at his feet to compose himself to speak. He was also preparing a pack of lies to tell Ford. He could not afford the public scandal of the disclosure of his misuse of military resources. Men sent to their almost certain deaths in one of the world's most hostile countries. The survivors of such a mission now out to scare and probably eventually murder him. No, the 'Holden and Waldron issue' would have to be resolved in some other way. They had obviously stayed silent to this point, he suspected from what he had seen and read about the events of 1898 that only those two could still be around. It made perfect sense to Patterson, Waldron's disability and the discovery of wheelchair tracks at two scenes. That was careless of Holden, unless deliberate. Holden's cold sense of duty and honour most likely stretched to revenge too. He would certainly find someone to deal with them quietly. But what to tell Ford? He coughed and began.

"In 1898, it's on record; I ventured past the Khyber Pass up onto the North West Frontier with a small group of light infantry men. The purpose was to see if there were friendly tribes there that would help Her Majesty's government develop industrial interests there, forge relations and bring prosperity to their negligible economy." This two-word description was said in such a condescending way Ford noted. "And obviously go a long way to improve our own economy further.

However, in the first native encampment that we discovered, a local fortune teller and fakir arrived that night claiming that we would bring the country nothing but bad luck and that the chieftain should be ashamed of himself for showing us hospitality." Patterson paused for moment. Ford wanted to keep the pressure on him to talk.

"So what happened then?" Ford almost demanded the answer.

"The fakir said that he would demand a fatwa, or death warrant be made out against us. The superstitious chieftain agreed and we had to escape pretty sharpish. We lost a man coming back over the pass. The unit got pretty spooked by the whole thing. I guess the natives saw me as the man in charge and this is all part of their savage hocus-pocus revenge attack."

Ford deliberately stood silently just looking at Patterson to see if he would add or subtract anything in the story. He was resolute, however, knowing that if Ford checked up the records would verify most of his lie. Only if Ford decided to speak to individual soldiers could he discover the truth. He would try to actively discourage him by presenting most of the records of his trip. Ford maintained eye contact and rubbed his chin as he contemplated the story imparted to him.

"So, you believe that these murders are being perpetrated against your people and perhaps ultimately you as a result of a fatwa issued under what I believe is called 'sharia' law?" Ford watched Patterson's pupils dilate slightly as he replied.

"Yes. Yes I do, Inspector. Hence, the savage and ritualistic nature of these killings. Look, when we get back to London I'll give you the details of this brief incursion we made into Afghanistan. I have the original orders and the final report by the corporal left in charge of the light infantry unit. There is little to it apart from verifying the mission."

Ford initially said nothing as he considered the minister's words. Slowly he nodded his head as he watched the now covered up crucifix finally exit the arena. He still didn't believe a word the conniving politician said.

"All right, Sir. I would appreciate seeing that when we get back please. You're free to go. Is your office going to take care of informing next of kin, etcetera?"

"Yes, Inspector, they will. Thank you. As you know we leave tomorrow. You shall have your information before the week is out."

Ford watched Patterson walk away towards the northern exit of the arena with Spicer following up in tow along with Bennetti. The two of them would see the Minister safely back to the hotel and his day's engagements. He bent down to look at the bizarre narrow, parallel tracks in the sand. As he could recall they appeared to be very similar to the ones left in Paris; he pulled his pocket diary from inside his linen suit knowing that it was exactly six inches long. He placed it on the inside edge of one track and then used it end to end a total of five times to measure the distance across to the inside of the other track. It gave an inside track width of two and a half feet. By a rough measure each tyre was approximately two inches wide. Ford's mind was fascinated and perplexed by the appearance of such marks for a second time. Could a paraplegic really be guilty of all these gruesome murders so far? They would have to be physically powerful if they were, and very persuasive. He considered the matter as he surveyed the arena and began to walk around it in concentric circles. There appeared to be nothing else to be found here; there were so many footprints in the sand that it was impossible to pin them to anyone; potential killer or accomplice. He moved off out of the bright hot Roman sun into the interior concourse and to the antechamber where the grim and callous butchery had seemingly taken place.

By the time Ford got there the limbs had been removed but the stench of burnt flesh still permeated the air. The subterranean stone room was unusually warm and he noticed the embers of a dying fire in one corner; the likely cause of the uncharacteristic heat. Again, as with the sand in the arena, there was no blood anywhere, but also no sign of a murder weapon. This disappointed Ford; he had optimistically hoped for such a clue. The type of bladed weapon might have helped prove or disprove Patterson's flimsy story. The room told nothing of the horrors that had taken place in there and only seemed to resemble a hovel where a vagrant might have cooked some rotten meat for himself overnight. There had to be more; Ford got down on his hands and knees to scour every corner of the room. Watching him was an extremely bored looking young carabinierie officer who as Ford looked up from his searching made eye contact, yawned and then looked away and glanced longingly back out towards the daylight.

Ford's efforts paid him back with a fortuitous dividend. In a darkened corner of the room tucked right up in the tight ancient Roman stone work where the wall met the floor was a discarded hypodermic needle. Ford picked it up to see if there was anything left inside the chamber; it appeared virtually empty. Optimistically he believed that some of the scientists back in London might get a trace of something from it. The Italian police official was still looking away from him as he examined the syringe. He broke the needle off against the floor and then pulled a cotton handkerchief from his trouser pocket to wrap the remainder within. Having done so, he placed it carefully inside his jacket pocket and stood up ready to leave. He brushed his trousers down, smiled and nodded to the Italian and left the antechamber.

Back in the sunlight as he prepared to leave the imposing Colosseum, Ford thought what a lonely miserable death that the ageing night watchman had met; his covered-over body was being stretchered out as Ford reached the sunlight. In the wake of the horrific and ritualistic murder of a visiting foreign government official, the old man's death would probably not even make the next day's newspapers and would pale into insignificance. Ford squinted as he came out into the light and felt the significant increase in temperature. He walked out into the now bustling Roman streets to make his way back to the hotel.

* * *

Bates had spent the previous day with his mind wandering at work as to the further contents of the explosive journal he had stolen from Patterson's office. He had not yet spoken to anyone else about it as he hadn't finished reading it fully, the handwriting at times had made it slow going. He decided to take the day off from work today to read it in its entirety and then form a plan of action as to what he was going to do with it. The massive consequence of such a political scandal in the public domain would once and for all, he thought, make him a household name. He would be the first person to solve the mystery of the so called 'Ministerial Murders.' Having taken the day off, he would not be the one writing the copy for the latest horrific events having taken place in Rome. He opened the weather beaten, leather cover of the journal to commence reading it again having decided to follow it from the very start once more.

Trooper John Waldron, 247616,

Special Raiding Party

Captain Holden's Inaugural Undertaking

September 20th Onwards, 1898

North West Frontier into Afghanistan

He read this first page over with its few words several times before being able to continue further with the full story. 'The Special Raiding Party'? Who the hell were they? The whole thing was surrounded by complete intrigue. He turned the yellowed page and read on. The writing beyond the carefully scripted title page was more ordinary.

<u>Special Raiding Party Role call:</u>
Captain William Holden (Cavalry)
Sergeant Major Nigel Green (Guards)
Corporal William Bayley (Light Infantry)
Troopers:
John Waldron (Engineers)
Jock Sutherland (Guards)
Cledwyn Jones (Welsh Fusiliers)
Peter Burwell (Light Infantry)

20th September
Today was a fairly uneventful day's trekking up into the Khyber Pass. As we leave colonial India I have felt compelled to begin to record the events of our passing days. All of us are in good spirit. The equipment we use is suitable and is working well and everyone is up to the task in hand. Mr Holden (the

Boss) is, as we have always known and seen, an excellent officer and is not prepared to ask us to do things that he cannot do for himself. The SRP is like a Marxist commune where we all share tasks. We hope that in two days we will be up and over the high ground of the North West Frontier and into the as yet unconquered Afghanistan. Mr Holden is certainly not underestimating those we might encounter there.

At this point it might be prudent to makes notes of the mission objectives in case we fail and all that is found is this journal. Sir Cecil Patterson, the Minister of War, has sent us out here on a quest for a substance that will help Britain become the leading industrial developers of one, the horseless carriage, and two the 'petrochemical' industry as he calls it. Under the mountains in an unpronounceable part of Afghanistan are vast lakes of what is called legendarily 'black gold' or oil. It is the key constituent in the manufacture of fuel for this new fangled 'internal combustion engine' used in the horseless carriage. He says that if it is there it will make Britain for the long term the most powerful industrial nation in the world and secure the Empire for many years to come.

For our safety, he has tasked us to say that we are from the Royal Geographic Survey to look for the stuff and once we have located it to bring back samples for analysis. The whole task seems easy enough although Mr Holden has stated that Patterson does have some vested interest. Most of us don't care as we joined the experimental SRP to do something different to regular soldiering. We've all spilt blood somewhere. If the whole thing goes wrong we've guns, supplies and if we don't return within a fortnight they'll be sending in some more lads to get us out. With our training and the leadership we should all do all right.

21st September

We have reached high ground in the mountains today and we are camping quite someway short of the summit. As we travelled in the Khyber Pass we encountered many people; singularly, in pairs, caravans, all sorts. As we gained height away we very quickly met no one. In fact, it is so arduous I wonder if there is an easier navigable route. It is very rocky with a lot of loose shingle underfoot. It often feels like two steps forwards and three steps back. The increase in altitude seems to make the air thinner and most of us on the very steep sections seem to begin to breathe heavily very quickly. The Boss is incredible though, he's like a bloody mountain goat. He just keeps going without tiring. He doesn't seem human sometimes. The stories about him excelling in his school days as sportsman must all be true. He gives consideration to the men at all times and senses when we are tiring and calls a rest break accordingly. He's even done the brew up twice so the chaps can all rest.

The Boss says that tomorrow we'll be over the top of the mountains and on our way down to lower ground and thicker air. Of that I will be glad; along with the other problems it is ridiculously bloody cold. I don't' envisage much sleep tonight. The sun has gone down and the temperature is still plummeting. Writing is becoming painful. My exposed fingers are going numb, must cover up before they discolour. Wally's sorting out the scran, more of the pemmican we are all carrying, then more bloody mint cake for dessert! Happy days!

22nd September

Morale was low this morning. Most of us didn't sleep a wink and even the Boss was beginning to look as if he was losing his usual resolve. What made it worse was the thought of going higher, getting colder and the air getting thinner. None of us relished the thought. We awoke to a damned whiteout. More pemmican for breakfast. It's amazing stuff, a bit of an acquired taste. The Boss says its origins are with the Red Indians of America and it is used by the lunatics who explore the Arctic and Antarctic. It's made according to the foods available at home, so for us it's lean beef or venison, bone marrow fat and cherries, blackcurrants and blackberries. After the conditions we've had I'll eat anything just to give us some energy.

The climb today was a killer, no doubt. I thought my lungs were going to collapse. We have all been carrying around eighty pounds of kit as well as our rifles. It would have been enough of a challenge to complete the climb unladen. Mr Green was sick on at least two occasions; the altitude seemed to really get to him. Jock and Cled spent most of the climb cursing every step in a typically Celtic defiant manner. The rest of us I think were bullied by the futility of their foul language! Once we reached the plateau at least we only had the raging blizzard to contend with, although that was enough on its own. Without the exertion of the climb we all felt the icy cold very quickly.

Dropping down over the next few hours was a lot easier although it plays havoc on your legs in a different way. Going up my muscles just began to burn with effort, but you drive on and go through the 'pain barrier' as the Boss calls it. But you don't feel the exertion on your joints. The prolonged descent was tiring the muscles at the front of my legs and making them feel like jelly, but also hammering my knees. Our first brew up gave as all a boost though, with the old banter amongst us having begun to return.

The camp. I write by candlelight in the early hours now in the hospitable surroundings of a nomad camp. Mahmood, our host, has been very kind and was educated in England it would seem. We have warm and comfortable surroundings and the food, a break from the pemmican, was first class. He has a very sweet young son, two beautiful 'adopted' daughters, both of who some of the prettiest girls at home could not hold a candle to. But there are his other two sons; Hamza and Omar. They are surly bastards and I have to say I can't trust them. We are destined to spend some time with them as they escort us to the legendary lakes of 'black gold' under the Kuh e Baba Mountains. They don't like us, what we stand for or our presence. I feel we'll have to watch ourselves around them.

23rd September

Our first day with our guides, escorts whatever you want to call them. They are not exactly conversationalists. We had a laugh amongst ourselves before leaving Mahmood's camp. We have been loaned camels for the journey to speed things up and make the journey more comfortable. Mr Green got thrown straight off a camel as he tried to mount it. Then Cled Jones got left hanging upside down along side of his one. The rest of us learnt a lot from their misfortunes! In fact I nearly wet myself laughing.

During the first break of our journey we formed a circle using the camels nose to tail as a windbreak. There aren't many of them with us, the brothers and one of their warrior chaps. The Boss managed to form an uneasy alliance with them but personally I still don't trust them, and I'm sure that he doesn't either. He's always been honest about our intentions, although they don't know that we are all soldiers. To seem less hostile we have assumed the role of a Royal Geographic Society exploration. It's a sensible cover and they seemed begrudgingly happy with it.

The rest of the day was just boring; the plains are scrubby and featureless. At least we have the benefit of transport now though. I think I'd have gone insane having to walk through such an ugly wilderness covering less than half the same distance. The camels are smelly, surly fuckers, like the brothers, but the famous 'ships of the desert' are a godsend.

24th September

Not much to write today to be honest. We passed some other small caravans but the land is still barren and featureless in the main, although we are now coming up on higher ground in the far horizon. We should be able to make it out in more detail tomorrow as we close on it. If the camels go well, and they might do having taken on some food and water today, then we might even make the base of our mountain destination. That would be great; we're not intending to have to do a summit again! We all seem to have mastered riding camels anyway. Not much call for that back in Blighty. Might have to consider a career with the notorious French foreign legion to utilise the new skill! Morale amongst the chaps is good; we know we're nearly there. The surly Afghans have lightened up and the weather has been quite tolerable throughout the journey.

27th September

I now write this journal as a matter of historical record for whoever finds it if the rest of us die. There are only three of us left. In fact, perhaps only one and a few fractions. The treacherous Arabs ambushed us two nights ago, the night of the 25th when half of us explored the caves when we first got there and the others stayed outside. The Boss is still able bodied. I have become paralysed from the waist down from a bullet wound in my lower back. What's happened to Nigel Green defies belief. They are savage evil people. He has told us of the events outside of the cave, but I think he wishes he was dead like Pete and Will. He has had his arms above the elbow and his legs above the knee severed with a red hot scimitar. It cauterised his wounds instantly otherwise he would have bled to death. It seems then they were preparing to whip him to death to prolong the agony they deliberately delayed. I will recount the facts as best I can.

Myself, the Boss, Jock and Cledwyn all entered the caves with the Davy lamps to prevent a fire. Nigel, Will and Pete stayed outside to prepare food. They noticed one of the three warriors had disappeared from the camp. It was only supposed to be a cursory trip inside. All hell broke loose outside first. Hamza again questioned the purpose of our trip, asking why we had gone in the caves with our rifles. It might be a good point, but with what happened it was just as well we did. The lone warrior returned with large scale reinforcements who took the three boys outside by complete surprise; Nigel said he was grabbed from behind and pinned down and forced to watch the unfolding attack, as was Pete Burwell. Bayley had a few seconds of a valiant defence. He took out two, one with a knife and the other with his sabre. He was then decapitated by a mounted Afghan and Nigel came face to face with his head as he was pinned down. Burwell and Green then really suffered as they stood their ground in complete defiance and overwhelming odds. They killed Burwell first forcing Nigel Green to watch it with a scimitar under his chin. He was tied to two horses and then split in two, his legs ripped from his torso at the crack of a whip. He died in Green's arms in terrible pain with massive blood loss and trauma.

They turned on Green whilst we were still in the cave, just prior to our contact. He was staked out on the floor and then each one of his limbs severed above their central joints with a red hot scimitar. No blood loss, lots of pain and fear. We saw the last of it taking place. They are the most evil bastards I have ever met with their vicious and calculating cruelty. He was then to be whipped to death with the only chance of escape on agonizing stumps. We got out before they could implement that sickening additional torture.

In the cave we found Patterson's black gold, oil, lakes of the stuff. The Davy lamps worked a treat. Then we found that some of the bastards had followed us. We drew our sabres with thought towards the possible ignition of the flammable stuff. We knew we had a fight with them as they came in with the other boy's Davy lamps; we assumed they were dead or prisoners. We dispatched a few by sabre, especially the Boss, and as they retreated and we'd recovered two lamps we began to make our way out. We came under a barrage of fire from cyanide poisoned arrows and Jock copped it with one in the throat. The Boss tried to save him but he was gone. Capt Holden then directed us to prepare for a charge out, rifles fired *from the hip and hopefully outrunning any ignition of the oil vapours.*

Then Cled got hit by poisoned arrows in both legs, the stinking Arabs had outflanked us. It only left me and the Boss to charge out, Cled was determined to take some with him. He stayed as we charged the exit and we heard him cock his rifle and let off at least four rounds. Then the cave interior went up. We heard Cled scream. He'd taken a lot with him, but the flames pursued us as we ran. Our speed, aggression, audacity and surprise at our action as we ran and Capt Holden leading firing from the hip routed them. Outside, our Lee Enfields and our marksmanship took out a load of them but that was when we heard Green's hideous screaming. We had to get to him and the barbarous brothers were maiming him. With precision shooting we both took out Hamza, five shots between us at least. We advanced using Holden's new found 'cover and movement' skirmishing technique to get to him. The adrenalin was amazing. I have never felt as alive. I took a round in the lower back as we received an attack from the rear; we dealt with them between us efficiently, despite my great pain, strangely little blood. That action, and strangely I think upon it fondly as a great British military engagement, was the last time I could use my legs it seems. Haven't been able to feel them or use them for over a day now. The whole event is worthy of half a dozen MM's and a couple of VC's.

Capt Holden, with me now crippled but still able to provide covering fire, carried on and took the bastards on single-handed now with both rifle and pistol. Omar and others escaped as Holden was forced, having caused a complete retreat with his tenacity to tend Mr Green. The sight was, and is, hideous.

All his limbs gone above the main joints. The smell of burning, human, flesh will stay with me forever. I dragged myself over to them.

There we were. The bloody Arabs had loosened all the camels as they fled. One able-bodied man and two cripples; no wonder for sometime Mr Holden had a complete break down. Ironically he was sobbing cradling his great personal friend Nigel in his arms, with Nigel, abhorrently disfigured, offering the great man comfort. I knew he'd bounce back though. He has buried the boys and counted the dead. We took out over twenty-five of the buggers and we don't know how many Cled accounted for in the cave.

He has man-hauled us for a day and a half now as we try to escape Afghanistan. We know we must lie low and wait for the rescue party, but the Boss has said we need to get back to the vicinity of the NW Frontier so by the time they get here they can get us safely over the mountains with the additional manpower. A good plan, if a little optimistic. Holden, now rational again, seems to have limitless reserves of physical and mental resilience. I feel sure that we'll get out.

1st October

A week man-hauling and we have found some Bedouins to trade guns for camels with. Nigel has completely withdrawn. I think the reality of his situation has hit over the last week. He will never be able to do anything for himself again. Mr Holden is a machine. I doubt I will ever witness such a display of ingenuity with his 'sled' and poles, physical stamina and resourcefulness with the Bedouins ever again. In fact, I know I won't. I still can't feel my damned legs or walk. That's it, no more drill for me! Although I don't much relish begging as an old soldier on street corners neither. Still got to get back yet and we aren't even near our point of entry. Hopefully the rescue team will be sent any day now. I can't imagine life in a wheelchair. I've been so active; I've marched for miles on campaign. God, it's a sickening reality. And no one will want to marry a cripple. Fucking Patterson. I've given up everything for him. I think sometimes I'd sooner be one of the ones left behind. Then I look at Green. No arms or legs. Perhaps I am lucky. He's got a girl at home with a kid he's never seen I think. He won't ever be able to hold a baby. Poor sod, perhaps I'm actually lucky. He still won't speak to either of us.

Mr H. is looking gaunt. We have to ration the pemmican and I think he's burning up a lot of physical reserves. He feeds Green with the dedication of a close brother, it actually makes me weep. I am bloody lucky really. Why on earth did I wallow just now in self pity? I hope God can free his mind and bring him back to us. How guilty do I feel? Stopping now, it's just a literary rant.

3rd October

The cut throat Arab's camp. With what Holden and I have just been through, secretly I'm beginning to wonder if we'll ever get out of this Godless country. We found our way back to the mountains that lead over into the Khyber Pass right at the point that we entered. And so we found that treacherous Arab's camp. Holden had that glint of revenge in his eye and the smell of a death giver around him as soon as we came in range of the place. All I could do was hole up with poor old Green and wait for him to come back.

I could see the camp fires and lamps within the tents; the Boss had disappeared into the camp. Not long after he had vanished from sight I heard rifle fire. I had no time to consider if it was Mr Holden's final action or not as Green and myself were ambushed by warriors. I have never felt so helpless. Pinned to the floor by one I was fighting off a scimitar attack by him with my bayoneted rifle, so all I could do was watch as the immobile and completely vulnerable Green was picked up by two more with a third drawing a dagger and stabbing him. They are cruel vicious bastards who are held in my regard below that of Patterson.

The dagger man's head exploded from a gun shot. This distracted my adversary who I then bayoneted in the guts, good and proper with a twist. It was Mr Holden, the other two tried to run but he took them out too. The two of us fought a brief action until they gave up an attack in the dark.

Green was mortally wounded. He died in the captain's arms with his last wish being that he tells his fiancée in Whitechapel what happened to him. We couldn't even bury him. We had to make a swift escape by the camel to another wadi where we once more had a brief few moments only, so it seems, to catch our breath. Mr Holden has come clean to me over who was at the camp; Patterson was there and he apparently seemed intent on making sure we could not live to tell any tales, but more importantly he was trying to negotiate over the oil as well. The Boss said he tried to kill him but he had to take out others first. He says that we will deal with Patterson when we return to

England. For all of our friends' sake, I am certainly with him on that. It will be the SRP's final assignment.

It was the last entry in the weather beaten journal. Bates sat opened mouthed with an adrenalin rush himself from the excitement of the amazing story he had just read. The evidence to besmirch the less than popular Patterson was a goldmine to an ambitious, in truth tabloid, journalist. He put the journal down and got up. At his drinks cabinet he poured himself a large single malt Isle of Jura. As he placed it to his lips and stared out of the window his hand was shaking.

Chapter Eleven

9.a.m, August 23rd

The ministerial party were now all back in London. In the security of his office, Patterson dismissed his protection team for the rest of the day until five in the afternoon. It suited both Ford and Spicer. Ford decided to indulge in a lesson with his fencing coach, having not undergone any tutoring for nearly a month. Spicer disappeared, Ford did not know to where and nor did he care. His former Whitechapel colleague's behaviour seemed to be becoming more aloof. Ford was not to realise that Spicer simply allowed him to disappear off from Whitehall to his home in Eaton Square, his intended venue prior to fencing, whilst he remained in the building and was summoned back to Patterson's office. There he found that the Minister was not alone; a tall well built man of around thirty with a hideous bladed weapon scar on his right cheek was also present. He had a military bearing and sported a look that coupled with his stature struck a chord of intimidation within those that met him.

"Ah, Spicer. Good. This is Major Hoare, I don't think you have met," said Patterson from behind his desk. Spicer offered the major his hand. The imposing looking officer reciprocated with a devastatingly firm handshake in return.

"Please to meet you, Mr Spicer. Marcus Hoare, Royal Marines, currently on secondment to the ministry. How do you do?" Spicer was a little in awe of the fearsome looking British warrior.

"Yes. Pleased to meet you too, sir." His hand ached from the introduction. Spicer and Hoare following the Minister's non verbal invitation then took a seat their side of the desk facing him.

"Gentlemen, as members of the Brotherhood, but more importantly shareholders in Empire Petroleum; a situation has arisen that needs attention." The two men sitting in front of Patterson listened intently. To gain favour amongst people in his employ, those that he knew were impoverished, such as Spicer; he gave a hundred shares to as a financial incentive at no cost to them. Equally, the Major was simply in his pay as a mercenary but with a greater mission than the one he was about to act upon with Spicer. "In 1898, I went on an abortive mission to Afghanistan the records of which I have had to alter slightly as it is warranting unwanted attention. It was a difficult undertaking and a total of three British service personnel with me died. But dead men tell no tales. Four survived the mission. Two have subsequently died in other overseas postings. Two more survive having left their regiment to go back to civilian life. Someone will ask questions of them and they must be persuaded not to talk. You both understand?" Spicer looked at Patterson a little concerned, he knew the Minister had an uncomfortable hold over him. Hoare looked on with a shallow and spiteful smile. His whole physical persona suddenly seemed to emit a penchant for cruelty. Patterson then passed the men in front of him two army service files.

"Two men as you see. They left the army together as they are both tradesmen. They have set up their own blacksmiths east of London in the sleepy village of Dagenham. You will go and dissuade them from passing on any information." Spicer looked at the file in front of him with apprehension. He was shrewd enough to guess that it would be Robert Ford asking questions about Afghanistan. He had been in earshot of the conversation between Ford and Patterson in the Colosseum. Both Patterson and Hoare could sense his reluctance to get involved. It would suit the ruthless, and habitually cruel by military reputation, Hoare to act alone.

"Minister and Mr Spicer. Let me be honest and state that with Mr Spicer's role in being part of your protection package and the threat still present, it maybe be best for me to deal with the matter in Dagenham alone." They were certainly the words that Spicer wanted

The Dressmaker Connection

to hear. Patterson, holding his hands almost prayer like to his face with his thumbs resting under his chin considered his suggestion. His mind drifted for a moment; he was due to have Karen come to the office in the next thirty minutes and he had left instructions 'not to be disturbed while she worked on some adjustments'. It was a good idea by Hoare; there could be violence required in getting the point across. It was probably not wise to allow a serving police sergeant to be involved in that.

"Very well. Spicer, please feel free to go whilst Major Hoare and I discuss some other matters." Spicer placed the file back on Patterson's desk. As he stood he could feel the cooling sweat running down his back, he had feared complicity in some underhand activity and that probability now seemed to have passed him. He left the office without a word being uttered by anyone. In the reception area he pulled a handkerchief from his pocket and wiped a few beads of sweat from the sides of his face.

Back in the office it was Patterson who resumed the conversation.

"Major. That is one matter put to bed. There is the other that I am sure you would like the update on as you will be leading the raiding force. I have secured funding through the highest echelons of the Catholic Church following my presentation of the business plan. It was the Cardinals in France and Italy that I needed to secure support from, so those in London and Canterbury, and then the large Eastern European diocese based in Prague will be a formality." Patterson stood and went to his drinks cabinet and poured them each a vintage Napoleon Cognac. The drink was gratefully received by Hoare as he looked and smiled in appreciation but with his cold and cruel eyes showing no emotion. "So with this funding secured and in place you may go ahead and continue to recruit our expeditionary, invasive and ultimately occupying force. The men can be offered pay double that of regular soldiers. Our future, Major Hoare, is looking very secure indeed." Patterson raised his glass and proposed a toast. "To the age of the internal combustion engine and the demands it will make, with Empire Petroleum at the head of the industry." They raised their glasses to each other in a show of mutual respect and support. Hoare savoured the taste and warm sensation of the mature spirit as it warmed his gullet and the pit of his stomach as it settled. Indeed, both men would have a fine future, just the little matter in Dagenham needed to be resolved.

Hoare had heard all about the tenacious Inspector Ford. If he hadn't yet received the report about the events of 1898, getting there first and arranging a permanent silence would not be a difficult obstacle.

* * *

The clash of sabres sent sparks flying into the air as Ford made a brisk but slightly desperate defensive parry of a rapid waist high thrust by his teacher, Andre Moreau. Moreau in his twenties and thirties had become the most celebrated swordsman in France; now twenty-five years later at the age of fifty-six he was the most respected fencing teacher in London, indeed in Paris too, the two cities between which he split his time as equally as he could. He was still an athletic and dashingly handsome man with jet black hair only now greying at the temples tied back into a typically eighteenth century masculine, French pony tail. A widower, having lost his beloved wife Lenora to consumption some five years earlier, he had vowed never to fall in love again; the heart ache of her death had been too great. Now without breaking a sweat, he attacked his student protégé Ford with calculating vehemence, forcing the talented Englishman into simplistic mistakes with the heavy, and still not yet natural extension of his arm; the sabre. Ford had grasped the lighter foil and epee very quickly and efficiently with excellent reflexes and good hand to eye coordination, but the grip, weight and lack of briskness with which the sabre moved had proved more difficult for him to master.

Behind his meshed fencing mask Ford was sweating profusely; the heavy, padded cotton protective jacket seemed to make his blood feel as if it was boiling with its warmth. His physical exertion and the warm summer sun streaming down on him as they sparred on the grass of the gardens outside his house in Eaton Square was beginning to take its toll. Moreau had decided to conduct the lesson at Ford's home, as was in fact usual. He couldn't see Moreau's face but he knew the inhumanly talented, celebrated swordsman would hardly be perspiring. Ford had spent nearly ten minutes sparring, receiving numerous strikes to his torso, thighs and left arm and he was beginning to feel frustrated and quite bruised. Aggression was beginning to cloud the calm and calculated approach that Moreau had always encouraged him to approach the craft of swordsmanship with. Moreau, despite not being able to see Ford's face, could sense his pupil's heightened aggressive frustration and was prepared to easily deal with any manifestation of it. He deliberately led Ford. Starting to back off further and further towards the borders of the garden with a barrage of aggressive thrusts and sweeps with no true methodology or style from Ford, he came to a stop just a foot or so from a thick bed of colourful red and pink roses behind him. It was time to teach Ford the lesson of not being clouded by misdirected aggression.

Ford telegraphed his intention of a deep thrust to try to catch Moreau, feigning weakness, harshly in the stomach protected by, not a traditional white cotton fencing jacket, but a masters light quilted suede gilet. The intention was easily read by Moreau; using a classic 'watch glass parry', he countered the violent and ill conceived thrust by turning the wrist of his sword arm as if looking at a wrist watch as his blade contacted with Ford's. Ford's forward momentum was directed to his side as he took hold of Ford's sword arm and twisted him sideways, throwing him to the floor with it. The uncomfortable action immediately caused the Englishman to drop his sabre and he landed, directed by Moreau's grip, in the rose bushes behind them. Before he realised where he was his opponent's sabre was contacting at his throat. The heavy cotton fencing apparel protected him from the thorns of the roses. Moreau held his sabre in place as he removed his mask. He was beaming at his protégé with a single bead of sweat running down the left side of his face. Ford, sweating profusely had to see the amusing side of his predicament and take on board the valuable lesson.

"Well. That's the first time I've been in the shit but come up smelling of roses," he said as Moreau helped pull him free of the roses. They stood apart, saluted each other with their sabres and then shook hands. They headed off to Ford's house only yards away.

"Robert, you have not had such an abject lesson in the miss-direction of aggression for many months. Yes, you must fight with tenacity, but think about channelling your desire to win a little more calculatingly. Look at what I achieved by leading you on and allowing you to tire and make mistakes." They walked up the few steps to the door of Ford's large town house with Ford ushering his teacher politely first.

"Mrs Adkins will have some refreshments for us, Andre. Please, the door is unlocked, after you."

They went through to the terraced, walled garden at the rear of the fine Victorian house. It was leafy and smelt of the various colourful traditional English garden plants that adorned the borders of the neat lawn. It was a tranquil spot in the busy city that Ford always found a wonderful retreat. He looked forward to entertaining Karen here soon. The two sat down on the fine wrought iron garden chairs set with comfortable cushions either side of an ornate occasional table. Mrs Adkins brought out a tray with two glasses containing ice along with an iced pitcher of her special recipe lemonade and placed it on the centre of the table.

"Thank you, Mrs Adkins. That is most kind." Ford said gratefully. Mrs Adkins, a lady in her mid sixties was a Godsend at keeping him planted in the real world in so many ways. Keeping the house wonderfully, cooking occasional meals or serving refreshments, or simply telling him to 'grow up' when he came in ranting petulantly about work issues.

"A pleasure, Robert. Is there anything else you would like?"

"No thank you. Please have the day to yourself, the weather is rather good after all."

"Very good. Thank you. See you tomorrow." The sprightly, mature housekeeper disappeared back in doors. Moreau initiated the continued conversation as they enjoyed the summer sun in the Victorian garden. Ford poured the lemonade.

"Robert, you must remain detached from your opponent. It is a personal one on one conflict but if you are drawn in to win quickly at all costs you will be destined to fail." Ford placed the heavy patterned glass to his lips and took a generous sip. The lemonade was cold and sharp and tantalisingly refreshing with its sourness. He took another mouthful and replied to Moreau.

"Yes. I must learn to apply the same mindset you taught me in foil and epee. The heavier cavalry type weapon makes me want to fight with less refinement and more brutality." Ford placed his glass back on the table swallowing hard with the bitter citrus taste of the lemon causing him to contort his face. He rubbed his hands across his eyes in a wearisome fashion prompting a question from Moreau.

The Dressmaker Connection

"You look tired and troubled. Do you have something on your mind? Is this what jaundices your normal skill today?" Ford cleared his hands from his eyes and looked skywards. He was indeed troubled.

"Frankly, Andre, yes. As you know I have been put on a detail with the Minister of War. Three members of his staff have been murdered in ritualistic circumstances and he has only just come clean as to a possible motive for someone. Personally, I can't believe what he tells me, although this afternoon he claims he will give me the official report to back his claims." Moreau nodded considering Ford's words.

"Well. Perhaps you must until you read this report give him the benefit of the doubt?"

"But why did it take three murders and not just one ritualistic one before he 'came clean'," Ford used his first two fingers of each hand in a mock parenthesis fashion, "on the whole issue. What it has done is raise suspicion in me and probably, if his claims are true, led to one or two more unnecessary deaths." Moreau, one of life's eternal philosophers, a trait that Ford considered came from his Gallic background, looked his pupil in the eye and spoke.

"You must wait and see, at least until after this afternoon." He took a generous swig of lemonade that elicited the same reaction to its bitter sharpness as it had in Ford.

"Perhaps you are right. I shall be in touch when I return from Prague, Andre. Thanks again for a valuable lesson, my friend." Both men stood up, Moreau first with his need to leave to attend a lesson elsewhere in London. They shook hands firmly.

"Take care, Robert. Remember, as in your pugilist days, controlled aggression." Moreau turned and saw himself out. Ford finished his lemonade and then took the tray into his well appointed Edwardian kitchen with its pristine white butler sink and mahogany fittings. He considered his teachers words as he heard a carriage depart from the front of the house and went upstairs to take a cool bath. He had a few hours yet until he was due at the Ministry of War.

* * *

Karen Wood apprehensively entered Patterson's building in Whitehall. She was running twenty minutes late and she knew that he would use it as an excuse to be particularly coarse in his penetrative intercourse. She could not think of it as making love as there were no pangs of affection between them in the act, there never had been. It was sheer brutal sex on his part which she tolerated to keep young Nigel looked after in his nursery in the Brompton Road. She felt sick to the pit of her stomach as she entered the building; she had to find a way for this violation that she felt each time to stop. She was in love with Robert Ford and deeply resented allowing another man to take her when she knew that deep down he was a man who loved her.

She reached the reception area of Patterson's office and was greeted by a disdainful Fiona Shaw; she knew that Shaw knew what her presence was there for and it had nothing to do with tailoring alteration. With no acknowledgement, Shaw made eye contact with Karen then resumed working at her desk. Karen felt deeply ashamed; she felt little better than a common prostitute. She knocked on the door of the office and entered as she did so. Patterson was sat behind his desk working on some documents in front of him. He didn't even look up as he spoke.

"You are late, Miss Wood. Why are you late?" Karen had no good reason apart from apprehension and the need to try to delay the inevitable. She said nothing initially just holding her hands in front her clasping her small leather handbag and staring uneasily at her feet.

"Well, girl. Do you not have good cause?" She didn't and she knew that she could offer no explanation. She was about to speak.

"Right. Lock the door and remove your clothes. Then come around here." Reluctantly she secured the door and then without ceremony stripped naked. He then for the first time looked up at her as she presented herself to him his side of the ornate mahogany desk. He looked at her exquisite form; despite the familiarity of taking her almost whenever he wished, her physical perfection still took his breath away.

"Come here," he instructed forcing her to step within arms reach. He touched her breasts with almost adolescent inexperience before running his hands further down her smooth hairless body. He then undid the fly of his suit trousers and barked a simply instruction to her.

"Kneel and pleasure me." Reluctantly Karen did as she was told as he viciously grabbed her flowing hair. She knew that the worst was yet to come as he made his usual demands and she swore to herself that this would be the last time. After a few minutes he forcibly pulled her head away by her hair and without provocation slapped her across her right cheek. She took the pain silently, but it hurt and her cheek began to redden. He spun her round so her back was to him and forced her over his desk. She heard him drop his trousers to the floor. She then felt the warm sensation of initial penetration within her, but then the sensation oddly stopped. Suddenly before she could react, he had pinned her so firmly to the desk that she could not move. With dread, she felt the initial sharp and painful commencement of anal penetration. She looked on at the carved wooden doors of his office and silently wept.

Chapter Twelve

Whitehall, 3.p.m

Robert Ford sat in the reception area of Patterson's suite at the Ministry of War. He had been called back early by telephone. Patterson then bowled out through the doors to meet him as Spicer appeared from the corridor. Fiona Shaw had long since gone. Patterson was holding a military file in his hand and passed it to Ford and spoke belittlingly.

"This is the official report on the short expeditionary trip into Afghanistan I spoke of in 1898. Please read it over, I don't know if it will help with what we discussed in the Colosseum. I need to go to my E.P office if you can let the driver know please, Inspector." Patterson then disappeared into his private bathroom. Ford was left staring at the particularly thin file and sensed immediate disappointment within himself on receiving it; he somehow expected more, a thicker file telling a more comprehensive story. Although eager to read it through, he knew that he had to secure the Minister's transport to Trinity Gardens opposite the Tower of London. Spicer then appeared from Patterson's office. Ford found this strange.

"Bob, do you know if his car he so treasures is downstairs to take him to the E.P building?" Ford asked of his subordinate.

"Yes it is. Out the front ready to take him. I'll see you down there if you like." Spicer stood looking at his colleague as if obtusely waiting for directions. Ford sensed the belligerence but didn't wish to address the matter now.

"Fine. You go down and I'll see you down there with the boss when he's ready." Spicer left the reception. Ford decided to wait until they got to Trinity Gardens to read the file. Patterson emerged from the bathroom ignoring Ford and heading straight off down the stairs. Ford followed him down and out into Whitehall and into the car. With a crunching sound, the driver put the car in gear and with a lurching action it moved off along Whitehall and then turned left in Horse Gardens Avenue. At the end of this road by the Thames it turned left and followed the Embankment all the way to Tower Hill and the Empire Petroleum office just off there with its gothic architecture and fine views of Tower Bridge.

* * *

William Bates strolled confidently into 'The London Times' Fleet Street offices with the priceless and incriminating journal in a leather briefcase tucked securely under his right arm. With the story and notoriety this would surely bring him he had travelled to work with an unhealthy sense of paranoia in the early afternoon that he might be robbed and he would lose his ticket to an editorship somewhere. He was right to be concerned, but he would never realise until it was too late that it needed to be concerned with his chief editor and his connections on two counts with Sir Cecil Patterson.

Alfred Baines had been the editor in chief of The London Times for the last two years. He had little regard for Bates and his tabloid background as he had risen through the ranks of broad sheet journalism in what he considered the 'hard and honest' way. As an adolescent he had joined The Times Group as a runner and tea boy. With age and experience Baines had become a messenger including such tasks as collecting scoop items from the Central News Agency. Having studied privately in the evenings he gained a basic journalistic qualification and was given an opportunity in his early twenties to cover low interest stories. It was an important first rung on the journalistic ladder which allowed him a slow but eventually meteoric rise to the top of the tree with the same newspaper. Along the way he had got to know many people well and form friendships and business relationships. He also met many important figures along the way; Queen Victoria in her late years, William Gladstone, Sir Charles Warren and even the celebrated Inspector Abberline of the Whitechapel investigation amongst many.

Unknown to Bates, one of Baines close personal and business friends was Patterson. They were members of the same Masonic lodge, played golf together but most significantly Baines was a major shareholder and sat as minor director on the board of Empire Petroleum.

Bates knocked on the half glassed door of Baines' office etched with 'Editor in Chief The London Times' and waited for a response. He could see the fifty year old slightly stocky man sat behind his plush desk looking over the morning's edition dressed in his high necked wing collar shirt and tie with a navy blue pin strip Edwardian suit. His grey hair was cut short and brushed to one side. He was cleanly shaven and obviously took great pride in his personal grooming. He was expecting Bates, the 'cheap tabloid' journalist as he considered him, as he had the made the appointment late the day before expounding the merits of 'an incredible story' he had discovered.

"Come in, William," called Baines without even looking up. He knew exactly who it should be. Bates opened the door and let himself in shutting it quietly behind him watching his key employer who still didn't look up, eyeing his paper's latest headline:

'HIDEOUS THIRD MINISTRY OF WAR MURDER IN ROME'S COLOSSEUM

Researcher slain with arms and legs removed in a bizarre and ritualistic fashion'

"Odd business these ritualistic murders surrounding the Ministry of War." Baines seemed to quite deliberately infer they were connected to the department as a whole and not its head. It mattered not to Bates; the conversation had immediately been initiated on exactly the topic he wanted to discuss. "Sit down, Bates. What's so special then to warrant the first entry in my diary for the afternoon, eh? Solved the mystery of the Whitechapel murders at last? Discovered that Queen Victoria was poisoned and not died of old age, mmm?" Bates was used to dealing with cynicism, after all he had been in journalism all of his working life.

"No, none of those things, Sir. But something sensational that solves the mystery of the Ministry of War murders I think, Sir." Baines head snapped up from the newspaper on the desk rapidly to engage Bates' conversation and assertion. This could indeed be big news.

"Tell me more, Bates. Tell me more indeed." He sat back in his luxuriant, quilted leather office chair that reclined automatically with his movement and maintained firm eye contact with Bates. Bates had to break this contact momentarily to draw the battered leather journal from the brief case he had laid on the desk between then. As the journal came out into the light he began to speak.

"I have evidence here in the form of a military journal written by a Trooper John Waldron of something called the 'Special Raiding Party' of a mission under the directions of Sir Cecil Patterson. It would appear that he decided to use a military resource for his own business ends to try to discover oil in Afghanistan, just a way beyond the North West Frontier. He then disavowed these men, trying to kill them after their mission had been attacked by local warlords when he had undertaken to travel there subsequently himself. He came across three survivors. It would seem one of them who had been hideously maimed was killed but the other two including the writer of the journal, who was crippled, escaped. The method of death for the soldiers in various circumstances matches the methods that have been used to kill Ministry of War staff."

To Baines this was indeed a huge and scandalous news story; but one he could never publish. He would have to take possession of the journal to read it to confirm what Bates had just told him. He would also have to arrange for Bates to be silenced. He was sure that Patterson could help him with that. He would have to make contact with his brother Mason, fellow shareholder and director today.

"Good work, Bates. In fact, excellent." Baines wished to lull Bates into a false sense of security. "I need some of the rest of the day to go over this as it is truly dynamite stuff. It is a scoop, and one that you and I need to keep quiet for now as we'll need to verify the authenticity of the journal. I'll have a read and make some quiet inquiries with the army over the chaps mentioned in the story, just to see if they existed or not. I can get it done today but it will take a few hours. We'll need to meet later away from the office but not too far from here, so I suggest around eight this evening underneath Blackfriars Bridge, down on the river there. We'll be away from prying eyes and after all walls can have ears. Is that all right with you?" Bates shifted a little in his seat, more from excitement that apprehension. Such 'cloak and dagger' secrecy was a first for him, especially from the top man of the newspaper. Excitement and greed overwhelmed any rational thought and he threw caution to the wind. Baines had him hooked. The day would not end in the way that Bates would have wished it to.

"Sounds exactly right, Sir. We must ensure its authenticity. I'll happily meet you as you plan later. Is there anything I can do in the meantime, Sir?"

"No, William. In fact enjoy the rest of the day out of the office and I shall see you tonight." Bates was further buoyed by Baines calling him by his Christian name.

"Thank you, Mr Baines. I will see you tonight." Bates left the office, and then the building taking himself of to a Lyons Tea House for a well deserved pot of Early Grey and a Bath bun.

As soon as Bates was out of sight, Baines picked up his telephone and tried Patterson's number at Whitehall. He had a direct line but there was no answer. He tried the number at Trinity Gardens. It rang several times before it was answered pompously.

"Morning, Patterson speaks. Can I help you?"

"Cecil, its Alfred Baines. We need to speak over an urgent matter. Can I come over?"

"Yes. I also have distressing news. An important document of mine has been stolen." Patterson's first port of call in his office was his drinks cabinet for a large single malt, the Laphroaig, his favourite. He could detect that things had been moved around in the cabinet as soon as he opened it. He discovered the journal had gone.

"Cecil, what have you lost? Is it a soldier's journal out of interest, about an operation in Afghanistan?" There was silence at the other end of the phone from Patterson.

"Yes…..Yes it is. How did you come across that then?"

"Cecil, I'll be over in twenty minutes and I will explain everything."

Both men put their telephones down. Baines grabbed his hat and a leather satchel type bag to put the journal in and left his Fleet Street office. Patterson strolled over to his window and looked out over the Trinity Gardens themselves and then over to the magnificent Tower Bridge, and all it's empirical symbolism. He took a generous sip of the peat flavoured single malt. The taste never failed to satisfy him, a little like Karen Wood's body. He felt a little more comfortable that the journal was with a Brother of the Craft, but how the hell had it got there?

* * *

Holden was back at the family home in Hertfordshire just outside of the village of Essendon. It sat upon rolling land just off the road that led from Essendon to the county town of Hertford itself. Holden Hall was a large, white, palatial stately home that sat part of the way up a slight incline overlooking the Hertford Road in the far distance. Its brilliant-white columned frontage borne out of Georgian styling could not fail to be a spectacular sight as it was approached along a long tree lined drive. He traditionally had a small apartment in the east wing of the house where he lived comfortably but simply. Almost his family considered bordering on Spartan. With the hardships he had endured whilst in the army, especially in Afghanistan, for him it was the lap of luxury. He had spun a fabricated story to his younger brother and sole surviving relative about leaving the army. He had told Francis of an abortive mission overseas for which they falsely held him accountable but believed he was dead. To live in peace he needed to maintain this charade, so if anyone came visiting the staff and Francis, they had no knowledge of his whereabouts. In truth he rarely used Holden Hall and so far no one had come looking for him.

Francis, or Frank as he was known, sat on the board of the bank in his older brother's place; as for all intents and purposes he was dead. Neither had a problem with this; it was a position that Frank had always wished to aspire to and it kept William anonymous. William Holden normally frequented a small family owned flat in Chelsea, in Ebury Street. He currently had Waldron staying there whilst he returned to the family home.

The brothers were close which had been the reason for the visit. Without telling Frank, William Holden feared that now he neared the end of his quest, a matter Frank knew nothing about, that his life could easily be in danger and he wished his younger brother to have positive memories of him. It was like the halcyon days for Frank of when his older brother first used to come home on leave from the army and they would enjoy weekends riding, hunting and fishing. Those activities were exactly what William had done for the past three glorious summer days with Frank. They had taken part in two fox hunts across the county, the pain of the memory of Genevieve in William Holden's mind of course throughout, then they had spent a morning game shooting on the estate. In the afternoon, they tranquilly fished in the Rivers Mimram, Beane and Rib. This final day, having had a fine dinner between them served by the staff every night, they were enjoying a 'detoxification' day at a local high-class spa just outside of Hertford, which was a facility attached to a hotel. They had begun the day with a countryside run; Holden still enjoyed the challenge of vigorous outdoor exercise and he knew it would do his often sedentary brother some good. It did aggravate the cough he couldn't shake off. This was at seven thirty in the morning when they had first arrived there. A hearty English breakfast followed, and then it was a stint in the sauna. Several sessions followed by repeated invigorating plunges into the icy 'plunge pool' then on to a full body massage each. Colonic irrigation was the final treatment before resting for part of the afternoon. The evening was spent in Hertford town itself.

They had a fine meal in a local bistro specialising in sea food. Moules Marinere was followed by Guernsey lobster and then a fine crème brulee for dessert. Each course had a small serving of sharp lemon sorbet in-between to cleanse the palate ready for the next flavour extravaganza. The whole meal was accompanied by a fine dry Chardonnay wine, and before coffee they drank a bottle of Verve Cliquot, 1898 between them. Frank found it odd that William on several occasions picked up the bottle and repeatedly ran his thumb over the year printed on the label until he had disfigured it. He still seemed his same loving brother, but somehow a little more distant occasionally, as well as much leaner, very tanned and with quite a weathered complexion; he assumed that was the years overseas. He would never have any grasp of William's hardship in Afghanistan.

"I have arranged a grand finale to the evening for us, Will." Frank spoke with a glint in his eye that intrigued his older brother.

"Are you going to tell me what it is?" Holden finished a large brandy after he spoke. He felt relaxed and ready for a challenge. He would not be disappointed.

"Go up to your room, brother. I don't expect to hear from you until the morning. You will be in good cheer I am sure." Frank stood and shook his brother's hand affectionately. William stood as they shook and then embraced his beloved younger brother tightly. He intended to leave early in the morning. He had prepared a letter for Frank; the envelope had written directions strictly to be opened in a month's time. He pulled back and held his younger brother at arms length and looked him in the eye.

"Whatever it is, I thank you. Frank, I want you to know I am proud of you and I love you, brother." Frank chuckled warmly at his brother's sentimentality. It was a chuckle that always warmed William.

"Hello, drink talking, eh?" William thought about that. No it wasn't; the alcohol having broken down inhibitions made him speak the truth. He embraced his brother once more and left the dining salon of the bistro for his room. It was not a long walk. The air cleared his mind a little and allowed him to shed the tears he wished to.

From the outside of the hotel he could see that his room light was on; despite the fact he was receiving a surprise he would approach with caution. The receptionist of the hotel showed him no unusual or ill reaction. When he reached the door of his room he listened by pressing his ear to the wood. He could hear faint stifled giggling. For once, feeling secure he threw caution to the wind. He flung the door open; indeed he was not disappointed. Nestling under the white sheet of his four poster double bed with the blankets discarded to one side were two of the prettiest of the stable maids on the Holden estate. They looked at each other and giggled out loud. He smiled warmly at them; they didn't notice that by life's experiences previously his eyes never smiled. He dropped his cape and topcoat to the floor.

"Good evening, ladies." He locked and bolted the door behind him. Frank was right he would indeed wake with good cheer.

* * *

Ford was sat alone in the plush reception area of Patterson's office in the Empire Petroleum building reading for a second time through the file relating to what was entitled on the cover page as:

'Operation Auric Noir'

The expeditionary mission led by Minister of War Mr Cecil Patterson to discover natural resources of oil for the purpose of refinement to petrol by Empire Petroleum on behalf her Britannic Majesty HRH the Queen Victoria, September to October 1898.

The opening cover had seemed so promising at answering the questions that Ford had in his mind regarding the apparent vendetta against Sir Cecil Patterson. The truth was, having read the short document cover to cover, that it just about backed up his story. He found the prose disjointed and inconsistent, and far from being in a diary form as he would have expected, Ford found that it was merely a cursory report. He couldn't help but feel that the original document must have been disposed of or heavily edited.

In September 1898 myself, Mr Patterson and six members of the Durham Light Infantry infiltrated Afghanistan by horseback having passed over the Khyber Pass and the North West Frontier. This was for the purpose of discovering the natural resource of 'oil' for refinement by Empire Petroleum. This would give the United Kingdom a 'head start' in the eventual race to dominate the burgeoning petrochemical industry born out of the invention of the internal combustion engine.

It saddens me to say now that we have returned the mission has proved less than successful. We spent our first night on Afghan soil in the company of a local Bedouin chieftain by the name of 'Mahmood Baryalai'. He showed us all great hospitality, but the single evening we spent there in late September quickly ended in disaster. A local fakir with a gift for clairvoyance attended the camp that night and instructed our host that he had been unwise in entertaining the 'infidels' who only came to rape the country for what they could. It made our host very stand-offish towards us for the rest of the night. He demanded that we leave the camp immediately and that if we did not he would demand a fatwa be placed upon us, especially against Mr Patterson who he identified as the head man amongst us.

The whole issue was compounded soon after the fakir left. Baryalai said that he had to pay attention to this man but he would be satisfied if we left in the morning, the first day of October. Suddenly around the fall of dark, our tent was attacked by foreign brigands that no one could identify. Privates Ryan and Gates were shot in the tent. Ryan died instantly and Gates died later of his wounds. Our host's son was killed and myself and Mr Patterson narrowly escaped death. This was enough to speed up our departure. We headed out with local warriors to find these men but failed to do so. Having failed in our search we made for the mountains and back to India.

This too ended in tragedy. Lieutenant Bromsgrove's horse shied whilst on the precipitous mountain trail throwing him to his death thousands of feet below. All of us men became nervous about making it home alive. Mr Patterson had been the only one riding with Bromsgrove ahead and assumed command as a result of a short spell in the cavalry as a commissioned officer and instructed us that it gave him seniority.

The Dressmaker Connection

None of us could be bothered to argue; four of us left with three now dead in what we were told was a simple surveying operation.

The rest of the cold and snowy climb over the mountains and back into the Khyber Pass was slow, uncomfortable but at least uneventful. I have no wish to return there. Ever.

It took us a fortnight to return to Calcutta. We had had to dispose of our dead before then with the increased temperatures. It didn't seem right; they didn't get a soldiers' burial.

This report is completed to the best of my recollection on 20th October 1898, by Corporal George Abrahams, nominal OIC following the death of Lt Bromsgrove, 24914, Durham Light Infantry, Tyne and Wear Barracks, Calcutta. The other returning unit members are:

Pvt Michael Spriggs
Pvt Stuart Higgins
Pvt Lawrence Wilcox.

Appendix to Abrahams Report, July 1902.

It is with regret that this report is concluded with the following information. Cpl Abrahams was killed along with Pvt Spriggs in enemy rebel action in East Africa in June 1902.

Higgins and Wilcox have since been discharged from the army and resettled in civilian life running a blacksmiths business in the Village of Dagenham Essex.

Charles Wilmot, archivist army records, MoW, July 1902.

Ford's disappointment didn't subside or increase with the second reading. Charles Wilmot had obviously risen within the ranks of the civil service to have worked for Patterson before being murdered. It seemed strange as he sat around in the reception area of Patterson's office, that there was no secretary there. This, mixed with confusion over the short report for what he considered a significant incursion into foreign territory, were in the front of his mind as a blue suited, smart and well groomed fifty year old man burst into the room. They were both equally surprised to see each other. Ford stood up leaving the report on the chair beside him and spoke first. As he did so he moved and made a physical block to the door of Patterson's office.

"Sorry, sir I won't keep you. May I ask who you are please?" Baines was caught out by the protective nature of this man that had the effect of eliciting an answer from him to the question.

"Erm… yes. I am Alfred Baines, editor of The London Times and friend and confident of Sir Cecil. Who are you, young man?"

"Detective Inspector Ford, Scotland Yard Special Branch, sir. May I see something like a calling card please?" Discovering who the man was, Baines was not surprised by the request and had no problem in obliging. Ford noted he seemed to keep precious hold of the satchel style case he carried. He produced an ornate and embossed calling card to Ford identifying him; he accepted it and knocked on the door to Patterson's office and showed him in.

"Thank you, Inspector. That will be all for now." Ford nodded his head in acknowledgement and shut the door. He heard it locked behind him as he stepped away. Oddly, Spicer then appeared; there was no way he was going to be able to listen in. Resigned to this fact, Ford gathered the few papers of 'Auric Noir' together and spoke to Spicer as he left the room.

"I'll leave it to you. I'll see you and Patterson in the car when they are ready." Spicer gave a nod of acknowledgement and then sat down and made of point of watching Ford leave.

Baines passed Patterson the journal from inside the satchel bag.

"Where the hell did you get it from?" Patterson almost jealously took hold of it and began to flick through it. He needed to ensure no pages were missing and he knew it inside out.

"My chief hack, Will Bates, brought it to me. I assume the only way he would have got it would be to have burgled your office here?" Baines was over at the drinks cabinet pouring himself an afternoon libation as he spoke. The Davy's vintage Tawny Port had taken his fancy and he

The Dressmaker Connection

served himself a generous glassful. He held it to his nose to savour its wonderful fruity oak smell before tasting it.

"Yes. He must have it's the only way." As Patterson spoke he came across the fake mail in his in tray. Initially the plain empty ones confused him. Then he discovered the lone one with The London Times logo on it's reverse. He passed it to Baines who had returned to the desk.

"I think that proves it," said Patterson as Baines examined it for himself. "What have you done so far with this hack of yours?" Patterson had venom in his voice as he asked the question. This was a dangerous lose end.

"Well, because of it's sensitive nature and the need to make other enquiries, namely this of course, I've told him to meet by the river under Blackfriars Bridge tonight at eight." Patterson now had the perfect solution, and the perfect man to make the rendezvous.

"Good. I have a man that can meet him there instead of you to tie up the loose end as it were. If you don't mind." Patterson had felt tempted to make the play on words by using the term 'noose end'. He decided not to as he didn't want to alarm his friend and partner Baines. He needn't have worried. Baines knew the likely outcome, especially for someone who dared to try to discredit the Brotherhood.

"Certainly not, Cecil. I'll happily leave it in the hands of your very capable man, I am sure."

Patterson made a very quick telephone call in a hushed voice whilst Baines refreshed their glasses. They each sat back once Patterson had finished and lit a cigar. Quickly the room filled with heavy acrid Cuban cigar smoke, like the average London gentleman's club. Patterson sat there considering that this latest intrusion on his privacy would be resolved by around ten past eight, and the tenacious and annoying Inspector Ford had for now been subdued with the report. Any enquiries he made from that should, with Major Hoare's assistance draw a blank.

Ford and Spicer eventually took Patterson back to his home address in Belgrave Square at just after six in the evening. They were then released from their duties for the rest of the day with uniformed police static protection officers discreetly positioned taking over whilst he was at home.

Ford made straight for Wilton Crescent to see Karen. He had had too many days away from seeing her and he ached for just a few minutes of her company. He was not impressed when she opened the door and he saw the bruise on the side of her face. She let him in and then fell into his arms sobbing. Initially she was unable to speak and he preciously and with a growing sense of jealously held on to her. He could guess what had happened and he was as equally determined as her that it should not happen again. She couldn't bear to stay within surroundings that seemed to be saturated with the stench of Patterson. That was not a problem. For the first time, she left and went to Eaton Square with Ford. Neither of them realised that they were under the observation of Bob Spicer as they did so.

Chapter Thirteen

8.p.m. Bates waited beneath Blackfriars Bridge with a sense of excitement and nervousness. The story seemed so explosive that he assumed that it would undoubtedly make the front page of The London Times; but he had a veiled concern that Baines might take all the glory for himself or assign the credit to one of the senior and much more respected, long standing correspondents. He looked out over the fast flowing Thames as he waited for Baines to appear. The sun was getting quite low as it dropped to a little above the West London skyline, perfectly silhouetting the St Stevens Tower that contained 'Big Ben' at the eastern end of the Palace of Westminster. He looked at his watch, it was getting on for five past eight; he was becoming nervous. Perhaps Baines was bypassing him completely and on returning to the office in Fleet Street the next day he would find himself fired. Coming from a humble East End background with his career in the main having been a climb up the greasy pole of tabloid journalism, he always had an inferiority complex about himself.

He leant forward over the riverside iron balustrade with elbows resting upon its cool rounded surface and stared out over the river once more. He didn't hear any footsteps approach as he stood there looking waterside. He had only been doing so for a half a minute, or so it seemed, when he turned round to be presented with a tall imposing man with a scar on his face and a significant military bearing. The riverside under the bridge was deserted and seeing this man alone Bates knew that this didn't bode well. Not only was Baines obviously intent in taking the real glory for himself, but also intent in ensuring that Bates would not be around to tell any tales. How wrong his summation was; he would find out in the last few moments of his life what the truth was. The scarred giant spoke first.

"Keep your hands at your sides, Bates, and turn around and face the river." Bates was compelled to do as he was told as his aggressor appeared to be holding some sort of weapon behind him. He was right, and he was about to discover what it was.

Marcus Hoare removed the long bladed Ghurkha's kukri from behind his back and flashed its shining blade in Bates eye line by the right side of his head.

"Now, friend," his assailant spoke in a menacingly calm way, "don't try to resist any instructions I give you. When this knife is traditionally drawn it should always take some blood. Don't provoke me to hold with tradition." Bates recognised the type of bladed weapon it was from years of reporting and occasional encounters with Ghurkha soldiers in the East End. Hoare had been to the scene earlier after he had received the telephone call from Patterson. He had already positioned a rope and noose under the bridge just above the balustrade at the waters edge. He had concealed it within the bridge's ironwork with a boat hook he had left tucked in at the drop of the steps that led down to the river front. With Bates facing away from him he pulled a large leather belt type strap; it was the kind used traditionally in the pinioning of condemned prisoners just prior to hanging. Bates noticed the knife disappear from his eye line and felt a misguided sense of relief. It was short lived as Hoare flung the belt around him rapidly and pulled it tight, pinning his arms to his side and immobilising his upper body. Bates was now beginning to panic.

"What are you doing! You can't kill me, I won't say anything! Just let me go!" He tried to run but Hoare had a firm hold of the now secured strap and he could move nowhere against this man's strength.

"Now Mr Bates, you are about to pay the price for trying to deceive and discredit the Brotherhood. It is a hard lesson to learn and you are paying the ultimate price to deter others of your kind who may try to interfere. Stealing and blackmail cannot be tolerated." Keeping hold of the strap, Hoare dragged Bates around while he picked up the boat hook and then drew the noose down into sight from the ironwork.

Bates worst fears were now realised and as he was man-handled to the rivers edge he began to plead for mercy one last time.

"Look, it's just work, it didn't mean anything! I'll leave London, go overseas. Just please don't fucking kill me," Bates began to weep and lost his power of rational speech at the end of his impassioned plea. It was wasted upon the cold and cruel heart of Marcus Hoare; when an assignment was given to him he had the reputation of seeing it through to the end without hesitation.

Hoare placed the noose over Bates head and tightened it up around the Masonic decreed condemned man's neck. At that point Bates urinated in his trousers through his sense of total and utter fear. He had continued pointlessly trying to struggle but Hoare's strength and ability to control his prey was overwhelming. Hoare tossed the boat hook to one side and then using both arms lifted Bates in a kind of matrimonial fashion and held him over the balustrade dangling over the water directly below. He had no intention of holding him there, the man had soiled himself. He let him go and Bates dropped and then hung like a long, leaded fishing weight dangling over the river. The drop was only short so there was no intention on Hoare's part of breaking Bates' neck. It was a slow choking death, so once limp and lifeless Hoare could remove the strap, push him out further over the Thames with the blunt end of the boat hook and ultimately give the impression of suicide.

Bates choked sickeningly for around two minutes, with his body bucking and kicking as he lashed out with growing futility in some attempted to try to save himself. It was all an autonomous response that Hoare had seen before in a military correction facility. Hoare was checking his watch from start to finish. He allowed Bates to hang silently for another two minutes after the kicking and choking had stopped; a total of near five. Hoare was very methodical and rehearsed in his approach. It had made him a useful assassin for the British Establishment to use without fear of compromise. He pulled the lifeless body of Will Bates back using the boat hook and removed the strap. He tossed it into the river; it began to flow away and then quickly sank out of sight. He twisted the boat hook pole with flair in his hand as if it were a ceremonial baton or spear and then pushed Bates out over the river with the rope sliding easily over the bridge's ironwork as he did so.

He pushed the lifeless hanging body just far enough to make it look as if Bates had tied the rope himself, stood on the balustrade's edge and leapt forward over the river; the momentum of which would cause the rope to slide forward on the ironwork, leaving the impression of suicide, overhanging directly the water and not the riverside.

There was still no one around having finished his work. Hoare tossed away the boat hook into the river as well and then strolled away. He crossed the road and walked off eventually along Puddle Dock and into the City of London. The next day he had his work in the countryside in Dagenham, Essex to consider. As he walked he had forgotten about the need for the kukri to draw blood. It pulled out again from its shoulder-holster sheath and gently drew the blade across his left thumb. Its sharpness meant he felt nothing. He placed the kukri back again and sucked the blood away with his mouth.

* * *

August 24th

Karen stayed at Ford's Eaton Square house whilst he went off to work. She would return there after she had visited the increasingly deteriorating young Nigel in Brompton Road. Ford was going to his office in New Scotland Yard on the river front over looking Westminster Bridge before attending Belgrave Square. Patterson wasn't due to leave home until after lunch and even then it was only to go to Trinity Square. Ford entered the hallowed red and white brick turreted building via Derby Gate opposite Downing Street. When he got to his office he found Spicer already there waiting for him. Ford was surprised to see him; it was supposed to be his day off.

"Bob, what are you doing here?" He spoke inquiringly as he removed his suit jacket on the warm August morning and hung it up.

"Two things you might like to know, actually. One is that William Bates, who we are very familiar with of old, was found hanging at midnight last night under Blackfriars Bridge. Apparent cause of death suicide." Spicer spoke with an air of pent up frustration.

"Christ all mighty. He never struck me as that sort. That is..." Spicer then interrupted before Ford continued.

"And I know that you are fucking Karen Wood." This did catch Ford very much off guard. But with speed of reaction borne out of the physical challenges of street fighting and fencing, his mind was able to respond to such an accusation.

"All right. I'm in love with her. Not just fucking her. What the fuck is it to do with you?" Ford was ready for a confrontation.

"I'll tell you what, she is our boss' mistress."

"Yes, mistress. Not wife. And not for much longer. Do you know he fucking beats her?" This mattered little to Spicer. This was about protecting the interests of his senior brother mason.

"Really, common bitch like that probably deserves it. Anyway..." before Spicer could continue further Ford had dragged him out of his seat and delivered two vicious body blows. Then he pinned Spicer up against a wall in a crossed grip, lapel strangle hold. Spicer was trying to pull Ford's arms off but he was too strong. Ford also had one leg forward of the other with his thigh pinning Spicer's lower body and legs to the wall. He couldn't move, he couldn't breathe and his ribs ached intensely. He felt sure that Ford must have broken one. Ford held his grip with an almost demonic stare and watched his colleague begin to change colour. Spicer tried to resist with fear of death but couldn't, Ford seemed to possess the strength of a madman. The incident prompted Ford to become lost in the recollection of his last fight as a pugilist near some twenty years before.

* * *

Spitalfields, 1883

Ford stood in one corner of the makeshift ring inside the deserted Spitalfields Flower Market, his opponent stood in the diagonally opposite corner with an expression of supreme hate. Ford had met this individual once before. His name was Bill Brooks and he had been the teenager whose nose Ford had split as an eleven year old nine years earlier in the 'Marquis of Granby' pub in Bethnal Green Road. He had been waiting all this time to 'take a shot' at the now famous street fighter Robert Ford.

Ford had fallen into street fighting almost immediately after his parents had died. When the lad was fourteen, and fortunately for him healthy and well developed physically to survive, William and Ann had been killed when an overloaded pleasure boat sank on the Thames on its way to the coastal resort of Rainham in Essex. It had been a devastating event for him to come to terms with spending many hours sitting down on the dock side at Wapping in some kind of misguided hope that the boat was about to return. He quickly found it hard to make money just with odd jobs and pest control with Jack so he turned to fighting; it offered high rewards for someone with talent, although a high risk of permanent injury too.

The crowd around the makeshift ring were achieving an almost frenzied state in the last minutes before the fight was scheduled to commence. Money was furiously changing hands in bets about the eventual winner. It was expected to be a long and bloody affair with the result being decided by the 'last man standing'. There were no clarified rules to adhere to except no biting. Eight in the evening, a bell was rung and the crowd fell silent. Both youths came out from their corners, light on their feet and their hands up ready to box. There were no taped or gloved knuckles here; it was bare bone and flesh to inflict maximum damage. Ford quickly had appreciated he would not want to pursue this career for long; eventually his hands would be an arthritic mess and he appreciated he stood to get significant brain damage in the long term, especially as better, quicker and hungrier opponents came along. Bill Brooks was certainly a hungry opponent. He wanted to better the legendary 'Robbie Ford' and get revenge for the incident nine years earlier.

They circled each other ducking and weaving and throwing range finding jabs for quite sometime before anyone attempted a concerted attack. Ford had no seconds as such with him and the dog, Jack, was safely ensconced in the old family home he retained in Cable Street. Brooks came in with the first attack. Fast volley of jabs then a good right hand punch tried to find its way past Ford's guard. He managed to catch Ford in the middle of his chest with the punch as it was deflected by Ford's left forearm slightly. Ford knew that at the split second that his opponent's attack subsided he should step in to try to catch him before he had time to properly put up a guard. It frequently worked for him and this occasion was no different. Breaking through Brook's defences he managed to land two punches on the other lad's nose. It shattered as it had done nine years before creating a bloody mess, although this time the more seasoned fighter as he now was, was used to the pain. Brooks managed a high almost 'hay maker' of a punch coming over the top left of Ford's guard that caught Ford above his left eye. Bare knuckle on bony forehead opened up a deep cut that immediately as it bled blurred Ford's vision in his left eye. Raising his guard a little as he suspected a volley of head shots, Ford didn't bend in his elbows enough as Brooks then landed two good punches into Ford's sternum.

The pain and the winding effect drove Ford back for a few seconds but he tightened up his guard to protect him from the next volley of strikes. He allowed Brooks to close in a little again and gave him a low swift, almost invisible to the crowd, kick to his lower left shin. It forced Brooks through surprise to drop his guard. Ford capitalised on this with an uppercut to the chin. Brooks' mind went into a spin. He became disorientated and suddenly found himself, for only a second time, on the floor. Ford moved lightly around him waiting for him to get to his feet. The crowd were going into a frenzied melt down; actually screaming for blood and literally for death.

Distracted momentarily and uncharacteristically by the mob, Ford found himself felled by the recovering, and now intent on victory at all costs, Brooks. Brooks had watched Ford moving around him and as he recovered he feigned disorientation for a little longer and then struck with a leg trap. He had opened his legs wide and then closed them in a 'scissor' like movement and brought Ford crashing to the ground. He then got nasty, but there were no rules other than the biting prohibition. He grabbed Ford under the chin and began to pull his head towards him as hard as he could digging his filthy sharp finger nails into his skin, so deeply that as he pulled he was drawing blood. He had a vice like grip. Ford struggled to loosen his grasp. Brooks was a powerful fighter with huge reserves of strength from portering at Smithfield's meat market. Ford sensed only one way out of this.

Using his natural athleticism, in a swift snapping motion he went into a backwards roll type move which kicked his legs up and round to catch Brooks in between his knees. The pressure on his lower back was immense and he knew he could not hold it for long, but he felt his life was in peril. The pressure from Brooks' hold felt like it would snap his neck. Ford even managed to twist his knees slightly which put immediate pressure on Brooks' neck; he heard a slight crack as he did so. Brook's screamed and released his grip. Ford let go his own and as soon as his legs were brought back down he twisted round and grabbed Brooks, still nursing his neck, and rolled along side him. He settled into a strangle hold on him from behind, one arm across the front of his neck with the other pushing his head forward to exaggerate the hold.

The crowd oddly started to subdue as they watched this action. They sensed that a 'real kill' could be upon them. In truth no one had the stomach for that. Ford could feel his opponent's struggle weaken as he fought a losing battle for breath. 'Can I really kill someone?' wondered Ford as Brook's became still. He immediately released the hold and jumped to his feet. The crowd was silent. Everyone was watching the apparently lifeless body on the floor. Suddenly there was a huge wheezing sound and Brooks took a massive gulp of air. He wasn't dead. He looked up as his eyes opened in fear of Ford. Ford stepped forward and Brooks cowered.

"Don't kill me! Please! You're the winner. Please, mate!" Brooks, normally fearless, was terrified having come so close to death. Ford offered him a hand and pulled him to his feet. Those having bet on Ford cheered at his victory. The back-street, illegal fight promoter paid Ford his handsome purse for the win. The crowd began to disperse from the lawless gathering, many drifting off to 'The Ten Bells' public house just over the road in Commercial Street.

Ford left briskly. He took himself off to Cable Street where he met the unconditional affection of Jack, his loyal dog. He took a warm soak in his large tin bath to relax and recover. He never fought again.

* * *

Ford felt Spicer's grip on his arms begin to loosen, he was close to passing into unconsciousness. Ford stunned at his actions, released his grip from his subordinate. Spicer fell forward coughing heavily to draw breath and bring stability back to his spinning, air starved mind. As he regained his full faculties the pain from the left of his rib cage became apparent to him again. Bent over, he looked up at Ford with hate, fear and begrudging admiration for his sheer physical abilities; no wonder he had tolerated and survived so much during the Whitechapel murders back in 1888. Spicer was no longer sure of what course of action to take. If he tried to discredit Ford he knew that after this second encounter he might not survive another. Ford possessed a menace that he had not witnessed in other police officers when provoked.

"Where do we stand then, Bob?" Ford stood back from his colleague as he spoke watching his every move for an aggressive response.

"I...er...We won't speak of this again. But you are on your own, Rob. I will say nothing. But if he finds out, then be it on your head."

"I can't believe you try to defend a man who treats a woman in no better way than the men of the East End used to, especially when drunk. Don't be fooled by his class and status. He is an untrustworthy and nasty man. Why do you think someone is out to kill him or his staff? He has some dark secrets, trust me." Spicer didn't want to get pulled into that kind of speculation. But with the introduction of the sinister Major Hoare, he suspected that Ford might be right.

"Rob, I just don't know," he spoke rubbing his tender ribs, "I just want to do my job and that's all."

"Right then. Enjoy the rest of your day off. I'm off tomorrow and then we're going to Prague the day after. Do your job, and I'll do mine." Spicer nodded in acknowledgment and paused. Then he spoke.

"There's a telegram from Inspector Reno from Paris on the desk there. He's given the measurements of those wheelchair tracks at the Sacred Heart. They're the same. Thought you'd be interested."

"Thanks Bob. I am." Spicer left the office. Ford wouldn't see him again until they left for Prague. He really didn't know where he stood with him anymore.

* * *

Marcus Hoare dressed in workingman's clothes watched the blacksmiths in Bull Street, Dagenham village from a distance. It was difficult for a man of his bearing and stature to blend in such common surroundings with such a rural population. He had managed it with a little forward planning since dealing with Bates; no washing and no shaving and stealing some working clothes from a relatively clean unconscious drunk along the Romford Road in Stratford on the way out to the countryside. The clothing included a wide brimmed hat that would help disguise his facial features when pulled down low to wear. Part of training during his many years as a Royal Marines officer had been with ship borne artillery and with basic explosives for the purpose of demolition of enemy strongholds. His knowledge had been refined with trial and error during practical exercises and during a voluntary deployment in India, where on several occasions he helped quell uprisings by the destruction of local strongholds or palaces from where the resistance emanated.

It was now eight-thirty in the morning and he had watched Messer's Higgins and Wilcox arrive at the forge that sat near to Howgego's cycle and motorcycle shop around half an hour before. Hoare had been much earlier in his arrival at the village blacksmiths. In fact, he had arrived under cover of darkness with his coachman with the odd nervous twitch, Joseph Netley, who had dropped him off and continued on to meet his sinister passenger later on. Hoare would walk up from Dagenham village and meet Netley on the road that ran past Lodge Farm outside the main barn.

Hoare had with him a medium sized canvas military haversack on his back when he alighted from the coach. There was no one around in the dark pre-dawn village to watch and report on his nefarious movements, which was exactly his plan. It was his intention to place a small explosive charge inside the unlit furnace wrapped in several layers of cotton wadding. As the furnace heated up and burnt more ferociously for the purpose of forging, the cotton wadding would burn away to a point where the small amount of explosives would become exposed to the heat and detonate. The explosion should be large enough to kill the two ex-soldiers working in there, thus confirming their silence, but also any one else unfortunate enough to be in the forge that early. With the common use of gas for lighting and heating he planned that with the destruction of the property being so great, and the instances of gas explosions being reasonably prevalent, the authorities would put the whole unfortunate incident down to such an occurrence.

He first of all checked the front door as a way in to the premises. It was a barn type building with the main doors being double wooden plank construction doors braced on the inside with diagonal planks, judging by the nails he observed. He walked all the way around the ancient barn type commercial building. There was a small door at the rear that appeared relatively unused. He suspected that this was intended as a fire exit. With a minimal amount of obvious damage on his part, and being a door that was seldom used or checked by the lack of footprints on the dusty ground outside adjacent to it, this was the most convenient way in for his plan. He pulled it outwards and met strong resistance. He shouldered it inwards and found the resistance weaker. Two more shoulder barges and the door went in. The rest of the plan was easy to execute having made the entry. He found the front of the furnace which was still warm from the day before and gave the closed iron handle a tentative touch. It wasn't too hot to grasp so he held onto the handle and pulled it open. Inside there were still glowing embers. He felt quite sure that they would not set off the explosive package prematurely.

He took the haversack from his back and removed the explosives. Inside he also had a Webley service revolver that he tucked inside the waistband at the back of his trousers. No one would get in his way during his escape. He placed the charge out of sight just inside the wide access door of the furnace and closed the door again. He put the now empty haversack back on his back and left the forge by the way he had entered. The sun was just beginning to rise as he exited outside. He looked down at the ground as he shut the rear door and saw his own foot prints in the dust; the only ones there. He looked around for something to rake the ground over but could see nothing easily to hand. He then took the haversack from his back and used that to smooth over the dust and disguise the footprints. Satisfied that they were gone, he disappeared into the farming countryside until well after dawn.

He returned looking like a dusty, weary traveller just before eight and sat outside of the 'Bull Inn' public house to get a simple breakfast; the landlord served breakfast to subsidise his difficult existence. He then watched from his table as the owners of the blacksmiths' arrived and unlocked the premises. They got the fire going in the furnace and then sat outside, one on an anvil, the other on a small oak barrel and enjoyed a cup of tea and what looked like good natured army type banter in the sun. Hoare looked on with no remorse even developing in his mind a picture for the imminent fate of these ex-servicemen, maybe even once brothers-in-arms in India.

Chapter Fourteen

The fire lit only minutes before and then fed with an abundance of fresh dry wood was beginning to take hold in the furnace. Hoare looked on noting that the furnace door was open, that was good as it would not contain the explosion too much, and the fire was growing steadily. If his intended victims stayed outside too long and the explosion occurred without them in the immediate confines of the blacksmiths premises, they could survive with injuries that might not prove life threatening. He was watching with growing concern that his carefully orchestrated plan might be foiled; but he had to avoid 'showing out'. He continued shovelling the food from his cooked breakfast into his cruel mouth in an undignified working class way which he detested, occasionally wiping the excesses around his mouth with his sleeve.

Then, as he finished chewing open mouthed on a particularly streaky piece of bacon, it looked as if his plan was about to come to fruition. The two jovial ex-servicemen finished their morning tea and both stood and walked into the premises. The fire he could see was really taking hold especially as one of them stoked and poked it with a long metal pole. It was a warm morning so the doors of the forge remained open. He drank from his dirty enamel cup; the tea made in it was strong and a little bitter and he swallowed a few leaves that were in its base that made him cough out loud. A couple of grubby dock type workers looked at him as he coughed and wheezed for just a few seconds. They returned to their own food and conversation, not particularly interested as to whether this individual was choking and about to die or not.

Everything, even to the veteran of many bloody campaigns as Hoare was, happened so quickly. A family party of a mother and four children then arrived at the forge with the children in pairs carrying a set of small garden iron gates. The children ranged from about four years old to nine. They were all laughing and joking with each other under their small piece of morning toil as the mother beckoned them with her finger into the forge. Hoare slammed the mug down on the table in front of him; the grubby Dockers looked around at him again this time with greater disdain. Even the cold hearted and godless Hoare did not wish to see the death of innocents. The plan was so far advanced now that the explosion was imminent, the protective layer of wadding would be on the cusp of having completely burnt through. 'The silly bitch!' he thought, 'why the hell did she have take her damned tribe in there this morning.' There was nothing for it. He would have to intervene claiming that he could smell leaking gas.

Hoare stood rapidly from his table with his chair sliding noisily back from behind him and then clattering to the floor. He moved with lightning efficiency from behind the table, passing the Dockers, barging them very slightly as he got onto the footway and ran as fast as he could.

"Wanker! Mind where you're going!" Shouted one of the Dockers after him.

"Tosser." Hissed the other under his breath as he stuffed some sausage and egg into his fat, overloaded mouth. Hoare had about sixty yards to cover to get to the blacksmiths and he ran flat out as fast as he could. His heart pumped hard feeling as if it was about to burst out of his chest over the short dash, a mixture of exertion and adrenalin. He was a fit and healthy man and in normal circumstances this brief piece of explosive activity would not normally weigh on him.

Hoare was about twenty yards from the forge when all four children ran out and came towards him. He felt momentary relief as they ran passed him away from the danger laughing and shrieking as they did so. But the mother had still not emerged. He could not leave them bereft of her; he had grown up on a sad and lonely, loveless basis himself. He was on the cusp of the entrance to the forge right by one of its open high gates when she emerged. She was sorting something in a cheap battered leather bag as she looked into his face startled; he was right on top of her. He stopped his forward motion almost instantly grabbing the edge of the pinned back gate and then took hold of her left arm saying nothing. He dragged her off with him back in the direction in which he had come. She screamed and tried to resist bringing the entire streets attention to bear on them. Everything was happening in slow motion now as Hoare ran as hard as he could almost dragging her along as she struggled to keep balance on her feet. The two Dockers, already disgruntled at his earlier behaviour, were out of their chairs and making their way onto the pavement to see what the commotion was. He made it just passed Howgego's shop and got to near to the post office when he threw her to the floor and then himself on top of her in an instinctive reflex action, as if prompted by some kind of sixth sense that the explosion was about to occur. With his back to it he hadn't seen Higgins and Wilcox come to the door of the forge.

There was a massive roar of noise then everything went completely silent to him, and in fact to those around them. He felt the heat of the explosion pass over him immediately followed by the sensation of the blast and then the rain of debris. He could sense that the woman was screaming but could not hear her. Everyone else in the street was also cowering on the floor or in doorways. The two ex-soldiers were blown clean out of the premises across the road and, according to Hoare's plan, were fatally injured. Wilcox was blown through a window and died of a head injury from impacting with an internal wall. Higgins was impaled on a length of iron tubing that was flung outwards perilously from the blast. Mercifully no one else was killed. No one knew what had gone on. Hoare got to his knees and looked down at the sobbing mother who looked back up at him with a seeming debt of gratitude, although not understanding at all what had happened. The children were lying on the floor huddled together and silent outside the Bull Inn, whilst the Dockers had stopped in their tracks not having any comprehension of what had happened. It would only be when Hoare had long left the scene and the police were trying to establish what had happened that anyone would consider a link between the mysterious scar-faced man with the haversack and the explosion.

Hoare walked briskly passed the burning building and when covered by the drifting smoke and out of view he ran to make his rendezvous and escape from the countryside with Joseph Netley, twin brother of the late John Netley killed the previous year in an accident, and well known to Robert Ford from his Whitechapel days.

* * *

When Ford arrived in Dagenham village only hours after the fatal explosion to visit 'Higgins and Wilcox Blacksmiths' he was shocked by what he saw. The bodies of the two, secretly murdered, ex-soldiers had long been removed by the police from the scene and the clearing up had begun. The local police had come out of their station some distance away in Bull Lane with a few constables and an inspector left at the scene. Conveniently for Ford the two Dockers and the mother with her shocked children were all still at the Bull Inn pub being comforted by locals and friends and waiting for police statements to be taken. Seeing the burnt out forge premises Ford strongly suspected he had made a wasted journey. He spoke to the local inspector.

"Hello, mate. Inspector Ford from Scotland Yard. Can you tell me what's gone on here?" Ford presented the inspector with his warrant identity card as he spoke. The local Essex inspector looked him up and down. He didn't like 'flash London detectives' in his back yard and his general demeanour and attitude would reflect that feeling.

"Yes, I can. But what brings you here, Mr Ford?"

"Certainly. I am involved on the peripheries with the investigation into the murders of Ministry of War staff. I am Sir Cecil Patterson's protection officer. I needed to speak to the two chaps at the forge about it with their army backgrounds." He found Ford's persona and general approach to be non-threatening, so the inspector relaxed a little and became less adversarial.

"Well, me old cock. You're out of luck there. Them two fellows is quite fucking dead from an explosion. We suspect gas, but there was some queer looking fellow running about just before it happened. Apparently it was like he knew it was coming. Saved a woman and her kids by all accounts." Ford was immediately suspicious.

"Where can I find her?"

"In The Bull down there," said the inspector pointing up the street. "Couple of my lads are there, tell them I sent you up." Ford offered the inspector his hand to shake.

The Dressmaker Connection

"Thank you, Inspector." They shook hands firmly and Ford then made off along the now war-torn looking Bull Street. There were shattered windows, doors blown in and still much debris lying in the road. Whatever had exploded it had been considerable indeed. To reach the Bull Inn, Ford had to pass Howgego's and the post office amongst other business and residential premises along the way. For the post office it was simply a case of sweeping up the glass from the shattered panels that fronted the building, whilst for the unfortunate proprietor of Howgego's had not only suffered the damage to his shop but also the destruction of some valuable stock in the window; two motorcycles and some bicycles that looked to the distressed owner to be beyond economic repair as Ford passed by. At the pub he was directed in by a constable on the door to the saloon bar where he discovered the Dockers, the woman and her four very quiet and seemingly shaken children.

Ford got all seven of them to sit together to try to elicit information from them regarding the mysterious stranger. By the end of a brief question and answers session with them he was certain of several facts about the stranger and the explosion. The man was not local, had never been seen before and by his accent and demeanour not a working man. He was striking in his tall appearance and military bearing. His presence was an odd coincidence to the explosion especially as he seemed to have some idea that it was about to happen by interfering with the family and their safety. If he was a killer, he was obviously conscious of ensuring that innocent parties were not hurt. An odd very English trait thought Ford, perhaps that of an honourable military man. Ford was in no doubt that these facts, coupled with the deceased being men that would have been key in supplying information regarding the threat against Patterson, meant that what had taken place here was a very carefully orchestrated murder, designed to appear as an accident. Ford left with less answers and only more questions to be settled.

* * *

London, Whitechapel

It was late afternoon when Holden and Waldron arrived in Commercial Street outside the notorious 'Ten Bells' public house on

Holden's quest to find Nigel Green's common law wife, and pass on the shattering news to her about his death. Neither had ever visited the area before but had heard much about it and its poor social fabric. Known by some as 'the abyss' they were under no illusion about having a comfortable time there. It was still frequented by thrill seeking moneyed men predominantly from West London 'seeking a thrill amongst the common working classes'. Both were dressed smartly but not garishly. Both more than able, from their vicious and violent experiences around the empire, to look after themselves, or so they thought. Both carried Webley service revolvers for if the need arose, to defend themselves robustly.

Alighting outside Millers Court on the west footway of Commercial Street, with the pub diagonally opposite, they looked for a safe gap in the traffic to cross the road, after Holden had pulled the wheelchair from the carriage and helped Waldron into it. Waldron jealously guarded his independence around his former commanding officer and insisted in wheeling himself around in his chair. The whole area even at a first glance was the complete antithesis of the West End of London that Holden was used to, and that Waldron had become accustomed to staying in Holden's Ebury Street residence. Just the smell of the air with its mix of the flower market, the less than sanitary living conditions of the local populace, the mess left by the constant flowing horse drawn traffic, created an unpalatable stench. They reached the east footway with Holden constantly glancing around to get a geographic picture in his head of the street layout. He knew he was looking for Fashion Street, and as luck would have it he saw it off to his right as they crossed the road. He felt he might as well strike while the iron was hot and begin to make enquiries along there. He turned to Waldron, craned his head down slightly and spoke to him. There was concern in his voice.

"Fashion Street is just over there, Wally. It's cobbled without much of a footway by the look of it. Do you want to chance your hand coming down it or shall I meet you in The Ten Bells," Holden pointed to the north as he spoke, "over there when I'm done?" Waldron wheeled himself slightly south and took a look at Fashion Street.

It was dark; a foreboding mixed business and residential street with gloomy and dirty bricked terraced buildings. He could see a few teenage lads milling about in groups and a few children playing in the street. There was something menacing and unseen about the street that made Waldron as a partial cripple feel distinctly uncomfortable, despite being armed. If he went with Holden he would struggle to wheel himself along the cobbles and he would be a liability to him if they were confronted. To complete the picture of danger, he noticed that two constables together patrolled along it, as opposed to the more usual one; and even in a pair they seemed to be at their guard. He detected that the concern in Holden's voice did not come purely from the physical layout of the street.

"I think I might be more of a hindrance than a help, Boss. I'll go into that Ten Bells and see you there when you get out. If I get bored I'll see you back in Ebury Street."

"All right. It makes sense. But still be careful despite the fact it's very public."

Holden then entered the top end of Fashion Street while Waldron wheeled himself off to the public house. He decided that the first 'rag trade' premises he came across would be where he would begin his enquires to trace Nigel Green's estranged wife, Karen. He felt that the news may well be uncomfortable for someone who, not knowing about the fate of their loved one, after six years may well have moved on geographically and emotionally. He only walked a matter of half a dozen yards when the second door that he came across had a tatty wooden plate on it signifying its commercial purpose. 'Jane Darrell, seamstress'. Holden was buoyed by the potential start to his quest. He knocked on the door and waited uncomfortably for sometime for an answer. Looking east further into Fashion Street he could see a group of young men walking along the north footway, the one he found himself on. Distracted by his defensive observation of them, he did not notice the toothless hag that owned the premises open the door. He was slightly startled by a blunt question bellowed unceremoniously in his left ear.

"Can I help you?" A dirty, ugly fifty year old woman stood hands on hips staring him in the face, waiting impatiently for an answer.

"Yes. Sorry to trouble you, madam, do you know anyone who works along here by the name of Karen? She had a husband in the army, overseas." The hag looked him up and down with suspicion.

"Had? Dead is he? You military filth, are you? Come to break the bad news, eh?"

"No. I am his former commanding officer and friend, Captain Holden. I do sadly need to pass on some bad news, however."

"I see. Well. Pretty blonde girl she is, used to work down there at Grundon's. Don't think she's there no more, got swept off her feet by some fancy West London politician. Go down to old Mary Grundon and ask her. Sorry can't help no more." Before Holden could even reply the door was shut firmly in his face.

For a few seconds Holden stared blankly at the tattered four panelled door that had just been slammed in his face. The awareness of the proximity of the gang of young men he had seen a minute or so earlier suddenly grabbed his attention. He wheeled round quickly so his back was to the closed door to face the four of them who now more or less surrounded him. All of them were around seventeen to nineteen years old, thin except for one, wearing dog tooth flat caps, white scarves tied at the throat, waist coats and bell bottomed trousers fastened with thick black leather belts that sported a large decorative buckle. They all wore the same buckle; a plain thick, heavy metal oval that if swung would certainly cause some harm. The fatter one of the group stood square on to Holden and moved his face forward in a deliberately intimidating way to speak and scare his potential victim. Their intention was to rob this visiting 'toff'; they had no inkling of the mistake they had made in choosing him.

"Well, chum. What brings you here then? Why you knocking on a workshop door? You lot are normally only here for the tarts, why don't you fuck off to The Ten Bells? In fact, why don't you just fuck off? But befo..." his words were cut short by the swiftness of Holden's attack; none of them had time to react. Holden brought his old SRP mantra of 'swiftness, audacity and surprise' to bear in a street fight.

He struck the fat one hard with a square on punch to his throat. It struck the young man's Adam's apple so hard that he thought it had ruptured and he fell to the floor clutching his neck and writhing in agony struggling to breath. Before he had even hit the floor Holden felled the one immediately to his right with a rapidly downwards, hammer-fist punch to the brachial nerve to the right side of the second attacker's neck. He blacked out unconscious from the strike before he

The Dressmaker Connection

hit the floor. The third young man to the left of Holden instinctively lashed out with a punch towards Holden's head but he was too slow. Holden had ducked down in anticipation of such an attack and then rapidly swept his left leg forwards and then back and took the legs of this third attacker and put him to the floor. The fourth gang member, as Holden had anticipated, chose to run and not to stand and fight. The third one, only knocked to the floor, found himself staring down the barrel of Holden's rapidly drawn Webley revolver.

"Now then, 'chum'," said Holden mimicking his first assailant, "you lads count yourselves lucky you are escaping with your lives. Before you go," Holden paused and noticed that this young hooligan, with his gang bravado, had urinated himself in fear of his life. The growing puddle around him caused Holden to step aside slightly. "Oh, dear. Are you scared, mmm? Never mind. Tell me, have you always lived around here?" The terrified young hooligan simply nodded. He was too terrified to speak. "Good. Ever heard of Nigel Green, a soldier and his wife around here called Karen?" The young man was now crying. The tears streamed down his much reddened cheeks. He nodded his head and coughed to try to speak.

"Grundon's. She worked at Grundon's with my mum years ago. Ask there, just along the road." Holden lowered the pistol.

"Good. Now you choose a righteous path and be helpful like that to all strangers. I ever see you and your friends strutting around scaring people I will kill you all." Holden spoke in a coldly matter of fact way as if discussing mundane working issues. The young man, and his now recovering friends that Holden ensured he too addressed, nodded gratefully. Holden turned his back on them and walked further east almost to the end of Fashion Street where it met Brick Lane and found the door to Grundon's workshop.

He had to wait for some time before the battered four panelled wooden door with its flaking paint was opened. He was presented with a quite statuesque woman in her late forties, cleanly dressed in typical Edwardian female working clothes with her long, brown but greying hair tied back into a single pony tail; it gave her sharp features and an accentuated aggressive look. She frowned at him as he made firm eye contact with her. She was the first to speak.

"Can I help you?" she folded her arms as she spoke.

"Yes. Mary Grundon?" Asked a quizzical Holden. She looked him up and down. He was dressed respectably and didn't look like one of the local police detectives. She felt unthreatened by him.

"Yes. And you are?"

"My name is Captain William Holden. I am trying to trace a Karen Wood with news about her husband." Mary Grundon knew that Karen had moved on bettering herself in the process with the thought in her mind that her beloved Nigel Green after two years with no word must be dead. This looked as if this was a long overdue visit to confirm that.

"Well, Captain, you've come to the right place to start with. She worked here up to about three years ago. Got a right good commission for a proper West End lady to fix and make all her clothes. Her husband was so impressed that he got her fixing up his suits too. She's moved up West as a result to be permanently on hand for them. To tell you the truth though, giving her a flat up West, there's more to that than meets the eye?" She unfolded her arms and leant against the door frame, there certainly seemed to be no sign she was going to let Holden in.

"I see. When you say more to it than meets the eye, what exactly do you mean?" Holden asked suspecting he knew the answer.

"Well, Karen is, if I may be blunt, fucking beautiful. Makes ya fucking sick really. She ain't from round here by birth. Her West End man is no doubt screwing her behind his wife's back, hence keeping her out West in a nice flat to get and do as he pleases."

"I see, who..." Before Holden could continue she carried on in an archetypal East End fashion; now that gossiping was in full flow she needed to pass on all the details.

"Still, it's allowed her to put her sick lad in proper full time care in a posh Knightsbridge nursery." The first clue, at last, to Holden as to where he should be looking next.

"Mrs Grundon, who are the couple that Karen is working for?"

"Oh blimey, proper posh and famous they are. He's a minister. Bloody Cecil Patterson he is. Got pots of fucking money by all accounts. Dead lucky she's been there, even if she does have to fuck the bastard from time to time." Holden stood staring blankly back at Mary Grundon trying to take on board the information that he had just been given. It seemed beyond the realms of possibility that not

The Dressmaker Connection

only was Patterson responsible for the deaths of his men but was now using the wife of one of his closest dead friends as a mistress. He felt an even deeper sense of loathing for this man; he even now knew who this woman was having had observed the undeniably beautiful blond within Patterson's entourage on occasions. At least now he knew exactly who to look for; he couldn't believe that the dressmaker had such a connection. But his greatest problem was trying to get to her to tell her the truth; she was part of Patterson's inner circle and might even know who he was and the danger he represented. He would have to be very cautious. "You gonna say anything about it then, yer bleeder?" Grundon was glaring back at Holden impatiently waiting for a reply. She did, after all, have much work to do. Holden snapped out of his distant thoughts to reply.

"I'm sorry, Mrs Grundon. That's all very helpful. I thank you for your time. Do you know where she lives exactly?" This was an important fact for Holden to try to establish.

"Nah, sorry. Knightsbridge somewhere. That's all I know. I take it old Nigel is dead then?" Holden had almost forgotten the purpose of the visit having established who Karen was, and knowing her by sight.

"I'm afraid so, yes. Quite sometime ago now. Afghanistan, 1898. Sorry."

"No surprise really. After all this time too. She guessed as much and I reckon she's moved on. Bleeder never actually married her you know."

Before Holden could reply she shut the door. Holden was left standing on the doorstep a little bemused for a few seconds. Then he turned and stood for some moments in the street. He watched the children playing and making mischief knocking on doors and then running away; he saw the youths he had dealt with earlier in the far distance in the west of the street; he had never been to this district before and turned and headed east along Fashion Street to try to find his way 'around the block' and eventually back to Waldron in The Ten Bells. Holden's enquiries in Fashion Street and his circular journey taking in the East End culture in Brick Lane and Hanbury Street and then back to the pub took him about half an hour. He would find Waldron already gone.

* * *

The entrance to The Ten Bells was, fortuitously for Waldron, by way of a set of double doors. He banged his way through them in his wheelchair leaving them swinging noisily behind him like the half doors to a Wild West Saloon, complete with all the clientele falling silent for a moment to see who had just entered town. He had experienced this kind of bizarre silent interest before, particularly as a uniformed soldier, but each time it still unnerved him; especially as a paraplegic. He wheeled himself up to the bar with the other varied types of drinkers, ranging from builders and casual workmen to servicemen and prostitutes, all quite obligingly moving out of his way. Waldron was physically strong so the only disadvantage he ever felt was a lack of speed and agility, but today inside the pub he didn't feel threatened enough to worry about it. In fact seeing who some of the clientele were he felt quite sure that he might find someone to help fulfil his sexual frustration by supplying some gratification for money.

However, 'first things first' he thought. He needed a drink. The friendly bar keeper would obligingly serve someone he suspected was an old soldier with a pint of the notoriously alcoholic 'Hells Teeth' ale. It was a dark, thick, menacing looking substance that played cruel tricks with the mind when drunk to excess; perfect for what Waldron wanted and he knew it. It would make him courageous enough to strike up some business with one of the girls. The obliging bar keeper served him with a pint in a marginally clean straight pint beer glass. Waldron paid for the drink with a crisp note from his worn brown leather wallet and instructed the bar keeper to keep the change ready for another. He pulled the glass off of the bar with his right hand and brought it up to his mouth and drank half a pint almost instantly without taking a breath. Its alcoholic effect struck him straight away as a result of the rapid ingestion. He could feel his head become slightly light; he liked it and promptly drank the other half a pint as quickly and slammed the glass down on to the bar surface in a convivial manner. The astute and alert bar keeper served him another paid for out of the first note he had received. He had now seen that the unusually smart cripple had means with him to get drunk and he would willingly keep serving him; after all he knew that he wouldn't fall over. Waldron was slower in drinking the next pint and savoured it much more. He had caught the attention of one of the local, prettier prostitutes in the meantime who now decided to saunter over from her place by one of The Ten Bells windows and join him.

Waldron very quickly noticed the pretty if slightly grubbily clothed twenty something year old girl walk towards him with positive eye contact and a willing smile. She was slender but with a good shape to her figure, wearing a dress that enhanced the natural swell of her breasts, some kind of heeled shoes or boots from the way she walked, and well kept long, straight, brown hair. She came and stood beside him, extended her right hand and introduced herself to him.

"Hello, sir, my name is Lucy. You look like you've come to Whitechapel to have a good time." She leant forward slightly as she spoke giving him an ample view of her alluring cleavage. Waldron felt a sense of arousal as he touched her hand and looked at her physical form. This was the first physical contact he had had with a woman since his crippling wound.

"Hello, Lucy," he said politely. He wanted to make a good impression on her despite knowing that she was out to make money from him by supplying her sexual services. He knew that it would be a loveless encounter; it did not matter. "Can I get you drink then?"

"Oh, that's very kind of you, sir."

"Please, call me Wally."

"Oh. All right, Wally, can I have a gin please." Gin, straight or otherwise was often the local prostitutes' favourite drink. On many, or even most occasions, it helped to dull the pain of the passionless encounters that they sold themselves into. The bar keeper was listening in around other conversations and within seconds a glass of gin was on the bar for her. Waldron watched hypnotised by her breasts as she pulled up a chair to sit slightly offset in front of him.

For fifteen minutes they drank and made small conversation with Waldron getting to the end of his fourth 'Hells Teeth'; the excitement of an almost certain sexual encounter drove him on to drink more quickly. The conversation eventually turned around to his disability. It wasn't something he was shy about and he had no problem talking to this pretty twenty-something about it.

"How did you end up in the wheelchair then, Wally?"

"Well, I was serving with the army on a secret mission in a country called Afghanistan when me and my mates were attacked. Some natives that we had got friendly with turned on us and slaughtered most of the men. I was a lucky one getting a bullet in my lower back but not being killed. It did leave me like this though. Bloody shame even if I do say so myself. Everything else works just not my fucking legs." The alcohol often made him swear as he slurred his speech a little. His last comment was exactly the cue that she had wanted.

"You say that everything else works then?" He knew what she was alluding to and didn't care. He was happy with the direction of the conversation.

"Oh, yes. I can promise you, that **everything** else works. Are you going to help to check that fact out then?" He saw no point in not being forward. "I certainly will, I know somewhere we can go just around the corner." She leant forward closer to him to continue speaking in a slight whisper. "It's a shilling for me to suck you off, or two bob for a fuck, I don't do it up the arse though, even if you're the bloody king." That didn't bother Waldron at all, he would be grateful for either oral or penetrative sex.

"How about three bob for both then?" Nothing ventured, nothing gained he thought.

"It would be my pleasure."

"No trust me, it will be mine," replied the almost trembling Waldron at the prospect of a sexual encounter. She stood up and was about to walk around to the back of the wheelchair to push him out of the pub.

"No, please don't, I can do that," said a proud Waldron.

"Oh. All right, my lovely. Just follow me then."

They left The Ten Bells through the double doors set on the corner of the building that led then to the corner of Church Lane and Commercial Street. It was still daylight and Waldron was wondering where they could be going to for some privacy. She turned right out of the pub and headed north along Commercial Street only a short distance up to Red Lion Court, a small alleyway leading off east from Commercial Street. It looked dirty and dangerous as it appeared not to lead anywhere. She turned into it as Waldron stopped for a moment in the main road.

"Are you sure we'll find some privacy up there?" He asked with concern and suspicion now in his mind.

"Look, follow me just a little way up. There's the door into an empty building up there that we can go into and be out of the way. Let's face it; we ain't going to lie down anywhere are we?" Waldron considered her words; she seemed to have a point really. Lucy disappeared only a few feet further along from where she had first stopped and entered the doorway she had mentioned. He wheeled himself up and followed her into the dark and damp looking abandoned building. Although the plaster was cracked and decaying and the floorboards were creaking and becoming rotten, it was private enough for them to engage in their business transaction. She had noticed already he had money and quickly got down to work.

Waldron began to tremble as she bent down in front of him onto her knees and started to unbutton his suit trousers. She looked up at him and smiled and already feeling a sense of arousal he now felt himself fully stiffen within his trousers. He was elated that his injury had not cost him his sexual ability as well as his mobility. She pulled him free from his trousers and took his penis in her mouth. As a former Victorian era soldier he was no stranger to the professional techniques of prostitutes as she performed the act of oral sex as well as any he had previously encountered. Having keenly observed her at work, he closed his eyes and tilted his head back with the overwhelming sense of great pleasure. His only concern now was that if she continued she may complete the deal before he had endured the pleasure once more of a 'fuck'.

Lucy was well versed in her craft; he need have no fear of that. She had been engaged in prostitution since she was fifteen and discovered that she possessed a natural talent for sexual pleasure. That was why she was able to charge a little more and pick and choose her clients. She stood up and lifted up her skirt to reveal herself to him with no undergarments. She stepped forward and straddled him over the wheelchair and lowered herself onto his erection. Her feet were off the ground with her spread across him, but he was equal to this. With his immense upper body strength it was easy to simply lift her up and down on top of him for them to achieve the effect. To him it felt heavenly and he groaned with pleasure; to her it felt reasonably good but it was just another fuck. She whimpered from time to time to please him and occasionally because it did feel pleasurable too.

As Waldron moved her up and down she then undid some buttons on the front of her dress and then pulled it down to reveal her breasts to him. They were generous and firm for her size and it was now too much for him to endure. Both of them could sense him about to climax. She briskly lifted herself from him as he came to avoid the unpleasantness of a later back street abortion. She then got off of him completely as he looked up at her with a look of astonishment on his face. She had just given him a sensation that he had not experienced in over six years.

"Lucy, that was wonderful. Thank you."

"My pleasure, darling. I know it sounds awfully cold," she said as she did up her dress and straightened her skirt, "but that's three shillings please." He knew that it was always a business deal and willingly paid her. She then coolly walked out from the building. As he re-entered Red Lion Court she had already disappeared from sight.

Waldron had a vague idea of where he was as he wheeled himself back down to Commercial Street. The afternoon weather was rather pleasant so he chose to take the air for a time before returning to Ebury Street. He would meet Holden back there later in the day. He recalled from the carriage journey to reach the East End that he needed to be heading south to eventually get back on route for Chelsea. His drunken mind and the euphoria of his sexual encounter were clouding his judgement. He wheeled himself from the east to the west pavement narrowly avoiding a collision with a carriage heading south and then a bus heading north. The abuse shouted at him by the respective drivers was unintelligible in his spinning mind. He found himself outside Spitalfields market with its very distinctive smell of fresh fruit, vegetables and flowers. It was bustling with market traders, but at this time of day few shopkeepers as they had already bought their produce. It was patronised by many buyers from London hotels buying their fresh ingredients for the evenings expensive gastronomic delights.

He safely crossed Brushfield Street and then mistakenly turned off and continued south in Toynbee Street; the main road had curved slightly left, but to the drunken cripple's mind he thought the continuation of the pavement he was on was the main road. He was now heading dangerously away from the safety of the busy primary thoroughfare.

He passed Millers Court, of no significance to him but the scene of the most outrageous of the 'Jack the Ripper' murders, rumbling his wheelchair over the roughly constructed Victorian pavement. He was paying little attention now to what he was doing. He allowed his wheelchair to get too close to the edge of the pavement in the top part of Toynbee Street as he entered it. The wheel dropped over the edge of the kerbstone and pitched Waldron out of his chair onto the hard cobbled road surface. He hardly felt a thing; he gashed the left side of his forehead and lay still momentarily trying to gauge in his drunken and spinning mind what had happened.

Holden emerged from The Ten Bells. He was curious as to where Waldron might have gone, and it was fortunate for Waldron that his appearance onto the pavement outside the pub occurred when it did. Holden in his instinctive survivor's way was scanning the environment outside of the pub. In seconds he saw his crippled former subordinate on the floor out of his chair. He also saw the lads that he had earlier encountered cross Commercial Street from outside of Christchurch, he suspected, to prey on the weak. This time Holden would be less merciful and tolerant. He crossed Commercial Street after them and followed the group into the top end of Toynbee Street where they had already surrounded the helpless Waldron and had begun to taunt him. Holden drew his Webley pistol as he reached the pavement, Waldron was probably too drunk, he assumed, to remember that he had a pistol too. He gave no warning, he had already done that. He felt quite confident that the constant drone of the horse traffic along the cobbles of the main street would drown out the noise of several cracks of gun fire.

Holden levelled his pistol at a distance of around fifteen feet from the youths and felled two before the others could react. The two he targeted received wounds to the centre of their backs, not killing them instantly but leading to a slow lingering death. The other two looked around in fear to where the shots had been fired from; they recognised their nemesis immediately. They attempted to run away south in Toynbee Street. Holden, still with the pistol levelled single handed, paused for a moment. He didn't normally like to shoot an enemy in the back. In his now confused sense of moral code it didn't seem like the right thing. In this case he forced himself to make an exception as he saw these weak young men as 'hyenas', preying off of the weak or misfortune of others. They had made about forty feet from him as he coolly engaged them one at a time in his sights. It took three shots to fell them both leaving him with only one round left in the weapon. He knew he wouldn't need it yet.

As the wounded and dying young men lay on the cold cobbles, Holden briskly lifted Waldron back into his chair and then pushed him off west into Millers Court to find their way through to the City of London and an escape by flagging down a carriage in Bishopsgate. Holden felt no remorse, only annoyance that Waldron had come close to letting him down again. He gave Waldron his clean handkerchief to hold over his head wound as the carriage made its way west and back to Ebury Street. He was concerned about taking him on the next and final overseas trip. Alcohol consumption would no longer be tolerated. Holden was about to speak when he began a violent coughing fit. He was forced to grab the handkerchief back from Waldron to hold it over his mouth. Coughing into it he pulled it away as he stopped to see that he had ejected some blood stained mucus. They both stared at the stained cotton, each knowing the significance of what they saw. Waldron spoke first.

"T.B then, Boss. Best you get some opium for that to relieve the pain." Holden couldn't bear to enter into conversation with Waldron at this point; he had put them in danger again and now he began to fear for his own health and ability to complete his twisted vendetta.

"Shut up, Wally. Just shut up." Holden stared out the window as Waldron eventually fell asleep.

Chapter Fifteen

August 27th, Prague 10.a.m

The Ministerial party all walked across the Karlov Bridge on their first full day in Prague; Patterson and Lady Patterson, Ramsey Phillips, Fiona Shaw with no researchers available at present, Robert Ford and Bob Spicer. Karen Wood had been forced to stay in London as her ailing son, Nigel, had had several days of increasingly poor health. She wanted to be able to see him every day and be close at hand if the worst came to pass. It pleased Ford, but only as it kept her safe from the increasingly violent Patterson when he made his sexual demands. With a murderous scandal surrounding this corrupt politician, as soon as Ford had got to the bottom of it he would use it as leverage for him to leave Karen alone. A comfortable roof over her head and money to care for Nigel was not an object for her any longer; Ford could pay for both with the continuing profits of his successful investments, and it seemed she would imminently move into Eaton Square permanently anyway.

The party were heading towards Prague castle and a meeting with the Austrian Secretary of State to discuss the sale of small arms technology by Britain for use by their armed forces. The Ministerial party admired the statues along the bridge, which spanned five hundred and twenty meters across the Vltava River, of famous personalities and Saints that featured heavily in Czech history. The bridge was distinctly Gothic and until 1741 was the city's only river crossing. Ford looked down at the calm flowing river below in between his eagle-eyed scanning of the area they were constantly moving into ahead of them. He had an ever growing sense of apprehension over this current protection assignment, although sometimes he considered it unfounded as so far each victim had been attacked alone. Would his adversary or group of adversaries strike at the protected party to achieve their ultimate aim, if it was the death of Patterson. As they passed St Ludmilla he noted how particularly impressive Prague castle was atop its hill location; a site that had been occupied by a castle structure since the ninth century. At the end of the bridge they passed under the Little Quarter Tower and made their way along Mostecka and eventually through to Thunovska and up the steps past the Panny Marie church to the castle. The climb was energetic but not exhausting. They were greeted at the first courtyard just in front of the Mathias Gate by a delegation of uniformed Austrian army officers. Their uniform was reflective of that of their German neighbours, most likely the influence of the Prussians over the years, and these men represented the equivalent to the English Chiefs of Staff of the military but for the Austro-Hungarian Empire. Unbeknown to Ford, this meeting was a low key diplomatic discussion of convenience to Patterson to mask his meeting with the Bishop of Prague. He had no intention of sharing English technology with the 'Arian upstarts' as he referred to them, so he would price it out of their reach.

Ford was about to be dismissed again for several hours until the party would be ready to depart. Being treated in an unconventional way with disregard for the preferred working practices of Special Branch protection was now becoming commonplace to him. He saw Patterson having a quiet conversation with Spicer before the Minister called Ford over to speak to him. What he also noticed between the two of them sent a cold shiver down his spine and confirmed his worst fears; as they finished their brief but intense conversation Patterson and Spicer shook hands. Ford could see and tell from the experience he had gained from Abberline that Spicer was also a Mason. Ford from then on knew that his colleague was bound to the Minister by duty, but more strongly by his Masonic oaths and allegiance. He would have to be very cautious. Had Spicer told the Minister of his relationship with Karen Wood? By the fact that Ford was still on the assignment he assumed not.

Around them were the Austro-Hungarian officers and as Ford approached Patterson he also noticed what appeared to be enlisted men dotted around the edges of the courtyard. There were also two men with military bearing in smart civilian clothes stood in the Mathias Gateway. They were quite obviously protection operatives for the other side.

"Inspector, we'll be in the secure confines of the castle from now until around four this afternoon. I've suggested to Spicer that if he wishes to stay here during this time, you can have the time off and then at four you can swap over. He can relax while you supervise the return to the hotel and security until late evening. Is that agreeable?" Ford looked Patterson harshly in the eye, his own slightly squinting with distrust. It was a reflex action that he couldn't help.

"No." Ford deliberately paused before continuing, watching Patterson feel distinctly uncomfortable with this slightly public disagreement. Just before the embarrassed Minister, actually lost for words, could reply he continued. "The principle is all right, but your choice of request to Spicer first to approve is unacceptable." Ford purposefully didn't address him as 'sir' at anytime. "If you choose to suggest such a course then you will speak to me first. I am your personal protection officer, despite any wishes you might currently have, and additionally by rank I hold ultimate responsibility for your safety. On the next occasion I expect you to speak to me first. The plan is, however, 'agreeable' so I will be here promptly at four o'clock. Good day." Before Patterson, who was completely lost for words, could reply Ford walked off into Hradcanske Namesti and towards the Schwarzenburg Palace.

Patterson looked on incredulously. He was stunned to have been addressed this way. In truth, it was only conduct that Ford was at fault with. His sentiments of how the issue of protection should have been dealt with, Patterson had to concede to himself, were quite correct. He coughed, regained his own composure and smiled warmly to the most senior officer as he turned back to them. This officer then led the way through to the Second Courtyard and then beyond into the inner confines of the mainly baroque castle passing by the Rose window of the Cathedral as they entered. The meeting with the military officials would not take too long. He paid particular interest to the Cathedral as he passed by it. In a little under two hours he would be meeting with the Bishop of Prague, Cardinal Lev Sklinski, to secure the final funding for his operation. The promise of a perpetual ten percent stake in the profits of Empire Petroleum to the Catholic Church had so far proved a good incentive; he saw that it should be just as lucrative to the diocese here as elsewhere.

The entire group spent the next forty-five minutes touring the castle until they settled in the Diet Hall of the Royal Palace, the 'Kralovsky Palac', for Patterson to enter into the formal discussion with the Austro-Hungarians over the sale of weapon technology. Whatever they were prepared to bid it was never going to be enough. They sat around a large ornate dark oak table in the room that dated from 1563 with its current interior. It had been rebuilt in that year by Bonifaz Wohlmut following a fire and the destruction of its original 1541 decoration.

The negotiations remained polite and cordial but as Patterson held his ground over the price of the weapon technology the room developed an atmosphere of unease. The members of the United Kingdom party shifted in their seats under the uncompromising stares of their opposition. Spicer had remained outside due to not being a member of the official Ministry team. He listened in from the other side of a heavy wood and iron door. Finally the chief negotiator for the Austro-Hungarians slammed down a large ledger type book he had in front of him and stood up. He was dressed in a very ornate and colourful uniform, typically Prussian with its Teutonic styling, and politely nodded and smiled at Patterson. He spoke through what was in truth a sneer as Patterson slowly stood to match him.

"I am sorry, Sir Cecil, that we cannot come to a mutually advantageous deal. Even some sort of compromise would have been nice over the price of the technology or an additional incentive to share it. It seems we will discover things for ourselves. If Europe ever falls into a great war, it will be interesting to see who has the most efficient weapons. For now it maybe you, but things change. Rapidly." He offered his hand to Patterson. He shook it in return and replied.

"I am sorry, General. But business must be reciprocal and I don't think we seem to be able to have our side of the deal matched. My best wishes to the Royal Family, please. Perhaps we might meet again."

"Perhaps not," said the General as his smile fell from his mouth and he disengaged from Patterson's handshake. He clicked his heels, turned and left the hall with the rest of the party standing and following him out.

The Dressmaker Connection

Now it was time for Patterson to lose the rest of his group for an hour or so. He addressed them whilst all still at the table.

"Sorry, folks, a deal with them obviously wasn't to be." It never had been, he knew that. He had devised the whole trip fooling them into meeting him just to get to Prague on an official basis. "So. I have to go to the St Vitus's Cathedral; I feel in the wake of the terrible events of the last few weeks that some prayer time and absolution in an unfamiliar church would be comforting. Please, I shall meet you all back the hotel. Your time is now your own. Patterson went to the door of the hall and opened it to show them all out in a friendly manner. After his staff had all walked out he was left facing Spicer. The less he always knew the better.

"Bob, I wish to be alone in the cathedral for half an hour or so. I'm sure I should be quite safe. May I meet you at the Mathias Gate where we came in when I am finished?"

Spicer considered the request for a moment and looked Patterson in the eye. This man had power over him in so many ways, although it seemed like a reasonable request. He had heard the Minister's reasons through the door being ajar when the General and his staff had left.

"All right, sir. I'll see you at the gate." Spicer then escorted Patterson from the palace to the Cathedral and left the Minister to his own devices in the ornately spectacular church building. The traditionally gothic cathedral had begun construction in 1344 under the direction of John of Luxembourg. Housing the tomb of 'Good King' Wenceslas it still wasn't truly completed with some art work yet to be commissioned and finished. Inside it contained much traditional architecture such as gothic vaulting, flying buttresses and patterned stone flooring. It was famous too for a fourteenth century mosaic of the last judgement by the main entrance.

Having been escorted to the door of the Cathedral by Spicer, Patterson entered and made his way up into the chancel. There a traditionally robed priest ushered him into an open confessional box. He sat down and pulled the door shut behind him. As soon as it had clicked shut the curtain was drawn back to reveal the drawn, harsh face of Cardinal Lev Sklinski dressed in fine velvet burgundy and black robes with a matching skullcap. He had rosary beads around his neck as well as an ornate brass or gold cross. The story that Patterson had so far spun to the other cardinals he had coerced money from was about to be used again as a subterfuge. Part of what he was offering was true but he was not going to allow them any religious autonomy in his soon to be conquered regions. He knew that it was the root of conflict too often. He would, however, give the church a healthy return on its financial investment in his project. Patterson initiated the conversation.

"Cardinal, it is kind of you to see me. I can assure you it is time well spent by listening to my proposal."

"So the other cardinals have told me, Mr Patterson."

"I call the project 'Operation Auric Noir'. With the rapid growth in the use of internal combustion engines there is the need to keep supplies of fuel for them readily available. It is my intention that Empire Petroleum will be at the forefront of this industrial demand. I am assembling a team of surveyors and engineers to be at the vanguard of exploration into Afghanistan, a wild and desolate country who may well respond favourably to mission work by churchmen during the industrialisation of their country. After all, they will need guidance on how to use their new found wealth from the people of the west and their demands for oil."

In truth Patterson's intentions were solely, with his private army being formed by Major Hoare, to secure the supplies of oil that Holden must have found under the Kuh e Baba mountains and defend it vigorously from the locals. Ensure its safe transfer to the west and to maintain a hold on this industrial 'gold mine' at all costs, using violence to do so with extreme prejudice. The population could go hang for all he cared. The inducement he had offered the various diocese could not be resisted and was based on a half promise; allowing them to establish a mission in the country. It would be, quite possibly, at the expense of their own lives. In truth he would not waste valuable defensive resources nurse-maiding idealistic priests. Since the invention of the internal combustion engine and the formation of his company Empire Petroleum, his use of his political position had always been about personal gain. With his ministerial responsibility had come resources he could use at no expense to himself on several occasions, such as Holden's original survey in 1898 and his subsequent follow up visit to establish the truth in the legend of the 'black gold'. Knowing that it now existed he would stop at nothing to try to gain as much control of the oil market as he could.

Sklinski looked at him with his piercing eyes displaying extreme caution, bordering on cynicism.

"Cardinal, for the sum of the equivalent of five hundred thousand English pounds, I will guarantee you a return of two hundred percent. So if you can give me that I will return to you the equivalent of a million and a half pounds in no more than twelve months. How much could the church do with that then?" The cardinal continued to stare at him once he had finished and initially said nothing. He was, however, very attracted by Patterson's offer. Indeed the church could do a great deal with that sort of return on its money; especially even after he had perhaps creamed off somewhere between five and ten percent for himself. No one would question his request to use church funds; he was the most senior priest in Prague. With that in mind if they did not know what the potential capital return was, then they would not miss some of it. Oddly, due to the fallibility of human nature even in some holy men, his counterparts in Rome and Paris had privately had similar notions succumbing to that most basic human sin; greed.

"All right, Mr Patterson, you shall borrow the money as you wish, with the undertaking that it is returned with the promised capital gain in twelve months or less. As we wish to organise missions in Afghanistan then we will expect the co-operation of you and your men." Even lying to a priest was no great hurdle to the calculatingly greed-filled industrialist that Patterson was.

"You have my word, Cardinal. My head of operations will be more than helpful once a stable 'bridgehead' as it were has been established." Hoare would certainly welcome them to their fortified supply depots as he established them, but beyond these enclosures the missionaries would have to fend for themselves.

"Good. Mr Patterson you will have to give me details of a bank so I can make the necessary arrangements. Of course records of this transaction will be kept to a minimum," what Sklinski meant by this was that they would be non-existent. He couldn't have his own little piece of profiteering detected. This was music to Patterson's ears. "And of course I'll ensure that you are notified of the money's availability."

"Thank you, Cardinal, it has been a pleasure."

"With that over with, my son, is there anything that you would truly like to confess?" Asked Sklinski, compelled to always complete his spiritual tasks. Patterson thought long and hard about his evil, deceitful utterly sinful life. He answered the cardinal with confidence.

"No, father, thank you there isn't."

* * *

London, late morning.

The Brompton Road. Karen Wood walked along the bustling thoroughfare on her way to the nursery from her residence in Wilton Crescent. Nigel was becoming progressively weaker so she now tried to spend as much time with him as possible. When the cruel Minister was away it was easy to spend most of the day with him if she wished. With the fine summer weather it allowed her to take him to the almost adjacent Hyde Park. The sickly boy loved to see the birds on the Serpentine and the red squirrels in the trees as Karen pushed him along in a child's wheelchair. She entered the fine red brick and white portico building with a sense of trepidation that she felt in the pit of stomach. It was as if today would be the last day she would spend with her tragic son. The day before he had hardly been able to speak as he struggled to breathe. He had become pale beyond belief. He had lost what little weight he had and was quite skeletal in his appearance. As a result he felt the cold intently and even on such a lovely bright summers day the slight breeze that was in the air was enough to make him shiver if he was not prepared properly for the outdoors.

One of the nursing staff showed Karen to his room that he shared with three other sickly children. Nigel was there alone and appeared restfully asleep, clothed on top of his bed clothes. The warm sunshine was streaming in through the window onto his bed illuminating him. He appeared quite angelic in the light and it was its warmth that allowed him to rest upon the bed clothes. The nurse stood behind Karen as she looked in tearfully at her son. It was words from the nurse that broke her concentration as she stared at the boy.

"He has been so looking forward to today, Ms. Wood. Because of not getting out properly yesterday he has been determined to wrap up for a day in the park with you." Karen bit her lip and could hardly speak. She walked over to the bed and gently sat on the edge and began to lightly run her hand over Nigel's hair as he carried on sleeping. It was a tear falling from her eye onto his right cheek as he lay huddled slightly on his left side that woke the boy up. It took him a second or two to focus and then he instantly recognised his mother.

"Oh, mama, how wonderful that you are here. I slept very well last night and I have prepared all my most warmest clothes to venture out together. Is that all right?" He coughed a little as he finished and his voiced had indeed sounded rasping. Karen wiped the tears from her eyes and swallowed hard to speak, coughing to clear her throat.

"Of course it is all right. I've been looking forward to it too. We'll have a wonderful day. We'll walk around the Long Water and the Serpentine and then stop for muffins or macaroons or whatever you want at the tea house." Nigel slowly and weakly sat up and kissed his mother on the cheek. He could see from the outset that she was very sad, and with the stoicism that frequently only children can demonstrate he spoke to her about her sadness.

"Mother, don't be sad. The nurses say that I will soon be on the road to getting better. A day out in the park with you can only help." His time spent in the care of the nurses in fashionable and expensive Knightsbridge had given him an air and an accent that belied his humble East End origins. Karen was proud of the 'proper little gentleman' he was at merely six years old. His small, weak physical stature belied his age; he appeared younger with the development of not more than a four year old in his size. Karen hugged him tightly and kissed him upon his forehead in response to his display of affection.

She stood up by the bed and held his hand as he stood unsteadily on his feet next to her. She had never seen him so lacking strength and it was a source of concern for her. As she looked up to the doorway she saw the nurse was still there, looking on she seemed to have a similar air of concern. They helped the boy to his wheelchair having wrapped him up warmly, topping him off with a heavy woollen travel blanket around his legs and Karen pushed him out into the street and off in the direction of Wellington Arch and Hyde Park. They crossed Knightsbridge itself and entered the park via Albert Gate being careful of South Carriage Drive and then the bridleway as they first entered the calm, Central London open space. The sun shone down on a bright and warm day for most, but with the breeze in the air all day that still felt cool to the terminally ailing child. Karen pushed Nigel past Rotten Row and up to Serpentine Road to begin their circuit of the park's expanses of water.

Despite his illness, Nigel was a studious, intelligent boy capable even at just six years old of soaking up and retaining enormous amounts of information. He had studied much about Hyde Park in the days leading up to the trip and now in an ever weakening voice he conveyed some of the facts he had learnt to his mother before falling asleep.

"Henry the Eighth acquired this park land from the monks of Westminster Abbey in 1536. It wasn't opened to the public though until 1637 under Charles the first. People came and camped out here during the Great Plague to be safe from the city. Rotten Row comes from 'Route des Roi' French for Kings Road, mother, from when King William the third moved his court to Kensington Palace and had a illuminated road created so he could walk safely to St James' Palace." Karen was so proud of how bright the lad was, but could tell as they reached the bridge in West Carriage Drive that separated the northerly Long Water from the Serpentine, that all his keenness to pass on his discoveries was making him tired and short of breath. He wheezed heavily as he began again. "Queen Caroline, wife of George the second had the lakes created in the 1730s." He began to cough heavily as he finished speaking. Karen stopped the wheelchair and gently rubbed his back for him.

"Save your breath for a little while, my darling. That was very clever of you to learn all of those facts and thank you for sharing them. Now do you think it's time to get tea and cakes at the clubhouse by the lake?" He was now coughing so heavily in an awful rasping fashion that he could not speak. He nodded his head in keen acceptance and his eyes, despite much pain and discomfort, conveyed his enthusiasm for having tea and cake.

They were able to easily find a table outside the Clubhouse tea room that overlooked both The Serpentine and The Long Water, where they were served by a waitress. It was still relatively early in the day and few people had yet gathered at the fashionable park café, lunch was some time away, so they simply shared the terrace with those taking morning coffee.

"Nigel, what would you like then?" asked Karen as a waitress came and stood at the table side. He seemed to have a sparkle in his eyes as he ordered his favourite snack item that he savoured when in his mother's company.

"I would like a glass of warm milk and two macaroons please." There was enthusiasm in his voice. "What are you going to have, mama?" Karen looked at the menu and paused for a moment. She wished that Ford was here to enjoy such simple, passive pleasures as a walk in the park in the sun as a family. Nigel had only heard of Robert Ford and was yet to meet the man who may become his stepfather, a family member he had never known.

"I shall have a Monsoon Malabar pot of coffee, please and a buttered scone." The waitress disappeared into the Clubhouse tea room as Karen and Nigel sat side by side at the table holding hands on Nigel's lap. It wasn't long before their order arrived and they both began to enjoy it. With his breathing difficulties Nigel was aware that he had to eat slowly to avoid the disastrous consequence of food or drink entering his delicate and damaged lungs by mistake.

They watched the birds on the lake side as they ate as well as those that were bobbing around in the water, occasionally disturbed by rowing boats. As the lad began to finish Karen could see that he was looking particularly pale and shivery, and yet he had looked so well when they had first sat down.

"Nigel, are you all right?" asked his concerned mother, taking hold of his hand more tightly. He was feeling ice cold.

"Mother, would you hold me?" There was a disturbing calm in his voice. She stood and lifted him out of his wheelchair ensuring that the blanket stayed wrapped around his shivering, weakened body. She sat back down into the wrought iron chair she had just vacated and held onto the boy tightly. She was trying to share bodily warmth. It was a warm day and Karen was confused that he should be suffering so. She would very soon have to get him back to the nursery.

"Tell me about Robert then, mama." He huddled tightly into her as she spoke clutching the lapels of her coat, as if trying to get inside it to gain additional warmth. He physically appeared scared and yet verbally gave no signs.

"Well, he's quite tall and lean, about forty, always smartly dressed. He's quite tough physically, he used to box and he fences, but he is a very warm and tender man. Generous. You'd like each other, he could teach you sport type things on summers days like this." She was rocking gently as she spoke to hopefully calm Nigel a little. His awful trembling was beginning to subside a little. He spoke in response, but his voice seemed very weak.

"Where is he from? Do we know it?"

"Yes, he comes from the East End, where I lived with your father before he went away with the army. Now he lives near to here and works from Scotland Yard. He's a real detective." Nigel had now closed his eyes. He nodded and vaguely grunted in a response to her answer. His shivering had stopped completely. Karen went cold at the thought of what might be happening, especially in mind to what one of the nurses had said.

Karen looked up into the clear blue, cloudless, August sky with her eyes full of tears. She continued to rock gently as she looked back down into Nigel's face. His eyes were completely closed giving him the appearance of looking blissfully asleep. He was making no rasping sounds; he was not trembling at all; he was not breathing any longer. Karen pulled him close to her and wrapped the blanket fully around him as she sobbed quietly to herself. She could only take comfort that his departure from life had been peaceful and in the arms of his loving mother, the place that most soldiers mortally wounded always cry for. In his tragic short life he had at least not wanted for anything. Having found someone in her life who loved her, the most difficult thing she would have to cope with in the next few days would be dealing with this tragedy on her own without Ford. She held on to the boy as the water lapped the shore and the world went by, oblivious to the sad passing of such an innocent.

* * *

Prague, 10.p.m

The Ministerial party were back safely and settled in their rooms at the hotel. Even Patterson was, bizarrely, back in his room early. Mark Vincent was on his usual overseas corridor duty again allowing Ford and Spicer to retire and relax. Ford, with the absence of Karen in the party, returned to his room. He took a hot bath and enjoyed a large, chilled glass of Hapsburg Absinthe over a generous glassful of ice and, for once in quite a while, he seemed totally relaxed. The window of the bathroom was closed which allowed a build up of condensation in the Spartan but well appointed bathroom. It gave it the air of a Turkish bath. It made the chilled Absinthe's intoxicating effect intrude on his mind in an accelerated fashion. He stared with relaxed eyes at the glass, the condensation upon which was exaggerated by the heat from the bath. He missed Karen not being there; her sensuality, her physicality and the emotional stability and calm that she elicited from within him. He would have to get out once he had finished his glass as he didn't want the indignity of drowning and being found dead in a bathroom in Prague, despite of the quality and comfort of the hotel.

He looked forward to his next fencing lesson. It was a discipline that taught him so much, elements that had he known back then, would have made him an even more successful pugilist than he was. He missed Moreau's wise counsel and most of all the opportunity to vent aggression in a controlled and worthwhile way.

Out of the bath and dressed in a towel wrapped around his waist, he looked at himself in the full length mirror in the bedroom. He was still lean and was proud of the fact, it helped engender within him his sense of being able to hold his own physically, especially knowing that in the world of protection he may have to fight at any time and in different ways.

The absinthe hadn't dulled his senses enough for sleep as yet, although he could feel its vaguely unsteadying effects. He put his glass down on the sideboard in his room and opened a small leather travelling bag. From a pocket he pulled out a slotted and perforated absinthe spoon and a bag that contained some sugar lumps. He placed a cube on the spoon and then rested it across the top of the glass. He poured some more absinthe over the cube, which then filtered into the glass. There were some vague remnants of ice cubes still within it. He grabbed a packet of hotel matches and held a burning match to the alcohol soaked sugar cube. It caught fire and hissed and crackled emitting a blue flame as it did so. He allowed it to burn for half a minute and then tipped the spoon into the glass. The rest of the liquid immediately ignited with a translucent blue flame instantly dissolving the remnants of the ice cube. Again he let it flame for nearly half a minute and then blew it out. He held the smoking glass up to his nose; the vapour was overpowering, pure alcohol. He placed the glass to his lips and drank generously from it. The burning heightened the alcoholic effect which hit him instantly and he felt drunk in seconds. He collapsed on to his bed with the glass still in his hand as his tired and spinning mind collected thoughts prior to falling asleep.

Ford remained deeply perplexed by the continuing series of murders. It seemed there was no one left to question over the minister's story relating to the events in Afghanistan in 1898; all the members of the expeditionary party were conveniently dead; the archivist of the original report was dead, and the report itself was scant. He was convinced from his years of policing that Patterson was withholding some vital piece of information. Something that would no doubt implicate him in wrong-doing, but at the same time point to someone who would have a motive for wanting to take revenge against him. Ford took another sip from the glass; the strong aniseed taste stimulated his taste buds while the alcohol relaxed his mind and body almost to the point of unconsciousness. What would Abberline have done? Perhaps his best course of action might be to seek the wisdom of the former detective chief inspector that had been so influential in his early career.

Chapter Sixteen

Spicer was elsewhere in the city trying to have a relaxing evening to allow his mind to once and for all establish where his loyalty and sense of duty lay. He strolled in the bustling late evening in the Old Town Square with its fine architecture and sense of space that allowed it to seem un-crowded. It was the architecture that he was particularly admiring; the Rococo stucco work of the light coloured stone buildings of the East side that led up to the frontage of the Church of our Lady before Tyn with its imposing gothic twin towers and solid gold effigy of the Virgin Mary. The church's true frontage was slightly occluded by the Romanesque arcaded houses with their eighteenth century facades. He then turned to the buildings of the north side which included the Church of St Nicholas and the art nouveau buildings designed by Oswald Polivka only six years earlier with their fine figurines and artwork in the gallery fronts of the upper façade.

Despite his mundane and less than cultured frontage, Spicer did appreciate fine buildings and the creativity that would go into designing and building them. But now it was time for a drink to relax and consider where his torn loyalties lay; he found himself taking a seat on the terrace of the Salvatora, a restaurant on the north side of the square. Spicer nestled into a comfortable wicker dining chair and pulled himself into the matching table. He opened the menu and instantly realised that this was a pointless act. He slammed it down in frustration and looked out into the void of the populated square on a warm late summer's evening.

He became aware of a well dressed figure stood beside him. He looked up to see a lean, well dressed but weathered looking man in a panama hat looking down at him. The stranger spoke as they made eye contact.

"Sorry, old man. Couldn't help but notice you seem a bit lost with the menu. My name is Liam Dwell-Dohin. I'm a regular in Prague and can speak a little of the lingo and know a little of the customs. Didn't know if you wanted any help?" Ford would have recognised this man immediately from Venice. But the slightly less dedicated Spicer had no idea that this man had been in his presence before; watching with predatory eyes from the near distance. Frustrated by his own lack of comprehension, and wanting something to eat desperately despite the wish for his own company, he decided to take up Mr Dwell-Dohin's offer. He stood and spoke, proffering a handshake.

"That's very kind of you, Mr Dwell er..."

"Dwell-Dohin, but please call me Liam." He took Spicer's hand and firmly shook it in return. William Holden, satisfied as he suspected that this individual didn't recognise him, sat down. "To drink I recommend that we ask for a half carafe of chilled Absinthe with some extra ice in the glasses. Prague produces some fine labels and personally I prefer it to the traditional Becherovka liqueur. I'm sorry; I didn't catch your name, sir?" Holden was deliberately very warm and friendly in his demeanour. He knew that it would assist to lull his victim into a false sense of security.

"Bob Spicer. Sorry. I need to relax so I'll go with your recommendation of the Absinthe. Then perhaps you could guide me through what to eat." Spicer felt at ease with this friendly Englishman. Holden's subtle use of questions and answers would, coupled with the alcohol, loosen the tongue of the policeman for him to elicit all the information he needed. A waiter attended their table and Holden spoke quite competently to him in Czech. Spicer was surprised and impressed and made out that he ordered more that just the Absinthe.

"I take you have ordered drinks and food then, Liam?" he asked quizzically.

"Yes. I hope you will excuse the liberty. I have skipped a starter and ordered us both a traditional main course. Its pot roasted fillet of beef served with sliced bread dumplings, a slightly sweet creamy vegetable sauce and garnished with cranberries. I have also ordered a red Frankovka wine to accompany the beef." Holden offered Spicer a cigarillo from a sleek silver case that he pulled from inside the jacket pocket of his grey linen suit. Spicer took one as he replied.

"Sounds great. I really need to just have a pleasant meal, a good drink and really, damn it I wasn't going to but, enjoy some relaxed conversation in the evening air, and watch the world go by."

"Well, not too many of our countrymen here so I'm obliged to help." Holden struck a match and offered it to Spicer first. He lent forward slightly and lit his cigarillo. He puffed it several times to get the end glowing and enjoyed the sweet taste of its flavour and the mind spinning result of the inhalation of the smoke. Holden lit his own cigarillo and shook out the match and tossed it into the cut glass ashtray on the table. The Absinthe arrived. The carafe was heavy with condensation from the ice cold drink within coming into contact with the balmy summer atmosphere. The waiter gave them each a glass filled with ice and then placed the carafe on the table along with a large clear bottle containing chilled water. They rested on the white, crisp, heavy linen table cloth and stained it slightly as the condensation ran down each vessel to its base. Holden took charge of the drinks, much to Spicer's relief, and poured them each a generous glass of the green aniseed base spirit. Holden picked up his own glass which signalled to Spicer to do the same and held it up to his dining companion. Holden made the toast.

"Well cheers, old man. Here's to happy holidays in the east." Spicer took a very generous mouthful of the cold, mind rupturing liquid.

Holden had ordered some Hapsburg which was renown as the second strongest with a rating of eighty-nine percent proof. It succeeded in making Spicer feel giddy in his seat, but at the same time it gave him quite a rush. Holden spoke again seeing the effect of the drink on his new found acquaintance.

"So, Bob. What line of work are you in? Are you in Prague on business or pleasure?" Spicer wasn't sure how to answer this question for a moment or two. He took another generous drink of Absinthe to help him make a decision. It did help as his mind again began to spin. 'Damn it. He seems like a reasonable chap. I'm not likely to see him again. I'll tell him the truth. It'll sound quite thrilling too.' Spicer coughed and composed himself to speak, already concerned that the two large mouthfuls he had taken might make him slur his speech. He put his glass down as he began, and to his horror, but also to his contentment, Mr Dwell-Dohin topped his glass up.

"Well. Liam. It's like this. I'm a policeman from Scotland Yard," he knew that the world renown 'Scotland Yard' always sounded good, "and I am one of the personal protection officers to Sir Cecil Patterson." Holden showed a false sentiment of being impressed.

"My, goodness. I didn't know there was such a thing. That must be quite a dangerous job. Are you here with work then?" A sense of creating an impression on a respectable middleclass gentleman made Spicer relax his guard and let his tongue wag too freely.

"Well, actually, I'm here with the Minister now. He's on official business here." Holden sat forward in his seat; he gave an air of naïve intrigue knowing that his own curiosity had some questions to be answered.

"Cripes. I suppose he is a bit of a target with all these killings around him. Who's looking after him now then?" Holden took a long drag on his cigarillo and then sat back. He lifted his head slightly and blew the smoke into the air.

"Ah. There is a team of three of us when we're abroad. Me, a chap called Ford who is in charge, and then another chap called Mark who does the night shift of sitting outside the Minister's room when he's asleep and me and Ford are on some down time. Works very well really." Spicer had another drink of Absinthe. He was in a full flow of drunken bravado. He got quite a sense of thrill from portraying his work as dangerous, exciting and highly specialised. To a layman as Dwell-Dohin seemed to be, he must have come across as a real hero. Where his dinner companion was concerned nothing could be further from the truth. To a professional such as Holden, Spicer was a loose tongued fool. By the next morning he would be dead from allowing himself to get too drunk and therefore compromised, and he would have betrayed all the intelligence that Holden wanted regarding the depth of Patterson's protection. He couldn't rely on his inside man to get all that right as the police seemed to play their cards 'close to their chests' regarding questions by the Minister's staff over protection. This, as he had hoped, was proving to be the perfect opportunity.

"My god. How clever. Is that what you do in England too?"

"No, works differently there. Uniform police guard his house all the time, me and Ford do the protection together through the day normally, like we do here, and there we're allowed to carry guns too. Overseas we're not always allowed." Holden didn't really need to know much more. The only downside was having to dine with this drunken, common policeman who would no doubt be edifying himself all evening. Still getting him drunk, perhaps even to the point of not being able to walk, would make the whole process of his demise much easier.

The wine came and Holden was given the opportunity by the waiter to try some first, he enjoyed the retention of such correct etiquette. The Frankovka with its deep red colour and aroma of plum and morello cherry was very palatable indeed. It would certainly complement the Absinthe in making this fool Spicer a drunken wreck, who would not know what was happening to him until he was suffering from a hangover and dehydration. The glasses were filled by the waiter and then the food arrived. They both tucked in, Spicer with little in the way of correct table manners, and enjoyed the traditional fayre in front of them.

A carriage was parked in the square with a sole occupant who sat on the driver's perch watching the activity on the restaurant terrace from a discreet distance. Waldron sat ready to bring the carriage forward when he saw the signal from Holden. His wheelchair was strapped at the back of the carriage under a blanket, so for all intents and purposes it looked like a simple load of cases or boxes.

"This is bloody good grub, Liam," slurred Spicer as some dumpling fell from the side of his mouth. Holden had to work hard to hide is disgust at the lack of class and manners being displayed.

"Yes, it is some of the best dumpling I've had." He noticed Spicer's glass was empty. He topped it up generously with the Frankovka. He needn't have worried; Spicer was beyond the point of no return towards a heavily drunken stupor. By the time he finished this last glass of wine he would have to be carried to the carriage, or at least heavily supported. Holden watched down his nose as Spicer finished the last of his food.

"Well, Bob. I can't manage a dessert, I don't know about you. I have to be off very imminently too." This panicked Spicer. He knew he was very drunk and he had bargained on a lift to get him back to the hotel.

"Oh. Er. Could I catch a lift with you back to my hotel? By embarrassing admission I don't think my legs would get me there, Liam." Spicer was struggling to be coherent and had to concentrate greatly on the simplistic and natural task of speech. 'Perfect' thought Holden. 'A willing passenger'. Spicer struggled for his wallet as Holden ordered the bill; despite being drunk he was keen to pay his share. Holden, ever the scrupulously honest gentleman, saw that he allowed Spicer to pay only his half as he took the money from the drunk's uncoordinated hand.

He helped Spicer to his feet all under the keen gaze of Waldron on the coach. He whipped the reins gently and rolled the coach forward and up to the edge of the terrace of the restaurant in the square at the kerb's edge. Holden comfortably and without suspicion assisted Spicer on board and Waldron drove off. Waldron left via the south-west corner of the square and found himself driving along Karlova directly towards the spectacular Karlov Bridge. They passed under the Old Town Bridge Tower, with its gothic magnificence designed by Peter Parler at the end of the fourteenth century, and then began rumbling over the cobbles of the bridge itself. Holden looked at Spicer who was slumped against the side of the carriage beside him; he was unconscious and didn't look as if he would be regaining any semblance of consciousness particularly soon. Holden stared out of the windows at the passing classical statues adorning the bridge on both sides. Pieta, St Joseph, St Ann, St Augustine to name but a few, and as they reached the Little Quarter end of the bridge they passed by the statue of St Wenceslas himself; perhaps the most famous of Czech icons.

The carriage skirted around the base of the magnificent Prague Castle in all it's baroque finery and the many buildings that constituted it, including the Lobkowicz Palace and St Vitus's Cathedral. The streets were dimly lit by 'Yablochkov candle' electric lights that seemed now, at well after 11.30.p.m, to make the streets appear shadowy and sinister. Having passed the most south western part of the castle Waldron turned the carriage north along the boulevard Kepelerova to eventually arrive at the tram depot at Stresovicka. Trams were the mainstay of public transport around the Czech capital and had been for many years, initially horse drawn with the system's inception in 1876 and then moving over to the first electric trams in 1891, the latter now constituting the mainstay of the fleet. Spicer was unconscious when they arrived. This would make it extremely easy to carry out their plan for continued revenge against the Minister, a trail of death that was now at its penultimate stage.

Chapter Seventeen

Spicer came around alone, uncomfortable, confused and in total darkness at a time that he had no way of determining. It was in fact just approaching five in the morning. He found himself blindfolded and gagged; his body was aching intensely all over from having been resting on a hard floor. He found his arms were outstretched, tied together at the wrists and then elevating upwards, as were his legs but tied at the ankles. He could not quite determine what he was attached to, but each end seemed metallic and the floor was obviously concrete. When the noise started he would only have seconds to guess where he was prior to a slow painful death. He had been tied to the rear towing hook of one tram in the sidings; this was where his arms were uncomfortably confined, whilst his legs were attached to the recessed towing eye at the front of the next tram in the sidings.

He was scared. Deeply terrified that he was about to experience an excruciatingly painful demise; he should have taken more notice of Ford. But it was too late. He had allowed his allegiances to fall the wrong way, influenced by what amounted to corrupted loyalty. He now realised as his stomach began to burn with the sense of fear and alcohol induced dehydration that he was about to die; he could warn no one and do nothing to escape it. His mouth was dry and he began to sob with his body convulsing uncontrollably. The trams being electric he didn't realise that the driver had climbed aboard the lead tram and was preparing to move. Still not knowing what he was tied between, it was only in the brief second before he was agonisingly killed that he knew that death was upon him. He felt the ropes at each end of his body go taut as the lead tram began to ease away from the sidings; the driver would feel nothing of the minor and momentary resistance offered by a taut human body. As the pain then only a split second after the ropes tensed set in, he screamed. The sound was so muffled that no one could hear him over the metallic rattling and clanking of the trams running gear. Then Spicer was torn in half.

His legs, as were Pete Burwell's six years before in Afghanistan, were torn out of their sockets in the hip joints and left attached to the rear most tram. The rest of him was dragged off in unimaginable pain along Stresovicka towards the centre of Prague. He lived and remained conscious for about two minutes before dying of massive blood loss and the enormous trauma of the blunt injuries he received. The authorities within the hour, having discovered the murder when a shocked crowd of workers waiting at a tram stop saw the car go by dragging half a man behind it, would trace the trail of ever thickening blood back to the tram depot. Prague had never before witnessed such a hideous and cruel crime. Once Patterson was aware of the nature of the murder, he would have a new assignment for the unscrupulous and coldly calculating Major Hoare, prior to the planned invasion of Afghanistan and its martial colonisation for industrial purposes.

* * *

August 28th, 10.a.m

Ford stood in the clinical, tiled Czech mortuary and looked down on the face of his dead colleague and the pained expression of agony that the face possessed. Spicer's body and features had been cleaned up by the attendants and a sheet covered the rest of his body. The sag in the middle of the sheet indicated where his body was detached from his legs. Gathered around the table with Ford were Patterson, Mark Vincent and a lone Prague detective who had an excellent command of English. Ford broke the silence desperate to discover what had happened, speaking to the detective.

"Inspector, what happened, please?"

"Mr Ford, your colleague was tied between two early morning trams and pulled in two when the lead one left the sidings while the other remained. He would not have died instantly, but quite quickly. I am sorry to say that we have reports of him screaming for a minute or two after it happened until he lost consciousness and died. Whoever did this to him was indeed someone acting with a high degree of cruelty." As the explanation was given Ford stared at Patterson the whole time. The eye contact had not been reciprocal; Patterson appeared scared, and more than ever as if he had something to hide.

"Well, Sir Cecil. What do you think of that? Does it have any relevance to you in its cruel and maybe ritualistic nature?" Patterson was slow to answer. Ford could see that he was trembling slightly and swallowed hard before he replied. His mouth felt very dry.

"Inspector, I do agree that it appears ritualistic. I am in agreement that perhaps someone is after me or my staff."

"Nothing to add, Sir?" said Ford with arrogant suspicion. Patterson momentarily looked him in the eye and left the room, either unable or not willing to speak to Ford any further.

"Thank you, Inspector," said Ford to the Czech detective, "my colleague here, Constable Vincent, will make the necessary arrangements with you."

Ford left quickly after Patterson. He loathed the man but his duty was to protect him. He met him aboard their waiting carriage and they made their way back to the hotel. Everyone was due to depart this morning according to Patterson's schedule, but everyone now just wanted to return to London that little bit sooner to try to escape the memory of the horrors on the visit to Prague.

*　*　*

September 2nd, London

Marcus Hoare was the equal of William Holden in ingenuity, resilience and guile; but he far exceeded Holden in his overdeveloped natural sense of cruelty. Having attended Essendon House he had discovered exactly where the elusive Captain Holden was staying in London along with his crippled ex-subordinate, and indeed established that they were both alive. It hadn't taken much cruelty on the part of Hoare to illicit the information he needed from one of the stable hands regarding Holden. The opportunity for coarse sexual gratification with her had also been quite pleasurable. From his instructions two days before to look for this man from Patterson, he now found himself almost within reach of achieving his goal of eliminating the final threat to potentially undermine the invasion he would be leading into Afghanistan. He stood in a doorway slightly further north in Ebury Street from Holden's apartment keenly observing the door that he knew either of his targets would emerge from. His plan was simple; he would follow the first out of the house at a discreet distance to a point well away from the premises. The coach carrying his henchmen would follow and observe the proceedings and as soon as Hoare struck it would roll up and assist in completing the kidnap. Patterson wasn't that interested in the cripple, he was to be disposed of to ensure silence, but Holden must be taken alive. Not for any sense of legal retribution to be taken against him, but because Patterson wanted to observe his murder with his own eyes to know that the shadow of death that was hanging over him had indeed now cleared.

It was a dull September morning as Hoare stood for two hours in the doorway of the residential premises, the owner of which he had paid a bribe, claiming to be a private detective acting for the famous 'Pinkerton's' Agency on a special and sensitive case. The well to do resident had readily accepted the story and the bribe from the smartly dressed, but imposing and slightly intimidating man with military bearing. Hoare's patience paid off. Nine a.m. exactly and the door to Holden's apartment opened followed a second or two later by the wheelchair bound cripple moving himself out and then, with a degree of difficulty, turning the entire chair around and reaching up to close the door behind him. Once he had taken care of the cripple today, it would make it quite viable to enter the flat by night and take care of Holden knowing that he was likely to be the only occupant.

Waldron wheeled himself off along Ebury Street, fortunately for Hoare, in the opposite direction from his point of surveillance. He moved driving the chair briskly and wilfully, the result of nearly six years of practice and necessity. As he turned the corner into Cundy Street that was when Hoare, who had now closed up on him, struck with his carriage borne support now bearing down on the unfolding scene. He pulled a bottle of chloroform from his coat pocket and soaked a large cotton duster with it over the last few steps he walked to catch up with Waldron. Hoare was fortunate that there was little pedestrian activity at that moment which allowed him to strike almost unobserved against the powerfully built cripple. Six years had forced his upper body to develop a huge reserve of strength and muscularity. With the speed of Hoare's strike it was of little consequence. He grabbed Waldron from behind and holding his head tightly into his own torso with his left hand he held the soaked duster as tightly as he could over his victim's nose and mouth with his right hand. Waldron's hands ventured for a few seconds onto Hoare's forearm and he had to struggle against the cripple's phenomenal but quickly failing strength to hold the duster in place. Calculating, he won out as the carriage pulled up alongside on the street corner. Two burly and muscular military types, some members of the now hugely growing private army that Hoare was assembling for the invasion, alighted and came swiftly over with an economy of movement, born out of hostile military operations, to help secure their quarry. They each clasped Waldron's arms to either side of the wheelchair with some chains and key operated padlocks and then, taking a side of the chair each, they picked it up and took it with the unconscious, crippled soldier back to the carriage. It fitted, only just, through the carriage door and then they, along with Hoare, jumped on board and the carriage lurched off in the direction of the Thames and a quiet slipway in Wapping, East London, some half an hours ride away.

The slipway they chose was just off of Wapping High Street before it met Wapping Wall by New Crane Stairs. It was a less commercial part of the river front, a deliberate choice to hopefully not be noticed by many as Hoare and his merciless team disposed of their victim. During the carriage journey they tied Waldron's arms and legs to the wheelchair with heavy cotton twine and then pulled a huge Hessian sack over him and his wheelchair to completely disguise the nature of their disposal into the river. So much rubbish was thrown into the Thames at times that no one would bat an eyelid at the peculiar shaped large sack. Hoare was quite confident that he administered enough chloroform to prevent Waldron coming to and making any unnecessary noise. They passed the 'Town of Ramsgate' public house as they rumbled along the cobbles of Wapping High Street and then turned right into Wapping Wall to continue east. They were stopping short of the busy 'Prospect of Whitby' pub to find their slipway.

As they turned off the main road into it Hoare felt the carriage pull up sharply, more so than he would have expected. The coachman, Joseph Netley, jumped down to speak with the occupants inside.

"Problem, squire. There's a group of men fixing up their old rowing boat on our slipway. What do you want to do now?" The somewhat unintelligent simple driver then continued with a ludicrous suggestion. "Do you want to dump him anyway?"

"Don't be so bloody stupid, you proletarian moron!" Hoare annoyed by the problem was now enraged by the driver's foolish suggestion. "You're the local man; get us to another quiet slipway or an empty dock or something. He's got to go today and bloody soon!" The perturbed Netley got back on his perch, exited from the slipway and continued east towards the Shadwell Basin through the predominantly wharf style buildings on either side of the road. Within seconds of pulling off Waldron was beginning to stir under the Hessian, he began to groan and they could tell he was trying to shift about in his semi conscious state. Hoare leant out from the carriage and shouted up at the driver.

"How long until we get to somewhere, Netley!" The driver knew that Shadwell Basin was only now yards away but was normally a hive of activity.

"Erm, perhaps a few seconds if it's not busy, squire."

"Be sure it's not, or you'll be with him!"

Netley made a left turn and they began to run parallel to the dock side of Shadwell Basin. One of Hoare's accomplices had been forced to punch Waldron on the chin, once he had located it under the sack, to render him unconscious again. Hoare looked out of the carriage, indeed it was a busy harbour of the Thames. They would take a chance and it would have to do. The driver pulled up right by the harbour's edge in as quiet a location as he could, there were still people bustling around within fifty yards of them engaged in various activities; porters, sailors, chandlers, all going about their business. Hoare needed a distraction. He turned to his henchmen.

"Right, you two, get out of the cab arguing and start a fight, get people distracted. I'll drop him out over the edge when you've got going." The burly ex-soldiers nodded in acknowledgment and before he could say anything had rolled out of the cab onto the dock side.

The plan worked perfectly and most people's attention was drawn to them. He then opened the carriage door on the other side and pitched Waldron in the sack out into the water just below them. The sack bobbed just for a few seconds before a combination of the weight of the old Victorian style wheelchair and the saturation of the sack and Waldron's clothes caused it to sink. Hoare watched as a few bubbles came to the surface and the sack was gone. Waldron felt nothing; already unconscious his lungs filled with water and he drowned without regaining consciousness. Hoare shouted to his henchmen who gave the act of misbehaving employees responding to their boss by disengaging from their fight and boarding the carriage. Netley cracked his crop by the horse's ear and the carriage rumbled off away from the Basin and up towards the Highway without any of the local people having noticed their true nefarious act. Holden was now the only element that stood in the way of Patterson's plan that would make Marcus Hoare a very wealthy man.

* * *

Karen had been staying with Ford in Eaton Square since his return two days before. She had been inconsolable since his arrival but having spent the last two days with him in the comfortable surroundings of his luxurious home she was beginning to slowly come to terms with the reality of her loss. Young Nigel had been buried quietly the day before Ford had completed his duties with the Minister. He had leave of absence since his return at the Minister's request as Patterson had no intention of leaving his Belgrave Square home for several days as he got over the shock and horror of the latest murder. The murder had made the press in London prior to their return, with both Ford and Patterson having seen copies of the coverage by 'The London Times' in particular:

'MINISTER'S PROTECTION OFFICER SLAIN IN ANOTHER RITUALISTIC KILLING

One of Sir Cecil Patterson's police protection officers was murdered in Prague during an official visit. The unnamed officer was allegedly tied to the front and rear of two trams and then killed by being split in two...'

Ford was staring at the headline on his coffee table while he sat on his green leather Chesterfield sofa with Karen curled up into him, cuddling tightly into his chest. They had no fear of Patterson making demands of her at present in the wake of what had happened overseas. This was coupled with Karen having got news to Lady Patterson that she would not be free to work for a week following her son's death. She had taken great comfort from Ford when she had come round to see him and break the news to him. She knew that he understood loss of people close to him following the events he had explained to her that had taken place in Whitechapel. He personally, however, could never empathise over the loss of a child. He had never experienced it and hoped that he never would. Ford was moved by the boy's death in that he never got the opportunity to meet him. He was also moved by the serenity in which the boy had slipped out of this life, in the arms and with the love of his mother.

Despite the wish to want to spend another day looking after Karen, Ford knew that today he had to go out to meet an old friend. Frederick Abberline, the senior investigating officer at 'street level' for the Whitechapel murders, was now the managing director of the famous European branch of 'Pinkerton's Detective Agency'. He split his time between his home in Bournemouth, professional commitments in Europe which included Monte Carlo, and his London office. With Ford having been in contact with him by telephone he agreed to meet up with his young protégé for lunch that day at the 'Café Royal' at the bottom of Regents Street, London. Ford was keen to get the perspective of this wise old detective on the murders and what might be fuelling them. Although not directly linked to Patterson's office, or so Ford thought, in anyway, he was also intrigued by the apparent suicide of Will Bates left hanging from Blackfriars Bridge. Although neither he nor Abberline would mourn his passing, the manner of his suicide seemed bizarre.

They were meeting for afternoon tea and when Ford arrived at a little after three o'clock, he found that Abberline was there already at their reserved table looking sternly towards him as Ford approached.

"You're late son. What's kept you?" He stood as Ford reached the table. He then extended his arm offering a handshake and as the two men clasped palms Abberline began to smile and then laugh at the face of concern that Ford had initially displayed. "You should know by now, Robert that I would only be joking."

"Yes, sorry, Fred. Came home to some bad news so I'm thinking very seriously. Sorry. How are things in the world of retirement then?" Ford began to relax.

"So, so. Can't complain, money's good. Wife is well. Bournemouth and Monte Carlo are both sunny. Best move I made really. Is the job still fucked?"

"Always was and always will be, you know that, Fred." The waitress came to the table to take their order.

"Gentlemen, what can I get you?"

"A conventional afternoon tea please, my dear," said Abberline in a fatherly way. The great detective was now in his sixties. He still sported his distinctive 'mutton chop' moustache and beard, it was now greyer and he was balder. The waitress turned to Ford.

"And the same for me please," was the reply. She walked off across the dining room with Abberline and Ford both watching her pert figure move away. Then they looked back at each other.

"Coppers never change do they?" said Ford.

"No they don't," replied Abberline. They both laughed. "So, brass tacks then, Robert. What did you want to speak to me about?" Abberline sat back in his chair and folded his arms. Ford took a deep breath and leant forward.

"Fred, what do your instincts tell you about Patterson and the murders that have been taking place of prominent members of his office?"

"Well, my suspicion is he's got something to hide. He is a politician and in his dim and distant past he's probably done something to alienate someone or some group. Now they're hitting back, although the whole thing is a bit extreme. If it ain't that, it might be a lone nut that doesn't like him and is killing everyone in a ritualistic way and saving the worst for him. Let's face it; they have got worse and more bizarre. As his PPO what's he told you then?" Ford took a breath looked down at the table and then looked back up at Abberline.

"Not enough. He reckons that he went to Afghanistan in 1898 and a holy man there put a fatwa up against him. He believes it's some foreigner carrying out this death wish on him and those around him.

I could live with that to a point with the death of the two squaddies in Dagenham as they were directly connected. Perhaps even the archivist of the report, but not the rest of them. They are innocent bystanders who don't even know where Afghanistan is so why should they be picked?" Ford was pausing for a moment.

"Where is Afghanistan then?" asked Abberline with a scowl.

"Oh, for god's sake, Fred…" Abberline burst into a smile.

"Only joking, mate. If I was you, I'd dig a little more over this Afghanistan thing. There might actually be a bit of substance to it. It seems partly credible." A large pot of tea, some cakes and the service to go with it turned up and the waitress laid the table out as they continued talking.

"Sorry I can't pay you Fred, for coming down."

"C'est la vie. Justice is never cheap, although perhaps on this occasion for the commissioner it is. Mind you, this is your shout lad."

"Might not be cheap for me then. Cheers." They both picked up a cup of strong, steaming traditional English Breakfast Tea and took a sip. "So do you think that he might have other documents that relate to something out there then? Something he keeps suppressed?"

"Yes I do. Look at the furore over the Tumblety papers back in '88. They were prepared to try to kill you for them. With that being the case then he might have something so secret that whoever or whatever it concerns will not let anything get in their way. That might mean the killer, or it might mean Patterson." Ford looked at Abberline puzzled over the last point. The veteran detective tucked into a cake holding it over his plate as Ford considered his words.

"What do you mean, exactly?" Abberline finished chewing and swallowed before he spoke.

"Look, all the ministerial staff murdered and then out of the blue Will Bates, our old journalistic nemesis ends up dead, why? Dig, Robert, there might be a connection between the two. I couldn't really care less about Bates but it is odd that he is dead, that's all. If I was you I'd go and have a look at his post mortem report. And while you're at it have a look at the details of all the P.M reports for the various victims. Might turn up another clue or connection. The cake's bloody nice by the way."

Abberline was quite right, thought Ford as he watched his old mentor demolish more cake. Why had Bates suddenly taken his own life in an apparent suicide? The time was fast approaching to confront Patterson about the whole affair, as well as about his abuse of Karen Wood. He had to solve this mystery as soon as he could. There were few potential victims left, but they included not only the Minister but those that remained close around him still. In the wake of the murder of Bob Spicer then he or even Karen, God forbid, could be next.

The old master and his protégé enjoyed the rest of the afternoon reminiscing about less political matters before going their own separate ways. They stood on the pavement outside the Café Royal in Regents Street just under its grand canopy.

"Goodbye, Robert," said Abberline, "and get the bastard. By whatever means that you can."

Ford was uncertain, as he walked away and Abberline left by carriage, as to whether the veteran detective referred to the mysterious killer or to Patterson.

Chapter Eighteen

Ford walked alone west along Pall Mall with the intention of going straight home to spend the rest of the day with Karen before returning the next day to his protection duties. Abberline's advice was spinning around in his mind. Why had Bates taken his own life? He was not renowned as a depressive and certainly, as far as Ford knew through his network of acquaintances in the media, he was not a man who had major personal issues of any sort. The man's only fault was his intrusive persistence. Ahead of him Ford saw the guards at their sentry boxes outside St James' Palace as he passed Marlborough House and turned into Marlborough Road leading to The Mall. It was the blood red colour of their tunics on the mild September afternoon that spurned him into action. Too much blood had been spilt.

Ford hurried into The Mall and flagged down a passing hansom and ordered the driver to take him off to the mortuary in Golden Lane within the boundaries of the City of London. He hoped to be able to see the body or the pathologists report when he got there; it was getting towards five o'clock and he realised that he might not get to see anyone that late. He watched St James' Park pass by on his right as the cab set off towards Trafalgar Square.

* * *

Holden was now wondering at five in the early evening what could have become of the unpredictable Waldron. Holden himself had gone out before Waldron in the morning to ride in Hyde Park and by the time he had arrived home after ten the house was empty. The ride had been a trying one. He had not ridden in the park since the days of courting Genevieve Glynn. It made him realise how alone he truly felt, with fate having robbed him of the happiness he should have achieved by a lifelong union with her. That tragedy, coupled with the bitterness and vengeance that filled his life, meant that any relationship he indulged in was purely for physical gratification. It was a mindset that he could not resolve, not perhaps, until he had completed his journey of revenge. He was curious and concerned for Waldron's well being, but there was a malevolence within him that also made him consider that if his crippled subordinate had disappeared along with his libellous actions, completing his task now it depended on being only in the UK would be much easier. This emotion generated a terrible feeling of guilt that was easily tempered by feelings of relief. Holden was losing his sense of right and wrong and soon he would not even be aware of the fact.

He stripped naked and looked at himself in the condensation soaked mirror on the wall of the steam filled bathroom, where he was about to soak himself in the bath along with a generous glass of Glenfiddich. He was still lean but the aging to the skin on his face from the years of hardship on the Indian subcontinent were contrasted by the smooth skin of his athletic body. It bore scars from his actions and he examined himself, changing position in the mirror to view them. He thought about what he had become; he couldn't define it. Fate had taken away the love of his life whilst Patterson had taken away his closest friends and his career. He climbed into the steaming bath and soaked in its luxurious suds. He could revenge the latter but do nothing about the former. Taking a large gulp from his glass and sending his mind marginally spinning, it annoyed him intensely, as did the ever present cough that again made his whole body convulse as he cleared his chest following the whisky. He would have some opium when he got out of the bath to dull the pain the cough generated. He looked down into the bath water following the bout of coughing. He was unsurprised to see that he had stained the water with red saliva.

Outside, Hoare observed from a carriage and could see the steamed up window with frosted glass that indicated to him that his next target was taking a bath. He would observe Holden's movements for a few days before striking; he would be a more difficult individual to deal with having read his service records. Having seen him enter the premises he looked remarkably well for a man who was listed as killed in action in the ministry's archives. However, circumstances were about to dictate that Hoare may not be the only man on Holden's trail.

Holden lying in the large, enamel, Victorian bath, slowly sank up to his neck in a prone position with his glass of single malt sat by the centrally mounted taps. It was time to relax for a few days before deciding to strike again. So far he had left nothing but dead victims in his wake, but to reflect the suffering of his men it was time to leave one alive. Perhaps the other protection officer; after all it would be wrong to consider killing one of the female staff. All the combatants in this campaign as in Afghanistan had to be men. He took a sip from the peaty tasting malt and savoured the burning sensation it generated in the pit of his stomach. Waldron would undoubtedly turn up, he was a survivor, a bad penny; he always came back. He would indeed, but not in the circumstances that Holden would have expected.

* * *

Ford arrived at the Golden Lane mortuary just before five thirty; the premises were open and inside he found a lone mortuary attendant who appeared to be on the verge of closing up. It was usual practice for such a caretaker to live nearby so that if necessary he could be roused during the night to provide access for the police or other agencies who may have a corpse to deposit. With this in mind Ford had no hesitation in delaying the man's departure. He showed his warrant card to the attendant and identified himself verbally.

"Evening, I am Detective Inspector Ford of the Metropolitan Police Special Branch. I wonder if you could help me. Do you still have the body of William Bates here please?" The mortuary attendant looked him up and down as he spoke. He studied his warrant card. Ford was all too familiar with this kind of individual; early fifties, very pale because he undoubtedly never saw the sun, slightly overweight and functionally dressed, but normally strong as an ox and only too pleased of some company in a profession that somewhat lacked conversation. Also the kind of individual that would be unfeasibly helpful to gain a greater sense of self worth. Approach them in the wrong way and they would attempt to wield the pitiful amount of power they possessed and try to eject you from the premises as soon as possible. The attendant had found his introduction polite. He would do what he could to help.

"I'll have to check the records, Inspector, but I think so. Can you bear with me?"

"Certainly. That's very kind." Ford looked around the interior of the building. It was functional and built in a very Victorian manner; tiled floors and walls to be easily washed down, the walls done in half green and half white and very ornately finished with a high degree of craftsmanship. In the open reception area that Ford found himself in, he could see three doors leading off of it with the doors to each open. To his left and right were two examination rooms laid out to conduct post mortems, and straight ahead was a corridor that was lined either side by body-sized pull out drawers. It was the chilled section were the bodies were stored until released and there looked to be space for quite a few. In the room in which he stood were several wooden filing cabinets that held the post mortem reports. The attendant had just entered the body store room when he stopped and called back to Ford.

"Would you like a cup of tea, Inspector?"

"Yes, I'd love one," Ford knew that being sociable would assist in getting results. He watched as the attendant stepped to one side and pulled out one of the body drawers. It held a body tidily on it but also a bottle of milk tucked in by the drawer front. The attendant picked up the bottle, shut the drawer and continued along the corridor. Ford looked on and gulped.

"The kettle is to your right, Inspector if you wouldn't mind just getting it going." The attendant called his request to Ford as he continued along the corridor. Ford looked to his right and sure enough there was a battered stove and kettle. He filled the iron piece of kitchenware from the scrubbing up sink, lit the stove and placed the kettle on it; the gas driven flames licked around its base.

A few moments later the attendant re-appeared in the reception area.

"Yes, old Bates' stiff is still down there, Inspector. Want your tea first?" The attendant fortunately retrieved the tea from within one of the filing cabinets.

The Dressmaker Connection

"I'll tell you what, old son," said Ford, "tell me which one it is and I'll go and have a look at him whilst you make the tea. Is that all right?"

"Certainly. Number twelve. He's starkers just to warn you. How do you like your tea, black or white, sugar?" Ford had no doubt as to how he would drink it today.

"Black, no sugar, please." Ford strolled off along the storage corridor. He found number twelve about twenty feet along the formaldehyde smelling corridor. He never got used to the smell of mortuaries, it was little different to that of Smithfield's meat market or any busy butchers shop.

He took a deep breath and pulled the drawer out. The familiar face of Will Bates stared up at him with its glazed and lifeless expression; his eyes were bizarrely still open. It sent a shiver down Ford's spine to see a man in death who he had argued with so vehemently on occasions in life. He was indeed naked except for the modesty of some underwear. Bates had severe lesions around his neck from his hanging injury. Ford wanted to look around the rest of the body for less obvious injuries that should perhaps not be there. He suspected from his conversation with Abberline that Bates had not taken his own life but had been murdered. He was looking for minor wounds to his wrists particularly, but he was surprised to discover other bruises that he would not have expected, albeit minor. Bates' wrists appeared unmarked but Ford noticed minor bruising to the lower part of his upper arms; as if he had been pinioned when he had been hung, an injury that he could not have inflicted upon himself. He examined the bruising a little more lifting one of the cold stiff arms as he did so. Sure enough just above the elbow there was minor bruising around two inches in thickness that indicated the use of a leather pinioning belt. Bates had indeed been murdered. What had he discovered? Ford heard a call from the end of the corridor.

"Tea's ready, Inspector. Do you want it down there or up here?" Ford put Bates' arm back next to his body and closed up the drawer.

"Up there please, I'm on my way back." He strolled up the cold corridor in which he could see the vapour of his own breath to rejoin the attendant. The black tea would be most welcome to warm his hands back up.

He walked into the reception area as the attendant closed and locked the body store up behind him and looked towards Ford.

"It's funny really, it's not like anyone can get out," said the attendant.

"No, but there is till a minor trade in cadavers, so I understand why you are required to do it," said Ford rubbing his hands together. The attendant handed him an enamel mug of tea.

"Do you want to see the post mortem report then, Inspector?" Ford suspected that it might be missing so he considered that it would be worth confirming his suspicions.

"Yes, I would please." The attendant went to one of the cabinets and pulled out the top drawer and began to have a sort through to find the document. Ford looked around the interior of the building again as the attendant conducted his search; it certainly required a special disposition to work in the profession that the building represented.

"Ah, I have found it. William Bates, that's right, isn't it?" He turned towards Ford as he spoke, a brown manila folder in hand.

"Yes. Excellent. May I see it?" The attendant passed it to Ford who placed his mug on a table and opened up the folder to begin eagerly reading through the report. The most important elements were the lists of pre-mortem injuries and the cause of death.

Ford had spent many years between 1888 and 1903 working within the detective department of the Metropolitan Police and was no stranger to pathologist's reports. He scoured the relevant pages of the report to find that it was not totally accurate by any means; he found this worse than the damn report perhaps having been missing. Within its text there was no mention of the bruising to Bates' upper arms at all, let alone whether they were pre or post mortem. No trace of any suicide correspondence had been discovered anywhere either, and when Ford read the text regarding the body's discovery, no one seemed to have questioned the distance the body was out from the bank side hanging under the bridge. From the information regarding this, coupled with his own experience and intuition, one had to conclude that he would have struggled to end up hanging where he was alone. The detectives at the scene seemed to be of the opinion that he had tied the rope having projected it to the superstructure of the bridge in a lasso style, then placed his neck in the noose and leapt forwards. Ford felt that this conclusion was vaguely possible but improbable. His face obviously betrayed his disbelief and puzzlement with the conclusions and the attendant noticed the air of incredulity.

"Something wrong, Inspector?" Ford was distant and did not answer straight away. He didn't wish to arouse any undue interest; almost anyone it now seemed could be involved in what was becoming a major conspiracy.

"No. Just a little saddened by the death of this chap. Very out of character one would conclude." Ford put the file down on the table in the reception area and finished his tea. "Thanks for your help, and sorry to keep you."

"No problem, Inspector. Anytime. Drop in anytime, its always dead quiet here in case you need a retreat on duty sir." Ford couldn't work out if the pun was intentional or not. He nodded and left the building into the warmer early September air. There was no doubt in his mind; William Bates had been murdered.

* * *

September 4th

Ford had been back with the Minister for only a day when he read the headlines on the front page of The London Times. As he studied the full size daily, he noted a small but intriguing column at the base of the page. The story began there but continued on page four, the text was a revelation.

> 'Discovered yesterday by the Port of London Police was the drowned body of a long missing serviceman. Identified by his leather 'dog tag' insignia, Sapper John Waldron of the Royal Engineers regiment was discovered on the foreshore below Tower Bridge at a low tide. Sapper Waldron, who has been listed as missing in action and presumed dead since 1898, was found strapped to a wheelchair that had dug into the sand, it is assumed, as the tide went out and snagged there, leaving him to avoid the indignity

of being swept out to the channel. Waldron is one of a group of soldiers who are all listed as missing in the North West Frontier region of our empire on the Indian sub-continent. How he came to be found back in London is a complete mystery but he had obviously been crippled at some point since 1898. Scotland Yard have taken on the investigation into the presumed murder as he had been strapped to his invalid aid which negated any chance of survival from the plunge into the Thames. Anyone with information regarding Waldron is asked to come forward. Next of kin have been informed. The Ministry of War has at this time not commented on his disappearance and the subsequent discovery of his dead body'.

Ford was stood in Speakers Court of the House of Commons in the shadow of the famous 'St Stephen's' clock tower so often misnamed 'Big Ben' after the bell within it, as he read the fascinating copy. Stood alongside him looking over his shoulder was Mark Vincent. He had taken over Spicer's position and his own had been assigned to a group of uniform central London constables as and when they were required.

"I bet I know which story you've been reading, Boss," said Vincent to Ford. He had a reasonable grasp of the mystery surrounding the events himself.

"Yes. Too bloody right I'm reading it. I'm fascinated by it. This could be the first key that unlocks the mystery. We need to get access to this man's records. Also I need to get the dimensions of that wheelchair. If they're the same then Patterson has some real questions to answer."

* * *

At that same moment Holden was enjoying an eleven o'clock cup of coffee on the terrace at the rear of his Ebury Street house reading the morning's edition of The London Times. He really wasn't taking much of it in; his mind was wandering thinking of many tasks. Where the hell was Waldron? 'The incompetent drunk with his penchant for now being a professional liability'. He had probably got himself arrested and then incarcerated for several days. It could be the only explanation. And how would he deal with meeting Karen Wood, the widow of Nigel Green? She was perilously close to Patterson and to the protection officer Ford; he would have to try to speak to her at a one off meeting unobtrusively alone. He knew that Patterson was in London and the UK only until Christmas so he had ample time to finish his quest for retribution.

As he was lost in his thoughts and his eyes idly scanned the paper he was drawn to the headline and article that Ford was also reading in different circumstances elsewhere in London.

'SOLDIER MISSING FOR SIX YEARS FOUND DEAD IN THAMES'

Holden avidly read on. The text was a bitter blow. He had suspected that by now Patterson had an inkling of who was responsible for the threat to him. This story confirmed these fears and now put the fact squarely in his mind that Patterson had unleashed an agent or agents of his own to find Holden, kill him and keep the entire scandal of the SRP, their abandonment, the oil and the abuse of power suppressed. He would have to act quickly but cautiously. Patterson's men had obviously killed Waldron but had been careless with the disposal of the body. He was also still mindful that he owed it to his late friend to tell his common law wife, of whom Green spoke affectionately a great deal, of what had become of her late husband. His concern also was how they had found Waldron. Had he been taken from outside his house? Had he been observed elsewhere? If they had found the crippled soldier they would find Holden, he would have to exercise extreme caution. He would try to come and go from the premises under cover of darkness and vary his points of entry and exit as much as he could. Disguise would have to be a consideration. He would be on his guard, carrying his pistol would have to be a permanent necessity, as well as a concealed dagger. If called upon he knew that he would use them with extreme prejudice.

* * *

Inside the Ministry of War in Whitehall, Ramsey Phillips was studying Patterson's forthcoming engagements for the next few weeks with keen interest. He was pawing over the leather bound desk diary on Fiona Shaw's desk as she returned to the reception area. He was unaware of her return and was startled when she coughed to announce her presence; although that was only after she had studied him with a scowl of curiosity on her face for a few seconds. He looked up in reaction to her cough and seemed calm and normal, smiling in her direction as he did so. She had perhaps become unusually concerned in the wake of the murders in people's interest in Patterson's movements. With hindsight this was a foolish notion in respect of Phillips. After all he had worked within the department for over ten years and was one of the people she should be least concerned about in taking an interest in Patterson's schedule. He was the Minister's under secretary. Phillips appeared not to want to speak, so she broke the silence.

"Everything all right, Mr Phillips?" He answered without hesitation.

"Yes. Absolutely. I was interested to see that we're off to Buxton soon, in the Peak District. That will be nice, good walking country with lots of fresh air. What's he up there for again?"

"Well, he wants to take the waters; he's doing a review in Bakewell and then going to a regimental reception there." Phillips pondered the reply for a moment. He seemed distant. Fiona Shaw hadn't seen him like this before. "Are you all right, Ramsey?" She thought the informality for once would get his attention.

"Yes. Fine thank you." He left the reception area and disappeared into his own private office.

Phillips sat down at his oak, leather topped desk and looked out of the window at the blue sky with sun streaming in through the leaded light glass pane. He then looked back down at his desk and unfolded the newspaper that lay in front of him. He looked at the date. A shudder passed down his spin. It was the anniversary of his dear first cousin Genevieve's untimely death in a hunting accident. The weather outside was so reflective of the fine day when it happened. Although having grown up on the poorer side of the blanket to her, they spent much time together in the formative childhood to adolescent years and had a firm, trusting friendship. Indeed he had been the first she had told about her love for Billy Holden. He had seemed like a good young man and was looking forward to having him as a relation through marriage. Both were stolen away from him so suddenly, or so he thought until he first saw Billy back from the dead. He never forgot the respect he had for Billy that lasted right up to the present day and he was astonished when Billy had related the story of how he and his men had been left for dead, and then Patterson had tried to have him killed. In truth he never expected Billy's revenge to take the form that it did, but whilst these people disappeared it always kept his own hard fought position safe, so he didn't object too much.

He looked away from the newspaper back to the window; so inviting was the sunshine and the blue sky that he got up and walked over to it to enjoy the view out over Horse Guards parade ground. St James Park beyond looked green and lush. The review in the Peak District was a thought clearly in his mind as his gaze became a distant stare.

Chapter Nineteen

September 5th, 10.a.m., Southwark Mortuary, Tennis Street, SE1.

The old mortuary building sat just off the rear of Guy's Hospital. Ford alighted from his carriage and gave instructions to the driver to wait. The Minister was safely ensconced for several hours at the Palace of Westminster which left Ford free to view the body of the late John Waldron. He had no time or concern to curry favour or exchange pleasantries with the staff at Southwark. He needed to be in and out briskly and establish a cause of death for this man and examine the wheelchair to see if there was a link to the tracks discovered at the murder scenes in Paris and Rome. His curt manner with the staff on arrival very quickly telegraphed to them that he was a man with purpose. They wasted no time on polite small talk. He was taken directly to the mortuary chamber in which Waldron's body was currently stored. The tray that held the body was pulled out from amongst a wall full of other such trays that resembled a macabre, giant, human filing cabinet.

The lifeless body of John Waldron lay clean on the tray giving no indication of his paraplegic nature. It would only be apparent if viewed from the rear with the ugly scar that he possessed on his lower back. Ford could see from the marks on his wrist that he had indeed been bound to his wheelchair. His upper body was powerfully built as a result of the need to propel himself in a wheelchair and he would still have proved difficult to subdue to strap down. There were no other apparent assault injuries. The post mortem report he was now browsing, handed to him by the sombre attendant, confirmed this fact. There was nothing as sophisticated as a toxicology report to indicate any other suspicious circumstances. Ford looked down at the body. It was an uninviting sight; discoloured and slightly bloated from its time in the River Thames. How would *he* have subdued such a muscular man? Ford turned to the attendant and spoke.

"Do you have anything I could swab his mouth and nasal passages with, please?" The pale, drawn, forlorn looking attendant with his dull eyes in very hollow eye sockets looked at Ford curiously without speaking. "I have good reason for wanting something." The attendant said nothing and walked away back to main reception and examination area. Ford looked at him walking away. He then stared around the building observing its ornate Victorian green and beige tiling, practical for keeping clean. He looked back down at the body. How the hell had someone missing for six years, having disappeared overseas, suddenly turned up in London?

Like a ghost the attendant appeared silently back at his shoulder. He said nothing and held out two wooden and cotton swabs in his right hand. Ford took them from him.

"Thank you." He then proceeded to wipe one around the inside of Waldron's mouth. Having done so, he held it up to his nose mindful not to get it too close. Ford couldn't detect any scent out of the ordinary, he felt a little disappointed. His disappointment would be short lived and he would be proved right in his suspicions. He took the second swab and carefully wiped it around Waldron's lifeless, dark right nostril. He again held it up to his own nose to sniff and caught a very distinct and powerful aroma; chloroform. As he had suspected, Waldron's killers had drugged him prior to securing him to his wheelchair. The river water had washed any traces out of his mouth but the residue of it remained in his nasal passages. He turned to the attendant.

"Chloroform. He was drugged." The attendant looked at him blankly. "Do you have the remains of the wheelchair here?" asked Ford. The attendant nodded and turned giving Ford no indication to follow, he did so instinctively.

He led Ford to another room in the building where the wheelchair sat in a corner amongst other discarded items of property. He left Ford in the room. The wheelchair was twisted and very rusty from its days in the river getting swept along and tumbling around in the water with its unfortunate passenger. Ford walked over to it and turned it upside down to examine the track of the wheels. He was pleased to observe that both large wheels remained with their resilient tyres. He pulled his notebook from the interior pocket of his suit in which he noted down the measurements of the tracks from Paris and in which he had also noted the wheel tracks in the Colosseum the day of the murder in Rome. Prepared for the occasion he had a small, short pocket tape measure with him too. He bent down to the wheels and with his tape measure checked the width of the tyre and the width of the track of the large wheels. It was a revelation; the details of the chair matched those of Paris and Rome.

Ford stood up after this Archimedean moment, suddenly with a much more confused mind. If this man was party to the hideous murders so far committed, despite his powerful upper body, how did a paraplegic manage to carry out the actions that he had? The answer was simple in Ford's mind; he was either an accomplice or perhaps another victim of a killer still at large. Ford knew that the time for drastic action was approaching, much as it had done earlier in his career when he had intended to raid Assistant Commissioner Robert Anderson's office to reveal the Masonic conspiracy in the cover up of the Whitechapel Murders. On that occasion he had been thwarted, but now with the deaths of so many having taken place, the potential danger to himself, Karen and still to the unscrupulous Patterson, action was required. There was no point questioning the Minister directly again, at least not at present with no further leverage, but his offices would be worth searching.

He left behind the less than animated staff who watched him leave with open mouth puzzlement and made his way back to the Palace of Westminster ready for Patterson's next movements. He would have a total of three offices to search over time. Ford wrestled in his mind as to which should be first.

* * *

Holden was as resourceful as ever in his humane quest of relaying to Karen Wood the truth about her common law husband's demise. His insider or 'mole' in the Ministry of War had kindly supplied him details of her address in Knightsbridge when requested. The need to finish the trail of retribution could wait temporarily while he completed his dying friend's last wishes. He left Ebury Street for one final time dressed in a smart lounge suit and with a small shoulder bag carrying the only possessions that would remain either dear to him or important; a small photographic portrait of Genevieve, a picture of the family home in its full glory during a splendid Hertfordshire summer, a cheque book, travel documents, additional ammunition for his concealed Webley and a picture of Nigel Green in tropical uniform taken in India in 1898 prior to the incursion into Afghanistan. On the reverse of the picture Green had signed it, 'my darling Karen, I will love you and little Nigel always'. Holden's varying methods of disguise and leaving under the cover of late or early darkness had persistently foiled the surveillance by Hoare and his group of military thugs. Today Holden decided to leave during daylight hours via his front door. Dressed as he was and carrying as little as he was, he gambled that his adversaries would assume he would be returning. With his cheque book and the family wealth that it gave him access to he could afford not to pack or return, at least for now.

As he left the front door Holden was careful to observe the world in his immediate vicinity; he spied nothing out of the ordinary. His intention was to hail the first cab that he could and instruct it to drive for him to see if he was followed. He did not wish to take additional danger to the widow of his senior NCO. Sure enough being the time it was in the middle of the morning he could see a hansom travelling east towards him as he made his way towards the pavement. He increased his walking pace to get to the roadside to hail its service. The driver pulled on the reins and brought the brawny, dark brown horse to a halt just beyond Holden with the carriage door perfectly in line for him to step into.

"Where to, squire?" asked the friendly ruddy faced cabman. Holden climbed aboard before speaking in a relatively low voice.

"Just drive, head towards Trafalgar Square please. Then I'll decide on where I want to go properly."

"Whatever suits, guv'nor." The driver cracked his riding crop close to the horse's right ear near to the back of its blinkers. The muscular horse responded and began to trot off with little apparent effort. The quality of the hansom, its driver and the health of the horse was very much a contrast to poor undernourished equivalents in the East End.

The Dressmaker Connection

Holden allowed the carriage to run on for a bit before taking a look behind to see if he could spot an apparent 'tailing' cab or carriage. Holden, with his combat experience, was always quick to observe either changes to the status quo or to the environment around him. With only half a minute's or so observation he spotted a vehicle that was shadowing their movements which he had noticed stationary diagonally opposite his house when he had left. He would have to try to lose them as efficiently as he could. To initially confirm his suspicions he got the driver to stop outside a branch of Holden and Glynn's Bank in Bressenden Place.

As he alighted from his own hansom he watched carefully as the suspicious carriage rode slowly passed him; he could not see who was inside and was almost convinced it was empty. He bribed the driver on route and entered the bank. He gave him strict instructions to remain there for at least half an hour or as long as he could. His intention was to leave the bank via a different door. He approached the counter that had a teller free and spoke politely to the smart young man that now confronted him. He pulled his cheque book from his bag and laid it on the counter. He spoke as he wrote a cheque out for cash.

"Good morning, Sir," said the teller.

"Good morning to you, young man. I would like to cash this please." Having quickly completed the order he tore it from his book a cheque made out for two thousand pounds. The young man looked shocked.

"I will just have to go and clear this with the manager, Sir," said the astonished teller. Despite it being a salubrious West End branch of the bank, it was not frequent that customers came in requesting that level of cash. Holden was concerned as to who might be watching and gave the teller an additional instruction before he walked away.

"Draw the manager's attention to the name and tell him that I wish no fuss to be made please." The teller looked down at the cheque and then back at Holden.

"Yes, Sir, I understand." Holden wanted to ensure he courted no attention, even that of a well wisher of either his or the late Genevieve's family.

He had paid attention to his environment from his first entry. No one else had entered since his arrival. Hoare was in fact one step ahead of him.

* * *

The previous day

"Well done, Major. You have indeed confirmed my worst suspicions that the man responsible for this trail of murder is in fact an ex-soldier with an unjustified grudge. Have you taken care of him yet?" Patterson moved towards the window in his Empire Petroleum office and lit a cigar as he finished speaking and looked out across Trinity Gardens to Tower Bridge. Hoare was seated in a comfortable new brown leather Chesterfield sofa as he observed the Minister's movement across the luxurious office. He had researched Holden and could not understand why a soldier with such an exemplary record would have turned into a sadistic killer. He begun to develop distrust of Patterson; but the financial reward that he was being given meant that distrust was parried by caution and not resignation.

"No. But I know where and how I will. He has been making enquires in Whitechapel regarding the common law wife of one of his late subordinates, so my sources have discovered. She is a dressmaker who has set up with some assistance in Knightsbridge, or so I understand." Hoare paused for a moment to observe any reaction from Patterson. Patterson had tried to be coy but the reddening of his neck as he continued looking out of the window and the sound of a hard swallowing action spoke volumes to Hoare. "It seems that on some fateful mission his entire unit was wiped out, or so the story goes, except for him and the cripple that we took care of. The dying wish of one of his men was to tell this woman what had happened to him. So Holden will show his face in time in the West End and when he does I shall strike." Patterson appeared a little nervous now.

"Really?" said the subdued Minister.

"Yes, really. Now there seems to be no records of him or his men going missing. Just army rumours that I have uncovered. I do know that this dressmaker is called Karen. She has a crippled son and lives in Wil…" Hoare was interrupted by a very agitated Patterson who rushed over to his desk and stubbed his partially smoked expensive Havana out in an ornamental ashtray and took over the talking.

"Wilton Crescent. Her surname is Wood and the crippled child has recently died. And she is my mistress. No collateral damage, Hoare. Do you understand?"

"But what if he tells her the truth of how his men came to die? She might in turn talk." Patterson became hostile.

"What do you mean the truth?"

"All right, this is for you to confirm or deny. The army rumour is that you sent a unit of six men to Afghanistan to find oil. They did but the natives turned on them and slaughtered all but two. They escaped thanks to the toughness of Holden back into India where one or two army contacts got them south to Delhi and then a passage home. Don't worry the story only seems to be legend. But everyone knows legends always have a basis."

"What the fuck do you want Hoare? What are you alluding to?"

"This man Holden is tough. To have survived as he did out there he has to be. Now he's turned native to scare you it seems. Don't forget who I am and where I have been, I know what the savages can do out there. He's trying to get to you by killing those around you in a fashion so that you got to know he's alive. So that you'll live in fear of when he will strike.

"Now two things. I don't know what you did to desert these men, but try that with me then you will have more than Holden to fear. Now the other. You want him dead so that will cost you an additional premium." Patterson knew that he was in a weak position; he faced a scandal, death and disgrace if any of this became public. Almost any demand would not be too much.

"What do you want? How much?" He was now sat slumped in his expensive leather quilted desk chair looking angrily despondent.

"Ten percent of E.P profits from Afghanistan and five grand for killing Holden and silencing him. And the girl might need silencing too." Patterson was enraged by the implication of the woman who brought him immense sexual gratification.

"No! The money and the profits yes, but the woman must be unharmed, whatever she knows."

Hoare was surprised at his sentimentality. He walked over to the ornate drinks unit and opened it to pour himself a drink. As he moved a bottle to get to a favoured malt at the back he saw the concealed journal. He pulled it free and held it up to Patterson.

"Put that back, Hoare." Patterson spoke coldly in a menacing way Hoare had not heard before.

"What is it?" Enquired Hoare surprised at this turn of potential aggression.

"It doesn't concern you, Major." Patterson levelled a pistol from no-where at Hoare as he spoke. The wily marine was caught, for once, completely off guard. He had faced far more danger in his past and was annoyed more that concerned.

"Minister, I'll put this back, but if you ever threaten me like this again you'd better see it through." Hoare put the journal back. He picked up a bottle of 1873 Glenfiddich and shut the drinks cabinet. He turned to face Patterson and maintained fierce eye contact as he proceeded to take a large mouthful from the bottle and then turned his back on the Minister and left the office.

The situation was now tenuous for Patterson. He lowered the pistol, put it back in a low desk drawer and contemplated his next move. He was especially annoyed with the marine officer as that was not only his favourite single malt but also his last bottle.

* * *

September 5th, Holden & Glynn's Bank

The teller counted the cash out on his side of the counter in front of Holden. He put a brown bank's money band around it and placed it in a plain brown envelope and passed it to Holden. Through the procedure Holden had kept a keen eye on the door into the bank and was satisfied he had seen no one that concerned him enter. He took hold of the envelope and placed it in the right hand internal pocket of his jacket.

"I have one more request, would you ask the manager to come over please?" The teller looked at him curiously; earlier he had wanted no fuss. He nodded in recognition of the request and then left his chair. A few moments later he returned with a thin, very upright man with a pencil moustache and slicked back hair who was the manager. He spoke in a very quiet and discreet tone to Holden.

"Mr Holden, a pleasure to see you after so long. What can we do for you?"

"Only a small favour. May I leave the premises via your staff entrance at the back that leads out into Allington Street?" The manager looked at Holden with a bewildered look in his eyes and then glanced quickly into the eyes of the teller.

"Yes of course, Sir. As part of the banking family then that is no trouble." The manager directed Holden towards a secure door that led to the private offices of the bank and then chaperoned him to the door that Holden wished to use. He opened it and stepped out in front of Holden and then offered him his hand to be shaken.

"A pleasure to be of assistance to the family, Sir." They shook hands vigorously and firmly with Holden then disappearing off into the quiet Allington Street. The manager shut the door firmly behind him.

Holden had certainly managed to give his prying adversaries the slip, but only on a very brief basis. Hoare was already in Wilton Crescent waiting for Holden to arrive. Neither could know that a third man was also making his way unexpectedly there.

* * *

11.30 a.m. Ford arrived at Patterson's office at the Houses of Parliament and was greeted by Fiona Shaw. She smiled as she spoke to him, seemingly untroubled by the murders that had affected the ministry.

"Hello, Inspector, the Minister is waiting in his office for you. He's just ready to go home now." Here was an opportunity. Ford could run the marginal risk of allowing Mark Vincent to take Patterson home on his own in the horse-less carriage he was so obsessed by whilst he searched his office here at Parliament.

"Oh, good, is Mark with the car?" enquired Ford casually.

"Yes, I believe he is." Fiona Shaw retuned to her paperwork. Ramsey Phillips appeared in the outer office.

"Inspector, I think the old man's ready to go if you are." This was Ford's chance.

"Right, I'll pop down and see Vincent and ask the Minister to make his way down when he is ready." Ford left the room to attend Speaker's Court, the small quadrangle in the shadow of St Stephen's Tower to speak with his colleague. He was happy for the Minister to move freely within the Palace of Westminster as it was secured by police on its gates and on roving patrols within as a result of the murderous activities that had been taking place.

Ford emerged out into the cool, shaded air of the quadrangle and saw Vincent waiting with the car and Patterson's driver. He wandered over as Vincent alighted to speak with him.

"Right, Mark a favour. I have some enquires to tie up here so I need you to get Patterson home on your own. All right?" Vincent looked at him a little puzzled. "Look, you'll be fine. I need to check something out with Phillips. I'll meet you up there in Belgrave Square." Vincent seemed a little suspicious but didn't voice any concern.

"All right, Boss. Take care." Ford nodded and turned away from the car to head back in. Vincent remained by the car awaiting the Minister's arrival. Ford deliberately returned into the building and took a corridor to avoid contact with Patterson so he didn't have to furnish some story to him about why he was leaving with only one protection officer. Sure enough as Ford emerged onto the first floor he peered out of window and having already heard the car start up he saw it drive out of Speaker's Court with the Minister onboard with Vincent, the driver and Fiona Shaw.

Arriving by the outer door of the Minister's suite of offices he knocked before attempting to enter. He was in luck; no answer. Phillips had to be elsewhere in the building. Ford gently opened the door and entered to find, as he expected, the outer office deserted. He walked over to the door to Patterson's and tried the handle. It opened and he entered. On entering two people received an equal shock; Phillips was inside sat at the Minister's desk searching through the drawers. Ford was stunned as to why he might be, but had less reason to be there than Phillips.

"Mr Phillips, what a surprise? Can I ask what you are up to?" For only a moment Phillips paused and stumbled partially over his words before coming more coherent.

"You can, I am looking for his schedule for the review in the Peak District, that gives me reason pretty much to be in here. What are you doing here still, Inspector?"

For the killer to have struck as he did and when he did, Ford had suspected for sometime that he may have an insider passing on diary schedules. How else would the killer know so much? Surely such an individual would not allow themselves to be caught so easily. It was going to be impossible for Ford, at least for now, to voice his suspicions as he should not be there either, and he had his own agenda. He thought it easier to play the whole incident down; he would have to conduct his search another time.

"Well, Mr Phillips, I am merely extending my interest in security. I'm sure you understand. As it's you it would seem that I have nothing to be concerned about, eh?" Ford's eyes deliberately belied the innocent working air he voiced. He wanted Phillips to know that he was onto him if he was the source of the leak, and that he would be watching him carefully. Ford smiled, but his eyes didn't.

"Very good. Inspector. I was just leaving." Phillips shut up the drawers and surreptitiously walked past Ford and out of the office. Ford knew that unless he followed Phillips out he stood to arouse the civil servant's own suspicion. He followed him out. An uneasy relationship would exist between them from now on.

* * *

Vatican City, Rome

Sunny, late morning in the eternal city. Within the hallowed and ornately decorated surroundings of the Sistine chapel gathered three key European catholic churchmen; Lev Sklinski from Prague, Victoire de Vicompte from France and Bishop Caravaggio of Rome. They met behind closed doors with Swiss guards preventing the entry of anyone into the famous chamber on Caravaggio's direction; the only person who could possibly defy the guards and interrupt them was the Pope himself. They sat around an ancient, hand carved, light oak table with large glasses of vintage ruby port. An enormous decorative decanter sat on the table between them. All were dressed in their finest purple robes with heavy gold crosses suspended around their necks intermingling with prayer beads. Caravaggio spoke first.

"Brothers, we take a dangerous step, a step that if it is successful will spread our influence into the most savage heart of Islam. This adolescent religion must not be allowed to expand and encompass resources that may be vital to Christianity and take any more of an oppressive hold than it already has."

"Agreed, Brother," said Sklinski, "but we do it at great financial peril to ourselves. If we fail we will be excommunicated for having brought shame on the name of the Christian Roman God." These men comfortably spoke with each other as 'brother' from their days as student priests in Rome some twenty years earlier, immersed in the intricacies of theology. De Vicompte was the last to speak.

"The assurances that Patterson has given us cannot fail. If they do we can merely state that we loaned money on the basis of helping to set up missions. If anything untoward happens then I have a plan utilising assistance from a captain within our loyal Swiss Guard to redress matters." He took a sip from his cut glass goblet. By the expression on his face the port's flavour was quite exquisite.

"Isn't the threat of violence a little ungodly, brother?" asked a concerned Caravaggio. He turned his glass in his hand resting on the table. The port lapped around its sides and clung slightly to the glass before retreating to a level meniscus as he stabilised his grip. Vicompte replied to this worry.

"This is not just about financial loss, brother. There are reputations at stake. For all that we have worked for, for the last twenty years, pushing you forward, Bishop, to be the next Pope. Just think, 'the pope who tamed the savage world of Islam?' No. If Patterson fails it's just an insurance policy to keep our honour intact. The money is not the important issue here." Sklinski was not convinced.

"How can you be so sure?"

"Because the money can be recreated, the finances of the church repaired. The purpose is well intentioned. Reputations once tarnished are lost forever. I will not allow it." De Vicompte was resolute in his belief. Caravaggio was to have the last word on the matter.

"Patterson's plan and assembly of forces appears faultless. We are discussing unwarranted concerns perhaps."

Silence fell uncomfortably across the wondrous Sistine Chapel. They all nervously drank some port. They seemed to be waiting for someone now. There was a cracking sound as one the huge wooden doors was opened and a Swiss guard stepped in and stood to attention just inside the door. Sixty-nine year old Pope Pius X entered. They stood up to greet him.

Chapter Twenty

2p.m. Holden arrived in Wilton Place by cab and was dropped off at the Knightsbridge end of the road at his request; his intention to walk the last few hundred yards down to the crescent. Hoare was operating his surveillance of Karen Wood's flat from a house on the corner of Belgrave Square and was undetectable. None of the players in the unfolding drama would know they were being watched. Hoare was not alone; he had one of his hired thugs with him, a combat experienced marine who had helped him dispose of Waldron. The two of them watched from a bay window of the ornate Edwardian house they were concealed in.

Holden began walking down from the bustle of Knightsbridge passing through the streets of private residences as he made his way to Karen Wood's flat. He was cautious and had his pistol ready with him as always, making use of reflections in windowpanes to see if anyone was following him; he appeared to be alone. He reached the junction of Wilton Place and Crescent and paused for a moment concealing himself within the building line before turning left. He looked along the new street and could see nothing suspicious.

Robert Ford was alighting from a carriage in Belgrave Square just short of Wilton Crescent and so he was out of sight to either of the other parties. He paid the driver and thanked him politely and looked across to the Minister's residence. He felt relieved to see his 'awful' car parked outside of it and a uniform police constable stood yawning on the doorstep. He felt comfortable that he could pop into Karen's briefly without being seen from Patterson's house.

Inside her apartment Karen was weeping. She was not alone. She was pinned over the back of a sofa in her lounge in just her corset with Patterson stood behind her. He had forced himself upon her in his usual manner, but this time was really going to be the last time. He was a particularly clumsy and coarse lover with an unhealthy obsession that he repeatedly indulged upon her. She could look through her lounge door to see partially into her kitchen as he rocked himself behind her and she tried not to think of the discomfort he caused as the tears rolled down her cheeks. She had a view of her block of assorted kitchen knives; all she could think about in her emotionally frail state following her bereavement, her relationship with Ford and this 'filthy fucker' still forcing himself upon her, was drawing the steak knife and cutting his throat with it when he was finished.

Patterson grunted slightly and with a couple more harsh movements he had finished. He said nothing, taking himself off to the bathroom, shuffling pathetically with his trousers and underwear around his ankles making it particularly difficult to walk. She found her dressing gown and pulled it around her having cleaned herself of his horrid union with him in her private en suite bathroom. There was a knock on the door.

'My god', her mind raced, 'I hope to god it's not Robert.' She went over to the bay window that overlooked the front of the block and peered through the net curtains. She could see a well dressed man she had never seen before standing on the step. Visitors out of the blue were unheard of at her door. She turned away and walked out of the apartment to go and speak to this stranger. Patterson, having flushed the toilet had not heard the knock.

It took her a minute to get down to the door where Holden shuffled slightly uncomfortably on his feet as he looked around him from time to time. Hoare and his thug, Marine Braban, opened the door and looked across at Holden. Hoare also then looked in the opposite direction into the Square and recognised the police protection officer he had seen around Patterson's offices, Ford. Hoare had to make an important judgement call; did he strike now or not? If he had seen the Minister enter the apartments at the rear of the premises then his decision would have been cut and dried but he was unaware of his presence.

She opened the door and the smartly dressed man turned and made immediate piercing eye contact with her. No wonder Nigel Green had continually spoke of this woman Karen Wood, she was the most erotic woman he had ever seen, oozing sensuality. For a moment he was lost for words and stood partially opened mouthed. She spoke first.

"Can I help you?" He could see that she had been crying. He found it odd she was dressed in a dressing robe so early in the day?

"Yes. You might have heard of me many years ago, I'm a friend of Nigel's. I'm William Holden."

She stared for a brief moment. Then her hands went to her mouth, her eyes began to roll and she fell forwards as she fainted. The lightning quick and athletically powerful Holden cradled her in his arms. A shot rang out that whizzed past his head and impacted in the hallway of the apartment block. Chaos was breaking out in Belgravia, a small skirmish was about to hit Edwardian London.

Ford broke into a run and reached inside his suit jacket to draw his Webley service revolver. He had seen the burly man cross the road towards him and thought little of it. With his hands momentarily engaged in the draw he was caught completely by surprise by the imposing burly man, Marine Braban, who punched him hard in the right side of his head. Ford was floored with his vision blurred. Braban kicked him in the stomach before he could react any further and took the wind completely out of him.

Holden had pulled Karen into the hall of the building and slammed the heavy polished, black painted door shut to afford some cover from view. The instant it was shut a bullet penetrated it again impacting into the wall. He picked her up properly carrying her in a 'crossing the threshold' style and took her as far to the back of the premises as he could.

Hoare having fired the second shot ran across the road with his Mannlicher automatic 7.65mm pistol in an 'off aim ready' position. The newly acquired pistol's sights were still not set correctly enough for him for ranges over twenty-five feet it seemed. As he crossed the road he looked to his left to see what Braban had done with the policeman Ford. Ford it seemed was lying on the floor writhing in pain as Braban circled him ready to strike again and finish him off. Hoare smiled a cruel smile that was to be short lived.

Patterson rushed out of the bathroom now properly dressed as a result of hearing two distinctive gun shots. He of all the people at that moment in Belgravia had the most to fear. This must be it. Holden had come for him and was battling his way through the defences set to hold him at bay. Patterson began to sweat and shake; he was experiencing real palpable fear. Unsure of whether to flee, possibly straight into the clutches of the enemy, or wait in the apartment he simply froze in the hallway looking at the open door. After a few seconds he rushed forward and slammed it shut.

At the rear of the buildings, sheltered between the main structure and a coal bunker, Holden cradled Karen Wood in his arms. He was looking down at her shaking her gently to try to rouse her. Her eyes slowly fluttered open and she looked up at Holden as if struggling to focus. Then she felt a small drop of water hit her face. She noticed this man was crying as she managed to bring his face into clearer view. She reached up and stroked his cheek. He moved against her hand like an affectionate domestic animal and closed his eyes. This was likely to be perhaps last time Holden felt a gentle female touch. It had been so long since he had been shown any sort of affection. Again Karen spoke first. He knew that they didn't have much time. It pained him as he had wanted to be able to break the news to her gently and have a few hours perhaps of civilized company and consolation. In the back of his mind he again cursed Patterson.

"William. He spoke of you often and fondly. How did he die?" Holden had to cough to clear his throat before answering.

"He died like a soldier, wounded and in my arms. He said for me to let you know that he had gone as he wished, and that he loved you very much." Still cradling her with one arm he pulled the picture of Green from his bag and gave it to her. "He wanted you to have this. To remember him as he was at his best."

She looked tearfully at the picture. She was trembling very slightly as she stayed with him.

"You're the man that is going to kill Patterson, aren't you?" He looked away from her. He was about to answer as she spoke further. "You can never be forgiven for the innocents you have killed, and I will never know why you did it. But promise me this. That man has brought me much harm. I assume it's because of him that Nigel is dead. He has abused me in a way that a common whore would struggle to be remunerated for. If you don't kill him, then the next time he comes here, I will." Holden immediately picked up something in what she said and the manner in which she said it.

"He's here now? Isn't he?" She was unable to look him in the face, she was sobbing looking into space and looking at the picture. He carefully sat her against the side of the coal bunker. Holden knew his answer.

Hoare looked back towards the front door of the apartments and began to stride towards it. He would be unaware that he was about to have to engage threats on two fronts. Braban looked north towards where Hoare had just been stood still and saw him heading towards the apartment. Ford, now in his full, cruellest self defence mode struck with the harshest force that he could. He trapped Braban's legs in a scissor movement within his own and brought him crashing to the floor. His intention then was to deliver as many punches to Braban's head as he could to knock him unconscious. Such a reasonable use of force was about to become inappropriate. His assailant was no slouch on the combat front. In swift movement he drew a bayonet from inside his coat and lashed out at Ford who was about to try to pin him down. It caught Ford across the left side of his chest and cut a minor wound through his clothing. He stepped back clutching his injury which gave Braban time to get on his feet. Braban charged him forcing Ford to dive and roll to one side to escape the line of attack. It was at this point, feeling an imminent threat to his life that he drew the Webley pistol, still holstered from earlier, and aimed at Braban. The threat of a firearm made no difference to him trying to call the policeman's bluff. As he ran at Ford again, a carefully aimed shot was fired that hit Braban square in the chest. He fell instantly and moved no further. Ford stood over him and aimed the gun at the back of Braban's head. Then he was disturbed by the sound of splintering wood and a loud bang.

Hoare had shoulder barged his way into the hallway of the building. He knew he was taking a risk and that Holden could easily be standing somewhere in the hallway waiting to place one carefully aimed shot. He had to take a chance and on this occasion fortune had favoured the bold. Where to go next though? He had seen Holden rescue the girl inside; he looked on the wall. There was a guide as to who lived where in the building. 'Wood. First floor, number three' he read it to himself. He gave no thought to clearing the rooms downstairs and ran straight up to the first floor. As he reached the landing he could see that the door to number three was closed.

He walked silently up to it and held his ear to door. He could detect nothing. He placed his hand on the brass door handle and tried it. It was locked. 'I've no time to fuck about' he thought, 'collateral damage'. He fired a shot through the door and heard a scream of despair on the other side, and then some footsteps running away. Hoare kicked the door in and saw a figure exit into a room on the right along the hallway of the apartment. He ran down there raising the gun as he rushed into the room. Cowering in a corner was Patterson. He wasn't even looking towards the door; he was just screaming in the corner.

"Please! Please, don't kill me! DON'T KILL MEEE!" Hoare felt instant revulsion to this cowardly reaction. He levelled the gun and aimed at a point just above Patterson's head. He fired. The screaming politician went quiet and looked up sobbing. His expression turned to disbelief in seeing Hoare. The Marine officer looked at him with utter distain. There was silence between them; Hoare broke it.

"You fucking weasel. This man Holden must be worth twenty of you." He spat to one side and walked back along the hallway.

Holden had made his way back into the house. This was it. He was going to finish it now, today. Patterson had brought so much misery to so many people in a variety of ways he had to die. He came cautiously into the downstairs hallway with his pistol at the ready. He still had a full chamber of six. He would count them along the way to be ready for a reload. He then heard a creaking of floorboards and looked up towards the stairs. The sun shining in was assisting in creating a huge shadow as Hoare came stealthily down the stairs.

Ford was running along the last few yards of Belgrave Square to reach Wilton Crescent and Karen's apartment, seemingly under attack. He didn't even stop to consider if Patterson was there. Karen was and that was all he cared for. He would kill anyone that was causing or trying to cause her harm. He had five left in the revolver and without the combat experience of the likes of Holden and Hoare he was unlikely to count them out, just find a random click as he reached an empty chamber, then react spontaneously to it. He was lucky that the sound of the door being crashed in by Hoare had snapped him out of almost pulling the trigger in a cold bloodied and unjustified execution. Ford reached the open and shattered door and burst in. He caught both the stealthy soldiers by complete surprise by his lack of tactical action and emotionally driven charge. Holden had decided to maintain his position in the hall towards the rear of the building, while Hoare was now at the base of the stairs in sight of Ford but keeping himself hidden from Holden.

At the sight of Ford and seeing the policeman with a gun in his hand, Hoare knew that Ford had used his pistol outside by the sound of the gunshot; he recognised it as that from a Webley revolver. He turned his Mannlicher on Ford and fired a single shot to discourage him from coming in. Having fired the one shot he retreated slightly upstairs to gain cover from him. Ford was undeterred and instinctively ducked but pressed on raising his pistol and firing to where he had seen Hoare. The shot impacted with the wall throwing up plaster and wood. The split second he fired the shot Ford realised that he was in grave danger advancing in the hallway with no immediate cover. He had drawn himself into this precarious situation through his desire to get to Karen. As he reached the base of the stairs ahead of him unaware of a pistol pointing at him, he saw another figure backlit by sunlight from a door to the right of him. First of all he couldn't make the figure out properly, but whoever it was shifted position slightly as some cloud cover passed overhead outside dimming the backlit effect. In a split second with the change of light he recognised the main features of this man as being the man he had seen and pursued in Venice. He now knew what the killer he was protecting Patterson from looked like.

The momentary distraction of this realisation allowed Hoare to step forward briefly. He then pistol whipped Ford with his automatic knocking him to the floor. A shot rang out from Holden's weapon that grazed Hoare's right forearm, he could see the fibres of his jacket singed and torn. Blindly Hoare pointed his arm around the corner and let off three rounds towards the rear of the hallway. They passed close by Holden who knew that with two potential assailants he would have to withdraw and finish Patterson another day. He ran back out to the rear of the premises looking down to Karen as he exited; she was sat with her back to the coal bunker with her knees drawn up to her chest and her arms folded in front her with her head buried in her arms. He wanted to console her but he had to escape; remaining in any way and for any reason would mean certain death or capture. The man that had initially engaged him he could tell was a military professional. He ran past her and exited through a gate that took him into Kinnerton Street.

Upstairs in the apartment Patterson was still slumped on the floor in the lounge. Opposite him was a mirror and he was transfixed on the smoking bullet hole he could see above him in his reflection. Having heard further gunfire downstairs he dared not move.

Hoare ran past the recovering Ford and out into the rear yard. He saw the girl on the floor but ignored her in favour of the open gate. He exited through it and looked left and right for any signs of Holden. He saw him running south towards Motcomb Street. He gave chase mindful that he had used all six rounds in his magazine and reloaded with a fresh magazine of another six.

Ford dragged himself to his feet and made for the open door. As he emerged into the yard he could see the gate open ahead and was about to run out of it when movement in his peripheral vision caught his eye. He turned his head swiftly to see that it was Karen.

"Oh, my god, no!" He rushed down to her as she looked up from her folded arms. He knelt beside her and she flung her arms around him sobbing; she seemed unable to speak. He desperately wanted to give chase to his two aggressors but knew that he had to get her inside. He helped her to her feet and then they entered the house. He slowly walked Karen up the stairs and into the apartment. He was not prepared to actually meet Patterson in there. When Karen saw him she screamed at him.

"Get out! Get out, you filthy bastard! Get OUT!" She was livid; Ford had never seen her so aggressively animated. Ford did not know what to think. What he did know was that he had to keep this horrible man safe, particularly in the light of the events of the last few minutes.

"Sir, go in the kitchen and wait there, please." Patterson looked at Ford; he got to his feet and left as requested. Ford sat Karen in an armchair.

Holden had made it to Lowndes Street when he heard another shot ring out. It shocked him as there were lots of the capital's public around now to easily be struck by a bullet fired hastily. He saw the lone shot impact into a nearby tree. Holden found himself some cover behind a red, iron post box with its 'VR' crest from the days of the last monarch and took a carefully aimed shot at Hoare. He surprised himself as the round whizzed past its intended target into thin air along Lowndes Street. Hoare ducked into the arched entrance way to a private house to give himself a safe place from which to return fire. He had five more rounds left before a reload; he was unsure how many Holden had; he assumed at least another five. The shot that had just missed him was the first he could recall from Holden.

"He won't touch you again, Karen, I promise." Ford spoke softly to her holding her right hand in both of his having placed his revolver on a table.

"I don't care if this madman does kill him; I just want him out of my life. He sickens me with his pitiful sexual experience and his coarse obsession. Don't let him back in here, or I swear I will kill him." She broke down in tears. Ford looked at her bowed head as she sobbed into her lap in an emotional and confused state. He knew that she was Patterson's mistress; surely this wasn't the only matter that had tipped her so dramatically into an emotional break down?

"Karen, is there something else? Do you want me to leave? You have had little time to yourself since little Nigel passed away?"

"No. I need you with me. I must stay with you; keep me away from him in your house." He paused before answering; he could tell that Patterson was at the doorway listening in. Then Mark Vincent appeared in the room.

"What the hell has happened here, Boss?" Ford had no time to explain.

"Mark, stay with her and the Minister. Keep them apart. I have to go and see where these gunmen have gone." Ford picked up his revolver and entered the hall to leave. He had been able to hear gun fire from two distinctively different hand guns in the distance and was in a state of confusion. There appeared to be two armed men that were battling each other. Was one with the Minister and the other the man out to get him? He needed the answer. As he was about to exit the apartment the Minister grabbed his arm.

"What does she mean 'stay with you?' She is my woman, Ford, just stay away." There was venom in his voice, he was regaining his composure.

"Minister, you may not be in a position to make demands. I mean, a mistress? Some other secrets you are not telling me about? Don't make threats you cannot carry through. Don't confuse you position with my authority." Ford pulled his arm away and ran out of the apartment, down the stairs and out of the rear of the building trying to listen for continued gunfire.

* * *

Holden and Hoare were in a stalemate on the streets of Belgravia. Neither were prepared to break cover and neither had fired another shot yet as they were both too well concealed. Panicking people ran around them in the street adding to the mayhem of the situation. Both were aware of the potential arrival of unarmed patrolling policemen at any minute; an intrusion that could only complicate the situation and force one of them out into the open. Holden had to escape. He needed to get away, to go to ground before finishing off his quest for revenge. He could ill afford to be engaged in a gunfight on the streets of London. He continued peering in Hoare's direction and saw his opportunity. Just behind his adversaries position was a uniform constable running towards them blowing on his duty whistle. He allowed the whistle to fall from his mouth and dangle by its chain and then shouted towards Hoare. He had no choice but to be distracted and turned towards the policeman. Holden broke cover and ran hard heading west and entered Cadogan Place; looking up in the distance he could see the building site of the new 'Harrods' store nearing completion, under the directions of its architect Charles William Stephens no doubt. A building site may be a good place to lose himself as he turned again and ran north in Sloane Street to escape his assailant.

Hoare turned towards the constable still with the Mannlicher in his hand. He levelled the gun at the policeman who stopped in his tracks.

"Now put the gun down, sir, don't be stupid. You'll hang for this if you do." The policeman spoke with amazing calmness as he faced the gun.

"Don't be stupid constable I don't want to kill you. I'm an undercover agent of the state in pursuit of an armed criminal, so stay away and let me get on with it."

"Show me some proof, first. You know there's more coming, you can't get away." The policeman was annoyingly persistent in his wish to detain Hoare.

Ford rounded the corner from Motcomb into Lowndes Street to see the confrontation. He knew that it was not practicable to try to engage this man with a verbal warning and with the constable stood there. Ford levelled his gun in both hands and took a shot. Hoare hadn't seen Ford enter the fray. The shot whistled past the constable's head and impacted into Hoare's left shoulder, high on the deltoid muscle so not passing through bone.

"Ah! Christ!" Hoare grabbed at his shoulder, dropping the Mannlicher in the process. Ford was nearly fifty feet away as the constable grabbed for the gun. Although wounded, Hoare was no stranger to injury coupled with the need to continue to fight. With limited use of his left arm he began grappling with the constable who had taken hold of the gun in his right hand. Ford was still running towards them.

Hoare and the constable struggled initially facing each other wrestling hand to hand and then Hoare turned so he grappled the constable from behind. A shot went off and the constable went limp. Hoare knew there was still one left in the gun. Ford levelled his weapon over the last ten feet but hesitated in firing as the gunman was using the constable's limp body as a human shield. Hoare, operating the gun in the constable's apparently lifeless hand, took a shot that just missed Ford. He let the body of the constable fall to the floor, drawing a throwing dagger from his waistband as he did so. Before Ford could react he threw the dagger that found its mark in Ford's right thigh, impacting in the muscles along the front of it. Ford fell to the floor clutching his leg in agony. Hoare grabbed the gun from the dying constable's hand and fled the scene in the direction that he had seen Holden take. With limited use of his left arm he reloaded a fresh magazine into the Mannlicher, but kept the old one as he had lost count of his rounds with the distraction of the wound.

* * *

Inside Karen's apartment there was tension. Vincent did not have the confidence to keep resisting the Minister's demands to 'see how my tailoress is.' Eventually he let Patterson into the lounge where Karen stood and was staring listlessly out of the window, eyes swollen and puffed, her thoughts far away with how this man was responsible for so much hurt in her life; sexual abuse and blackmail while her son was alive, a feeling of low self esteem from his constant depravity, the death of her husband and now the misery of being tied to him having found love with a decent man. She felt a hand on her shoulder and instantly knew from its feel that it was Patterson. She turned and lashed out with her fists. He wasn't a weak man where women were concerned and he very quickly got control of her arms and held her still with a great deal of discomfort to her. She felt weak and alone and gave up resisting and began to sob again, collapsing in front of him as he held her up by her arms.

"Now you listen to me, you cheap little slut, and listen well." She couldn't look at him and continued to sob. "If you have fucked our policeman guardian angel then I suggest you stop. You would be nothing without me and have nothing, so you will do as I say."

"I have nothing because of you. I no longer care anymore." She fought for breath as she finished this short retort.

"Do you really want to go back to stitching and whoring in the East End, eh?" He drooled slightly with anger as he spoke.

"I never whored myself there, only here with you, you bastard."

Patterson hauled her up slightly more by her arms forcing her to take some of her own weight, then he let go of her left hand and slapped her harshly across her face. She didn't scream out, just cried a little more. Vincent heard the sound of the slap as he stood outside of the room. His fists were clenching and releasing; he had never had such a situation to deal with and did not know how to react. As a beat constable he had dealt with frequent domestic assaults and had stepped in to prevent a great many, but never one involving a high ranking member of the government who had officially sanctioned protection. He could hear Karen whimper some more as Patterson forced her to stay on her feet. Another slapping sound; Patterson had struck her again. Vincent prepared to step in now infuriated by the man's cowardice. His mother had often been beaten in front of him by his father and this abuse of a woman in a similar fashion was too much for him to bear. As he considered walking into the room with memories of his mother's beatings, he recalled them, in an out of body experience, observing himself as a nine-year-old boy.

* * *

The nine year old Mark Vincent cowered in a corner of a run down kitchen in a shabby terraced house in Islington. His face already felt sore, as he had received a slap just for being in the house from his drunken father, a stocky man of average height with poor personal hygiene that was exacerbated by the smell of alcohol abuse. He was unshaven and dirty from his toil as a chimney sweep. His skinny son had been of no use to him today having sprained an ankle the day before and was unable to walk. The chimney sweep's dinner was not ready as he arrived home from the pub and he had begun to exert his displeasure on the only two people in the house; Mark and his mother.

The lad had been easy to deal with; a swift back-handed slap had put him onto the floor and had exaggerated the pain in his ankle as he fell. He had dragged himself into the corner to sob and try to hide behind a tatty butchers block. He watched as his callous and violent father approached his mother who had her back to a plain brick wall next to the ancient iron stove. His father slapped her twice across her face forehand and then backhand, she stood defiantly in front of him not touching her reddening face. She had been brought up to accept the behaviour of her husband. She knew that it didn't make it right but was afraid to fight against working class conventions. His father was obviously not satisfied with her silence. Then the punches began. The side of her head, then her stomach and then her back as she fell to her knees. Mark looked on helplessly crying loudly in fear for himself and his mother's safety. When his father started kicking her he could take no more. He looked up to the top of the butcher's block at the aging knives that it held. He got quietly to his feet and pulled one out; a steak boning knife that glinted slightly as he turned it and gazed upon its ten inch blade. His father was unaware of his son's actions. Recalling some of the stories he had heard at school of ancient Rome he knew he could stop his father without killing him. He walked quietly the few feet across the kitchen to his mother and father, his mother lying on the floor eyes screwed shut gasping to breathe, his father now just stood over her. With one swift movement the boy slashed out with the knife across the back of his father's two thighs ensuring the knife slashed deeply. His father screamed out and fell to the floor; it had achieved the desired effect of severing both his hamstrings.

The memories of the events following the attack on his father were always vague; he could remember the man not being around much once he returned from two months away at a boarding school.

* * *

He was now stood in the lounge of Karen's apartment, back in the present and looking down he realised that he had a knife from her kitchen in his hand. He had subliminally, whilst lost in his thoughts, fetched one from her block. 'What the fuck am I doing?' he thought to himself. He tossed the knife down and strode over to Patterson about to hit her again. He grabbed his raised arm from behind and spun Patterson around who let go of Karen. She fell limply to the floor crying. He put the Minister in a painful arm lock with his right arm wrenched high up his back and marched him out of the lounge. In the hall he threw Patterson harshly to the floor. He landed face down and then turned himself over staring up at Mark Vincent with venom in his eyes. He appeared initially lost for words so Vincent spoke.

"It is part of my protection duties; really it is for your own good. Because if you continue to beat her anymore then I will kill you." Patterson didn't know what to say.

Chapter Twenty-One

Ford clutched his right thigh. The pain was immense with the knife having buried itself deep in his quadriceps. Helplessly he had to watch Hoare get away. He held his breath and pulled the knife out of his leg; he screamed in agony as he did so, the pain so great he nearly passed out. He had to breathe heavily to regain his composure. When he had, he dragged himself over to the prostrate constable. He took his pulse and checked his breathing. There appeared to be nothing he could do for him. He grabbed the constable's whistle and pulled it free from the dead man's tunic. He blew repeatedly upon it until eventually several other officers arrived. One was a sergeant. Ford spoke to him and showed him his warrant card.

"Get me back to four Wilton Crescent, Sergeant!"

"But your leg, sir?"

"Fuck the leg, get me there and I'll sort it out later." The sergeant helped Ford get to his feet and then supported him as they limped back to Karen's apartment.

When they arrived back there, there were numerous officers on scene. The Minister had been taken home to Belgrave Square; he would have some explaining to do to Lady Patterson as the press were beginning to swarm the scene too. Vincent was the one who had taken Patterson back so Karen was sat in an armchair alone with a constable making a pot of tea in her kitchen; the universally British way to put things right it seemed. She looked up as Ford hobbled into the room. She could see his heavily blood stained trouser leg.

"Oh Robert!" She ran sobbing to him and flung her arms around him and cried into his shoulder. She managed to speak a few more words. "What is going on, this world has gone mad! What happened to you?"

"I wish I knew; I turned up here to see you to find two men trying to kill me and each other it seems, then that son of a bitch Patterson was here in a completely unscheduled way. If he carries on like that he won't have to worry about warding the killer off, he just invites him by moving around without any protection." She helped Ford sit down in a chair and then went to fetch a cotton sheet and a bowl of warm water to tend his wound.

Alone in the room for a few moments, he stared out of the window. He would get the truth now from Patterson whatever the cost, and that man would not go near Karen again.

* * *

Hoare found himself approaching the back of the nearly completed Harrod's store in Hans Crescent. He seemed to have lost Holden but kept himself close to street furniture and building lines to try to be able to quickly acquire cover if a shot missed him.

On the third floor of the new department store Holden looked out along Hans Crescent from a window that was on the corner with Basil Street to see if he could spot his wounded pursuer. He knew that he had been caught with a glancing shot, but that would probably only prove to be an advantage if his assailant ended up in a hand to hand fight with him, although the wounded man was tall and looked powerful. He would try to take him with a gunshot from his position. Holden had got access into the building without being challenged; the third floor was complete and now being fitted out and finished off. He had found a quiet office that afforded him his view. Being side streets, Basil Street and Hans Crescent were quite quiet. Pedestrians were conspicuous along them; then Hoare came into view. Holden observed from his movements that his adversary knew only too well he was vulnerable in the street, so he would have to make any shot count. The tall powerful man was also scanning his environment above eye level, only too aware of the potential for a kind of 'sniper action'.

The Dressmaker Connection

Holden reasoned that if he could kill this man now it was one less obstacle preventing him from getting close to Patterson. He also reasoned that this man must have been employed with the raison d'etre of finding Holden in the wake of the murders. He was certainly not being employed officially by the state by the measure of his actions. Holden could see that Hoare was now getting into the realistic range of a pistol shot from him; he also realised he had made an obvious error. The window in the office was still closed. He had two choices, shoot through it giving his adversary a minimum of warning, or open it slowly hoping that its movement was undetected in Hoare's peripheral vision. The first option was his only real choice to be sure of maximum success.

He reloaded the revolver to be sure of a maximum number of shots and brought the weapon up into the aim. Hoare continued along the building line of Hans Crescent oblivious to his impending possible demise. Holden cocked the hammer action on the Webley to be sure of the greatest level of accuracy through a minimum of trigger shake or snatching, and focused himself with the iron sights. A head shot was out of the question, it had to be at the body, the centre of mass for greatest chance of success. Hoare was comfortably in his sights about seventy feet away; Holden pulled the trigger.

The glass of the office window shattered immediately giving away his position. The split second that the glass shattered Hoare threw himself to the floor diving forwards with the bullet whistling only just past him. He got to his feet before Holden could get another shot off and ran to the building line of Harrods and out of Holden's sight. Holden exited the office he was in to prevent himself from being trapped and made for a set of signposted stairs. They were on the opposite of the building from where Hoare would enter and would afford him a greater chance of escape. He gave up on the idea of killing the tall man now, in so doing he could end up in the hands of the authorities with whom the area would soon be swarming.

Hoare ran up the first set of stairs he could find, gun in hand with workmen and foremen shouting after him. 'Oi! You can't fucking go up there!' But no one challenged him physically having noted the gun. When he made it up to the third floor, with a mind for spatial awareness he found the office very quickly but as he suspected it was empty. He would have to give up the search for this dangerous man Holden for now. His shoulder was aching; he knew that his new priority was finding medical attention.

Holden made it swiftly into Hans Road, which was on the other side of the store, and then into Knightsbridge itself to hail a cab.

"Where to Guv'nor?" asked the cabby as Holden clambered on board.

"The Great Central Hotel, Marylebone Road, please driver." Holden was out of breath as he spoke.

"Right you are, sir." With a crack from his riding crop the cab lurched off heading east along Knightsbridge with its lone occupant feeling a sense of escape.

* * *

September 7th, Patterson's Empire Petroleum office 10.a.m.

The Minister didn't want to meet with his supposed inner circle anywhere near Parliament. That was where most of the intrusive press coverage seemed to be concentrated at. The report in the previous day's London Times had not been positive for the Minister but was favourable for the police:

'WAR BREAKS OUT IN BELGRAVIA PART OF THE GROWING MYSTERY SURROUNDING MINISTER PATTERSON

The mystery surrounding the attacks upon the office of Minister of War Sir Cecil Patterson intensified yesterday with a sensational shooting, and the murders of an innocent beat constable and a former marine in a normally safe and respectable London street. Inspector Robert Ford of Scotland Yard fought a running gun battle with two mysterious men that began in Wilton Crescent and continued up to the back of the nearly completed Harrods store. In the process a former marine who attacked Ford with a bayonet repeatedly was shot dead by the inspector, who is charged with the care of Patterson, and fought against two further assailants. They escaped after one of them stabbed the hero inspector in the leg having murdered a beat constable, yet to be named, moments before as the constable wrestled to get a gun from him. Scotland Yard have, as yet, declined to respond to any press questions. Patterson was at the scene of the skirmish, apparently cowering inside number four Wilton Crescent, for reasons unknown. Neighbours have said that the occupier of the premises is romantically linked to the Minister, who has always presented a respectable family life with his wife. Neither the Minister himself nor his office have yet to comment either, but it is believed they are taking legal advice. It is yet another twist in the bizarre saga that has surrounded this government office. So far the death toll has now reached six. The investigation continues and Inspector Ford, a veteran officer once involved in the investigation of the murders of 'Jack the Ripper', is believed to be currently considered for a bravery award.'

Present in the lavish office were Patterson, Ford, Vincent and Phillips. There was silence between them as Patterson had already stated that he was waiting for one more person to arrive before the way forward was discussed. Ford's leg hurt, it was heavily bandaged and bruising more than anything else was the main source of discomfort. He had been treated at the Charing Cross Hospital just off of The Strand; the nursing staff had been very helpful, flattered to receive a genuine hero in their triage.

The sound of the door handle being turned and the door opening drew everyone's attention to see who was about to enter. Ford leapt to his feet painfully in disbelief and drew his revolver as Hoare stepped into the room.

"You can put the gun down, Inspector Ford. I am not here to threaten you or anyone else. I am here at the request of the Minister. I believe today's meeting is about resolution to the current crisis. For those of you who don't know my name I am Major Marcus Hoare." Ford kept his pistol trained on Hoare as he spoke to the Minister. In the meantime Vincent had drawn his own. Hoare was calm in the face of two pistols being pointed at him; the reality was that two policemen would not shoot him in cold blood in this office. It would be an action that would render them as guilty as he was.

Ford no longer felt obliged to treat Patterson with any cordiality. He felt sure that Patterson would be sensible enough not to enquire about his directness; the time for politeness had passed.

"Patterson, you must be fucking joking. What the hell is this killer doing in here? I assume for me to take him into custody for the murder of an innocent beat duty constable?" It was Hoare who replied first.

"Oh come on, Ford. You saw what happened. It wasn't a deliberate act. If I was out to kill don't you think you'd be dead too. Lets face it I had the chance. The poor fellow was collateral damage." Ford could feel his rage developing within. He pulled the hammer action back on the Webley.

"Collateral damage? So if I kill you now do you think I could justify that in the same way? 'Heroic policeman shoots dead gunman previously seen in gun battle at Minister of War's mistress's house?' That would get me clear of a cop killer like you," Ford said addressing Hoare and then turned to Patterson, "and finish your career, you son of a bitch," Ford was looking at Patterson as he finished.

"Ford, put the gun down. And how dare you speak to me in that way. So what if she is my mistress. It's hardly uncommon. The only unusual factor is for a psychotic former army officer to be out to kill me and therefore expose me publicly at the same time." Ford lowered his gun looking at the Minister in disbelief. Watching him do this, Mark Vincent trained his own firearm on Hoare.

"What do you mean? You know who the hell it is don't you?" Ford holstered his weapon and walked behind Patterson's desk and grabbed him by his lapels. He lifted Patterson onto his feet and then slammed him into the wall behind him. "Explain yourself, Patterson. What the fuck do you mean?"

"I'll tell you what he means, Ford. I know what his dark secret is I suspect. Put him down, let's all put our guns away and talk about this over a drink," said Hoare in an inappropriately casual and calm fashion. Ford scowled at Hoare. He looked across at Vincent who acknowledged his look holstering his weapon. Ford let go of Patterson's lapels who proceeded to straighten his clothing out in a very pretentious manner. Everyone observed Hoare walk up to the drinks cabinet and its facia. He lowered it to form a serving area placing five tumblers from the case affixed to the wall above the drinks cabinet. It contained an assortment of elegant Waterford cut glass drinking ware. He noticed a new vintage bottle of Bowmore single malt whiskey in the cabinet he had not seen before and he pulled it out and read the label. "A new acquisition, Minister? Bowmore 1883. Very nice. We should enjoy this, gentlemen." He poured everyone a generous tumbler leaving the most generously filled one for himself. He passed them round and toasted the group. "Well cheers, everybody." Hoare savoured the peaty taste of this freshly opened malt. It was different from the Glenfiddich he had finished previously, mostly as a result of being made with different natural spring water.

Hoare put his glass back down on the cabinet and bent down to look to the rear of it. He was not disappointed; the leather bound journal that he had previously spotted was still there. He was amazed that the Minister had not moved it.

"Very lax, Minister. Keeping the most secret document you possess in the same place? Shame on you. That journo that I had to take care of found it, I saw it. Well even the likes of the police would have found it." Ford advanced towards Hoare but was stopped in his tracks by Vincent grabbing his arm.

"You, tosser Hoare. Don't you dare belittle us. You've just confirmed my suspicions about William Bates. It was quite obvious he had been murdered. When you got a pathologist to overlook injuries, either lie about them or have the report destroyed. Even the weary Igor's who work in the mortuaries would be able to tell that he was pinioned. I believe it is you that needs to sharpen your act."

"Mr Ford, I assume that you are sharp enough to realise that I have been set to do your master's dirty work. The cripple, the journo, old soldiers in Dagenham, and now a man named Holden as a next target. Isn't that right, Minister?"

Patterson had been standing quietly sipping his single malt naively hoping that this point, the one that Ford had raised so vehemently about his complicity, would go away.

"Come on Patterson, coupled with the killer, who I presume is this man Holden, and your lackey Major Hoare, we have eight murders on our hands from their efforts. I assume that the explanation is, one might say in the understatement of the year, somewhat serious and perhaps convoluted?" Ford's aggressive stance had given way to resigned weary cynicism; one the most natural traits of a veteran police officer. Patterson took a deep breath and looked around the room.

"Hoare, bring the journal please." Hoare pulled the battered, leather bound document from the cabinet and began to walk it towards the Minister. "No. Give it to Ford to read." Hoare passed it over to the detective inspector.

"I don't suppose I can have a quick précis from someone?" Inquired Ford. The Minister stayed silent. Hoare coughed and began.

"Well, I can tell you what I suspect the gist of the truth behind the events is. Based on long standing army rumours and by my own involvement in events, and from what I suspect that journal contains, then this is what I believe this entire scandal and trail of death is about.

"Back in 1898, you Minister sent a group of highly trained but experimental soldiers led by this Captain Holden out to Afghanistan to discover whether or not there were rich reserves of oil there. Legend stated that it was pooled underground but easy to get to. Formed in lakes its known locally by its bizarre viscosity as 'black gold'; hence 'operation Auric Noir'. Very cliché. I would imagine you promised to get them out, or send help if there was trouble. There must have been trouble; they were compromised in some way. But you left them there to rot. Rumours have it that all but two were killed in a brutally savage local fashion which leads to the air of ritualism in the killings in Europe. Apparently you subsequently went in there and tried to have Holden and the other survivor killed, but you failed. He escaped back to Europe eventually by use of his own guile and army contacts to come and seek out a campaign of revenge against you. He's certainly been successful so far.

"His name is William Holden. He is a captain, with a distinguished service career and an enormous amount of natural leadership qualities, resilience, but above all else a natural soldiering aptitude. Holden comes from a moneyed background but his personal life prior to military life was not without tragedy. In the wake of struggles of the last six years, and no one knows how long it took him to escape Afghanistan and India, he is out to kill in revenge for his men's suffering and neglect. I tell you all now, without our vigilance from here on in, he will succeed. He is tough and resourceful and highly dangerous from his soldiering efficiency. He must have a very positive state of mind to be prepared to kill as he has done ritualistically to scare you. If I was you, Minister, I would be grateful for the presence of myself, Ford, Vincent and other protection officers that may or have come along. And all this because you wanted to maximise the profits of Empire Petroleum by cornering the market early on for the use of fossil fuels. Now, how far from the truth am I?"

Patterson had to pause for a moment while he digested the elements of Hoare's theorem. There was no doubt that the Marine Major was almost one hundred percent right. He stood to be ruined if the journal, or any mention of what had so far been discussed, leaked beyond this room. He looked into each of the faces of those gathered in his office; they looked back at him in an expectant manner. He composed himself.

"Well, I will leave you all to read the journal, but Major Hoare is almost absolutely right regarding the facts to now." Confirmed Patterson. Ford interjected.

"How many murders were we up to when you realised that you might know who had started this blood bath that spreads across four European cities?" Patterson was reticent to answer. He lied; his most potent weapon and one that continually served him well.

"Three. At that point I knew that Holden was out to get me." Hoare remained silent; he knew factually that it was not true. Ford allowed the silence in the room to create discomfort, Patterson's slight tell, a minor twitch in his left eye gave away the lie.

"With the bizarre nature of that first one, you must have had an inkling, you son of a bitch. Certainly after the second one. How the hell did you think you'd get away with me not finding out the truth?" Ford was speaking rationally but coldly.

"I hoped that there would just be an incident and that you would kill him. When I realised how efficient he was, that was when I asked Major Hoare to find him." Patterson's eye maintained its minimal twitch. Hoare interjected.

"Of course, Inspector, that was after he had employed me to lead the major incursion into Afghanistan. After I had taken care of the journalist." Ford looked around the room in disgust with his feelings towards these men.

"State sponsored murder. That is what you are employing your henchmen for, Patterson. Bates, the cripple Waldron, the so called accidental shooting of the constable in Belgravia, the attempt on my life outside Karen's home, forcing me to kill in self defence. This is going to stop. Once it does I swear I will bring you both to task."

"Ford, don't be so common. Men like us don't get brought to task," said Hoare. "We have a common enemy. Defeat him together and I will live in self imposed exile. You'll be lucky to fix the Minister, he's a Freemason. But of course you knew that, and you have a poor track record against them." Hoare lit a cigarette as he finished; he did not expect Ford's lightning response. Ford charged him whilst he concentrated on the flame of a match and knocked him to the floor. He pinned his arms down with his legs and grabbed his lapels in a cross-armed fashion. He pulled them hard un-crossing his arms as he did so beginning a very effective strangle hold. Hoare tried to struggle but it was futile against the efficiency of Ford's method of attack. His struggle became more and more violent as asphyxiation very quickly began to take hold. Mark Vincent rushed forward and dragged Ford off Hoare who was left coughing and choking on the floor lifting himself onto his left elbow and holding his neck with his right hand. Vincent held onto Ford by his arms waiting for him to calm before letting go. Patterson was the first to speak.

"That will achieve nothing for god's sake."

Hoare cut in.

The Dressmaker Connection

"Watch your back; you are only a thug policeman. When we have Holden then you and I will face each other again." There was menace in Hoare's voice. Ford was unafraid; his formative years had knocked most of that emotion from him.

"We must come up with a plan to stop all this. You may attempt your retribution later, Ford," said Patterson. "For now you are as much of a target as the rest of us."

That was the first truthful and salient point Ford could recall Patterson making. With the list of victims including a police officer then Holden knew no bounds; it was any male it seemed associated with the Ministry. Ford considered his words. No one expected Vincent to speak, he was new to the immediate circle of the Minister, but Ramsey Phillips who seemed conspicuously quiet was the first to make a suggestion.

"Look, may I speak? If we are looking for an obvious way of luring this man Holden into the open, then use a fictitious venue. Let's make it somewhere we can use and plan to our advantage. The Carfax-Smythe family of Tudor Castle in Kent are old friends of my family. The castle sits on an island on a lake with only one non-waterborne way in over a bridge and through a gatehouse with a portcullis. We cancel the review temporarily and hold some sort of seminar or Ministerial meeting there over several days and see if it smokes him out. Easy to defend and hard to get into." Again, as had happened so frequently in the office, a silence descended as they all considered the suggestion.

Hoare could immediately see the sense in it from a military strategist's point of view, as could Ford from the years of consideration to 'safe houses' in the protection world. The cowardly Patterson liked the idea of increased invulnerability. Perhaps, following such as suggestion, Ford's suspicions surrounding Ramsey Phillips were unfounded.

"All right, when can we go?" said Ford.

"If you want to get him out into the open to make an attempt on the Minister we have to publicise the fact," said Philips, in truth knowing that it would cover his own tracks perfectly. With public awareness of the case there was an excuse for Holden to know if the 'conference' was publicised; without doubt the policeman and the mercenary would start looking inwards for answers. This tactic would put them off any internal scent. "I'll convene a meeting with the chiefs of staff with a false agenda. When they get there we'll treat it as a social engagement to put them at ease. All we can then do is wait and see what happens."

"All right," said Ford, "having the overriding autonomy for the protection package then I say we'll work with it. Make the necessary arrangements, Mr Philips. I the meantime, would you all leave me alone with the Minister please, we have something to discuss."

Hoare, Vincent and Philips all left the opulent office leaving Ford and a nervous looking Patterson behind. Patterson sat uneasily in his green, leather-quilted chair at his desk as Ford shut the door behind the last to leave. Ford walked over to the desk and leant, stood up still with his hands flat on the edge of the desk peering over it with a quiet air of menace.

"I'm going to cut you a little slack, Patterson, so listen well. That press report is not favourable. I plan to take you down at the end of this, but if you do as I say you'll still have a marriage and not the expense of a divorce. Leave Karen Wood alone. Dismiss her as your supposed seamstress. I can cover the nonsense of a romantic link by stating you were attending to pay your respects over the loss of her son, and because you had a guardian role for the lad. It's a load of shit I know, but it will work. But you'll only have the scandal of Holden to deny then. Lady P. will be appeased, so will Karen and so will I, partially at least. If you refuse it will be on your own head. Touch her again and I'll make sure Holden finds you. Do we understand each other, Minister?" It was a cold hearted and clinical proposal. It suited the nature of the man it was addressed to; he didn't have to think about it for long, although he would miss the sexual gratification.

"All right, Ford, you win. The little slut is yours."

Patterson felt sure it wouldn't be for long. Although he had seen Hoare taken off guard, he knew that once this ghastly interconnected affair was over Hoare, out of his own self interest, would take care of Ford and blame Holden. That would leave him free to indulge in the pleasures of the dressmaker again.

"Good day to you for now," said Ford as he nodded slowly to Patterson, turned and left the room with the journal in his hand to read. Its contents would give him a full understanding as to the motive and origins of the hideous acts he had witnessed. In the doorway he spoke before closing the door. "Oh, and by the way, I am right in suspecting that this journal will help me understand how a long crippled soldier ended up washed up in the Thames?"

"Just read it, Ford. Oh, and do bear one thing in mind, when you are supposed to be able to remain detached, when you go public how will you explain your liaison with a member of my staff? Surely that isn't very professional? How **will** that affect your professional standing, eh?" Ford could not believe he was being out-manoeuvred by a Freemason again.

"You fucker." He left the room, conceding inside that 'the bastard' had a point.

Patterson smiled a Machiavellian smile as Ford left the room and then got down to some E.P paperwork. The phone then rang. It was Lady Patterson.

"Hello, darling......it is a nonsense what was printed......yes, you know I love you deeply......Look, Inspector Ford is going to make a statement and explain my link to Karen, and why I was there the other day.......Well, darling it's obvious if you think about the poor girl's loss........ no she can't do your clothes for a while.........No apparently she needs a little more time to grieve.......I'll see you this afternoon and we'll chat more then.........Take care, bye now...."

Patterson replaced the candlestick style, brass telephone on the desk.

"Gullible bitch." He carried on looking at his share certificates; E.P was annoyingly looking a little low this month.

Chapter Twenty-Two

Holden Hall, Hertfordshire

Holden was talking to a tearful and shaking stable girl inside the grand Georgian stable block. There was the over-powering stench of horses in the air. His brother, Frank, looked on helplessly as he had been unaware until now of the intrusion by Hoare. The merciless marine had simply attacked the hapless girl in the stable block who had unfortunate knowledge, for her, of William Holden's return to England. She had explained how a tall powerful man had held her down and put her in a painful restraint holds until she told him everything of the recent events at Holden Hall, and knowledge of Master Holden senior having a house in Ebury Street, London as she had heard the brothers talking about it. She broke down as she alluded to the fact that the man had then raped her. She had been near to inconsolable as William Holden had taken the girl in his arms and she sobbed violently into his shoulder and chest, holding tightly onto him like a frightened child. Frank looked on with a look of concern.

"Why would this man come here to find out about you, Will?" It was a question that he knew he had to ask to gain some insight into the girl's sorry condition. William Holden paused to gather his thoughts before speaking.

"All right, here's the crux of it. I was sent into Afghanistan with a group of specially trained soldiers to look for reserves of oil on behalf of Patterson and the government, but in truth to further his own Empire Petroleum interests. The natives turned on us and slaughtered all but two of us eventually. He promised to send a rescue party that never came. All that did come was him and some soldiers who tried to kill us to silence us, but I got away with the other survivor." William could see Frank concentrating on his explanation. He knew that his younger brother was clever enough to deduce one element he would leave out. "We came back here, and he discovered that we were alive. He can't face a scandal so he had the other survivor killed and now he's after me. That's why that man came here. He is a callous, conscience free bastard. You'd be in your rights to shoot him on our land." Frank looked his brother in the eye.

"Don't you think it's too late for him not to face a scandal? He already is with the murders you have set in place! How could you? I used to look up to you! You are no better than him! Killing all those innocents, why did you just not go for him if you had to do something! You have brought shame to our family, Will."

"But, Frank, I can…"

"GET OUT! LEAVE! I never saw you and I never knew you survived if this man comes back. Our parents would turn in their graves. Do what you have to do to clear your own warped sense of right and wrong, but don't come back here!"

Frank took the young girl, who was oblivious to the heated attack by her current employer, and left the stable block. William Holden looked on helplessly out of the door of the block with tears in his eyes and a lump in his throat as the two headed towards the main house. He sat down on a hay bale and his head dropped into his hands as he began to sob himself. He had finally lost everything, the respect of the remainder of his family and any hope of returning to live or visit the family estate. In his troubled mind there was one thought that was unequivocal; this was the final nail in the coffin for Patterson. His quest for vengeance must now end, no matter what the cost.

The sobbing led to a coughing fit, which in turn forced him to hold a handkerchief to his mouth. He coughed up more blood from his lungs than ever before and the rasping hacking left his chest feeling very painful. As he regained his breath but still felt the pain, he removed a pipe from his pocket and prepared a small 'blaze' of opium. He could not realise that the drug might be easing his pain but increasing his mental instability.

The Dressmaker Connection

* * *

September 9th, Ministry of War, Whitehall

Ramsey Phillips had not seen who had entered the Minister's office. All he noted as he entered the reception area where Fiona Shaw was busy typing, was a hand carved, mahogany 'do not disturb' sign hung on Patterson's office door. It was a very unusual event. Fiona looked up at him as he entered and was not forthcoming as to who was inside. She spoke to him on a separate matter.

"Have you set a date with the Carfax-Smythes for this Chief's of Staff event at Tudor Castle yet?" He certainly had, and this afternoon he had to make his scheduled rendezvous with Holden to pass him the details. He had no remorse for having culpability for his colleagues' deaths, with his obsessive ambition to climb the civil service ladder to the top, it kept his up and coming potential threats at bay.

"As a matter of fact, I have. Much sooner than we anticipated. The 20th September. If you let the head of the army and the navy know via their respective offices then we'll convene for two nights on that date. I'll get the details of who will use which parts of the castle for accommodation. Pass the date in the press and 'spin it' accordingly about something to do with military restructuring for the good of the Empire. We don't really want the buggers to know that it's a social event for the chiefs to draw out this Holden chap." Fiona Shaw was unmoved by his answer; it was what she expected.

"Sounds good, I'll get that moved along." She returned to typing at her heavy, iron typewriter. He looked at her and then back at the 'do not disturb' sign. He had to know who was in there.

"Fiona, who is in with Sir Cecil? Unusual to see that sign?"

"It's the Prime Minister. I think he is quite outraged by the events of the last month or so and is telling the Minister that he'll have to consider his position. Trouble is he has to be delicate as he's a share holder in E.P."

Phillips nodded his head in acknowledgement and then turned and left the office. He needed to clarify with the castle who would use which rooms so that he could pass the information on to Holden. Phillips and Holden had a protocol between them for meeting secretly in London for the exchange of information on Patterson's movements.

They had no intention for the process to take up to twelve months but had made a plan based on certain London parks alphabetically with the first park on the list representing the month of January, the second in the list February and so on. At each park there was a designated point for a 'dead letter drop' where either of them could leave details of a place to meet or a telephone number to call but the message had to be left on the tenth day of the month. Phillips would have to leave a message for Holden to meet outside 121 Westminster Bridge Road, Lambeth; the station terminus for the London Necropolis Railway. The code in relation to parks and letter drops worked as follows:

Battersea Park, January, message folded and left by the east-facing step of the bandstand;

Bushy Park, February, message placed behind the scoreboard of the cricket pavilion that borders the park (home of Hampton Wick Royal cricket club);

Chelsea Physic Garden, March, message placed under the coarse black piece of granite prominent in the rock garden:

Crystal Palace Park, April, message placed in the mouth of Waterhouse Hawkins statue of 'megalosaurus';

Green Park, May, message placed by the bottom hinge, furthest west of Canada Gate;

Greenwich Park, June, message placed at the base of the front of the General Wolfe statue overlooking London in the distance;

Hyde Park, July, message placed at the back of the 'speakers corner' sign at the north-eastern most point of Hyde Park;

Kensington Gardens, August, message placed under the trunk of the elephant on the 'Asia' corner of the Albert Memorial;

Kew Gardens, September, message placed at the Pagoda tucked below wooden slat flooring on the top storey;

Postman's Park, October, to be placed on the under side of the bench seating that itself was below the plaque erected to Mary Rogers;

Regents Park, November, message left at the rear of the box office behind the upright guttering;

St James' Park, December, message left above the cistern of the first gents toilet that faces Horse Guards Road.

Outside of this dead letter process communications overseas had tenuously been done by Ramsey Phillips passing a message to Holden surreptitiously at his hotel. After contacting Tudor Castle he would have to get himself out of the office briskly and over to Kew Gardens to deposit the appropriate message.

Phillips made his way the very short distance along the oak panelled corridors to just past the communal office usually shared by Ministry of War researchers, when they had any. At present he had the luxury of a great deal of privacy with their demise and the current difficulty in recruiting more. His office was immediately next door and normally each office could be over heard by the other through a wood only dividing wall. He entered his office and made his way to the desk near to the window. He sat down and pulled out a large leather desk diary from a drawer and opened it up to the back where he had a list of contact telephone numbers; amongst them he had the number for the Carfax-Smythe's personal assistant, Peter DeBrett, at Tudor Castle. He knew DeBrett well from their professional associations over the years. A congenial telephone call followed as Phillips dialled and then heard DeBrett answer at the other end.

"Hello, Tudor Castle."

"Hello, Peter, its Ramsey here, how are you?"

"Hello, old boy. Very well. How are you?"

"Yes fine thank you. Look, can you let me know which rooms the Minister, the head of the Navy and the head of the Army will be using?"

"Certainly. The key people will all be housed in the main castle that juts out from the island, while you and the ministry staff will be housed in the Maiden's Tower on the edge of the castle island. Is that all right?" Not enough detail yet for Phillips.

"Yes, fine, but which rooms will they be having? Or most importantly where can I tell the Minister he will be?"

"Oh, that's simple. He'll be on the top floor of the castle in the King's room, that's the one decked out in blue with the cream coloured canopy." That was the key information that Phillips needed. His meet with Holden, although always potentially hazardous, would be worthwhile.

"Thanks, Peter. We'll see you on the 20th around lunchtime." Phillips put the phone down.

He would have to be brisk away from work in order to get to Kew Gardens before they closed to leave his message at the Pagoda regarding meeting at the Necropolis railway. It would be an excellent place to meet. The south side of the river was not populated in the same way as the north side for commerce or entertainment, and with the morbid nature of the venue he had chosen, it was unlikely that their meeting would draw any unwanted attention.

Tudor Castle, just outside of Maidstone in Kent, had started life as a Norman fortification in 1119 constructed by one of William the Conqueror's barons, Robert de Crevecouer, built on two islands within the confines of the River Len. It fell into the hands of the English Royal families from 1278 until the 1520s from when it remained permanently in private ownership. The modern romantic appearance of the castle was based around the original Norman foundations; at one end of the islands sat the main castle built into the river's water almost connected by an arched gallery to the second portion of the main residence. Centrally to one side of the island sat the Maiden's Tower and then at the opposite end to the castle was the gate house and now permanently built stone bridge. In days of yore the land connection had been a wooden drawbridge. Phillips knew that Holden would be pleased with the location. There was only one way in and out other than a cold swim or the use of a boat. He also suspected that with the Minister billeted in the outcropped portion of the castle with nothing obstructing its span into the river, the use of artillery was a possibility. He had forgotten that the killing would have to be of a ritualistic nature. Phillips would have no clue as to how Holden would actually tackle the castle, and no inkling of his intentions when he did.

Phillips ensured he was out of the door of the Ministry of War by 2.p.m to allow him bountiful time to get to Kew, and not so early as to arouse the suspicion of the police protection officers. It was only Detective Constable Vincent there today, with Ford having a few days off to convalesce at home from his knife wound.

* * *

Robert Ford sat in the shade in the landscaped garden of his Eaton Square home having almost finished the journal for a second time. Karen was lying out on a wooden deckchair. He was expecting Moreau imminently for a sabre lesson; he was looking forward to it as although his leg was still stiff and sore, he felt the activity would do him the power of good. Reaching the end of Waldron's account of the violent events of the SRP mission to godless and lawless Afghanistan, he now understood entirely the significance of the ritualistic murders. He was still amazed that the devious Patterson had kept it secret all this time; his interests in the region and his obvious abuse of his political office were almost too much to comprehend. What Ford didn't realise was the connection to Karen Wood.

Mrs Adkins was there finishing her every-other day chores when she came through into the garden with Moreau, Ford nor Karen had heard the knock at the front door. Ford got stiffly up from his chair. Moreau immediately noticed the awkwardness of his movement, so far removed from his normal lithe economy.

"Robert, are you sure you want a lesson today? You look injured enough already without me giving you additional bruises?"

"Thank you Mrs Adkins," Ford addressed his wonderfully efficient housekeeper first. She smiled and returned to the house. "Yes, Andre, I do. It will get me a little more mobile and it feels like an age since I had any tuition or did a disciplined sporting activity. So please, indulge and bruise me. Let's go out to the communal garden."

"Very well," Moreau nodded as he replied and they both entered the house to access the communal garden, via the front door, in the centre of the grand square in which he lived.

Karen, although only marginally dozing, was disturbed by the men's talk and stirred. She stretched and yawned in the warm sunlight and then sat up and took a look at the pleasant, sweet smelling garden around her. Her gaze eventually fell on the teak wooden table and chair that Ford had vacated and the journal that sat upon the table top. She stood up and walked over to it and picked it up. She saw that it was very weather beaten as she opened it to the first page. She read through the introductory title and eventually down to the role call; and there it was, 'Sergeant Major Nigel Green'. Her blood ran cold. She sat slowly down in Ford's chair and flattened the journal out on the table and began to read. She could never have been prepared for the content.

* * *

Vatican City

The three scheming Cardinals were all still resident in the Catholic Church headquarters in Rome. They were all keen to try to be together for the initial phase of the plan in which they all had so much invested, but they were all to a man very interested in the declining health of Pius X. They wanted to be in the midst of the Papal enclave should the worst imminently occur to ensure the decision was made to elect Caravaggio as the successor to the current pontiff.

The three were all sitting comfortably in a lavish lounging room; all ensconced in high backed, studded leather chairs with a fire burning set off to one side of the room whilst the remaining walls were adorned with Italian renaissance art. Most of the rest of the furniture was either made from high quality oak or mahogany; the dark redness of the latter would seem in keeping with their deep coloured and luxurious cardinals' robes. This morning the three lifelong, ambitious friends with a mutual obsession for the domination of the Catholic Church between them and the eventual overthrow of all other faiths for worldwide Catholic religious control, were distracted by the latest news from London. Vicompte was the first to speak over the matter.

"This plan seems more and more fragile that we have decided to participate in. There is too much death and scandal around Patterson. I think it is time we prepared for the worst." Caravaggio sat impassively still apparently taking in the news; Sklinski nodded in agreement. He was no longer convinced of the viability of the plan and their investment. They needed to ensure the return of their money. Sklinski was the first to respond.

"Yes. I fully agree. Patterson is now a liability to us and he strikes me as the kind who might even consider dragging us down with him should he fail. Whether his obsessive killer succeeds or not we must ensure the return of our heavy financial investment and his silence." Caravaggio finally put his paper down and looked at his two lifelong friends.

"Very well. I shall instruct the captain of the Swiss Guard to set our plan I have called 'recovery and retribution' in place. He has some very good men by all accounts."

Sklinski and Vicompte looked at each other and then both at Caravaggio and all nodded in agreement. Their reputations in the face of the wild developments surrounding Patterson could not be put at risk. They would have to consider an alternative plan to spread the way of Catholicism.

* * *

The sabre blades sparked as they made contact repeatedly with each other in the overcast conditions of light that had occurred since Moreau and Ford had begun their training session in the communal gardens of Eaton Square. A small crowd had gathered to watch the two men duelling as the speed at which they fought gradually increased; the endorphins now coursing through Ford's body with the adrenalin rush that Moreau's undoubted skill offered, had dulled the pain in his injured leg. Moreau himself was amazed to see his pupil move with his usual speedy efficiency so quickly, it had almost taken him off guard early on in their session. Less than half an hour before, it appeared that Ford would struggle just to walk through his comfortable terraced house. Ford was never a stranger to pain, physical or emotional. His years as a street fighter and the hardships he had endured during the murders in Whitechapel in 1888 had shaped him to be the man he was. One thing had changed again, however, he had the love of a woman that he adored in return and would do anything to protect.

"You are fighting like a man possessed, Robert, but with rationale that I have not observed before when so aggressive. What has changed?" Moreau was beginning to sound uncharacteristically slightly out of breath as he spoke; Ford was actually countering his challenges in a very efficient manner considering his relative newness to the sabre. Ford was perspiring heavily with his physical efforts and with the subliminal resistance to pain.

"Andre, for the first time for many a while, I had a real fight for my life in Belgrave Square. It has made me all too aware of the preciousness of life again and the need to guard it jealously but with clarity of thought. If I can overcome you when duelling, then I can bloody well defend myself against anyone." Moreau smiled as he moved with lighting reactions to counter Ford's very accurate and considered attacks. But being the master, he knew that with Ford's fatigue he would gain the upper hand; fight an opponent long enough and let physical attrition do its work. It was a waiting game. He was lulling Ford into a false sense of security by seeming to be permanently on the back foot. He knew that with the wrong type of impetuous lunge, his favoured method of disarming would work as it always did. And, with Ford, yet again. Both men were sweating heavily now sporting quilted white cotton fencing jackets. Each could see their building fatigue with the lack of use of fencing face guards. The weapons were not edged or pointed but if they struck home they would still cause serious injury. Neither had yet scored any sort of injury on the other as the blades continued to flash together and create metallic noises that seemed occasionally to echo around the square. Even one of the local beat uniform constables now stood at the fence to the gardens to watch the fight. To him it was a familiar if irregular sight to see Detective Inspector Ford with his fencing teacher.

Moreau could sense that the time was right. Having offered two marginal attacks against Ford that he allowed his pupil to defend with ease, he feigned being pushed back from one of Ford's lunging attacks. It was working; he could see the very slight widening of Ford's eyes as he misguidedly sensed victory was near. He allowed himself to be pushed back to the point where he knew a tree was off set behind him. Then Moreau struck as Ford made an impetuous lunge; he could not believe that Ford was about to fall for the watch-glass parry again. Moreau deflected Ford's blade harmlessly inside his left arm again and grabbed hold of Ford's right arm locking it inside his left and throwing him off balance. This time though instead of allowing him to fall to the floor he directed him so that he hit the tree with his back facing outwards in time to receive the tip of Moreau's sabre under his chin.

"Jesus Christ, Andre! How do you do it!"

"This time, Robert, you were my equal, so I had to play the long game. Make you tire to allow your confidence to rise from apparently effective attacks and then, voila. Need I explain any more?" He dropped the blade away from Ford's chin transferring it into his left hand. He took Ford's right in his own and shook it heartily. The small, gathered crowd clapped in appreciation of the master class they had witnessed and began to dissipate.

"Thank you, Andre. That is valuable."

"It will perhaps be the most valuable tactic you can learn. There is little more to offer a natural fighter like you other than practice until there are no errors." Moreau let go of his hand. Ford picked up his own sabre.

"Thank you, that is flattering. Will you come in the house for some refreshment?"

"No. You have not seen, my carriage has arrived and is waiting. That is unusual for you. Don't forget your peripheries. I have another pressing lesson. Good day to you Robert. Take care I shall see you soon." Moreau walked off to his waiting carriage with a style and aplomb that Ford could only dream of; although he knew he moved well he lacked the grace of Moreau with his natural, gliding, loose limbed demeanour. Ford waved the coach and his tutor off and then re-entered the house.

In the garden he found Mrs Adkins comforting Karen Wood. She was sat with the sobbing dressmaker on a mahogany two seat bench with her clutching the girl in her arms. Ford was alerted as he walked over to the journal of Trooper Waldron sat open and at its end on the table next to the two of them. Mrs Adkins looked up at him as he approached. She then spoke to Karen.

"Karen, Robert is back now. Let me leave you alone with him." Karen sat up nodding her head gently then wiping her red and swollen eyes with a handkerchief as Mrs Adkins herself then stood up. She approached Ford.

"I'm sorry, Robert, I found her like that. Inconsolable it seemed. It's that journal isn't it?"

"Yes, Mrs Adkins it is. Thank you very much. Perhaps you could just pop the kettle on for me, knock up a pot of tea and then head off if you wish."

"Thank you, that's kind. I'll do that. Maybe see you the day after tomorrow." Mrs Adkins then strolled off into the house as Ford sat down next to Karen.

Chapter Twenty-Three

Mrs Adkins had brought out a fresh pot of Lapsang Souchong just before she left. She served it on a plain wooden tray in a Port Merion tea pot with matching cups and saucers. There was an additional plate that held some all butter flapjacks partially dipped in dark chocolate. There was no milk and no sugar; Lapsang was never drunk with milk and neither Ford nor Karen took sugar. One of the many things Ford enjoyed about Mrs Adkins' housekeeping was her magnificent attention to detail.

Karen had stopped crying but still had a very red and puffy face. Ford stood up momentarily from the position he held next to her on the bench holding her in his arms.

"I take it you would like a cup, darling?" It was the first time that Ford had ever addressed her with a term of endearment. Even in the wake of her latest grief the affection this showed to her made her skin tingle and brought her out in 'goose-bumps' and she knew that despite all the sadness she felt that this was the man she could spend the rest of her life with.

"Yes, of course, please," she sounded as if she was getting over a cold as she spoke with her sinuses having been working overtime with her crying. Ford poured them tea using a metal strainer into the finely decorated china cups and then passed her a cup as he sat back next to her.

"So can I assume that Nigel Green was your ex-common law husband and the father of your little boy?" Ford spoke softly as he wished to gently coax the answers from her.

"Yes. I never told you but that man who was in the building the other day when Patterson came to my door had called only minutes before all the shooting began. He was the man 'Holden' spoken of in this book and he had come to break the news to me that Nigel had been killed. He was kind and gentle, but he had a look in his eyes, like he didn't care for life anymore. His eyes were lifeless. I think Holden is on a self destructive path and god knows from reading that awful diary I know why. All his men and his friends butchered because of that bastard's greed. The only sad thing is that Patterson can't suffer each of those individual fates that Holden has inflicted." She paused and drank some tea. Ford looked on at her with concern. Patterson's abuses had obviously taken their toll.

"Look, why don't you get out of London until this is done? You don't need to stay here. I'll pay for you to go anywhere to get away." She looked at Ford and made fierce eye contact with him. She placed her cup and saucer and then his on the table and took his hands in hers.

"Look. I'll go if you come with me. We can give all this up. You know that you can. Let someone else protect that bastard and solve the case."

A chill ran down Ford's spine; this was déjà vu with Mary Kelly. 'Leave London and let someone else sort it out'? No, his sense of duty, again too strong, wouldn't allow it. He would stay, solve the enigma but keep her close to do it. She would go to Tudor Castle with him and he would have a final confrontation with Patterson about her if necessary.

"Karen, I can't do that. But I will keep you close. You are not in danger. Not like Mary I told you about. When I leave London you come with me. When this is over," he paused. Suddenly his mouth dried up and he felt 'butterflies' in his stomach. The moment had come and she sensed a slight trembling in his hands. "When this is over, then marry me."

Karen squeezed his hands tightly and he could see her eyes welling slightly with more tears. Then she threw her arms around him and hugged him tightly; he responded with the same action. They stayed locked in each others embrace as Ford heard the front door quietly shut. Mrs Adkins had left. He let go of her and stood up. She stood up too, in front of him. He picked her up in his arms and carried her into the house and up the stairs to the master bedroom. He laid her gently on the bed and took off his shirt and took the belt from his trousers. She looked up at him in excited anticipation. He closed the bedroom door and cocooned them in their own world, albeit only temporarily; it was theirs and no one else's.

* * *

September 10th

Holden arrived at Kew Gardens a little after 11.a.m on a fine autumnal day. He knew the 'dead letter' rules as well as Phillips did and he acknowledged that he needed to get to the Pagoda briskly. One of his key concerns was that an inquisitive child could always find their messages before they did. He had no information to pass back to Phillips so he knew he was attending the pagoda for the next snippet of intelligence on the Minister or for arrangements regarding a meet at another venue. He entered the Royal Botanic Gardens of Kew via the Lion Gate that lead to the park directly off of Kew Road on its west side. It was the southern most entrance to the park with its square brick built arch over which sat an ornamental Lion made of coade stone and dated from 1845. It was sometimes known as pagoda gate as the path via this entrance was the closest direct way to the oriental folly. The pagoda was born out of the eighteenth century fashion for garden 'chinoiserie' and was designed by the architect William Chambers. Completed in 1762, it stood 163 feet high with ten storeys each of which going upwards was one foot less in circumference than the preceding one.

Holden reached the base of the pagoda; the crowds throughout the park were light as he stared up at the towering structure gaining a false perspective of its height by his proximity to it. He looked around him; there were few people nearby and he had not seen anyone enter the structure as he approached it, nor had he noticed anyone making their way up to the viewing point at the top. He entered the pagoda and began the long climb up its circular staircase to reach its highest point. The temperature was mild and as he reached about three-quarter distance he could feel the first few beads of perspiration on his lower back and could tell that his forehead was beginning to feel clammy. As he passed by the open aspects of each floor he enjoyed the various views they afforded relative to compass points; to the north the Thames and the edge of Brentford on the river's north bank, to the east Mortlake and views towards central London, to the west Syon Park and House and the Old Deer park, and then to the south affluent Richmond and Richmond Park. These lush, green open areas made him sad that he would most likely never see the family estate at Holden Hall again as he neared the end of his quest. He reached the top of the mock oriental structure where he found silence other that the gentle whistling sound of the wind at this higher level as it was directed around the tower.

He searched the wooden slats of the floor of the top storey where he found himself regaining his breath and coughing annoyingly painfully; he had never previously become so short of breath after such physical activity. He found it un-nerving and knew that his time in the unhealthy Indian sub-continent was perhaps now catching up with him. The effects of tuberculosis were taking a firm hold. It did not take him long to find the message left by his informant, Ramsey Phillips, concealed within the flooring. It was inside a plain white quality envelope that bore no writing on it. He opened the envelope to find the message written on equally good quality writing paper and in a familiar hand, just as he had seen previously pushed under his door in Rome.

Meet midday on the 12th September. 121 Westminster Bridge Road, The London Necropolis Railway Terminus. Too much information for a letter. There is the need to speak regarding Tudor Castle, Kent. It will be your best opportunity. There is need for caution.

Regards,
R.P.

Holden read the letter over twice before folding it up and placing it carefully within an inside jacket pocket. He began coughing again as he completed his descent from the pagoda; it felt quite uncomfortable and he felt the rasping quality again to his coughing and slight wheezing.

He reached the comfort of the base of the tower in a matter of minutes, cautiously looking around for anyone paying him undue interest, just as he had when he had reached each floor during the way down. On each fresh new landing he had looked out over the park and the immediate area of the pagoda for anyone that seemed to have stayed obtrusively in situ. In truth he had seen no one. He felt comfortable back on the ground floor as he strolled out and decided to return to Lion Gate to leave the park. He had more of a spring in his step now he was out of the tower but as he reached the gate he felt a light headed sensation and he began coughing quite harshly. He pulled a handkerchief from his pocket to cover his mouth and the annoying loud sound of his wheezing. He coughed heavily into it trying to clear his uncomfortably tight feeling chest; it was as he did so he felt the sensation of fluid coming up through his throat with the exertion. He thought little of it until he examined the fluid he had coughed into the cotton hanky.

As he had begun to fear; the curse of Asia he had brought back with him was taking a heavy toll. There was blood in the handkerchief, but in greater volumes than before. He had the first signs of the very serious onset of tuberculosis.

* * *

September 12th

1.p.m. Robert Ford and Karen Wood walked arm in arm through St James' Park away from Whitehall and towards Buckingham Palace. They were on the north side of the park and were walking almost parallel to The Mall. The weather was fine and the park was busy with the late summer crowds, many of whom they could see just ahead of them were gathered around a narrow but tall red and white striped tent. It was a 'Punch and Judy' show, a very familiar, popular scene and form of entertainment in Edwardian London Parks. Once they were in range the two of them stopped at the back of the crowd that was gathered watching the strange comedic puppet show.

In the few minutes that Ford and Karen watched the show, all the key characters and events seemed to take place for them to witness. Mr Punch was beating Judy. The baby was left to its own devices as he did so. The crocodile appeared, then the policeman, Joey the clown and a bizarre string of sausages. All of these additional characters were subject to extreme violence from Punch, including the clown who was supposed to be his friend. They all were portrayed with odd squawking voices, the legacy of the 'swizzle' that the puppeteer, or 'professor', would hold in his mouth. Both Ford and Karen had not witnessed this form of entertainment for many years. They had arrived towards the end of the performance and so only got to stand and watch the last of it over about ten minutes. They stood silently watching the bizarre show demonstrating so much use of violence and wrong doing. They watched the surreal curtain call made by the puppets before they continued their stroll back towards Eaton Square.

"That is a really ironic show for us to have witnessed, Robert," said Karen as they continued on their way.

"Oh, really? Why is that?" Ford felt that he was reading, perhaps naively, less in the events that he had been involved with than she was. She made her point about it and it made him see events in a different light. Karen explained.

"Well think about it. There's Mr Punch or Patterson, morally corrupt and with little regard for anything. He gets away with literally murder. Look at what he does; take the crocodile as being his resources overseas. As long as he gets what he wants he'll use violence to obtain it, so he beats the crocodile to have his own way, or turn the poor bastard into some new shoes.

"Then there's the baby. Punch cares nothing for it. Then there's the policeman who gets a beating for trying to do the right thing. Then the friend, you know the clown character; he gets attacked again for trying to stop Punch from doing the wrong thing. Look at what he gets for his troubles. The whole Punch and Judy story is almost a parody of our lives with 'Patterson Punch', the 'Lord of Misrule' and a 'trickster'." Ford considered her words.

"That's quite a deep interpretation. So am I the policeman who gets a beating?"

"Yes, of course you are. This man Hoare you speak of, and Holden, they are the crocodile. I'm the foolish woman who had to tolerate his ill temper and sexual demands, his bloody Judy, with the beatings too."

"Has he ever beaten you?" asked Ford. His manner was sterner now at the intimation that Patterson had used violence against her. She was reticent to answer. There seemed enough problems as it was. "Well? Has he?" She wouldn't look Ford in the eye as she spoke.

"Yes, a little. Your friend Mark put him straight the day of the shoot out."

"Really? We shall have to look into that." Ford began to move them along breaking back into a walk. She forced them to stop and turned and stood in front of him holding his hands in hers.

"No don't make things any worse. Let the final acts of this awful drama play out first. If you weren't so bloody dedicated to protecting him perhaps it would end." Ford was partially enraged at this and squeezed her hands tightly as he spoke in a harsh tone to her. It was the first time he had.

"Listen to me, Karen. This isn't about wanting the bastard to live, although if he does the disgrace of this whole saga will bring him to his knees. This now is about being at his side when this twisted killer Holden strikes to complete his quest for justice so that I can bring him to task for the murders of innocent members of the ministry; including a policeman. Don't forget that." He turned away holding on to one of her hands and began to stroll on again. "He is purely now a mechanism to bring this whole sickening fiasco to an end."

They walked silently for sometime until they left the park and were making their way along Buckingham Gate and the side of the palace towards the Victoria area. The world continued around them as Ford came to the realisation that he had to catch Holden and try to expose Patterson as best he could without a press connection to himself. It was shame that the nemesis he still had responsibility for had ensured quite accidentally that his only immediate link to the press by years of association was dead.

* * *

One hour earlier

Phillips arrived at the entrance to the London Necropolis Railway first and stood smartly dressed below its fine, classical façade. There were, as to be expected, funeral parties arriving on a frequent basis that seemed to all consist of grief-filled, working class types. All with an unhealthy pallor to their already drawn complexions, with the females locked in melodramatic wailing as they prepared for the railway journey to the burial grounds in the Surrey countryside. Phillips hoped that

Holden wouldn't be long as he couldn't bear to be around the working classes for too long.

Holden had gone to ground following the shoot-out in Belgravia and had not been seen by Hoare or any of his men despite their best efforts. He had decided to take a suite in Claridges under an assumed name and had for several days kept himself confined there but for the brief trip to Kew Gardens. There he had begun to have trouble sleeping as a result of 'night sweats' another telling sign of the tuberculosis as well as a loss of appetite despite ordering meals from room service regularly. When they arrived he struggled to make a dent in them. He realised that he was losing weight but it wasn't until he met with Phillips that he had to give consideration to how much he actually had. He left the hotel dressed in a dark blue suit with the usual smart accessories but with an overcoat as he had begun to become sensitive to the cold.

Holden tapped Phillips on his left shoulder as his friend was looking south towards Kennington Road underground station, which was currently under construction at the convergence of Bayliss Road, Kennington Road and Westminster Bridge Road. Phillips turned; a little startled to be confronted by a man he instantly recognised but was shocked by his drawn, pale appearance. The true extent of his weight loss was at that moment disguised by the overcoat.

"Christ, Bill. Are you all right? You look bloody awful!"

"I'm fine, and how are you, Ramsey?" Holden replied with obvious sarcasm.

"Sorry, old chap. But you do look a little under the weather." They shook hands as they spoke.

"Yes, just a passing virus or something." Holden was reluctant to discuss the true nature of an illness he was only too aware of from his years on the Indian Sub-continent.

"If you say so. Shall we walk? I can't bear being around the wailing proletariat. Let's head towards Lambeth Palace. The grounds there are pleasant and discreet along with the route there. We'll walk and talk on the way, and then once we've popped out of the back streets if you want to go I understand." Phillips looked into Holden's eyes as he spoke. They were dull and lifeless, in a way he had never seen on anyone before.

"Yes, that's fine. But I may not wait around as you suggest." Phillips did not question this reply coupled with a degree of furtiveness that he had never before witnessed in the calm and collected Holden. He guessed with the last set of events surrounding the Minister, Holden was on edge and keen to get his task completed.

They turned north from the Necropolis Railway and walked the hundred yards or so to Upper Marsh and turned left walking west towards Royal Street. Holden was silent waiting for Phillips to initiate the conversation and pass on his valuable final piece of information to him that would give him his opportunity.

"In the wake of the fact it seems that we have little else to discuss then here's what you want to know. Patterson will be staying in the main castle on the top floor that over looks the main part of the lake. The other members of the military top brass will most likely be in that building too and the rest of the entourage including the police will be housed in the subsidiary part of the castle which is far enough away to be safe." Holden nodded as he walked with a slight stoop as he had never done before. He coughed into a handkerchief he pulled from a pocket and tried not to reveal its surface. Phillips caught a brief glance and saw a trace of blood on its cotton surface.

"Bill, are you certain that you are all right?" Phillips spoke with concern.

"Yes. I'm fine, a little chest cold. What about security? Where are the main protection officers going to be?" Holden spoke with a slight hoarseness to his voice.

"The main men at night, as Ford and Vincent will probably be sleeping in the annexe castle I just mentioned, will be uniform patrols. There are likely to be some uniformed policemen from Kent patrolling the castle island and an armed Metropolitan Officer posted outside Patterson's room in the castle. Nothing I'm sure you can't deal with."

"Mmm." Holden rubbed his chin as they walked. He was weaker than he would normally like to be and would have to be cautious. "Yes, I'm sure." In truth he would have to get some sort of medication; not to cure him but to try to be on top of his game. "When is this meeting taking place? And where? You haven't confirmed that it's Tudor Castle in Kent yet."

"Yes. It is, sorry in my," Phillips hesitated before continuing, "in my haste to get walking I forgot those details." In truth it came from the fact he was so shocked at Holden's ill complexion and appearance. He knew he had already offended his old friend over this and was not going to pursue his physical well being further. "It is Tudor Castle. You know where that is down near Maidstone. They are all arriving there the morning of 20th September for the weekend." Holden looked distant, deep in thought as he replied.

"Good, a long enough period for me to be stealthy. I don't know why but I have this superstitious suspicion that Patterson could be my equivalent to the literary 'Green Knight'." Holden made eye contact for a moment as he spoke and could see Phillips frowning at him at this remark. "Have you never heard the poem about the legend of 'Sir Gawain and The Green Knight'? Look it up sometime, you'll see what I mean. A kind of nemesis, hard to kill perhaps." Phillips was lost. Was his old friend just babbling? If he had the chance he'd try to read it.

They reached the back of the grounds of Lambeth Palace, the home of the Archbishop of Canterbury and both came to a stop in Royal Street with a view of the Thames just to the north. Holden stopped and extended his hand to his life-long associate. Phillips took hold of it as they then firmly shook hands.

"Well, Ramsey, thank you. You have been a great help in my quest, although I am amazed that, as you have learnt about what has gone on and my intentions, you have persisted in giving me information?" Phillips paused before he answered this point. He had his own selfish interests at heart. Holden was indeed suspicious of this and would have to give the matter consideration. When he finished he intended to leave the country. He did not want Phillips to perhaps offer assistance to the powers of law and order.

"Bill, I have my own interests and agenda. Let's leave it at that, eh?" Holden held onto Phillips' hand just for a moment longer than would be normal as he digested this final statement.

"I'm sure, Ramsey. See you on the other side." He let go of Phillips' hand and strolled off towards the Thames. Phillips called farewell to him.

"Yes. Goodbye, Bill." Holden disappeared as he reached Lambeth Palace Road and turned west.

The Dressmaker Connection

* * *

September 15th

In his private office at the Vatican, Caravaggio heard a knock on the heavy oak door. The Captain, or Hauptman, of the Swiss Guard entered with one of his junior non-commissioned officers. Hauptman Schiltz and his subordinate marched smartly across the office to stand in front of the plush mahogany desk that divided Caravaggio from those that entered. The cardinal sat back in his high-backed, leather-quilted office chair as the two elite Swiss, mercenary soldiers came to attention. He eyed them up and down as they stood upright, smart and rigid to be inspected. The captain was in his mid to late thirties, slim and fit looking and the product of Arian genes. The NCO was far more Anglo-Saxon with dark hair, in his mid twenties, with his striped blue, yellow and red uniform disguising a large muscular frame. They wore their traditional basinet type helmets with the younger guard carrying the halberd, their standard sentry weapon. As a fighting or protective unit of men, the guard had a distinguished reputation and significant history.

The Swiss Guards were (and still are) Swiss mercenary soldiers who served as bodyguards, ceremonial guards, and palace guards at foreign European courts from the late 15th century until the present day (in the form of the Papal Swiss Guard). They generally had a high reputation for discipline and loyalty to their employers. Some of these units also served as fighting troops in the field. There were also regular Swiss mercenary regiments serving as front line troops in various armies, notably those of France, Spain and Naples until the 19th century who were not household or guard units.

Various Swiss Guards had existed. The earliest such detachment was the Swiss "Hundred Guard" (*Cent-Garde*) at the French court (1497 – 1830). This small force was complemented in 1567 by a Swiss Guard regiment. The Papal Swiss Guard in the Vatican was founded in 1506 and is the only Swiss Guard that still existed in 1904 (and continues to exist). In the 18th century several other Swiss Guards existed for periods in various European courts.

"This is Feld-Weibel Sepp Dietrich," said Hauptman Schiltz. "I think you will find that his experience and disposition will be ideal for your assignment, your emminence." Caravaggio stood up from his seat and began to walk around his ornate desk, it seemed, to inspect these men more closely. He then spoke as he changed his direction from the guards towards a wooden cabinet that matched the desk over by one of the teak pannelled walls.

"Stand at ease please, gentlemen." He opened the cabinet to reveal a shelf containing a large cut glass decanter with half a dozen matching tumblers around it. The decanter held a light brown coloured liquid. Caravaggio pulled three glasses forward onto the shelf formed by the cabinet door hinging downward. The two guards followed his command and then looked towards the cardinal who was finishing pouring the last glass.

"Gentlemen, please come and take a glass and let us sit comfortably," he gestured and walked towards some soft furnishings that the men had passed to enter the room. Dietrich lay his halbard on the floor as Schiltz picked up the two drinks, then passing one to his colleague. They joined Caravaggio sitting in armchairs. "Finest Normandy Calvados. On an empty stomach it warms your heart and helps clear the mind." Caravaggio turned to address Dietrich sat almost directly opposite him. "This may sound ungodly, but let us get to the point. You have been trained to kill, an assassin by trade with a former military unit prior to joining the Swiss guard?" The young Anglo-Saxon nodded with a frown of concern on his face. "There is no need to fear, young man. The work you are to undertake is with the churches' blessing and, therefore, forgiveness. Let me begin."

* * *

Trinity House, London, 10.a.m

Patterson sat staring across the desk at Hoare. It was less than a week to the planned trapping operation at Tudor Castle. Hoare was there to report on the military build up he had begun on the North West Frontier; he would also be present with two of his men to provide additional protection at the castle. Patterson, although intensely interested in Hoare's news, was also preoccupied with the threat made to him by the Prime Minister; he must consider the tenability of his position or have the consideration made for him. Hoare noticed that

The Dressmaker Connection

Patterson's gaze passed right through him, he could see that the corrupt politician's thoughts were elsewhere. He despised what this man stood for and only tolerated it because it paid him well and would allow him to retire from arduous work of any kind early. It seemed that there was the possibility that Patterson could be the vanguard of a new breed of politician, who as a cabinet minister could influence the introduction of statutes that would allow politicians to pursue their own agendas free of public scrutiny; effectively acting above the law but operating behind it. He could see that he needed to grab Patterson's attention. He had a sizable leather-bound ledger type book open on his lap in which he had recorded his latest troop numbers, locations, supply and armament situation. He slammed it shut with a loud bang. The action achieved its objective and Patterson focused on Hoare's face having physically jolted at the unexpected sound.

"Do I have your attention then, Minister?"

"Yes. You bloody well do." Patterson coughed and shifted in his chair getting comfortable again. Hoare re-opened the ledger and then began to read from the pages he was previously analysing.

"Right, I shall begin. There are five hundred men camped just short of the entry to the Khyber Pass in northern India. They currently have the use of a Lee Enfield rifle each and the officers and NCOs amongst them, numbering twenty-five also have side arms. All have uniforms, albeit slightly varying styles from their former or recent service days and there are food supplies for ten days currently at the camp. Of the five hundred, forty are involved solely in logistics so are fairly continually backwards and forwards at the moment. The officers on the ground are looking to amass a month's rations before we go in and begin establishing centres of control and then ensuring that each man personally has one hundred rounds, with an additional two hundred rounds in the supply section.

"This amounts to quite an expense and the current budget from E.P has almost gone. I need money to continue the supply operation and pay the men." He looked up at Patterson. The corrupt M.P and industrialist was sitting elbows resting on the desk and his hands clasped together in a prayer type fashion and held in front of his mouth with his chin resting on his thumbs. He took a deep breath and sat back. E.P was already into the operation for a lot of money, but that was not the point; he had massive financial resources that he had coerced from the Catholic Church. But the more he spent out on the operation the less there was for him and the other members of the board to fall back on. He would have to settle for the fact that it was long term proposition and invest further and substantially.

"Bare bones then, Hoare. How much?" The former marine officer made steely eye contact with him, it made Patterson shift again.

"Realistically, to encourage the men and ensure their continued loyalty by being paid regular rates, coupled with all the logistical issues, and then added to the additional duties you have made me take on, then we need seventy-five thousand pounds wired to India for the logistic officers immediate use for pay and supplies, and of course an additional retainer for me." He paused for effect to have the satisfaction of eliciting an annoyed response from Patterson.

"You greedy bastard! How much?" Patterson looked away from Hoare deliberately to exaggerate an air of disgust.

"For me right now, an extra three thousand pounds."

"That's outrageous!" Patterson stood sharply up from his seat. Hoare remained calm and seated, simply raising his look slightly to maintain his icy eye contact with a desperate and greedy man. Patterson paced over to his drinks cabinet and poured himself a large shot of Isle of Jura single malt. He lifted the weighty cut glass Waterford tumbler to his mouth and drank hastily from it. He swallowed hard not savouring its peaty taste, wincing as the excessively brisk ingress of strong alcohol burnt his oesophagus on its way to warm his stomach. He could tell that Hoare's eyes had followed him around the finely decorated room and their glare felt as if it was burning deeply into him. He knew that in reality Hoare had been partly responsible for preventing him from having been killed days earlier in Wilton Crescent. He turned to face the man who would eventually be leading and supervising the incursion and subsequent industrial colonisation of Afghanistan.

"All right. A one off payment of that amount, **after** we have been to Tudor Castle **and** successfully taken care of Captain Holden. Then after that it is your monthly salary until you earn your bonus for the first oil coming out of Afghanistan." Hoare considered his offer, deliberately taking an uncomfortable amount of time to answer. He approached Patterson, stood by the drinks cabinet and calmly poured a large drink for himself, knowing that this would irritate the man who could not do without him. He took his time savouring his drink and looking at the liquid in the glass with admiration as he swallowed a conservative mouthful.

"You know, Minister, that is rather good. I agree your terms. Should Ford's attempt to bring you to justice at the end of this sordid saga succeed, and then you are on your own. Once the initial oil wells are established at the 'harvesting sites' are secure, then I shall leave it to one of my subordinates. I will prefer a quiet life of retirement, most likely away from these shores. I wish no stigma attached to me when you fall from grace."

An uncomfortable silence descended over the room as Hoare poured them both another drink and they each took their time to savour it. Both had extremely different considerations crossing their minds, strangely both were absolutely selfish in their individual ways.

* * *

Vatican City

"An English industrialist has promised Rome religious autonomy over the Middle East as it becomes subjugated by industrial colonisation. However, recent events suggest that he may not be good to his word. The church has provided money for a mission to be established for us in advance," Caravaggio was deliberately obtuse with the truth. "In readiness that he is not good to his word and to avoid recriminations upon Rome, we must have someone on hand to silence him. Permanently. Do you understand what I am suggesting?" Dietrich paused before answering.

"Yes, Holy Father, I do. I assume the methodology is immaterial, so long as he is silenced?"

"You are quite correct. But you must not be caught or found out in anyway. There is to be no reflection upon the power of Rome."

"That should not be an issue. I undertook training in the Far East in all types of assassination techniques when despatched there by my former employers, the Austro-Hungarian Empire. For the honour of you and the Papal Holy Father himself, consider your request complete. How am I to travel and live in, I assume, London?"

"There is a house in Hobart Place, the Victoria postal district belonging to the church for use during discreet visits, a convenient location as you will discover for dealing with the target. You will have a multitude of disguises waiting for you there; policeman, cab driver, butler in service and many others should you need them. Assess your target and choose the most appropriate." Dietrich nodded as he kept eye contact with Caravaggio; his look was a little glazed, as if staring right through his master to something catching his attention beyond. Then he spoke.

"Your eminence, the name of the target please?" Caravaggio took a deep breath and looked at Schiltz before speaking and then back to Dietrich. Schiltz's gaze also fell on his subordinate to see his reaction.

"Sir Cecil Patterson, Minister of War. You will have to tread carefully, he is well protected." Dietrich nodded slowly and then sank his highly alcoholic calvados without saying a word; the rich spirit seeming to have no effect on him. No one said anything else from then until some minutes later when the guards left Caravaggio to his administrative papal duties.

Chapter Twenty-Four

Patterson dismissed Ford and Vincent while he was within the protection of his own office building; he had taken on additional security on the door of Trinity House and within it by recruiting, through Major Hoare, some fierce ex-military types. They masqueraded as Commissionaires, the organisation established by benefactor Captain Sir Edward Walter to give servicemen after the Crimean war honourable and gainful employment.

The protection officers had stayed together and hadn't ventured far. In fact they were just around the corner from his office in a white and gold fronted 'Lyons Tea Shop' in Crutched Friars on the corner with Seething Lane. The tea shop sat on its standard position on a corner with two entrance doors, serving exactly the same menu as every other Lyons premises. Ford and Vincent sat at the back of the premises at a table for two positioned against the back wall with no doors behind either of them. It afforded, by habit, a complete view between them of the entire premises with no weak point of either of them having their backs to an unguarded blind spot or point of danger. Each had a steaming cup of tea in front of them.

"Mark, can I ask you something about the day of the gunfire exchange at Karen's place?" Vincent was taking a sip of fresh, hot tea as Ford asked the question. He put the cup back onto its saucer and swallowed and then responded.

"Sure, Boss. Go on."

"She told me that Patterson was getting heavy with her, and you stepped in." Vincent was suddenly concerned for a moment that Ford was about to admonish him for his actions towards the Minister. Then he recalled the lack of respect that Ford had and the unenviable position that he was in protecting Patterson's life. He also recalled Ford's long term view on the assignment and realised he could answer freely and honestly.

"Yeah, he did get physical with her and I did step in. I can't be dealing with all that domestic 'man on woman' violence, Guv. Saw way too much of it as a kid and it ain't right. So I walked in and told him so and that was that. I'm sure that it was the right thing to do." Ford listened intently to this reply. He looked Vincent in the eye as he spoke and now he had finished he delayed just for a moment breaking that eye contact. He looked down at his steaming tea, pointlessly picked up a tea spoon and began stirring his drink; there was no need, he didn't take sugar.

"You did the right thing, Mark. It isn't right for anyone. Especially not that cowardly fucker. Changing the subject, do you want to read the SRP journal? It certainly will enlighten you as to this man Holden's quest."

"Yes, it would be useful."

"Right, tell you what, have it at Tudor Castle to read over in your room. I'll give it to you when we arrive."

"All right. It can wait. I'll read it then."

Silence fell between them. They each took a sip from their cups of tea and then immediately looked towards the door when they heard its warning bell chime as someone entered. Policemen's habits of people watching never waned, and in the protection world it was a skill that might just keep them alive.

* * *

September 20th, Tudor Castle

The three Rover '8' 1.3 litre 'horseless carriages' arrived in front of the Island Wing having crossed the moat bridge and driven around the croquet lawn. The three cars carried between them Patterson, Ford, Karen Wood and Vincent; Phillips, Hoare, Fiona Shaw, a uniformed, although currently covertly dressed, Metropolitan armed officer called Aled Stone, and the head of the Admiralty, Sir Digby Standage-Jones.

The cars chugged and rattled around the lawn until they came to a stop by the main doors and a pleasant silence descended. The various occupants of the vehicles alighted; all looking tired from a tedious mechanised journey. Ford had tried to persuade Patterson to use the train to Maidstone and then either a horse drawn or car transfer to the castle but he had refused, wanting to continue 'embracing the new technology that would change the world'. Ford could not see how anything so dirty and noisy could possibly change the world in any positive way. He suspected they would become, over time, more powerful, larger and faster and create anarchy on the roads amongst those foolish enough to use them. He understood fully that Patterson's enthusiasm derived from his industrial interests.

Staff came to each of the cars to collect baggage and deposit it in the guests' various rooms. The rest of the military staff had already arrived and were waiting in the library to have late morning coffee with the minister and his delegation. Other members of staff showed the car passengers to their rooms to freshen up. Ford went with the minister while Vincent ensured that Karen Wood got settled. She would not be alone; when off duty Ford would stay with her in place of his own room. Staff and guests alike disappeared into the stone built Tudor Castle, once a hunting lodge of Henry the Eighth. The Minister and his immediate staff in the 'Moat Wing' that was built over the water, while everyone else was boarded in the 'Island Wing'. Posted in various points around the immediate site of the castle were ten Kent policemen; four around the outer moat on walking patrols, two on the castle side of the moat bridge each issued with Webley pistols, and the other four armed with Lee Enfield rifles posted to tactical aspects of the castle overlooking the moat and surrounding lands. Each looked in a different compass point direction. These ten would each be relieved every four hours by another ten and then after a twelve hour shift another twenty officers would come on duty to take over the protective responsibilities Kent Constabulary had been assigned.

In preparing this operation Ford had taken no chances; Holden would be caught and not allowed to complete his bloody campaign. No one, not even Hoare, really knew the extent of the adversary they were up against.

* * *

The Library, 11.30a.m

The Minister and Ford were the last to arrive. Around the library already taking piping hot, black, finest Columbian coffee were Standage-Jones and his staff officer, a Naval Captain, and Field Marshall Owen Bowen-Long and his staff officer, a Guards Major. They stood up as Patterson entered the room and all politely shook hands. Also present were Lord Carfax-Smythe and his estate manager Peter Debrett. Ford spotted Vincent stood discreetly in the background. Karen was nowhere to be seen. Patterson walked up to a fine oak table where the coffee pot was being kept warm and attended by a member of the castle staff. He was poured a black coffee and left to add anything else himself. He walked away with it as it had come and sat among the gathering in the library. Ford got a cup of black coffee and then went to stand with Mark Vincent. It was time for the Minister to come clean to his two most senior military officers as to why they were there.

"Gentlemen. Let me first of all thank you for attending this lovely setting. You will be surprised to discover that you and your staff will be able to enjoy its amenities and land to the full over the next three days. We are not here on official business. We are here as a result of an initiative driven by Inspector Ford, Mr Phillips and Major Hoare.

"As you all well know, my staff and I are currently in the grip of a wave of murderous violence perpetrated by a wayward madman." He was not going to tell either of his chiefs or their staff that they knew who it was. The chances were good they would know Holden, ask questions and perhaps even sympathise with him. "I have invited you here to see if this madman may attempt to strike against me here. He will quickly be aware of the uniform outer patrols but perhaps not the police armed security within other than the Metropolitan protection officers. We have an additional four riflemen and, of course, Major Hoare, who has an extensive military background of operational experience.

"You may be potential targets, but Inspector Ford is confident that it is only I and my immediate staff." In truth he knew the key target must now be only him; the rituals relative to the deaths of each SRP men had now been fully re-enacted. Ford having read the journal was also very aware of this. "Major Hoare will issue you all personal side arms in the form of Webley service revolvers for your own protection. Use them only if necessary, having tried to identify your target first as friend or foe. I am sorry to put you all in this spot but this man must be stopped and Tudor Castle presents a perfect opportunity to defend ourselves and apprehend this man." Bowen-Long was the first to reply.

"Jolly good show, Minister. Haven't had a bit of action for yonks. Look forward to the challenge."

"Here, here," added Standage-Jones. The hosts, Carfax-Smythe and Debrett, seemed ambivalent to the news. Phillips had already explained the exact purpose of the visit to them and they had felt they were merely being 'public spirited' in helping.

Ford was not happy with what he had heard and approached the Minister who was now sipping his coffee and catching his breath.

"Sir Cecil, I need to speak to you please," Ford gestured to move away from the crowds in the seats to along to two rows of bookshelves out of earshot. "No one consulted me on dishing out guns willy-nilly, Minister. That is not safe or clever."

"Oh come now, Inspector, surely it's best we're all protected. It was Hoare's idea and rather a good one I thought. They're all versed in using guns."

"Yes, in battlefield combat, not in an urban civilian environment. They're liable to kill someone they shouldn't."

"It's too late, the decision has been made. Go and give them some advice if you are so concerned." Patterson stormed back to the gathering to see Hoare issuing the firearms and spoke very cynically to them all just to make Ford's position more difficult than it already was. "Oh gentlemen, the inspector has some views and advice for you, don't you, Ford?"

Ford emerged into the room from the rows of books with his empty coffee cup still in his hand. He had been forced to speak. He laid it down on the oak table and looked at all those gathered. They were in fact looking to him with expressions of interest on their faces despite the Minister's belligerence. But Patterson had made his mind up for him as to what sort of advice he would offer.

"Well. May I simply say this? Don't point them at anyone you like, and don't pull the trigger unless it's someone you don't want to see again." He walked out from the library leaving everyone to look at each other with an air of bewilderment.

* * *

Phillips found himself alone in the library in Tudor Castle during the late afternoon. He browsed the shelves full of leather-bound editions of classics and encyclopaedia when a recollection occurred to him regarding some words from Holden. 'Sir Gawain and the Green Knight'? He seemed to be in the ideal location to try to discover the fabric of the story. He browsed the shelves to locate the encyclopaedic section amongst the row upon row of dusty faded leather spines. Eventually he discovered a whole unit dedicated to such references and using his index finger traced his way along the shelves to find the index volumes. Finding the volume containing 'G' he looked up 'Gawain and the Green Knight' and checked its reference number and volume. Again using his finger, he found one of the two volumes that encompassed 'G' and lifted it from the shelf. The entry for 'Gawain' was quite early on in the volume and having found it he flicked the pages over to see how long the entry was. It was sizable, over several pages beginning with a basic definition and then an in-depth explanation of the writing of the poem, its legend and subsequent interpretations in depth. He read the first paragraph over twice to himself to understand the gist of the story.

> 'Sir Gawain and the Green Knight is a late fourteenth century alliterative chivalric romance outlining the adventures of Sir Gawain, one of the knights of King Arthur's round table. The single copy of the original manuscript survives held at the British Museum written in its North Midland Middle English dialect.
>
> 'In the story Sir Gawain accepts a challenge from a mysterious warrior who is completely green. The "Green Knight" offers to allow anyone to strike him with his axe if he will take a return blow in a year and a day. Gawain accepts the challenge, and beheads him in one blow, only to have the Knight stand up, pick up his head, and remind Gawain to meet him at the appointed time. Gawain's struggle to meet the appointment, and the adventures involved, cause this work to be classified as an Arthurian tale involving themes of chivalry and loyalty.
>
> 'The story begins in King Arthur's court at Camelot as the court is feasting and exchanging gifts. A gigantic

Green Knight armed with an axe enters the hall and proposes a game. He asks that someone in the court take the axe and strike a single blow at him, on the condition that the Green Knight will return the blow one year and one day later. Sir Gawain, the youngest of Arthur's knights as well as Arthur's nephew, accepts the challenge and chops off the giant's head in one smashing blow, fully expecting him to die. But the Green Knight picks up his own head, reminds Gawain to meet him at the Green Chapel in a year and a day, and rides off.

'Almost a year later, Sir Gawain sets off to find the Green Chapel and complete his bargain with the Green Knight. His journey takes him to a beautiful castle, where Gawain meets Bertilak de Hautdesert, the lord of the castle, and his beautiful wife, who are both pleased to have such a renowned guest. Gawain tells them of his New Year's Day appointment at the Green Chapel and says that he must continue his search the next day. The lord laughs and tells him his search has ended: the Green Chapel is not more than two miles away.

'The lord of the castle goes hunting the next day, and proposes a bargain to Gawain before he leaves: he will give Gawain whatever he catches, on condition that Gawain will give to the lord whatever he might gain during the day. Gawain accepts. After the lord has gone, the lady of the castle, Lady Bertilak, visits Gawain's bedroom to seduce him. Gawain, however, yields in nothing but a single kiss. When the lord returns with the deer he has killed, as agreed, Gawain responds by returning the lady's kiss to the lord, but avoids explaining its source. The next day, the lady comes again, Gawain dodges her advances, and there is a similar exchange of a hunted boar for two kisses. She comes again on the third morning, and Gawain accepts from her a green silk girdle, which the lady promises will keep him from all physical harm. They exchange three kisses. That evening, the lord returns with a fox, which he exchanges with Gawain for the three kisses. However, Gawain keeps the girdle from the lord. The next day, Gawain leaves for the Green Chapel with the lady's silk girdle. He finds the Green Knight there sharpening an axe, and, as arranged, bends over to receive his blow. The Green Knight swings to behead Gawain, but holds back twice, only striking softly on the third swing, causing a permanent scar on his neck. The Green Knight then reveals himself to be the lord of the castle, Bertilak de Hautdesert, and explains that the whole game was arranged by Morgan le Fay. Gawain is at first upset, but the two men part on cordial terms and Gawain returns to Camelot, wearing the girdle as a badge of shame. Arthur, however, decrees that all his knights should henceforth wear a green sash in recognition of Gawain's adventure.

'It is believed in folklore the setting for the alleged 'Green Chapel' is 'Lud's Church', a deep natural chasm hidden within a dense wood in the Peak District.'

Phillips read on but discovered no more references to Lud's Church within the authoritative text. The reference to a real location further aroused his curiosity and he replaced the 'G' volume and returned to the index to look up Lud's Church. Sure enough he discovered an entry and he soon had the book from the shelf to read what it said.

There was little depth to the explanation but enough to at least confirm its existence.

'Lud's Church is a deep millstone grit chasm created by a massive landslip on the hillside above Gradbach, Staffordshire, England. It is located at SJ987656 in a wood known as Back Forest, in the White Peak, towards the south-west fringe of the Peak District National Park about 6 miles west of the A53 between Leek and Buxton. Over 100 yards long and 18 yards high, it is mossy and overgrown, wet and cool even on the hottest of days.

'The Lollards, who were followers of John Wycliffe, an early church reformer, are supposed to have used this as a secret place of worship during the early 15th century, when they were being persecuted for their religious beliefs. 'Lud's Church may have been named after Walter de Ludank or Walter de Lud-Auk who was captured here at one of their meetings. A wooden ship's figurehead from the ship *Swythamley* formerly stood in a high niche above the chasm, placed there by Philip Brocklehurst, then the landowner, around 1862. It was called 'Lady Lud' and was supposed to commemorate the death of the daughter of a Lollard preacher.

'Ralph Elliott and others have identified Lud's Church as the Green Chapel of 'Sir Gawain and the Green Knight'.'

Phillips closed the book and asumed that Holden had a fixation with the poem from his sense of chivalry from an early age, coupled with an obsession to kill the man who had become, as Holden had put it himself, his real life nemesis; as the story so readily identified between its two protagonists.

* * *

Sepp Dietrich emerged into the daylight of Victoria Station's outer concourse, London. A bustling city much the same as Rome outside of the Vatican City; crowds of people, the smell of the railway, the noise of the horse drawn traffic on the cobbled streets; the madness of twentieth century life that when inside the walls of the citadel state that he preciously and proudly served didn't exist. He wore a smart suit and carried a modest leather suitcase and a satchel. He had no grasp of where Hobart Place was from where he stood so he walked towards the main traffic junction and found a policeman to ask. The constable dressed in his high neck tunic, traditional pith style helmet with its blackened out 'GR' crested badge and duty band displayed was tall, imposing and due to his physicality commanded respect that those of an average height or less often didn't. Awkwardly the constable was stood on a raised island across a live carriageway from Dietrich. Foolishly he tried to call to the officer. Hearing his call was impossible with the clatter of the traffic.

The constable cupped his hand to his ear to signify for Dietrich to speak up. He still wasn't able to make himself heard. The constable eventually rolled his eyes and crossed the road to come to him. Dietrich was about to speak when the large and surly looking Edwardian constable spoke first. He pointed to his right ear as he began.

"Human ears. Not dogs, or bats or bloody great big lop eared rabbits ears that can capture loads of sound. Sorry. Now what do you want?" With Dietrich's non-colloquial command of English this was lost on him.

"Hobart Place, sir." The constable looked him up and down.

"Got some friends with money then, eh? Hobart Place. Mmm."

"Yes, please," he said smiling to be polite. The constable frowned; he didn't seem to like the smile. Dietrich reverted to an impassive look.

"Right up to the top end there and Hobart runs across both ways."

"Thank you." Dietrich strolled off briskly.

Reaching the 'T' junction formed by Grosvenor Gardens and Hobart Place he looked left and right to try to spot numbers. He subsequently turned left and found the number he needed along on the left. He climbed the three steps to the immediate doorstep and pulled the metal bell pull that hung to one side of the shiny black door. He heard no footsteps approaching when within a few seconds the door was being opened. A very pretty, young nun opened the door; he could see just under her cassock that she was barefooted. It explained a lot.

"Come in, Mr Dietrich, I have been expecting you."

* * *

Midnight; following a sumptuous banquet everyone was in their rooms. The lone Metropolitan uniformed officer, Constable Stone, was 'on post' outside Patterson's room armed with his Webley and his standard duty whistle to attract attention. At this time of night the castle had an eerie serenity from its silence. The officers on walking patrol on the outside of the moat were conveniently silhouetted by the light emitting from the castle's interior and exterior lights.

Following an earlier reconnaissance operation by Holden, this was exactly the opportunity he had expected. He lay camouflaged in a copse of trees on some high ground that gave him a two-hundred and eighty degree panorama of the castle. With his ingeniously silenced Lee Enfield sniper's rifle fired in conjunction with a specially constructed Leica telescopic sight he had personally had commissioned with the company, he would be able to take three of the four police sentries and then advance on foot to finish the last one by hand with a combat knife. His old instincts that had served him well in Afghanistan were again alive and kicking and he felt more energised than he had done in weeks. His adrenalin was dulling any ill effects of the Tuberculosis. Along with this specially constructed weapon, he possessed three Webley Mk IV service pistols; with pouches on the military webbing he wore over his Afghanistan style fatigues containing rounds of 'speed loaders'. Clusters of six rounds held together he had devised for quick re-loading in a frenetic gunfight situation. He had learnt much from Belgrave Square. Other pouches on the rear of the webbing by his lower back held a multitude of ancillary equipment.

With no enhanced night vision capability in 1904, Holden had to bide his time with the movement of his three targets across the lighting from the castle to provide a sharp silhouette. He relaxed himself in his prone sniping position with the barrel of the rifle resting across some Hessian sacks he had filled with earth to provide a stable firing platform. He controlled his breathing taking long and languid breaths to assist in his completely still bodily state to avoid any misdirection of the shot. He took up the slack on the trigger with his right forefinger. He waited for the helmeted silhouette to pass what appeared to be windows to a kitchen. His only overriding concern at this point was over penetration. If he had not taken that into account he would be found out with the first shot. He had flattened the tips of each of the .303 rounds to ensure they hit their targets and remained within them. There was a very quiet thud from the muzzle of the rifle and a subdued muzzle flash as he squeezed the trigger and let the first round go to find its target, hopefully first time. If not, again his plan would be compromised.

He wasn't disappointed in his abilities. His impeccable marksmanship had not deserted him. The silhouette fell and disappeared in the blackness below the window. At three hundred yards he was close enough with the wind blowing towards him and no other ambient noise to tell if his target had cried out with the impact of the shot. Again his anticipated plan had worked and the victim of his accuracy had fallen silently. He shifted his position silently right to prepare to fell his next victim. He took himself through his same monastic, disciplined sniping drill. Within ninety seconds of the first, the second target was felled.

* * *

Ford lay propped up against the padded headboard in the double bed in Karen's room naked under the covers. He could feel her warm, naked body pressing against his own and with an arm around him over his stomach as she slept, as if for protection and reassurance. Moonlight streamed in through the leaded-light windows and bathed the bed and it's occupants in an esoteric glow. It allowed him to look down at her. The covers had slipped slightly down from either of them and he could see the smooth skin of her arms, upper torso and the edge of her Celtic tattoo. He was so in love with her that it made him feel vulnerable. Lying next to her in the moonlit, in the ornately decorated and oak panelled bed chamber of a castle was a place where if someone said to Ford that he had to 'be frozen in time at this juncture forever', he would not complain. There had been so much happen since the beginning of this assignment that it was enough for several entire careers to have experienced. With his invested wealth he had to wonder why he still risked his life. The answer was easy: until this assignment he had had no one to share it with. Fate had now conspired to change all that. When this was over he would consider tendering his resignation.

He had been sat in bed for quite some time and the temperature was falling. He moved himself down to lay properly alongside her causing her to moan very gently in her sleep and shift position. He pulled the covers over the two of them and settled himself down.

* * *

Holden readied himself for his final shot before he would have to move forward and engage the last walking sentry in person. He settled his breathing and waited again for the perfect moment with a sharp silhouette. Fortunately for him fortune favoured the bold; as he squeezed the trigger the light behind the unsuspecting police constable went out but the shot had already been discharged. It found its target; but he had no way of knowing if it had. He had to pause and wait for some kind of reaction. If it had missed then the constable would have been aware of something whizzing by him and within seconds would sound an alarm. The seconds ticked by. Was he compromised? The seconds turned into a minute by his moonlit Rolex. Nothing. He must have found his mark. He left the rifle behind and moved forward in a low crouch drawing a Bowie knife as he did so. This next killing would have to be very close and personal.

At fifty yards out he crawled forward on his chest and stomach in a classic military stealthy 'cat' or 'leopard' crawl. In the dark it allowed him to get within forty feet of his target. Now he observed the police outer perimeter sentry's movements for a minute or so. The pace at which he walked, the distance before he turned around, the amount of clothing he had on; would it get in the way of cutting his throat? It looked like it could with his high-necked tunic and cape.

Suddenly a brilliant thought struck him. He put the knife away.

* * *

Patterson woke after an hour or so of restless sleep and realised why he could not settle. That common little slut was here and desperately out of his grasp to enjoy defiling her to achieve his usual sexual gratification. It was no good, he would have to leave the room to see if he could coerce one of the castle's staff. With his position and power and the usual false hope he promised them he might get somewhere. His mind concentrated only on his own sexual desire to the detriment of all other reasoning. He was naked except for his dressing gown now that he was out of bed. He pulled on his slippers and went to the door. The door jamb surround, as he approached it, gave the telling sign of a light on in the castle's corridor as it highlighted the doors edging on three sides. He unlocked the door and pulled it open.

'FUCKING HELL!' Patterson let out a huge and frustrated sigh before running his hands through his greying hair and speaking in an indignant tone.

"Oh, fuck. I forgot you'd be there. Don't suppose I can go anywhere or get any bloody privacy." Aled Stone stood up from his chair opposite the Minister's bed chamber door and spoke calmly in reply.

"Sorry, Sir. You know the rules and Inspector Ford's orders. This is a trap so best you stay there for your own good."

Patterson shook his head in desperation and re-entered his room slamming the door behind him. He forgot to lock it though. He stormed into the en-suite bathroom turning on the light and looked at himself in the mirror. He did look tired, but his skin was also flushed red with his emotions. He undid his dressing gown and let it fall to the floor. He felt the coldness of the porcelain sink against him which initially shocked him. Then aroused him. He took hold of himself and muttered under his breath, 'haven't had to bloody do this for a while.'

* * *

The constable had just turned his back from Holden's direction. He knew he would take nearly fifty seconds to cover his pacing away from his start position before turning again. Holden leapt to his feet and ran briskly and silently across the grass and then took the constable in a headlock and pulled him down. His tall, crested, beat-duty helmet fell to the floor, and although he flung his arms around Holden in a form of retaliation it was too late. With a vice like grip of the constable's head and a rapid rotation he broke the man's neck and let him fall silently to the floor. He looked down at the lifeless constable. In the dark he only needed his helmet and cape to bluff his way to the castle side of the moat bridge. He undid the cape fastened around the constable's neck and removed it, and then instantly sweeping it around his body to put it on and fasten the cape to himself. He grabbed the helmet and put it on. He began striding towards the bridge, a matter of a hundred yards.

He pulled one of his Webleys from its holster, leaving two on the hips and one under his left arm. From another pouch he removed a silencer for the weapon he had again devised and constructed himself for just such an event. He screwed it into place around the barrel of the pistol with the thread that he had cut on each to match. He was now only twenty feet or so from the bridge. On the far side he could see the two constables looking bored and disinterested. They obviously thought the whole case was over hyped. One was leaning against the castle walls and in the moonlight Holden could see that the man was struggling to stay awake.

He stepped onto the bridge. The constable who was more alert called out.

"Who's that? What you doing here? We've all only been on post for two hours." Holden dared not attempt a reply. He sped up his pace and when mid-way across the bridge and around twenty feet from either of them he raised the pistol from under his cape. He let two shots go at the first man, the first a sense of direction shot and the second an aimed shot. The first found its mark, centre of mass in his chest and the second struck him in the neck. He collapsed silently. The second constable much to Holden's surprise had managed to draw his pistol. With another 'double tap' Holden felled him too. He was now free to enter the castle. He reloaded the pistol as he walked allowing the empty and live rounds to fall to the floor; he had plenty of pre-prepared speed loading ammunition for his pistols. The forces he had so far encountered he had been able to observe over a twelve hour period prior to the commencement of his one man assault. The inside of the castle and the personnel within would be a complete enigma to him.

Chapter Twenty-Five

It was no good. Ford could not settle to sleep properly with the moonlight streaming into the room from the gothic shape window across the bedroom. He should have pulled the curtains in the first place before they went to bed; in his excitement of clasping her naked form and making love to her he had completely forgotten. He slowly and quietly got out of the bed and walked still unclothed over to the diamond patterned leaded-light windows. The silhouetted rolling countryside looked mystical in the moonlight. As he grabbed the curtains with two outstretched arms he happened to look down to the moat and the area illuminated just beyond it. He could see a prone figure, or so he thought, on the banks of the moat.

He rubbed his eyes and looked again. The ancient glazing didn't help. He opened the window for more clarity. 'CHRIST!' it was the prone and completely still figure of one of the outer sentries Kent Police had posted. He scoured the area as much as he could and saw nothing else out of place, but he was certain all was not well and that this officer was not simply napping. He needed to get dressed briskly and grab his gun. He pulled on some trousers and a woollen pullover and grabbed a pair of shoes; there was not time for anything else. He moved to the bed and grabbed his Webley MkIV from under his pillow. He had to ensure no panic. Gently he cupped his left hand over Karen's mouth to stifle any noise she might make as she woke while he gestured her to be silent with his right forefinger in front of his mouth as he made a 'shush' sound.

"Say nothing. Get dressed and get under the bed until I come back. Don't argue and don't deviate from those instructions." With a brow furrowed by fear she nodded her head quickly and frenetically. He moved away from her and grabbed some more bullets from his briefcase. He went to the door and left to go to Mark Vincent's room.

* * *

Holden now had a free run of the castle itself. He purely had to move with caution and stealth to ensure surprise and not being detected. His goal was so clearly in sight. He walked under the gate house and skirted around the croquet lawn at the waters edge allowing him to quickly go to cover if necessary. Looking across at the Island Wing the number of lights illuminated was now far less than only an hour ago. Hopefully less targets to end up as collateral damage would be wandering around. He hugged the edge of the building line in a crouch and tried the windows of the rooms that were unlit. Little did he know at this point he evaded the view of one of the Kent riflemen who was overlooking the croquet lawn. On his third attempt he found a window that would open having established it wasn't locked; he peered through the glass before opening it any further. Although the room was dark his night vision was well adjusted now and he could tell that the room appeared to be empty. He eased the sash style window up slowly to keep any noise to a minimum until he had pushed it far enough to slip inside and close it behind him.

Ford quietly knocked on Vincent's door. The bleary eyed Edwardian protection constable came to the door. He looked awful.

"What the hell's wrong with you," said Ford in a whisper.

"Too much bloody port to try and get to sleep two hours ago that's bloody what. Anyway, what do you want, Boss?"

"We're under attack, Holden must be here, and I can see that one of the outer sentries has gone down."

"Christ! I'll get my gun and get some clothes on. What's the plan?"

"Right, do you know where all the riflemen are?"

"Yes."

The Dressmaker Connection

"Good. Go round and warn them all, but tell them to stay put, if they start moving about we'll end up in the midst of a shooting gallery. I'll go and back up Stone with the Minister."

"What about Karen, or Hoare?"

"Karen is taken care of. Hoare can go fuck himself."

"But Guv, we need to have him on side and know what he's doing tactically or he might add to the danger for us." Ford hadn't thought the one part of the plan fully through that applied to Hoare.

"Good point. Go and see him first, then round up the Kent boys." Ford made off along the corridor to the walkway that would transfer him from the Island Wing into the Moat Wing. The saving grace for Patterson's location here was that Holden would be unlikely to try an amphibious assault and with three sides surrounded by water it should be easy to defend.

Ford found Stone at his post wide awake sat outside Patterson's oak and metal braced door. The young constable was surprised to see him as he came into view at the end of the corridor and he stood up as a result.

"Inspector Ford, what are you up now for?" Ford was mildly out of breath. Dressed casually, Stone immediately saw the Webley in the waist band of his trousers. "Bugger. I take it all is not well then, Sir?"

"Understatement of the year, Stone. Holden is here and he is systematically picking us off. We need to go in and make sure Patterson is all right and then hold him here at bay until his killer arrives."

"Have you dialled out, Sir, for more help?" It was a good point, but there was a flaw in this suggestion.

"Unfortunately the Carfax-Smythe's are resistant to the march of progress in the twentieth century. They have no telephone. Is the door open?"

"Funny you should say that. He popped his head out a little while ago and was right annoyed I was here, like he'd forgotten. He shut the door again but I certainly didn't hear him lock it." Ford nodded sagely.

"Good. Hang on here for a moment. No. Follow me in and then watch the corridor from the cover of the doorway."

Ford opened the oak panelled, iron studded, arch-shaped door and slowly entered. The room was dimly lit from an open bedside lamp. It was enough to show that Patterson was not in his bed. 'Bollocks!' thought Ford, 'where is he?' He looked around the very comfortable and generous bed chamber, his gaze turning away from the four poster bed across the area occupied by a coffee table and two leather upholstered Chesterfield armchairs atop a Turkish patterned rug, to the door jamb of the bathroom and the hint of light that it betrayed around its edges. He drew his Webley and walked towards it. As he got closer he could hear the subdued sound of a man grunting. He reached the door, pushed it open gently with his left hand as his right held onto the pistol, pointed at the hip by his arm along his side then bent forward from the elbow at ninety degrees. He could not believe the sight that greeted him. The pale but lean, naked body of Patterson masturbating. Despite the potential danger of the evening, Ford could see the amusing irony of what he had discovered.

"Well, well. I always thought you were a wanker, Minister." The surprised Patterson whose eyes had been screwed tight shut suddenly opened his eyes wide in shock and then bent down grabbing for his dressing gown. He was flushed red with huge embarrassment; he could not believe he had been caught in such an adolescent, boarding school situation. "I suppose this is because you couldn't get out of the room to get to her? You couldn't help yourself, could you? You pathetic, filthy bastard. I really don't know why I have bothered for so long."

"Because it's what you are paid for, Ford!" Patterson screamed as he barged past him into the main bedchamber. He switched on the light with a flood of illumination washing over the moat twenty feet or so below. He grabbed a decanter on a sideboard and poured a large brandy from it into an ornate cut glass tumbler. "Get out, you common little man in a superior world."

"I don't think you are in any position to judge that tonight," replied Ford calmly. "Besides, do you not wonder why I am here so casually dressed with a pistol drawn?" Patterson stopped mid sip. In his flushed and embarrassed state he hadn't. The reality of real danger now occurred to him.

"He's here then? Holden? Go and get Major Hoare in here!"

"Don't worry, Vincent's gone to get him, Stone is outside. We do get paid to look after the likes of you; but his quest is about justice for the others. Sometimes I feel that if he gets you then tough. Trouble is I won't have that on my reputation. It won't happen on my watch. Whatever, I'll make sure he doesn't get you. I want to see the public scandal do that."

"That's as maybe, Ford. You are not pure white in this, remember?" Ford paused for a moment then approached Patterson and cocked his Webley's hammer and raised the gun to his face.

"Killed in the crossfire? Perhaps I don't care after all. It's not like I need the job now, I may not be whiter than white, but at least she and I are both single, and in love." Patterson turned visibly pale with the gun inches from the bridge of his nose.

"You wouldn't?" It was hard to get the words out as his mouth was completely dry. Then there was a voice from the door to the corridor the sound of another hammer action being cocked.

"No he wouldn't," it was Hoare with his Mannlicher automatic pistol raised and pointing at Ford. Ford remained solid.

"Action beats reaction, Major."

"We'll see," there was an icy calm in Hoare's voice. Then the sound of another hammer action being cocked. Hoare heard it the loudest as it was inches from the base of his skull. Everyone recognised the voice.

"We will. Put the fucking gun down!" It was Mark Vincent. Patterson now felt brave. He turned away from Ford and walked to the window and looked out across the moat. Everyone lowered their guns and then safely eased their hammer actions closed. The sound of distant gunfire focussed everyone's attention.

* * *

Safely inside the house, Holden gave consideration to trying to keep the number of enlisted policemen he killed to a minimum. In his twisted mind he realised that sometimes taking their lives due to the circumstances was a 'fate a complete'. He had pulled from his webbing, held in a large canvas pouch that sat on the small of his back, a handheld miniature crossbow. Whether loaded with conventional arrows or the lighter poisoned tip ones he possessed it was a fantastic weapon due to its stealthy capabilities. He looked down at the body of one of the riflemen, the officer that had been overlooking the lawn. Tactically his position was an obvious choice, so Holden had moved slowly and quietly walking along the edge of floors and stairs, his back to the walls to reduce any noise to find the officer. Looking in from an open doorway he'd fired the silent crossbow and struck the man in the small of the back. He'd fallen almost instantly clutching his back and stiffening quickly, falling unconscious. The poison was made up from a dilution of scorpion venom and other natural extracts; he had learnt about it as he escaped back through India many years ago with Waldron.

However, before he could reload the crossbow, he heard a single shot. It whizzed past his head as he immediately reacted to it, diving for cover to one side of the room. He could only draw his pistols to react and as another rifleman entered the room levelling his already cocked weapon, Holden fired three shots each finding their mark. The rifleman dropped his gun and fell onto a chaise-long to his right. Blood quickly dripped onto the floor from his wounds as Holden got up to check his pulse. He holstered the pistols and reloaded the crossbow. He did concede in his mind that this was almost pointless as anyone around would now be running amok potentially with guns. He needed to move with extreme caution around the building to avoid detection if possible. Another thought struck him as he was about to walk out. He looked back at the officer knocked out by the arrow and rubbed his chin. Then he shut the door and walked over to him, after all with the change of shifts the only ones who knew that he wasn't one of the Kent Police officers were the two remaining Kent officers, Patterson, Hoare and probably Ford.

Stone rushed into Patterson's room from his cover just inside the door but shielded to the occupants by the oak door. Ford reacted to his movement instantly.

"Get back in the doorway and keep a watch on that bloody corridor. Right, I don't think that there is anywhere particularly safe, so I suggest we hold the Minister here. There is after all only one way out and in." Hoare was the first to reply, addressing Patterson at the same time.

"He's right, Minister. We can easily hold out here. He's a fish in a barrel as soon as he comes down that corridor." Patterson was beginning to pace with nervousness. He was less convinced.

The Dressmaker Connection

"You don't know this man. One of you watch the bloody windows and the moat. I'm telling you he could come from anywhere." Vincent went to one of the windows and peered out over the moonlit water. There was no sign of any activity outside anywhere. Patterson then strode into the bathroom and locked himself in and called from behind the closed door. "I'm staying in here. Get me when you've got the bastard."

Patterson was in truth completely mortified. Holden's intention to strike absolute fear into him had now been achieved. He sat himself down on the cold stone floor in one corner of the bathroom against the equally cold tiled walls. He drew his knees up to his face and buried his head in his arms resting on his knees. He quietly sobbed.

Outside in the bed chamber there was an uneasy silence as Vincent watched the moat, Stone guarded the door and Hoare and Ford stood with their weapons drawn waiting for the first one to speak. They were quietly uncomfortable with having coming to an agreement. Ford broke the silence.

"The only thing we can do is swap with those two every few minutes or so to take turns watching and ease the pressure a bit." Hoare simply nodded in agreement.

Holden, now in a police uniform, casually strode the corridors of the Island Wing to make his way into the Moat Wing. As soon as he left the room shutting the door on the officers he had already silenced, the other attendees were entering the corridors. He first encountered Standage-Jones and his staff officer, he noted armed with a pistol.

"What the blue blazes is going on, constable?" The admiral demanded.

"Nothing to worry you, sir," replied Holden, "just a little drill. Please go back inside."

"Bloody stupid idea. You bloody police are so blithering incompetent." He turned on his heel and re-entered his room leaving his staff officer in the corridor. He looked Holden up and down and reluctantly re-entered his room too.

Rounding a corner he soon ran into the Field-Marshal, Owen Bowen-Long. Holden took a dislike to the man as soon as he saw him, he remembered him as a General doing a review many years ago. He knew that he would be too pompous and ignorant to remember a mere adjutant of a regiment.

"What's going on, officer? Something dangerous or stupid?" Holden was seething. He had his silenced pistol in his hand which was resting inside his tunic and desperately wished he had his crossbow to hand instead to silence the bastard. Before he could answer, another door opened and the army staff officer emerged. He was a Major who had gone through Sandhurst with Holden, and, about to speak, he instantly recognised the weathered and drawn SRP captain.

"Christ! Bill! You're supposed be bloody dead?" He could afford no further comment from the major, those words were enough. He drew the Webley and struck the major as hard as he could downwards onto the side of the neck to render him unconscious with a brachial stun. It worked; the major buckled at the knees and fell to the floor unconscious. Bowen-Long tried to tackle Holden but he was too fast for him. He turned and kicked out with a sideways stance at the ageing officer as he advanced and struck his left knee, forcing the joint against its natural movement. The old man yelled with pain and fell down. Holden delivered another strike as before to render him unconscious.

He strolled off along the corridor and entered the Moat Wing. As he did so he re-holstered the silenced Webley in favour of the cross bow again as was his original plan. His timing could not have been more fortuitous; a voice from behind called to him.

"Hey, Bob where are you going?" He turned to see one of the other Kent officers. The officer had assumed he was a colleague; he levelled the crossbow and fired one of the poisoned lightweight arrows straight and true. It struck the officer in his abdomen and he collapsed within a few seconds. 'Christ! How many more were there? And what about the protection officers?' He loaded one of only three remaining arrows and walked on into the picturesque building constructed over the water. With the only gunfire coming from within the buildings, the final rifle-armed officer was himself stalking the corridors. Sadly for him Holden came up behind him. The officer felt a sharp pain in his lower back and then collapsed.

Within minutes, Holden then found himself about to enter the corridor that led to Patterson's room. Now in the Moat Wing, at each corner he cautiously took a look around before committing himself along it. That tactic now paid dividends as he spotted Stone in the doorway looking, as luck would have it for a split second, the other way. Holden abandoned the crossbow and drew the silenced Webley again. From the other rear pouch he pulled a smoke grenade that he intended to use to create confusion in whatever room he found Patterson in; he knew he would be well protected. Initially walking down the corridor he would bluff out the young officer he had seen to draw him away from the door and take care of him. He entered the corridor and began to walk towards the doorway. The young officer, Stone, instantly spotted him. Fooled into thinking he was one of the Kent officers he left the cover of the doorway to enter the corridor to greet him. He was playing straight into Holden's hands.

"Sir! It's one of the Kent lads." These were temporarily his last words. Holden let him come right to him before again delivering another brachial stun, although this time, once down, he kicked Stone in the jaw just to ensure his unconsciousness.

"Stone! Stone?" Ford, Vincent and Hoare all looked at each other when there was no reply. Ford was about to go for the door when he heard something bounce into the room and then there was a flash and a loud bang. The room filled with smoke and his ears were ringing; so loudly in fact that any other noise was almost inaudible.

Ford felt a hard strike in his face that sent him backwards to the floor, and he could taste the iron flavour of blood in his mouth. As he looked back up from the floor into the smoke with everything happening it seemed in slow motion, he almost could not believe what he was seeing. The figure that had put him to the floor darted quickly through the smoke and Ford heard the muted sound, through his temporary tinnitus, of glass smashing. He could just about make out the figure of Mark Vincent, having been charged down at incredible speed, crashing out of the window that overlooked the moat. Then he was gone.

Hoare was standing directly above Ford and began firing with his automatic Mannlicher pistol. He could see that his bullets had struck a figure in the smoke twice in the torso resulting in a strange metallic sound before Hoare's gun, over technological for its day, jammed. The figure fired back at Hoare with one shot. Ford saw Hoare's head snap backwards and then he fell to the floor, smashing his head heavily against a post of the ornate bed as he collapsed. Ford levelled his Webley at the figure. He hesitated. 'Fuck! It was the sunglass wearing man from Venice!' This uncharacteristic hesitation cost him; his pistol was kicked out of his hand. In a reflex action, born out of his pugilism, the hand devoid of a gun, as it regained nervous commands from his brain, grabbed at the leg that had kicked him. Catching it at the end of its swing, Ford pulled it hard, as hard as he could. He achieved his end; he got the figure to the floor. 'Captain Holden' he thought, 'we meet at last'.

Chapter Twenty-Six

Holden, hyped up with adrenalin, was momentarily caught out by this reaction from a man he believed he had significantly disabled. He had no inkling of Ford's combative past when he had viewed him from a distance on many occasions, but had given consideration to Ford seeming to possess a meaningful physical presence. He very quickly, despite being partially prone, lashed out with his right hand still holding the Webley to try to 'pistol whip' his opponent in the head swiftly to concuss him. Ford's lightning reflexes punched out at the wrist of Holden's right hand instantly numbing it and forcing him, through a spontaneous nervous reaction, to drop the gun. Ford was now in his spiritual element; one on one, hand to hand fighting. He rolled quickly over and pushing Holden to the floor, now on top of him pinned him down. Momentarily letting go of Holden's left hand, he laid a devastating punch into the right side of Holden's face. His head rolled to his left and a slight spray of blood was emitted from his mouth. The moment that his left hand was free was enough to counter in some way. With a clenched fist he drove his left thumb hard into Ford's groin to deliver a sharp distracting pain into his femoral artery. It was enough to make Ford flinch backwards. This slight movement was enough for Holden to buck wildly and throw him off. Then they were both quickly to their feet.

Ford was into a boxing stance instantly, as was Holden, a southpaw that took Ford by surprise. 'He must have boxed in the army' deduced Ford. In the generous space of the bed chamber they began moving around and launching range finding jabs at each other.

Holden knew that he would have to deal with his opponent quickly; a long 'spar' would take its toll on his breathing. He went in for an all out attack briskly. He struggled to get any punches through Ford's well versed defence. As soon as he dropped his own guard just very slightly, Ford struck with a devastating blow to his upper chest. It knocked the wind out of him and forced Holden back a few steps to catch his breath. Ford rushed forward. Holden dropped to his knees in a squat and stepped sideways and kicked out with his left leg deadening Ford's right thigh. He pounced on Ford from behind and gripped him in a stranglehold with his right arm across Ford's neck and his left arm forcing Ford forward against it exaggerating the constriction on his breathing. Suddenly the door from the bathroom opened revealing a terrified looking Patterson. He saw Ford and Holden locked in a life or death struggle; he was in fear of his own life now that Holden was only a few feet away. He lunged forward and grabbed for one of the pistols on the floor.

Ford felt the stranglehold ease slightly; Holden had released the pressure of his left arm. Ford knew something was up and he had to get free. He jabbed hard with his left elbow at Holden's body and only felt a hard surface as he did so. 'What the hell did he have on under his clothes?' Suddenly Ford was physically whipped around by Holden to face the nervous, gun toting Patterson; one of his worst fears. Then he felt something sharp jab him in the back and he began to feel nauseous. Before he lost consciousness a gun shot went off and in a surreal state of mind he felt he could almost see the bullet pass by his head. Then he blacked out.

Holden rushed forward quickly with the limp body of Ford and drove it into Patterson knocking him off balance. The cowardly industrialist was now apoplectic with fear.

"Don't kill me, please don't kill me!" He sobbed and broke down. Holden forced himself to show remarkable restraint as his adrenalin flowed furiously and the desire to kill the man he had last seen in a Bedouin tent six years ago was almost overwhelming. But this man was the Green Knight.

"You sickening, bastard!" He rushed forward reaching into a small pouch right in the front of his webbing and withdrawing a hypodermic needle and syringe. He discarded its protective cap and then plunged it up to the end of the needle into Patterson's arm through his shirt sleeve; he was now dressed in trousers and a shirt. The Minister screamed out and then became unconscious in seconds. The room fell silent.

Holden looked around the room. It seemed very still and calm with three bodies unconscious around him. He found himself breathing heavily and wheezing a little. Now he had to make good his escape. He could hear splashing around outside. He looked out of the window and saw the officer he had driven through it trying to get out of the moat on the far side. Nearest the castle was a sheer wall with no escape; the far bank wasn't much better with a sheer side designed for it to be impossible for potential invaders to escape once fallen in. Vincent wasn't going to trouble Holden. He grabbed an overcoat from a hook for Patterson and put it on him, then placed some shoes on his feet. Then he went to the dining room he had passed earlier where he had seen a drinks trolley to collect and use as a perambulator for Patterson.

He was confronted by someone panicking who saw him in the police uniform.

"Don't worry, it's all under control," he assured them. He managed to convince the Naval Chief of Staff's aide and Carfax-Smythe who had ventured out too.

Phillips, on the sound of all hell breaking loose, had made his way to the dining room where he had seen in a cabinet a set of prized shotguns used only occasionally by the Lord of the castle. He suspected in the drawers below the cabinet there was ammunition too. He had felt compelled to at least arm himself, although technically amongst whoever was shooting there should be no one who would bring harm to him.

He knew from previous visits that being accommodated in the Island Wing he only had to go down a floor to get to the grand dining room. He had, however, moved around the corridors and stairwells with caution with the sound of distant gunfire from the Moat Wing. He had never witnessed frequent high intensity gunfire before and it made him realise the mettle that the average British soldier must possess to not only fight but often undertake pioneering tasks under gunfire. He found some shells for a shotgun and loaded its twin barrels. He foolishly took cover in a corner of the room shielded by a drinks trolley having turned the lights off.

It was about ten minutes later when he saw a figure furtively enter the room. He heard shouting in the corridors only moments before. The figure seemed to brandishing a pistol. In a defence mechanism he subconsciously clicked the safety of the shotgun to fire. Holden with his heightened senses from the evenings combat heard the distinctive sound immediately. Then, in moonlight that slightly polluted the darkness of the room, he saw movement in an opposite corner. Assuming it was another policeman and with only the pistol to hand he fired. The muzzle flash of the first lit the target for a split second to get a second aimed shot off and then another. Holden heard a figure fall. The flash had worked both ways; Phillips had seen who shot him.

Holden advanced on the corner to get himself the trolley. Phillips bled silently on the floor, fearing of a coup de grace. He didn't realise from his injuries that was academic. Holden emptied the trolley and got it up to the bedchamber. He loaded the Minister on board and left the room for the main entrance. He had one wide set of steps to descend on the way. He tipped Paterson off and let him roll limply down as he dragged the trolley down. Then he loaded him back on and went out to the stables. A stable hand was there.

"The minister needs a hospital. Get me a carriage prepared now!" The fearful groom, faced with an abrupt policeman, did as he was told and within a couple of minutes Holden was making good his escape with Patterson.

The carriage was ideal with its design to get him all the way to the Peak District. He would only have to stop very briefly in London to collect some clothing and food for the journey. He shifted on the perch of the carriage; the body armour he had constructed was now feeling uncomfortable with the drop in his adrenalin levels. He carried on north reaching West Kingsdown before the discomfort became too much. He pulled over on the outskirts of the village and jumped down from the carriage. He removed his jacket and cotton shirt to get access to his home-made protective vest. He based its design on a combination of technologies.

Directly against his body was a moulded layer of 'boiled leather' which once cooled formed a hard, slash resistance armour about five millimetres in thickness. The layer atop of this was two sets of cotton wadding stitched into panels and sewn together to form a gilet of a construction not unlike a fencing jacket but thicker. The outer layer was an articulating suit made of thin, mild steel, of the style of a roman legionary iron cuirass or 'lorica segmentata'. The three parts together, fastened at the sides, formed an effective body armour resistant to knives and pistol rounds. It had been an expensive piece of kit to produce and he knew that it would be useful again. He threw it into the back of the carriage next to the unconscious Patterson. He replaced his shirt and jacket, remounted and rode on cracking the reins to get the horse trotting on.

* * *

Ford came to with an awareness of his head resting on the thighs of someone kneeling to tend him. Then he realised what had awakened him; smelling salts. He felt almost physically sick. He looked up into Karen's eyes. Mark Vincent was offset to one side of the room, his clothes soaking wet, as he tended Hoare who was propped up by a wall with Vincent cleaning a flesh wound to the side of his head. Ford then, within a few seconds, had a full recollection of what had happened and where he was. He sprung to his feet with Karen looking back up at him in shock.

"Patterson? Where is he?" No one answered. "Come on! Where is he?" Hoare broke the silence.

"He's gone. So is Holden. Kidnapped. A groom prepared a carriage and they left in that. The bastard was disguised as one of the local coppers." A voice from the bed chipped in as Stone sat up.

"The bastard fooled me like that. He approached me in the corridor and shot me with a poison arrow. It ain't half flipping sore." Ford recalled Stone falling silent before all hell broke loose in the bedchamber; Stone having acknowledged what he thought was one of the Kent police.

"How many dead then?" asked Ford. He thought there might be a body count by now. Vincent knew exactly, having got the information from one of the Kent officers who had purely been hit with a poisoned arrow.

"One of the Kent lads is dead with a broken neck, another dead from wounds when shot in the house. The others, well three were knocked out and have come around, same as you, the other five are still alive with various injuries and blood loss from pistol or rifle wounds. He's a bloody one man army." Ford shook his head.

"I know that Patterson left them to die and that Holden's men suffered terribly, but Jesus Christ, how determined is he to kill him? And why did he not kill him here?" Ford paused. "Is everyone accounted for then?" Vincent wasn't sure.

"I couldn't say for sure, Boss."

Ford left the room to march the corridors and account for the other guests, the staff and castle owners. Very quickly knocking on the doors for all the bed chambers, he was relieved to discover no one else dead. Bowen-Long and his staff officer complained about their injuries and Ford was little surprised by the staff officer's reaction when he spoke.

"Inspector, that man who has committed all this carnage is back from the dead. Bill Holden, he was presumed dead in India or Afghanistan, up somewhere on the North West Frontier six years ago. Always a bloody good man in all respects. He must have gone raving bonkers."

"Indeed," replied Ford, "it seems so. Do you know anything of the story as to why he and his men were there?"

"Sorry, no. Just some special recce or something. Poor bastard."

"Poor Bastard!" replied an astonished Ford.

"Yeah, he's had some rubbish luck in his life. No excuse, I know."

"I think that's the understatement of the year, Major." Ford headed off to try to find Ramsey Phillips, the only one he had so far been unable to account for. Sadly, it seemed to all that learned his fate, it didn't take long.

* * *

Phillips had received a mortal wound in his chest and a glancing shot in his left arm. When Ford found him, he was bleeding heavily from a gaping gunshot in the right hand side of his chest. The wound in his arm seeped only a little. The shelves against which he had initially fallen and then slumped to the floor now propped him up. He was babbling incoherently as Ford approached him and was wheezing heavily from the air-sucking wound linked directly to a collapsing lung.

"The Green Knight………Gawain didn't kill the Green Knight…….. only me and other innocents………..he's insane. Gawain must be stopped." Ford cradled him in his arms as he bent down to see if he could tend the wounded man. He crouched down and leant him sideways against his leg to keep the blood that had filled his punctured right lung out of his left. Ford could see from a vast patch of blood on the floor that he was beyond help. Looking at Phillips' back, towards the top of it was a large exit wound leaking blood incessantly.

"Ramsey, what are you talking about? Gawain and the Green Knight?" The words seemed like that of a dying man's delirium; Ford was almost right, he was dying but not delirious. In his traumatised state he could only recall the facts of the last conversation he had with his friend near Lambeth Palace.

"William. He's mad. He wants to kill his nemesis and will stop at nothing. If only I hadn't..." Phillips words tailed off. Ford heard someone enter the room.

"If only you hadn't what? Ramsey?" Phillips eyes were slowly closing. His head then slumped to one side. Ford pressed a finger into his neck; there was no pulse. Phillips was dead. Ford's mind raced. Had Phillips been so foolish as to really have passed on the details of all the Minister's movements over the last months? In his suspicious detective's mind he considered it a possibility. Holden having followed them everywhere and successfully managed to complete ritualistic killings? To ensure success he would have to know in advance where they had been travelling to as opposed to just following with no clue. And anyway how would he have got passage to the European venues by pure chance on the day of travel or immediately after? Coupled with Ford stumbling across Phillips in the Ministers office it all made sense. He would never know for sure but he was certain that Phillips had been the insider.

Ford's own stare had become slightly distant. He looked up to see Vincent and Hoare, with a bandaged head. Hoare spoke.

"You look distant, old man?" Ford snapped out of his glazed look.

"Yes. I was. What the hell is the story of 'Gawain', and some 'Green Knight'? Anyone?" Well read on many classics, Hoare offered an answer straight away.

"Its part of the Arthurian legend. Gawain has to confront his opponent who he was previously challenged by and if bettered had to face again, or a story to that effect. The library here will have something on it to explain it more fully I'm sure."

Ford laid Phillips gently to the floor as Karen walked in. She gasped and held her hands to her face covering her mouth and nose. She stared at the corpse and lowered her hands slowly and then looked up at Ford. He spoke first.

"You've seen him and I'm sorry. Could you go and see Fiona and let her know what's happened. I don't want her to see the same." She nodded and left the room. The three men then went to the library.

"Are we looking for a poetry book?" asked Ford.

"No," said Hoare, "we'll look it up in the encyclopaedia. It'll take hours of trying to find the right poetry book." Being an educated man and having appreciated the set up of the library previously, Hoare went straight to the right shelf as Ford and Vincent looked a little lost and indecisive. "Its here gentlemen." Hoare took the volume over to a large oak reading table and placed it on the table's leather inlaid surface. The three men crowded around and read the entry.

* * *

At Hobart Place, Dietrich was sleeping soundly in a very comfortable, ornate, wooden bed under soft and generous bedding when the crack of the door lock turning and a shard of light being projected across the room woke him up. He sat up slightly and could make out a silhouette peering into the room. The door opened wider and the figure entered. In the light that briefly illuminated the room from the hall he could see that it was the young nun who had first greeted him when he arrived. He reached to the side of the bed that she was stood by and switched on small bedside lamp. It illuminated her and she shied very slightly.

"Are you all right, my dear? I have not seen you since I arrived?" he spoke in clear, concise, textbook English.

"Yes, Mr Sepp. I am fine."

"Then what brings you here after a few days?"

"My masters told me that you may have what you want." He looked quizzically at her. She undid the rope that tied her cassock tightly around her waist and then shrugged the garment from her shoulders.

He breathed in as she did so. He had noticed on the first day even with her nun's headdress on that she was a very naturally pretty girl. Now she had walked in with blond hair flowing and was stood completely naked in front of him and she did indeed take his breath away. She was fair skinned, very slim with no apparent hair on her body, with round pert breasts; her innocent nudity aroused him greatly. She approached the bed and as she did so he moved across very slightly to give her room to get in under the covers with him. She lifted the sheets and blanket, slid herself onto the mattress next to him and moved up close. He felt the warmth of her naked smooth body touch his own. She looked up at him as he leaned over her and she cupped her hand around the back of his head.

"What is your name, sister?"

"Sister Amy." She pulled him towards her and kissed him.

* * *

"So. He must view Patterson as this 'Green Knight' and himself as 'Gawain'," said Ford.

"Yes," Hoare scratched his head as he replied, "and if that is the case as seems likely we need to get up to Derbyshire to this 'Lud's Church' to stop him killing Patterson." Ford nodded as Vincent watched and listened to the two of them speaking.

"Yes, and I would guess that he has gone in the carriage. He couldn't get away with the train. So, if we get ourselves into London on the train from Maidstone and then change mainline stations and crack on up to Buxton."

"Sounds good. I take it that no word of this must get out, Ford?" asked Hoare. It was a very valid point.

"Absolutely. We must swear all these people to secrecy and just get him back. We'll worry about the consequences of it if we are too late when it happens." Ford turned to Vincent.

"Mark, gather everyone together somewhere and tell them what is happening and not to pass on anything of it. I'll head into town with Major Hoare and then onto Derbyshire."

"Right, Boss. Anything else, want me to come with you?"

"No hold the fort here. Major I'll meet you in the stables in fifteen minutes. We'll get to the station and wait for the first train into town." Hoare nodded and the three men went their separate ways.

Ford met Karen in their room. She was about to take a bath and was wearing a silk kimono dressing gown. 'My God she's so desirable' he confirmed in his mind.

"I'm back to town with Hoare as soon as possible and then on to Derbyshire. We're going to finish this madness."

"Why Derbyshire?"

"In his mind, Holden seems to have to complete his vendetta in a place up there. His ritualism on this occasion has bought us some time. We're hoping to be there at the same time or earlier and stop him." She threw her arms around him.

"Be careful. I love you, Robert." He squeezed her tightly.

"I love you too." They kissed. Then he broke away from her. "I need another favour?"

"What?"

"Let me jump in the bath quickly first." She smiled and nodded her head towards the bathroom as if to say 'just get in there'. He did, stripping naked in the main bed chamber before entering the bathroom. She admired his lean body from behind as he walked away and played with her hair as she did so.

* * *

"You are *fucking* joking, mate!" The 'East End' in Ford just slipped out.

"No I am not, you rude git!" shouted back the railway man on the doors of the very closed Maidstone station. "There's engineering works all weekend and that's final. You'll have to wait until six o'clock Monday if you want a train to London. I don't care who you are there is no service." Ford was fuming. He hoped they'd be better in a hundred years from now and cheaper. The railways were becoming 'fucking useless' in his mind. As for people like the station master who had no real power, they seemed to always need to assert what little authority they did have, and do it in such a way that he just wished to punch them.

"Well, Ford. It looks like another torturous ride back to London in the cars." Hoare deep down was equally dissatisfied but refused to show it. The car that had brought them and its driver was still waiting behind them. They jumped aboard and he headed for London.

The Rover chugged and shook as they made their way through Maidstone to pick up the 'London Road'. Hoare turned to Ford.

"What weaponry do you have? Are you considering us going straight to Euston when we get back?"

"Yes, provided the trains are bloody well running from there. I've got my Webley and eighteen extra rounds." Hoare nodded his head.

"Good. I've got my Manlicher and some better quality rounds that shouldn't jam, better brass cases. I want to grab a rifle on the way. We'll drop in to my place; it's only round the corner from the station in Marylebone."

"All right," said Ford, "but if we can, we take him alive."

Chapter Twenty-Seven

The Vatican

In his plush office Caravaggio, now promoted to Papal administrator, awaited the arrival of his two fellow cardinals. The double oak doors opened and Sklinski entered accompanied by a very tired looking de Vicompte. They were all waiting for the imminent passing of the Pope, but more importantly, now worried about the future of their investment. Patterson had been out of touch since Prague so they had no news of when to prepare missionary parties to leave for Afghanistan.

"Your eminence," began Sklinski addressing his now more senior friend, "any news from the Swiss Guard, or from Patterson himself?"

"No, my friend," Caravaggio shook his head, "there is not. But I have sent fresh orders to Sepp Dietrich, our insurance in London. He is not to terminate the business agreement we have permanently until he has recovered as much of our money as possible." De Vicompte spoke.

"Have you taken steps to ensure the Guard's fullest loyalty?"

"Yes, I have. He has a woman at his bidding and I have promised him a cut of what he recovers for a well earned early retirement."

"Very wise, my dear brother. A healthy incentive is always a good proposition. Sex and money are the two best draws." Caravaggio and Sklinski both looked at their friend who sounded as if he spoke from experience. He quickly noticed their curious expressions. "Of course, that is only so I am told." There was a silence across the room.

"Brothers," said Caravaggio breaking the monastic atmosphere, "can I offer you both a cognac?" The mood instantly lightened and they fell back into their casual friendly ways born of many years of association over large Napoleon Brandies.

* * *

It was very late afternoon. Ford and Hoare had already called by Marylebone for Hoare to collect his 1898 Mauser-Gewehr 98 five round magazine rifle. It was fiercely accurate and carried great stopping power with its 7.92mm rounds bolt fed into its chamber. They now arrived at Euston Station at 5.30p.m. This time Hoare made the enquiries about the train times and availability. Both men were tired, stressed from what had happened in the last twenty-four hours and carried with them the burden of a great state secret with the Minister's kidnap, and the ultimate responsibility for saving his life.

Hoare walked back towards Ford; sporting a fedora type hat he had collected from home to cover his bandaged head. His face told the story of bad news before he even spoke to Ford.

"The trains from here are up the spout too. The last one of the day left ten minutes ago. It's the last one as someone jumped in front of a local train that was a minute or two behind it on the same track. They've closed the track to remove the fatality, which by the time they're done means the service can't reach through to Buxton before it shuts there." Ford initially remained silent. Hoare could see a vein throbbing in his neck quite obtrusively; usually the indication that someone was at the point of losing their temper. Ford turned and walked away and composed himself by some pacing around. He then walked back up to Hoare.

"Right. How long to get to the Peak District by carriage then, do you reckon?" Hoare took in a deep breath through his nose as he considered Ford's question.

"He left in the early hours. He can't really use any other form of transport easily. All day today, all day tomorrow and then maybe getting to his destination late on the third afternoon effectively." This brought reassurance to Ford.

"All right. We meet back here tomorrow at eight for the first train out. We can be lying in wait in this Lud's Church by evening tomorrow night. That way we won't miss him and should hopefully stop any killing taking place." Hoare nodded his head.

"A good plan. We'll be fresher tomorrow with clearer thinking. We'll need good outdoor stuff for a night in the open though. Get packed properly Ford."

Ford could not dispute that Hoare was the natural in the area of surviving outdoors with all his military experience. Ford would follow his lead and directions until the confrontation took place. They left for their separate London addresses, the car dropping them both off.

* * *

Ford was greeted by a pleasant surprise when he entered the ornately period decorated, tiled-floor hall of his house. He closed the gloss black four panelled door behind him, it's brass fittings clanking as he did so. Karen was in the hall waiting to meet him. She flung her arms around him with no questions as to what he was doing home just pleased to see him. Mrs Adkins popped her head around a doorframe beyond them leading to the kitchen and spoke with her warm tones and familiar smile.

"A pot of Lapsang and scones for you both, Robert?"

"That would be lovely Mrs Adkins."

* * *

24th September

Robert Ford had been in a deep and restful sleep before he awakened. Nothing had disturbed him; he just came out of a restful slumber by his own accord; he had visualised his time for waking prior to sleep. Seven a.m. He had become quite accustomed to such self programming. It helped to keep him sharp in the dangerous profession in which he now indulged. As he shifted slightly in the soft and generous double bed in his luxurious West London house, he could feel the warmth of another body pressing into the front of his own. It was soft and smooth, and as his eyes became accustomed to the early morning light that filtered through the curtains he remembered how he had come to be here and not yet in the Peak District. He was very satisfied to find himself here.

She was beautiful, possibly one of the most naturally beautiful women he had ever seen since his brief affair with Mary Kelly. Blonde, with a slim but curved figure; as he looked down he could see the generous swell of her breasts and her long lithe legs. Her slightly olive complexion would not have been out of place in the Mediterranean and the thought of her wild sensuality excited him knowing he had yet again made love to her only hours before. Her back was pressed into Ford's chest with its smooth contours; he looked it up and down and saw the large Celtic tattoo on the small of it; such an unusual feature in a woman of that time but deeply erotic. Its pattern and colours were sensual upon the canvass of her radiant olive skin; it seemed to re-enforce the sheer sexual allure that she possessed. In her sleep she must have sensed him waking and moving slightly she rolled over to look at him, her long blonde hair streaming across her elegant, natural facial features. Her eyes opened and Ford saw again those deep blue pool-like eyes that he had first seen many months ago and had drowned so easily within consumed by sheer passion. So much had happened between then and now and he found it hard to believe that he lay next to her, looking into the eyes of the woman whose looks and personality had driven him to distraction seeing them abused so much by someone else. It had been nearly sixteen years since he had felt these kinds of emotions. Suddenly, as they lay there clasped in each others arms, he realised that not only was he in love, but infatuated with Karen Wood, and he would do anything not to give this woman up. Then he recalled that he needed to be on a train leaving from Euston Station in an hour.

He had packed a brown leather holdall with outdoor clothing and dressed in smart casual country wear ready for his journey. He kept the Webley in a holster concealed under his jacket. He also had, in a specially designed carry case, one of his fighting sabres in a scabbard; it might also prove useful in a confrontation. Karen had left the bedroom for the kitchen as he readied himself. By quarter past seven he was drinking a cup of black Columbian coffee she had made for him in the comfort of his conservatory. It was a bright, warm, pleasant morning. The realisation crossed his mind, as he enjoyed the perfection of the moment in Karen's company enjoying the simple pleasure of good coffee in the early morning that he might not return. He was up against a formidable adversary in Holden and in the back of his mind he knew that he could not fully trust Hoare. He knew that in a few minutes he would be departing and this was not a sentiment he wished to share.

"My love won't you excuse me for a moment?" He stood as he spoke. Karen simply smiled as he put his coffee down and went to his office on the first floor that overlooked the Eaton Square gardens.

Ford opened his mahogany in-laid bureau and sat down pulling out some personalised writing paper from one of its compartments. He began by addressing it to his solicitor.

ROBERT FORD ESQ.   14A EATON SQUARE
                                                BELGRAVIA
                                                SW2

                                                24th September 1904

Dear Mr Hendricks,

Paul, I am writing to advise you of an amendment to my current will provisions. In the event of my untimely death, in this instance whilst resolving my commitment to protecting Sir Cecil Patterson, 80% of my entire estate is to pass into the hands of Miss Karen Wood, whom I wish to inform you I was due to imminently marry. The other 20% is to be placed amongst East London charities, especially those supporting Health and Education. Your fees will of course be deducted from the estate in advance of these wishes.

I thank you for your assistance over the years.

Your friend
Robert Ford.

He placed the letter in an envelope and addressed it to 'Mr Paul Hendricks, to be opened in the event of Robert Ford's death'. He would post it through the door of Hendricks & Co. in Wigmore Street on his way to Euston. He heard a hansom pull up outside; it was time to go. He went back downstairs and pulled Karen Wood, who was stood in the hallway, into his arms and gave her a firm embrace. He kissed her passionately for several seconds and then pulled away slightly, but keeping her in his arms.

"I love you, Karen. I will see you in a few days, this whole affair finished."

"I love you too. See you then. Don't be late!" They laughed together at this suggestion. He broke away, put on a waxed cotton jacket, picked up his bags, opened the door and walked out closing it behind him. Karen stood in the hall and looked on at the closed door feeling a sense of unease.

* * *

Hoare was already seated and settled on the 8.a.m train from London, Euston to Buxton as Ford marched along the first class aisle, with his bags swinging around glancing off the wooden panelled corridor, to meet him. He looked at the overhead rack to see where there was space to hoist his bags up to. He saw what he guessed were Hoare's by the leather rifle case and placed his own bags next to them. He removed his jacket and placed it up there too and then sat down opposite his ex-military counterpart. They sat by the window of a six person first class carriage with the aisle or corridor in the offset style on the other side of the carriage from them. With the door to their compartment shut it afforded them some privacy, at least until someone else sat down. The train then jerked as the slack in the coupling was taken up and it moved slowly off of the platform.

"Had any breakfast, Ford?"

"No, just coffee, Major." Ford could not bring himself to refer to him as 'Hoare', as although a different spelling, his years in the East End had brought him to dislike the word, and he would only use it in anger.

"Well come on then, old chap, I'll treat you to a Full English in the restaurant car." Ford didn't want or need charity from this man or anyone, but could tell a genuine gesture when he saw or heard one.

"Very kind. Let's go, I am bloody hungry in truth." Hoare stood up and eyed Ford's luggage curiously as he did so. He guessed the policeman was armed with a pistol still on his person but he could see that Ford had packed some kind of edged weapon.

"Expecting to engage our man in some kind of dual then? What is it? Epee? Sabre? What?"

"No flies on you, Major. It's a sabre. You never know; if we can take Holden alive I intend to so he goes on trial. Can't guarantee that with firearms in a gunfight."

"You must be very sure of your sabre skills then, up against an ex-cavalry man?"

"I am, aren't you? Obviously not, carrying a rifle"

"Just being practical. Anyway, what makes you think you'll get a chance to take him alive? Patterson and…" Hoare suddenly stopped and was reluctant to finish the sentence. Ford knew exactly what he was going to say.

"Patterson and you? Is that it, Major? Because you're both in it up to your necks?" Hoare seemed to hesitate before replying.

"Look, I'm a servant of the state like you. Charged with getting him back, like you. I'll disappear when we're back. Leave Patterson to face the music." Ford squared up to him; the pugilist in him coming out.

"Listen, you are nothing like me. You were a servant of the state but now you are a mercenary. A blunt instrument wielded by the greedy, highest bidders, so don't flatter yourself. You forget that you killed a police officer." Ford maintained ferocious eye contact with Hoare who he could see became annoyed and uncomfortable.

"All right, policeman, you are right. I suggest we have breakfast and don't discuss this again until Holden is dealt with. The moment our job is done then watch your back."

"Yes and you watch yours too." The two men made their way silently to the restaurant car, the train bumping its way along the tracks heading up through North London, tossing them against the sides of the corridor as it did so.

* * *

Moving Patterson on his own by carriage for Holden was not a straightforward task. Once at a safe distance from Tudor Castle he had bound and gagged Patterson to ensure no opportunity for escape or to call for help. He then knew that at least every four hours he would have to inject him with more curare, a poison derived from a South American plant that causes temporary paralysis and loss of all motor function.

He had two overnight stops that meant that Holden could not afford to leave the carriage with its concealed interior for more than three and half hours at a time. This interrupted his sleep patterns and made him tired, a fatigue that was already fuelled by the increasing effects of TB. He took comfort on the last day of travel that his quest would soon be complete. Patterson would offer little resistance in a duel with three days of no food or water consumption. His opportunity to defeat the 'Green Knight' in single combat would be an achievable one, and then he could seek medical assistance and retire into overseas obscurity.

As he drove along using 'off the beaten track' thoroughfares to take him north to the Peak District, he looked at his watch and he could see the time for some more medication for Patterson was imminent. He would need to pull off into some woods or behind some empty farm buildings to ensure privacy for his work. The concentration of the driving coupled with this new need for additional observation made him sweat heavily in his ever weakening state. He knew that he would have to resort to drugs such as laudanum to retain his own strength and lucidity.

Along a back road linking the villages of Milton Keynes and Newport Pagnell, he found a perfect set of abandoned barns. So perfect that they gave him the opportunity to drive into one of them and be completely out of view which meant he could take his time with Patterson's medication, and more importantly take some rest himself. He jumped down from his perch once inside and walked around to the carriage door. He opened it up to see his ward beginning to be able to move very slightly. Patterson's eyes were wide open, however, and as he saw Holden climb aboard and stand over him; the fear within them was quite palpable. He couldn't yet talk and could only really wiggle his fingers and toes. He was powerless and in Holden's complete control.

"Well, Minister, it's so good to be in each other's company again, don't you think?" Holden's conversation was completely rhetorical. "After all, the last time we saw each other properly we parted so quickly, you trying to finish me and my remaining crippled and maimed men off, you bastard!" The hate welled up inside Holden quickly as he pictured the final moments of Nigel Green's tortured last days. He punched Paterson in the face striking him square on his nose and sending a stream of blood across the left side of his head as the blow forced it that way. Patterson began to tremble, the only movement he could muster and watched helplessly as Holden prepared a syringe. This had been the first time he had been conscious to watch him. Having drawn the liquid into the syringe's chamber he watched as Holden ejected a small amount of fluid in a spout as he held up the needle to test it. Then, swiftly he bent down to Patterson who saw the needle rushing towards his neck. Holden jabbed it hard into the carotid artery and thumbed the plunger on the syringe rapidly to inject the curare into the minister. The scratch of the needle was the last sensation that Patterson felt or was aware of.

* * *

The dining car was bright and airy with a fine wooden interior coupled with plush velvet upholstery to meet the needs and expectations of the first class diners. Hoare and Ford were directed to a table next to a window that offered a good view of the country passing outside, slightly occluded by the net curtain hanging to ensure a little privacy. They both ordered a full English cooked breakfast and were left with a pot of strong Kenyan coffee and an over-stacked rack of toast. They tucked into this spreading, their slices generously with thick Channel Islands butter. The uncomfortable silence remained. Hoare was forced to break it.

"What do you hope to achieve by bringing me down with Patterson?"

"Nothing. It's about justice for the murder you committed in Belgravia, that's all."

"Ford, it wasn't deliberate, for god's sake. We were all engaged in a raging gun battle if you recall."

"Yes I do recall, complete with an injury to my thigh you bastard." Hoare shook his head.

"I'll cut you a deal. There are nearly a thousand soldiers being paid to go into Afghanistan living in some pretty tough conditions on the North West Frontier. When this is over I am supposed to be going to lead them. Undoubtedly we will be withdrawing with Patterson's corruption and misappropriations made public. Let me ensure that process takes place safely. Otherwise we could have another Holden or perhaps several on our hands. Mmm?" Ford breathed out heavily through his nose and stared out of the window across the Hertfordshire countryside. He felt a degree of emotional blackmail. He felt the urge for clarification of the term 'misappropriations' but then quickly assumed it would be the abuse of treasury money. Only Hoare would be the other one to know about the Vatican money assuming it was safe to lose and spend on the private army. Upright cardinals would never resort to violence; he felt safe about that. He was right; they didn't, but employed others who would.

"Having read about the SRP men I can't face that notion. Go but never set foot in England again, Major Hoare. I shall ensure all ports have you on file."

"Thank you, Inspector." Hoare knew he would be safe. He had a plan. Their full English breakfasts arrived. Devilled kidneys, scrambled eggs, sausages, a pair of kippers and some fried potatoes were served up on fine bone china plates in front of them carrying the crest of 'GNWR'. They both tucked willingly into their food.

* * *

Karen returned to Wilton Crescent to pack the last of her possessions and move in with Robert Ford. She had two battered medium sized suitcases to fill, plus the tailor's mannequin, a sewing machine in its case, and a large wicker box of sewing materials. She had packed all of her clothes into both cases placing some cherished photographs in one, mostly of young Nigel, and her perfumes and other effects in the other. She was just beginning to stack it all in the hallway for loading onto a carriage when she heard a knock at the door. She answered the large, four panelled wooden door to see Lady Patterson standing on her doorstep. She was shocked to see her, and actually quite scared with all that had happened. Lady Patterson stood on the doorstep without forcing her way in and politely spoke.

"Karen, may I come in?" Karen felt humbled and tripped over her first few words.

"Ye...yes madam, please do." She ushered Lady Patterson in who walked slowly past her and then stopped in the hallway. She waited for Karen to close the door and then walk past her showing her into the lounge. Karen was in a quietly anxious state; she suspected full well that this would be an explosion of rage at her regarding Sir Cecil.

The Dressmaker Connection

Lady Patterson sat down in a dark green Chesterfield armchair. Karen sat adjacent to her in a two seat sofa of the same style. Comforting for Karen, Lady Patterson began the conversation.

"Karen, first may I say again how sorry I am about the passing of young Nigel."

"Thank you, Lady Patterson that is very kind."

"I would also like to say now to clear the air between us that I am very sorry for what you have endured with my husband. Ever since the birth of our children we have been unable to feel comfortable with a physical relationship together. To be honest, he is such a clumsy and thoughtless lover that, having borne him children, I could stand his advances no longer. I am very sorry that in the wake of this he used financial and emotional blackmail against you to get what he wanted." Karen was amazed.

"You know about all that?"

"Yes. I decided to delve into his personal records after the dreadful shooting episode here. He isn't good at concealing things at home. From bills and scribbling in an occasional journal I know exactly what has been happening. I am very sorry."

"Madam, that is very understanding of you. I am sorry to have dishonoured you."

"My dear girl, worry not. The saving grace for me is that it has kept him away from me physically and there is no scandal about it as yet. Whether there will be? Who can tell." There was silence between them.

"Madam, what are you going to do now?"

"That rather depends on if he lives or dies. I'd sooner the bastard didn't come back in all honesty. Make my life easier. Probably little scandal and lots of money." Karen reeled trying to take all this in. "This is a very nice little flat. I shall keep it open for you if things don't work out."

"My Lady, what do you mean?"

"You and Inspector Ford. I may have lacked sexual activity for many years, at least with him, but I can still tell when there's a spark between people. I assume that is where you are off to?" Karen looked at her slightly open mouthed. Had it been that obvious? She must have been making a lucky guess as to her move.

"Yes, madam. It is. We are to marry."

"My dear girl," Lady Patterson got up and approached Karen kissing her on the cheek and then taking both hands in her own. "I wish you every happiness." She held on to Karen's hands for a few seconds before letting go and walking elegantly out of the room. A few seconds later Karen heard the door to the flat open and then quickly close again.

* * *

Having finished their breakfast both Ford and Hoare were back in their almost secluded first class carriage by virtue of the continued absence of other travellers. Ford sat down by the window, loosened his tie and began to feel the march of fatigue wanting to force him to rest for more than just a few hours; no doubt exaggerated by the need to digest a large breakfast. On arrival back in their compartment Hoare pulled a shoulder bag down from the overhead rack and placed it on the seat next to him. His intention once Ford was asleep was to use a charged syringe, with which he had drawn into its chamber fifty percent bleach and fifty percent lemon juice and vinegar mixed together. Within the chamber they would react to produce chlorine that he would inject into Ford in between two of his fingers to try to avoid a clear verdict on his death when he was discovered; alone apparently having died asleep. With Ford out of action it would allow him a free run to rescue Patterson and then disappear and leave England behind forever. Hoare observed Ford yawning as he looked out at the passing countryside.

"You look like you could catch some rest, old chap."

"Yes." Ford struggled to reply beyond the single word. Hoare was quite right.

"Well get some rest, man. Its hours yet." Ford really didn't need any encouragement. He rested his face upon his hand propped up by an elbow on the armrest and closed his eyes. His other hand rested casually on his thigh.

* * *

In the lounge of the comfortable Vatican retreat in Hobart Place, Sepp Dietrich read each day's newspapers with great interest. Still there was no further news of Sir Cecil Patterson anywhere to be found. It made him unusually suspicious that all had not gone well during the chiefs of staff conference at Tudor Castle, so widely publicised. Dietrich was no fool, he realised that the intention of the publicity was to draw out the ministerial killer; like everybody else, he didn't realise that the killer wouldn't need announcements in the media to gain his information. He racked his brains for another source of information on the Minister's whereabouts. He could think of none. He got up from his armchair and headed into the hall. Wearing a suit with a shoulder holstered pistol, he grabbed an overcoat from a peg by the gloss black painted front door and then opened it, he left through it into the street slamming it firmly behind him. He would go down to the Ministry of War building in Whitehall and watch it for the next few hours to observe the movements in and out; he should see Patterson enter or leave at some point.

* * *

Hoare had been keenly watching Ford for nearly half an hour. He seemed to be in a deep sleep. He opened up his shoulder bag and removed the pen sized leather box that the syringe was in. He knew that it was fully charged and ready to go as he observed it sitting on blue velvet inside the box. He took hold of the syringe in his right hand and threw the box back into his bag with the other. The train bumped along with constant rhythmic sound and minor jolting as it passed over the equidistant track joints. He moved one place and sat directly opposite Ford and eyed his right hand spread across his right thigh with enthusiasm. Perfect; he would jab the needle into the skin in between his index and middle fingers and then simultaneously push the plunger down. Within a minute or two Ford should struggle for motor function control as his breathing would become interrupted. As soon as he was unconscious he could throw his body from the train. As always he had thought of everything. Nearly.

As he plunged the needle into Ford's hand, an opposing train passed them causing a rocking movement of the train, a reaction that was physically exaggerated by the sounding of its train horn too. In turn this exaggerated the effects on Hoare and Ford. Ford jumped and instantly came out of his sleep with a start. This wrenched the needle from Hoare's hand before he could depress the plunger and it fell out of Ford's hand and onto the floor. There was a momentary standoff pause. Then the battle for life began.

Chapter Twenty-Eight

Dietrich reached Lower Grosvenor Place within a minute of leaving his retreat and was struck by a brainwave; he knew the address of the Minister's home residence but was unsure of its location. If it was close perhaps he should go there first. He returned to the house and knocked on the door; Sister Amy opened the door dressed in her unflattering habit.

"Sepp? Can I help you?"

"Amy, where is Belgrave Square?"

"It is only a few minutes around the corner. Would you like me to walk you there to find it?"

"That would be very kind. Thank you." She stepped straight out of the house, closed the door behind her and they walked off in the opposite direction heading west.

"Why do you wish to go there, Sepp?" She didn't look at him but at the road ahead as she spoke.

"Amy, you know why I am here?"

"No, I only know to tend to your needs while you are here. Your mission is very important so I am told, it must be for a member of the Guard to be sent here." Should he tell her? After all, his 'mission' was a little ungodly. He decided not to explain.

"Yes. It is an important mission." They turned left into Eaton Square, north side, walking along past its plush, large, white terraced, grand town houses flanking them on either side. Horse drawn carriages and buses passed them in both directions occasionally punctuated with the odd motorcar. Eaton Square became Upper Belgrave Street and then spat them out into Belgrave Square itself, with its even grander detached corner residences on it sides. Dietrich looked around but only cursorily so. He was missing detail in his haste.

"Which one is it?" Amy looked at him oddly but he was unaware of her expression scanning the square.

"Is it not obvious? It's the big, detached house in that top north-east corner; the one with the police patrolling outside." She was quite right, in their subtle, dark uniforms he hadn't really taken their presence in.

He began to walk towards the house. Fortunately for him Amy followed him. He reached the corner of Grosvenor Crescent and Belgrave Square when he was challenged by an officer from behind him, Amy with was within feet of him.

"Sir, can I ask why you seem so interested in that house?" The voice from behind startled him and he jumped very slightly as he turned to face the uniform constable behind him. Before he could speak Amy interjected.

"I am sorry, Father Sepp is visiting London for the first time and he's with me. He had been told of the grandness of this square and wanted to see it for himself." The constable looked at her as she stood at Dietrich's side. He bounced slightly backwards and forwards on his toes with his hands clasped behind his back. He looked Dietrich up and down.

"So why aren't you in the old cleric's get up, Father? The dog collar and all that?" Dietrich was now quick to go along with Amy's story.

"I am on holiday, officer. Merely travelling not partaking in God's work." The constable looked him up and down again.

"Mmm. This lady obviously confirms all that. Don't really want to search a man of the cloth."

"What do you mean, officer?" asked Amy.

"All persons, in the wake of things, showing interest in the square and this house," he pointed to the Minister's house, "are being searched for obvious reasons. But with who you are, I don't think it's necessary." This was a lucky escape for the covertly armed Dietrich.

"Thank you, constable very kind," said Amy. The constable walked on.

"We better go," said Dietrich in a relieved fashion. He turned and walked back the way they had come. Amy turned and followed him.

"You all right?" she called after him.
"Fine. I need to get to Whitehall."

* * *

The syringe rolled around on the floor beneath Ford and Hoare. Hoare had pinned Ford into his seat with his bent left leg and was attempting to repeatedly punch the police inspector. Ford was equal to this with his arms up, the back of his forearms protecting his face and chest. Hoare was a physically big man, powerfully built with natural core strength and quickly Ford came to directly experience this fact. It was a kind of physical punishment that he was familiar and strangely comfortable with. What he didn't like was the smell of Hoare's breath bearing down on him with the blows; it was a phenomenon that he could not defend easily against with the distaste it engendered.

Ford had read the uncalculated nature of his opponent's attack that lacked a basic form of defence. He knew when to lash out very quickly from these observations. Hoare raised his tiring right hand; from the lack of structure in his attack that was when Ford struck savagely with a long and lightning fast left hand jab. It caught Hoare completely unaware and with its impact Ford felt him move back from him slightly, reducing the weight pinning him to his seat. He sprung forwards forcing Hoare backwards landing on his own opposite seat.

Hoare tried to put his right leg up to defend himself as Ford came forward, but Ford fully expected this and lashed out with a hammer fisted punch into Hoare's calf. It deadened the muscle and forced it to one side. Ford stepped in between Hoare's legs and began punching him in the face and upper chest. He landed several blows before the stunned Major could properly defend himself. Blood began to seep from Hoare's nose. To Ford's surprise he blocked a volley of strikes and managed to roll to one side. He then stood and turned to face Ford taking up a classic 'Queensbury rules' boxer's stance. Stood ready to continue the fight, Ford was reminded of Hoare's imposing physical presence once more. From his years of pugilism, however, he was undeterred.

They began exchanging punches and range finding jabs, both moving lightly on their toes. Ford knew he had to play the long game and take some punishment to tire his opponent. They traded punches with no one gaining the upper hand. Ford knew it was time to get dirty.

He observed Hoare's footwork in his peripheral vision. He recognised quickly a weakness he could exploit. Every few seconds Hoare's stance turned slightly sideways; he would use this to put him to the floor.

Ford's reaction to this movement when the moment came was devastating. As Hoare moved to this slight angular stance, Ford dropped to his haunches and then lashed out forwards with a hard straight kick into the side of Hoare's knee. With the unnatural movement that Ford observed with the strike, and Hoare's subsequent reaction, he knew he had applied the right tactic.

Hoare buckled instantly with the forced, incompatible articulation of his knee joint that in the process stretched a ligament. He fell to the floor with Ford dodging sideways to avoid him as he tumbled forward. He was grimacing in pain. Ford actually jumped onto a seat to avoid him.

Despite the pain, Hoare was quick to react; he too was a seasoned campaigner with life threatening experiences. He grabbed one of Ford's ankles and yanked it brutally pulling him off of the seat. He crashed onto the seat with his lower back and felt the pain reverberate through his coccyx. He then landed next to Hoare who now had the syringe back in his hand. Ford grabbed at both his arms with his hands and entered into a bitter wrestling match with the Marine Major. They both knew that one of them was now going to die; each expected it to be the other. Ford's advantage over Hoare's natural strength in these circumstances was the saving grace of being on top. Hoare, despite Ford's best efforts had the needle dangerously close to Ford's neck. They both struggled hard with each other, both with veins swelling in their necks and foreheads with the strain. Ford managed to push the needle a little further away. He suspected that he just had a little more endurance than his opponent.

This assumption in seconds proved to be correct as he managed to push the lethal syringe away and begin to turn Hoare's own hand on himself. Ford could see the concern developing in Hoare's eyes, he could see the beads of sweat across his brow, and much to his fury he could also still smell Hoare's stale breakfast scented breath again. Both were now shaking violently with the efforts they were applying; each knew there could now only be one living victor.

Ford's superior endurance rather than strength within a few seconds had him pointing the needle at Hoare's neck. With only an inch or so to go Hoare's eyes expressed real fear as they strained sideward to see the location of the needle. He needn't have bothered putting them under such eye-popping pressure. He jumped and for a split second relaxed and immediately re-tensed as the needle entered his neck. He looked up at Ford his eyes now wide with fear; he knew that he was about to die an excruciatingly uncomfortable death if the syringe's plunger was pushed. His mouth dried instantly and he struggled even to whisper a plea to Ford.

"Please…please, don't do it Ford. You'll kill me in seconds." Ford looked down on him almost with disbelief.

"Don't kill me? Don't fucking kill me? What were you about to do to me?" Sweat dripped from Ford's brow onto the back of one of his own hands that clutched Hoare's holding the needle.

"You're a policeman! You can't kill me!" There was panic in Hoare's voice. He physically tried to resist again but Ford's hold could not be broken. Ford managed to place one of his thumbs onto the plunger of the syringe. Hoare gasped. "Don't! Please!"

In a rapid movement Ford pulled the syringe out of Hoare's neck and flung it against the carriage door. The glass phial shattered and its contents spread onto the floor and down the door, fizzing and making a hissing sound as it did so. Ford punched hard and fast at Hoare's jaw and nose. He inflicted some vicious damage and laid his opponent unconscious. He rolled him over, pulled a set of handcuffs from his belt and clasped Hoare's arms tightly behind his back. He stood up and looked down at the man unconscious from his handiwork. Then behind him he heard the compartment door slide open. Ford turned quickly ready to strike in case Hoare had some of his henchmen secretly on the train. He faced a panic stricken ticket inspecting guard.

"Don't hit me mate, please!" begged the guard whose colour instantly drained from his face. Ford looked him up and down.

"What's the next stop?"

"Erm? Northampton. Why?"

"I am a police officer and this man is under arrest for murder and sedition. When this train stops you go and get the police here straight away. He is a danger to society." The guard looked even more panicked.

"Oh, all right, officer. Whatever you say. About ten minutes away."

"Good," said Ford wiping his sweating forehead with a handkerchief from his pocket, "Now leave me alone." He wanted to search and disarm Hoare.

* * *

The train stopped at Northampton station and the guard brought the police to Ford's compartment as requested; however, it took an hour. Ford had found nothing incriminating on Hoare; he was disappointed but not surprised. He gave no value to Hoare's pistol and handed the corrupt marine officer and all his belongings over to the two policemen of the Northamptonshire constabulary who came to the compartment. A gruff bearded sergeant and a young 'wet behind the ears' constable confronted Ford and the now lucid Hoare sat, still handcuffed, on one side of the compartment. Ford had also gagged him.

"Sergeant, I am Detective Inspector Ford of the Metropolitan Police Special Branch. What I am about to tell you is of national importance and secrecy. Do you understand?" The constable looked petrified by the thought of enduring such responsibility; the sergeant frowned and clasped his hands behind his back and rocked on his toes.

"Well, Inspector. What seems to be the problem then?" asked the sergeant, holding his chin up in an attempt to try and seem important; everybody likes their little piece of power, but the truth is that the office of 'warranted constable' of any rank actually has significant responsibility. An issue that the train guard was naïve of as he tried to enter and take part with an over inflated opinion of his own importance. Ford barked at him.

"Get out! This is a matter of national importance!" The rail operative slid the compartment door shut and skulked off. Ford turned back to the two officers, the young constable trembling slightly. "Gentlemen, I cannot express to you enough the delicate position the state is in. This man is involved in a conspiracy to create a private sovereign state in the Middle East for industrial purposes. In the process many people have been killed. This man is guilty of complicity in some of these murders.

He must be taken back to your most secure gaol and held there pending a secure transfer to face questions and charging in the Metropolitan District. Do you understand?" The young constable remained looking scared, like a rabbit caught in a beam of light at night. The sergeant, by expression, looked to enjoy the prospect of being part of a major investigation. He spoke.

"Yes, sir. Northampton has a secure gaol. Does he need to be incommunicado until he is collected, sir?"

"Certainly he does, good thinking, sergeant. Get him there as soon as possible and I will continue my journey north."

"Very good, sir." The sergeant pulled Hoare up from his seat whilst the constable grabbed his luggage. The three then disappeared off along the corridor and then off of the train. Ford looked around the compartment. He was in a bit of a daze. His mind was now filled with issues that had to be addressed; the build up of innocent troops with the promise of riches on the North West Frontier, the defeat and arrest of Holden and liberation of Patterson, Patterson himself 'facing the music', the trial of Patterson, Hoare and others for their seditious acts, the trial of Holden for multiple murders.

He sat down and rubbed his temples with his head in his hands, his arms in turn resting on his legs. The train was now running significantly later. In the back of his mind with past experiences, would there ever be justice? Whose side was he on? He flinched and stared out of the window as he felt the train jerk as the steam driven locomotive began pulling its lengthy load out of Northampton Station and ultimately to Ford's destiny.

* * *

Dietrich was bored with watching the Ministry of War building. Amy had returned to Hobart Place on the journey from Belgrave Square. He had been walking up and down the main thoroughfare of Whitehall for over an hour, passing between Horse Guards Avenue and Great Scotland Yard. He had seen no movement in or out of the Ministry Building and he suspected that all was not well with Patterson's office. He had no safe way of finding out. He decided to return to Hobart Place himself and relax for the rest of the day. He would scour the newspapers the next day for information.

He walked casually west towards Parliament Square passing the top of Downing Street as he did so; an innocuous looking central London residential street. Large town houses in a dark brick set back on the right that led down to a footpath through to Horse Guards Road and St James' Park. At the mouth of Downing Street on the left were the Foreign Office Buildings. Built in their grand Italianate style, Dietrich was impressed by the architecture, almost seeming to rival that of the Papal Museum of the Vatican. No gates or other barriers obstructed entry into the street in which the Prime Minister of Britain and the Chancellor of the Exchequer lived. He was almost tempted to walk along it for the sheer satisfaction of passing by the home residence of a head of state.

Having been challenged by a police officer once today and extricated from an awkward situation by Amy, he decided against that course of action without her there. He strolled into the sunlit Parliament Square and enjoyed the grandiose view of the seat of British government on the north bank of the River Thames at Westminster.

* * *

Ford alighted from the train in Buxton at just after 5.p.m. The plan had never been to go straight to Lud's Church. He knew that he had half a day in hand so could leave at first light the next day. He had to keep the entire nature of his visit a state secret so he had no liaison with the local police arranged. He took his bag, his sabre case and Hoare's rifle; he loathed the idea of using it but decided that it was a sound tactical option. Ford strolled along the platform amongst the diverse mix of travellers from all classes that had just alighted from the train, looking no different to any other middle-class gentlemen. He was pleased, it was a look that did not court any unwanted attention, apart from some young urchins keen to make a penny carrying luggage for passengers with potential wealth.

A scruffily dressed boy of about ten approached and took hold of the handle of his travelling bag.

"Carry that for you, mister?" He tried to tug at it as he spoke. He had no chance of finding Ford parting with anything, especially not a sabre and a rifle.

"Sorry, lad. You'll get no work from me today. I bare my own burdens." The boy let go looking disappointed, dropping his head slightly. With his own humble background Ford always had a weakness for these types of characters. He reached into his pocket and pulled out a dull penny. "Hey, boy." The lad turned to face him still looking upset. Ford then flicked the coin at the lad and spoke as his did so, "catch." With well-practiced lightning reactions born out of necessity the lad caught the coin swiftly and looked into the palm of his hand with a beaming smile.

"Thanks, mister!" He ran off along the platform out of sight squeezing through the ticket barrier hidden within the crowds.

Ford had chosen quite deliberately for Hoare and himself not to travel with official government or police travel warrants. This was to avoid any unwanted attention of what might be viewed as help whilst in the Peak District. With the delicate nature of the kidnap, murders, industrial imperialism and ever-present Masonic-establishment interference, even though on his own he had to work alone. He knew that it was a choice made with great risk. He presented his ticket at the barrier as he passed through without anyone batting an eyelid. He strolled through the station's internal concourse and emerged into the outside word and the bright sunshine of a late summer's day. The forecourt of Buxton station was a hive of bustling Edwardian activity, especially so with the town's added attraction as a 'spa retreat' to take the health giving waters.

Built on the River Wye, and overlooked by Axe Edge Moor, Buxton had a long history as a spa town due to its geothermal spring which rises at a constant temperature of 28 °C. The source of the spring is behind Eagle Parade and piped to St. Ann's Well opposite The Crescent near the town centre. Initially developed by the Romans around AD 78, the settlement was known as Aquae Arnemetiae (or 'the spa of the goddess of the grove'), although little evidence remains to be seen. The town largely grew in importance in the late 18th century when it was developed by the Dukes of Devonshire, with a second resurgence a century later as the Victorians were drawn to the reputed healing properties of the waters. Buxton was also noted for much of its spectacular architechture such as; The Crescent (1780–1784) which was modelled on Bath's Royal Crescent by John Carr along with the neighbouring irregular octagon and colonnade of the Great Stables; Buxton Opera House which was designed by Frank Matcham in 1903. He was a prolific theatrical architect and also designed several London theatres, including the London Palladium, the London Coliseum, and the Hackney Empire; The opera house is attached to the Pavilion Gardens, Octagonal Hall (built in 1875) and the smaller Paxton Theatre. The Pavilion Gardens contain 23 acres of gardens and ponds and were opened in 1871. Buxton railway station, the design of which impressed Ford as he strolled through it, was designed by Joseph Paxton, who also designed the layout of the Park Road circular estate. He was perhaps more famous for his design of Crystal Palace in London. The Natural Baths, by Henry Currey, sit on the site of the original Roman Baths. The building was opened in 1854. The 122-room Palace Hotel, built in 1868, is a prominent feature of the Buxton skyline, situated on the hill above the railway station. It was designed by Henry Currey, architect to the 7th Duke of Devonshire. The Palace Hotel was Ford's destination for the evening.

Ford walked a good dozen or so paces across the forecourt scanning his new environment. He was trying to pick up clues as to the direction of the Hotel; he spotted the answer in the form of a uniformed constable who was stood on the edge of the forecourt where it met the station's approach road, a road that led to Palace Street. Before Ford reached the constable, a brash be-suited business type man strode up to the officer and blurted out a question in an abrupt fashion; as he spoke he faced East whilst the constable faced west towards Palace Street.

"Palace Street and the Palace Hotel?" The constable replied equally brashly and as quick as a flash without looking at the rude enquirer.

"Straight on." The business man strode off without even acknowledging the constable's answer. Ford wandered up the last few feet to him.

"Did I hear right, please officer, the Palace Hotel is straight on?"

"You, did hear me right, it's straight on, but in the direction I am facing." The constable smiled as he bounced slightly on his feet. Ford understood exactly the reason for the constable's first response; after all, he hadn't lied to the business man, he had just failed to clarify the answer as a result of his brash rudeness. Ford looked east to see the business man striding on with no sign of stopping. He smiled too.

"Thank you, constable. Have a good day." The constable nodded in acknowledgement and Ford made his way to the Hotel.

Chapter Twenty-Nine

Hoare sat quietly and sullenly in the claustrophobic compartment of the black Mariah as it made its way from the railway station to the police station in Northampton. He had pushed his luck with Ford. He was now guaranteed to be implicated by the annoying East Ender-made-good policeman, and so he had nothing to lose in plotting an escape. His best bet would be to feign illness. The nature of the carriage made it impossible to tell where he was; no decent window to be able to see out of. But when he sensed through sound and feel that they were driving over cobbles he knew that they must now be in an urban environment. Running away in town was easier than across open fields.

He knew the answer. Shallow the breathing and slow the pulse by relaxing. With experience as an accomplished member of the Royal Marines swimming team it was easy for him. If he feigned unconsciousness or semi consciousness then they might remove the cuffs and get to him to hospital or a doctor. It was worth a go. He relaxed himself totally and began to feel strangely elated. By the time he reached the police station yard he was prone on the floor of the Mariah, and waited for the police to open the doors. He heard the handle and latch being operated.

"Fuck!" came a cry from the young constable. "Sarge, he's collapsed!" The sergeant rushed around to the back of the Mariah to see for himself. They looked down on Hoare who was lying face up with his cuffed arms across his chest.

"Oh bollocks!" said the sergeant. He climbed into the back and felt for a pulse in Hoare's neck. "His heartbeat is very slow. We need to get the cuffs off of him and get a doctor."

"Take the cuffs off out here, sarge?" the young constable was puzzled.

"Yes, you clown, because if we don't he might croak on us, and The Yard won't be happy about that."

"What 'yard'?"

"Scotland Yard! You numbskull!" The annoying exchange taking place between them meant that neither was fully focussing on what they were doing. Squinting through his closed eyelids, Hoare could make out that there were only two other officers immediately to hand in the station yard and that the access gate was wide open. Their petulance with each other was going to play into his hands.

"I don't fucking know what yard you mean do I, sarge! It's not like I deal with London coppers and their prisoners everyday!"

The lad obviously fed up with his sergeant, was not really paying full attention as he released Hoare's handcuffs. Just for a moment Hoare allowed his arms to flop uselessly to his sides and stayed eerily prone. The lad moved his ear near Hoare's mouth.

"I think he's fucking dead, sarge," said the young constable. The mature sergeant fed up with the whole affair and not concentrating, stepped up to them.

"Let me take a look," he was in kicking range. Hoare lashed out with a vicious forward kick with sole of his shoe that struck the sergeant's knee which bent the joint against its natural movement. He yelled in pain and fell to the floor. Before the young constable could fully react Hoare had pulled him face down to the ground and ripped the cuffs out of his hand. He immediately got one on to the lad's right wrist and easily took control of his flailing left arm and secured the second bracelet. The young officer was face down in the dirt of the yard with his arms pinned tightly behind his back. The sergeant called to the driver of the Mariah and the other officer that was loitering in the station yard.

"Quick! Get hold of the bastard!"

For a brief moment Hoare gave consideration to standing his ground to disable these other two before escaping. The problem with that was if others poured into the yard from the building he could be trapped and recaptured. He decided to run; he bolted for the gate and in a few quick strides and still accelerating into a sprint he was out into the main street. The two officers gave chase. However, once they reached the gate and the street they had already lost sight of Hoare in the bustling thoroughfare. The sergeant saw them pause at the gate.

"Well go on you wankers! Get after him!" They moved out of his line of sight splitting up to cover each direction. It was the driver who within a few seconds re-acquired sight of Hoare just fifty yards or so up the road. His quarry was moving at a fast, distance pace, not a sprint, to obviously be able to maintain a good speed and gain distance to disappear, but not tire quickly as he did so. The driver, a mid thirties officer of medium build and carrying little weight, increased his own pace to try to close him down. He deliberately avoided calling so as not alert his quarry, who might then in turn speed up.

The horse-powered traffic passed beside them on the cobbled street as they kept to the footways. Before he could close the gap he lost sight of Hoare as they crossed a major road; Hoare got across but the driver was forced to stop by large omnibuses being pulled. These also occluded his vision and he lost sight of Hoare. As the traffic cleared he regained sight of the road on the other side and found a gap to cross. But he had lost sight of his fugitive. Not for long though.

He passed a narrow alley from which Hoare emerged. He stopped dead to turn and face Hoare, but as he did so he was greeted with a large piece of sawn timber striking him in the face. He fell, not unconscious, but in agony from a severely broken nose. He felt sick, his head was spinning and he could feel the warm blood coursing between his fingers as his hands held his face, and he sensed the taste of it as it also ran into his throat as he lay on the floor. He looked around as he became accustomed to the pain but his quarry had disappeared.

* * *

Deserted barns, South Derbyshire

With Patterson out of action for several hours, Holden took to making a fire, cooking some food and making a cup of tea. It was late in the afternoon and he would probably stay here until first light before completing his journey and reaching the final stage at Gradbach Mill, following the stream through the valley up to Lud's Church. He sat staring at the fire as he occasionally stirred the stew pot that dangled from a make shift tripod above it. He thought of the men of the SRP and their humorous fireside exchanges.

Northern Punjab, 1898

The men of the SRP had been able to horse and mule trek for quite some distance before abandoning their steeds to go over the mountains of the North West Frontier, passing from the Khyber Pass into Afghanistan. Their first day of marching, carrying all their belongings on their backs, started at lunchtime. Holden knew that it would be safest to make a camp before reaching the dangerous high ground and the final push over the top, through plummeting temperatures, over difficult and dangerously loose terrain and infrequent precipitation.

They found an outcrop of rocks that formed a semi-circle. Very quickly using their rucksacks they completed the circle making somewhere to huddle in. Before they bedded down for the night and with the fire snuffed out, they would all take their canvas 'poncho' sheets designed to be tied to trees to form rudimentary shelters. With six of them and using pegs and rope they would eventually be able to make the semi-circle completely enclosed.

In the meantime, Will Bailey got a roaring fire going from various pieces of wood the group scavenged over a radius of several hundred yards. The sun was falling over the horizon forming a marvellous red canvas behind the beautifully, hazardous Afghan mountains with differing shades with the height of the sun and the loose cloud formations. The men were all gathered around the fire waiting for a kettle of water to boil. It was Cledwyn Jones who began the banter around the fire, loading the first rounds of antagonism.

"So Pete," addressing the youngest member of the unit, "how many days you got in the mob then?" Pete Burwell was quick to reply.

"Its not days, you cheeky, old, Welsh bastard, its several years actually."

"Oh, fuck off! I'm entitled to more days off than you've got in the army!"

"Oh all that, from an Irishman that couldn't swim," chipped in Londoner John Waldron.

"Oh, hello? The cockney wanker speaks. Pearly king, self appointed tosser," replied Jones.

"Tell me Cled," said Waldron, "how come you look like you're getting fat!" Jones replied as quickly as a flash.

"Because every time I go round and fuck your wife she gives me a big bit of cake!" Everyone roared with laughter except Waldron. He tried an equally cutting reply.

"Make her wear a sheepskin jacket or a jumper just to make you feel at home do you?" Will Bailey entered the fray.

"I don't know about a sheepskin or jumper, hopefully she's wearing a blindfold, poor cow!"

Holden's pot over the fire came back into focus as he drifted back into the world of reality and 1904. He missed those days and his men terribly; more importantly he missed enjoying good health. He began coughing heavily and pulled a handkerchief from his pocket. He placed it over his mouth. When he finished it he examined it as he had done many times now. There was an alarming amount of blood on it. Time was short.

* * *

Hoare still had plenty of money in his wallet. No one, as luck would have it, had taken it from him during his brief time in police custody. He made directly for the railway station having gleaned directions on the way from several local people. Nobody batted an eyelid at this man in his respectable dress and with a calm demeanour. He gave away no indication of desperation or being a fugitive. His goal was clear; abandon Patterson; steal whatever money he could find in Patterson's home or office, two venues to which he was not considered a stranger; make for Dover and get to France. From there he would take the Orient Express to get himself to Turkey and close to the Middle East. He would join the military units there and attempt a much smaller incursion. They would verify the presence of oil and then sell their ability to allow access to these reserves to the highest commercial bidder. Simple. He would not only lead the whole enterprise but become the controlling figurehead, standing to make the most from it.

Hoare strolled into Northampton Station, St John's Street, nonchalantly but paying scrupulous attention to every detail in the environment that surrounded him. He had to avoid doing this too much at the ticket office so as not to look furtive. As he stepped away from the window, he saw a group of six police officers enter the station concourse; he recognised three straightaway. The driver, the boyish constable and the now limping sergeant; they all looked ready for fight as did the three new policemen. All of them were brandishing their truncheons except the sergeant. Hoare suspected that he was armed with a concealed pistol. Hoare was armed with nothing but his own guile and sense of self-preservation. He needed to avoid a violent confrontation in somewhere so public.

He looked around him. There was a door only a few yards away marked 'staff only'. He took the gamble that it was unlocked in somewhere so provincial. It paid off. He turned the cold brass doorknob and entered. There was no one inside and it was a staff restroom. Railway official's uniform was hung up on one side. The ideal disguise for him was there, a large sized overcoat and a ticket inspector's cap. Both fitted. He wandered back outside.

The police had split their forces into three pairs. The limping sergeant was paired with the driver. They were fortunately the furthest away from him at the far side of the bustling concourse. The station itself was relatively small so the moderate crowd that there was easily filled it up. Of the two pairs nearer to him only one officer was likely to recognise him. Their division of forces had been woeful, why had each pair not had an officer that would recognise him. More fool them. He knew which platform he wanted. He strolled towards the waiting train passing straight by the pair that included the boy constable. Not a feint of recognition, the lack of eye contact and examination of a railway official was probably key to that.

He strolled unmolested along the platform and onto the train and the first class compartment for which he had bought a ticket. He didn't drop his guard. The most natural and obvious thing for the police to do was examine each departing train, especially one for London. He sat facing down the platform so he could observe the approach of any officers from the window. A pair was heading his way within a few minutes. He hoped no one else had boarded.

He allowed them just to get a bit closer. When they were a matter of a few yards away he got up. He moved into the second-class compartment and began checking tickets. Everyone was unmoved by his action. It worked perfectly. The two officers outside strolled on and while his back was turned the sergeant and the driver walked behind him along the inside of the train. He saw them in his peripheral vision and then turned his head fully as they exited the carriage to be sure they were leaving to enter the next one. He continued his charade until he saw all four of the police walking back along the platform towards the concourse. The train began to move, there was a jolt as the slack in the couplings was taken up. He could hear the sound of the locomotive as it began its toil pulling the carriages, and the driver sounded the train's whistle. Smoke from the steam engine then breezed passed his window as the train picked up speed. He smiled as he relaxed into his seat. He would keep the disguise for the other end, although it was unlikely that the police in London would yet be looking for him. Ford had instructed the sergeant to keep him in Northampton incommunicado. No one in the south would yet be looking for him.

* * *

Midnight; Patterson came round and could feel most of his body except his legs. He was still inside the confines of the carriage. He felt for the door handle and turned it slowly. He felt the door go light and he slowly eased it open. He was presented with the glow of the embers of a dying fire that illuminated the sleeping Holden in an eerie red hue. His kidnapper looked sound asleep. He might not be able to feel his legs, but he could drag himself over to the fireside and strangle the bastard. Then, when the feeling in his legs returned he could escape and raise the alarm. Holden's murder would be a justifiable homicide in self defence. No court in the land would convict him of otherwise.

He had to ease himself out of the carriage slowly to avoid creating unnecessary noise from its suspension. The numbness in his legs included not being able to tell when his feet hit the floor and then as he got lower his knees bending; he had to watch himself in the fading firelight to check his progress. Once onto the floor of the barn properly, he slowly dragged himself across the floor to reach his sleeping captor. He had a bizarrely happy, adrenal feeling as he neared Holden, knowing that for once and for all this was going to be over. He would cover up the whole thing in a way that suited him, spinning a story of unjustified aggression towards him and his staff by a deranged ex-soldier. Using his forearms he inched up to a point where he lay beside the apparently prone and sleeping Holden.

He looked around in the fading, ember light for any kind of weapon that might have been left around; there was nothing to be had. He moved up as close as he dare in readiness to attempt to strangle Holden. Suddenly his ambition seemed to have been overruled. Before he could raise his hands to strangle Holden, he had spun around towards Patterson with a leading right arm that, as he turned, pinned the Minister to the ground by his throat. Within a split second Holden was upon him with his knees either side of his body pinning him to the floor, with his arms locked in beside his body.

Patterson still had no sensation in his legs so he could not resist by kicking out. As Holden towered over him he was aware of the apparently indestructible soldier having a coughing fit. A chance to demoralise the crazed officer.

"What's the matter then, Holden? The Middle East and India kill you after all?" Misguidedly Patterson expected a verbalised answer, what he got was the sound of more coughing then a hushed silence. Then there was the sound of someone spitting and the next thing he knew he was hit in the face by a liquid of some sort. He knew exactly where it had come from. "You filthy bastard, Holden! You'll die before you get to finish me."

Holden wished to dehumanise Patterson as much as he could during this journey. He refused to respond verbally to him. Patterson could see him draw something from his pocket in the shadows and the next thing he knew he felt a scratching sensation in the sinews of his upper left arm. Holden had given him another but larger dose of curare. He was unconscious before he could even think of a reply. Holden then placed him, with a growing physical strain, back into the carriage.

* * *

Ford woke at 4.59.a.m. He lay there waiting for the unruly sound of the brass alarm clock to commence. The din that it made at five was lamentable; but his usual programming the night before when working under pressure had worked. Ford washed, shaved and dressed before making his way down to a specially arranged early breakfast. He carried with him his sabre case that also held a scabbard as well as his favoured edged weapon; he also had his pistol, some handcuffs, a few basic first aid items and a fighting dagger all in a leather satchel bag. The last item he picked up was Hoare's cased rifle. He left most of his luggage as he fully intended to return and use the hotel before leaving for London, when Holden was successfully in his custody. He would house him temporarily in Buxton gaol. He wore the outdoor style clothes he travelled in as well as taking his waxed cotton hunting jacket. From the kitchen he would take a few supplies to see him through the day while he lay in wait for Holden to arrive with Patterson; a flask of coffee, some oatcakes, a couple of ham sandwiches and a couple of slabs of Kendal Mint Cake.

At 5.25 he was tucking into a traditional English breakfast, not dissimilar to the one he had enjoyed on the train. Today was the ultimate test of his own personal resolve. Despite the extremes of all his previous life and death experiences, none of them seemed to possess the sense of reticence that the feeling of confrontation with William Holden was presenting Ford. He had faced the man in a single fight only once but had been so close by when other events had occurred. He now wondered whether his own resilience and physical abilities were enough to match this seeming 'superman'. He finished his breakfast, pulled the napkin from his lap, stood up and pushed the chair under the table. He pulled on his wax cotton jacket and left the dining room.

On the forecourt of the hotel he stepped aboard a local hansom cab and the driver made for the Rose and Crown pub on the main Buxton to Congleton road. Ford examined a map he had purchased in the hotel as he tried to sit relaxed inside the cab. A visitor guide also provided him with a brief description of his destination. 'Lud's Church; an immense natural cleft in the rock on the hillside above Gradbach, in a forest area known as the Black Forest. The feature has been formed by a landslip which has detached a large section of rock from the hillside, thus forming a cleft which is over 15 yards high in places and over 100 yards long, though usually only a few yards wide'. He was wily enough to have also brought a compass in case he lost his bearings once he made his way up from Gradbach Mill.

The cab journey was uneventful but also uncomfortable so Ford was glad to strike out on foot once they reached the Rose and Crown. His instructions to the cab driver at this point as he alighted were clear.

"Wait here for me until nine this evening. Here is ten pounds now and you'll get half as much again on my return. If I don't return then call the local police and they will eventually reimburse you for your time." The driver simply nodded, accepted the money, secured his vehicle and then made for the pub that was about to open to offer walkers breakfast.

Walkers. Ford had not given consideration to any potential 'collateral damage' in his planning for today. Lud's Church was a curio and so may well be visited by innocent thrill seekers and walkers while he confronted Holden. He would deal with that problem when it happened. He trudged off away from the main road towards Gradbach as the sun shone down on a bright, crisp morning. It was now gone eight. He expected that he had plenty of time to get there and then set himself up and lie in wait for Holden to arrive. How he would confront him, he wasn't sure.

* * *

Getting Patterson into Lud's Church was not an easy task. Holden had had to take a mule drawn cart across the bleak moors of Gradbach with the corrupt politician under heavy sedation as he had been for the three day carriage journey from London. Holden's mind had for many weeks lost any sense of reason when it came to completing his quest for revenge. Any sane and straight thinking man even wanting to exact harsh revenge would either have finished the matter at Tudor Castle or at a location not far from there. He had for a month or more become completely convinced in his mind regarding the avenging of the disownment of the SRP that he was Gawain and Patterson the Green Knight. Patterson having laid down the challenge for him to survive, which he had done, he now had to complete that challenge by ensuring that 'the knight would never trouble anyone again'. Therefore he had to defeat the Green Knight in the fabled location of 'their earlier encounter'; Lud's Church. His mind was in terminal decay due to mental stress and his physical deterioration caused by the T.B.

There was only so far he could take the mule and cart once he left the course of the main road by the Rose and Crown public house. The path beyond this led to Gradbach Mill, and he knew that he would have to get clear of any inquisitive eyes of those milling before he could abandon the cart. He was running parallel with the River Dane for a time through a winding, lush and rolling valley and within a third of a mile he could tell it was safe to discard the cart. He unhitched it from the patient mule that stood staring aimlessly ahead, swinging its tail as Holden worked around it. Soon the mule was free of the enclosed cart, which he propped against a tree stump and an outcrop of rock to keep it level. Then he opened the cart and pulled the semi-conscious Patterson from the interior in a kind of fireman's lift. He then deposited the industrialist over the back of the mule which brayed as it took on a new burden. Patterson was slumped with his head and arms dangling over one side, his body across the beasts back and his legs hanging down on the other, in a kind of classic western 'gun-slinging bounty hunter brings the wanted back to town – dead' style.

Patterson was still under the influence of curare that ensured a kind of temporary paralysis without the awkwardness of rigidity. It would not be long that as the effects wore off, he would initially become mentally lucid before any physical recovery. This was perfect for the progressively weakening Holden to be able to deal with him to inflict fear before death.

As he led the mule by its reins, he examined the track in front of him as he walked. The earth was damp leaving the top layer to form a thin coating of mud that allowed the imprint of footprints. As he moved further he realised trying to determine if there was a party of any significance in front of him was pointless; there were prints everywhere. The constant climb uphill as he moved further away from Gradbach quickly took its toll on his debilitated lungs. He coughed and wheezed from time to time ejecting blood as he did so. Ironically the treatment of the day was exposure to open, clean air to try to improve lung capacity and deplete the bacteria. He hoped that as the ground levelled off as they neared the chasm his breathing would improve. He examined Patterson every five minutes or so with a cursory glance at his face. His eyes were now open and expressed fear at the precarious position he found himself in. His mind now working fully knew that his time was short. He held out no optimistic view of being saved from the clutches of his self-created nemesis.

* * *

There were no signs for Lud's Church once Ford reached it; he had checked his position with map and compass and was quite certain he was on top of it. He looked around the wooded area he found himself in and then spotted some bushes with an unusual gap in between them. To one side grew a small tree, to the other side of the gap the bushes died away to a path. He walked up to the gap. As he neared it he could see that there was a path through the bushes. He entered. As the ground sloped away he could see that it was taking him into a narrow passageway between two steep rock faces, and that beyond the ground dipped further away. He made his way cautiously down, his bags rubbing against the sides of the damp rock faces. The floor had given way from earth to damp and moss covered rock. He was cautious with his footfall to avoid slipping as the rock formed natural stepping steps beneath him that lacked any adhesion.

The further Ford descended the more light began to shine back at him as the narrow cleft suddenly opened up into the vast chasm. It was truly a mystical sight; a light mist filled the void created by the land being torn apart, the rock of volcanic origin seemed broken and torn in slightly jagged straight lines and covered on its flatter surfaces in moss. In some places the moss had given way to the full-grown intrusion of vegetation. As the steps levelled off there was a long expanse of flatter ground which appeared dreadfully narrow as a result of the imposing sheer sides of the chasm. Ford acknowledged how easy it was for this to have become to some a mythical site. He admired it alone with no sign of any other human activity and only some faint bird sound as company. The next question in his mind as he strolled the length of 'the church' was where to lay in wait. He followed the cleft round a near perfect ninety degree corner to the alternative entrance and exit. It was a wide extension of the main chasm that opened up into woodland with a rolling descent in one direction down a wooded hillside. A foot path led off around the sides of the chasm in the direction from which he knew he had come that appeared well trodden. His mind was made up; he would wait at the turn giving him a view of the full length of the 'nave' and sight of both approaches. There were some large rocks at the base of the walls at this point he could sit on and keep his weaponry out of sight. It was late morning and just a waiting game. He hoped the attendance of curious hill walkers would be at a minimum or non existent. He would not have to wait long for his quarry and his captive to arrive.

* * *

Holden reached the tree and bushes at the western end of Lud's Church, the entry that Ford had used less that an hour before. He surveyed the ground around him. There were no tell-tale signs of recent activity obvious to him. He tied the mule to the tree and looked at Patterson as he did so. Paterson's feet and hands were bound and in turn he was secured to the mule. Holden could see from his wriggling type movements that the curare had mostly worn off. He pulled out a bayonet from a scabbard on his belt and cut the ties securing Patterson to the mule. He instantly slumped off of the creature, sliding feet first to the floor. His feet and knees buckled as soon as they hit the floor and he landed in a heap. He gasped with the shock and the pain it sent up through his legs.

"You bastard, Holden. Why don't you just get on with it and kill me?" Holden was beyond any reason. The mild use of opium to dull the pain of the T.B added to his delusional state.

"Shut up." He spoke in a calm and monotone way. He then reached down with the bayonet and cut the rope tying his legs together. "You'll die soon enough, but not until you have faced me one last time."

"You're mad! Fucking mad, Holden!"

"Get to your feet, knight."

"What?"

"Just get to your feet!" With his hands still secured behind his back Patterson awkwardly got to his feet. He staggered around for several seconds as he regained his balance after several days under the influence of a paralysing drug. He dare not question Holden again. Holden drew a sabre from his own scabbard and pointed it at Patterson. "Into that gap, and where it drops away to stone, wait." Patterson did as he was told. Holden removed a long bag strapped across the mules back that contained a rifle and another sword. He carried it in his left hand

and followed Patterson into the entrance to the chasm. He coughed as he did so and then spat blood from his mouth. The narrowness of the entrance to the chasm reminded him of the entrance to the caves in Kuh-e-Baba; that seemed a lifetime ago.

* * *

In the silence that surrounded Lud's Church Ford had heard the exchange between Patterson and Holden. In a dutiful sense only, he was pleased that Patterson was still alive. His heart began to beat faster knowing that he was about to face Holden again. He drew his sabre and also had Hoare's rifle close at hand, cocked ready to use, in case Holden appeared with a firearm. He then moved behind the rocks and crouched down to be out of sight until Patterson and Holden moved into the centre of the chasm. There was no point issuing a challenge to Holden too soon, he had to ensure that he could maximise the safety margin to Patterson.

Ford watched as Patterson emerged at the bottom of the stone steps with hands tied behind his back, with Holden behind him, sabre in hand pointed at the Minister, and carrying a long bag in his left hand. Ford undoubtedly had the advantage of good cover at his end of the 'nave' whilst Holden had none. What Ford hadn't considered was that Holden would use Patterson if engaged by a firearm as a human shield.

Chapter Thirty

As the two figures walked nearer to the centre of the natural nave, Ford took hold of the rifle in his hand. He raised himself up into a kneeling position from behind the rock, still keeping a low profile, and aimed at Holden. He followed him in the sights as he moved just offline with Patterson. Within a few seconds he was settled with his sight picture and issued a simple verbal challenge to Holden.

"Captain. This is Inspector Ford. Stand still and drop your sabre." Ford was not prepared for Holden's move. With lightning speed he dropped his bag, sheathed the sabre as he stepped directly behind Patterson and then drew his pistol and jammed the barrel hard into the back of Patterson's neck pointing upwards. This would guarantee an instantly fatal shot if he pulled the trigger. Ford flinched a little and felt his hands loosen and then re-tighten on his rifle. He tried to keep Holden in his sights but it was impossible; Patterson was providing him cover as a human shield.

"I suggest you lower your weapon, Inspector. You are now in no position to make demands. I can kill your professional ward before you have the confidence or ability to take a shot at me."

Ford's mind raced; he could feel perspiration almost instantly appear on his brow. Should he take a shot so it would over penetrate through the shoulder of the Minister and deliver, hopefully, an incapacitating blow to Holden? There was no guarantee of that result.

"Captain Holden, this is over. Let him go. I understand that you and your men were wronged, but this is not the way to resolve it."

"Oh please, don't patronise me inspector. I am a dying man. The subcontinent has killed me. Because of him," he jammed the gun hard into Patterson's head, forced it forward causing the Minister to give a painful grimace, "and lets face it, I am to face the gallows, at least for crimes of revenge here. So it is over, you are right. But on my terms." Ford had to think. Holden might pull the trigger at any moment. The sabre.

"Captain, you are a man of honour, are you not?"

"What of it?"

"You seek satisfaction from your nemesis, a knight. Can a champion not fight in his place?" Holden's drug addled mind whirled for a moment. A champion fighting on the Green Knight's behalf? He wasn't a king or even a lord. But the sense of a true combat drowned his sense of reason.

"What are you proposing Mr Ford?" Holden began shuffling on his feet behind Patterson, moving his weight from one to another. He knew in his mind what might be suggested. The prospect of a decent sabre duel frankly excited him.

"I'll fight you. Let him go. He can watch, and if you win then you can do as you will. If you lose, then I take you into custody and let the wheels of justice turn."

"No. If I lose, you deliver a coup de grace. If you can't challenge me on those chivalrous terms then prepare to meet your end prematurely, Inspector." With that, Holden began to march Patterson forward quickly, still with the gun to his head, still using him as a shield.

Ford panicked. He looked through the sights and took aim. He took a shot. The sound echoed around the chasm. There was a single scream; the advancing figures stopped. He lowered the rifle to see clearly the outcome of his marksmanship.

* * *

The Vatican, afternoon

The three cardinals enjoyed the late September afternoon sunshine in the famous Vatican gardens. The gardens dated back to medieval times when the area was cultivated as vineyards and orchards. The area changed from walled, cultivated land to ornamental gardens in the

1400s for the enjoyment of the Pope and to form locations for Papal ceremonies. Sklinski, de Vicompte and Caravaggio stood overlooking the Eagle Fountain designed by Jan van Santen. They were spread along the cobbles in front of it all looking into the water with the peaceful sound of it coursing through their ears. Caravaggio spoke first.

"So, the Papal father seems to have pulled back from his illness. It looks like there will be no conclave after all." The other two nodded stood with their hands behind their backs. Sklinski responded.

"For a man of sixty-nine who seemed frail with illness he has truly done well. The Lord himself must have intervened." De Vicompte remained silent. Caravaggio broke the pause in their musings.

"Well, Victoire? You seem unduly quiet?" De Vicompte turned from the others and began to stroll away from the fountain into the lush gardens. Caravaggio and Sklinski looked at each other and followed him. "What's the matter, Victoire?" The Frenchman stopped on the lawn at the base of a bronze statue of St Peter. He turned and addressed his friends with a look of concern.

"Friends, I am disappointed that you, Lorenzo, have missed an opportunity to become Pope. I feel your inspired leadership would be good for the faith, especially with all of our views on Pius X's reforms. But there is a more pressing matter that stands to disgrace us. What is happening in London is my concern. There is still no guarantee of the recovery of our cash and bonds."

Caravaggio had absolute faith in the Swiss Guard.

"Have no fear. By fair means or foul, we and our beloved church will not be disgraced. Matters in London are in hand. There is someone there to oversee that other than Sepp Dietrich."

"Who?" asked Sklinski.

"I cannot betray an operative that acts secretly for us in London. The matter will be resolved." Caravaggio spoke with supreme confidence. It seemed to ease the troubled mind of the French cardinal. The three of them then continued walking across soft grass to reach the sublime tranquillity of 'The Casina' or 'Nymphaeum', the ornate oval courtyard with its beautiful baroque architecture that joined together the main elements of the 'Villa Pia'.

An iron table and four chairs had been set there with a waiting service of afternoon tea for the three highly placed churchmen.

"Gentlemen," began Caravaggio, "let us sit and enjoy the tranquillity of our surroundings. We do not need to concern ourselves with issues that will not come to pass." It was only de Vicompte who could not share this optimism as he drank tea that he had no desire for in the warm Roman sun.

* * *

Patterson was screaming and almost limp in Holden's arms. The rifle bullet had penetrated his left shoulder and passed through it but had missed Holden. Holden was still holding him as a shield despite Ford having lowered his weapon. Ford knew he would have to face single combat.

"Very foolish, Inspector. You now have a principal who is bleeding, possibly to death, but still in the arms of his captor. You almost make me feel like shooting him myself. You have put us all at risk." Having seen Ford lower the rifle, and having advanced to within twenty feet of Ford, he maintained his hold of Patterson but now levelled his pistol at the police inspector. "Tell me why I shouldn't shoot you dead, right now?" Ford had to think on his feet in this ever moving situation.

"Because fighting him with a sabre in his hand would be unfair, he has been injured and is weak. Fighting me would still be vaguely a challenge."

"And what do you know about sabre fighting, policeman?" Holden sneered as he spoke, his military arrogance assuming a humble copper would never be so practiced in such a skill. Ford was enraged by his sense of superiority. He stood dropping the rifle and picking up a sabre from out of sight to Holden behind the rocks. He pulled himself up to his full height brandishing the sabre with its blade glinting in his right hand.

"Well, captain, why don't we find out?"

Holden's eyes' narrowed. Patterson was clutching his wounded shoulder. He pushed the Minister away from him to the floor and holstered his pistol. He turned his back on Ford and strolled casually to the bag he had dropped under Ford's watchful gaze. Ford stepped over the rocks and approached Patterson. Before he could speak, Holden had reached the bag, withdrawn a sabre himself and was now walking back towards them.

"I accept your challenge, Ford. This will either be immensely rewarding and or very curtailed and unsatisfactory." The mix of an earlier intake of opium and adrenalin had dulled the pain and dysfunction of the TB. Holden felt himself again preparing to take on another in honourable single combat. The two of them faced up to each other and gave a salute with their sabres holding them to their faces before taking up combative stances. Both actions took Holden by surprise; perhaps this man did know something of duelling. Ford's mind raced with the voice of Andre Moreau and his words of wisdom.

They circled for a few seconds before the first clashes of metal took place. Holden made the first attack. It was rapid and efficient. Ford defended tenaciously and the image of Moreau fighting him came into his mind; this man was as quick and ruthless in his economy. Ford knew he would have to play the long game to win through fatigue and mistakes in his opponent's defence and attack.

Patterson crawled to the side of the chasm and propped himself up against its rocky side. He was beginning to shiver despite the day being mild; it was blood loss and shock. He watched the flashing blades in front of him as the two men fought with fast, controlled aggression. He no longer cared who won. If it was Holden he prayed for a quick death, if it was Ford he hoped for the attention of a physician as soon as possible.

After a few minutes of mortal combat both men were sweating heavily. Ford made a quick and violent lunge in one of his attacks that Holden parried with the classic watch glass manoeuvre. Ford, having been taken by this so many times was equal to it. As Holden tried to trap his arm, Ford swept a kick with his left leg striking the side of Holden's right that put him off balance, so much so that not only did he release Ford's arm he lost his footing and fell to the floor. Ford tried to kick the sabre from his hand but Holden rolled and then sprang to his feet. As he stood once again 'en guarde', Ford could hear a slight wheezing in Holden's breathing. It gave him hope, if he could keep the fight going he sensed his health and fitness would win out.

The sound of their blades clashing echoed through Lud's Church, the sound of each strike with his weakened condition, made Patterson flinch as he half sat, half laid helplessly on the floor. As he tried to watch the protagonists his vision was becoming increasingly more blurred; he sensed he was dying. He was not going to let Holden get away with this. With a supreme effort he began to drag himself towards the rocks that had sheltered Ford. He knew that there was a rifle there.

Ford looked at the face of his adversary as they clashed and held blades locked against each other. Holden was pale, sweating profusely and looked fearful. Ford could not afford to be complacent; the look could be a ruse, and one that he would not be fooled by. They pushed away from each other, both grunting heavily as they did so and began circling again. They were both too immersed in their own life and death struggle to observe what Patterson was doing. Holden came forward with another unrelenting attack, Ford wondered if perhaps the man who seemed to be weakening might have the endurance and skill to outlast him and win. The thought of defeat distracted him. Holden found a chink in his armour, sufficient to disarm Ford like a novice. A lunge forward had been weakly parried, and a counter twist had thrown Ford's sabre out of his hand.

Holden smiled a cruel smile and began walking Ford back towards the side of the chasm. He opened his mouth to speak but before he could emit any words there was a gun shot. The rifle slug that struck Holden in the side of his chest put him to the floor. Ford looked at him and then quickly towards the direction of shot in disbelief. He saw Patterson with the rifle resting on the rocks for support trying to cock the weapon. He began walking towards Patterson.

"What have you done?" asked Ford menacingly. He had desperately wanted to take Holden alive, whatever the risk.

"Saving my skin you pri..." there was another gunshot this time from behind Ford that struck Patterson square in his forehead. Blood spewed from an exit wound in the back of his skull and as more blood leaked from the entry wound he collapsed dead.

Ford turned rapidly drawing his own pistol to confront Holden. He had no need to worry. Holden had already collapsed back onto the floor having taken the shot and was wheezing from his sucking chest wound. The lack of pain and the few minutes of life he had left were merely fuelled by the opium. His pistol was discarded next to him.

Ford rushed to Holden and cradled him in his arms. The dying captain spoke as blood trickled from his mouth.

"Nice try Ford. You almost did it. A worthy adversary indeed. Thought you always looked meaningful. You could have beaten me, except for your last novice lunge. You could have saved him, but look. He couldn't let things take their course even to save himself."

"William, why did you set out on this path?" Ford could feel the warmth of Holden's blood seeping into his own clothes.

"They all knew. They all knew that we were betrayed, none of them saw the horrors that I saw, and that's what they deserved for their betrayal. Especially Philpot, he buried the whole story. Even edited it so no one would really know. They all needed to feel the pain. The whole campaign allowed the fear to build in the toads."

"If he knew it was you because of the journal, why didn't he tell me?" Holden took a breath which made a sickening sucking sound from his chest wound and Ford could hear him beginning to rasp.

"Weakness and corruption. He didn't want people to see his failings. It's too late. You must expose him Ford. You ha......" Holden's words tailed off as he began a short but violent bout of rasping coughing. The sight and sound was hideous as Ford was forced to see the fear in his eyes as he seemed to vomit blood as if he was drowning. Then Holden fell quiet, his body that had violently convulsed became calm and still. He became limp in Ford's arms as his eyes shut slowly.

Ford took a deep breath and sighed as the whole scene felt vaguely reminiscent of his best friend's death on the filth-ridden streets of Whitechapel in 1888. He looked down at Holden's lifeless body; he couldn't help but feel pity for this once honourable and respected man who had become so twisted by revenge. He reflected on the SRP journal. The six men whose bravery it recounted deserved honourable recognition, unlike the man who had sent them to their deaths.

Ford laid Holden gently to the floor. What a bloody mess. This wasn't over; there was much to do in London. He had to bring the only other person who could stand trial to justice; Hoare. He had to expose the whole failing of Patterson, his murderous corruption, his greed and his outrageous empirical plan. A tourist rounded a corner of the chasm as Ford stood, his attention initially being shared between the two lifeless bodies. The shock struck walker stopped in his tracks, with a crowd of others then bumping into him from behind.

"Get me the police, now!" shouted Ford, brandishing his warrant card. The scared looking tourist and the party that rounded the corner after him stared at Ford and then nodded and left. They had seen the barbarous outcome of Holden's last stand. Indeed the police were required.

Chapter Thirty-One

September 28th, London

Hoare immediately hailed a cab as he walked out of Euston Station to take him directly to Belgrave Square. He hazarded a guess that there was yet no news of Ford's actions successful or otherwise in The Peak District. He was complicit in Patterson's deception of the Catholic Church and knew that he had to access the funds he had purloined as soon as he could. He would go straight to the Minister's house and quiz the very trusting Lady Patterson. He planned to dupe her into believing her husband was subject to ransom and that Ford suggested they pretend to be ready to pay to entrap the kidnapper. In discovering where Patterson's ill-gotten money lay he could take hold of it and then leave England.

The uncomfortable cab's tired suspension and its iron rimmed wooden wheels did not supply Hoare with the most comfortable journey and he was grateful to arrive at the Patterson's, pay the morose driver and then make it to the front door. The police presence had been withdrawn with the hunt for Holden well and truly outside London and the belief that there was no threat to Lady Patterson or the building. How wrong the ministerial and police powers were. A new source of ruthless danger was soon to enter the building.

As he took the path to the front door Hoare didn't notice the lone figure in a long coat loitering in the square's park area just the other side of the carriageway. Sepp Dietrich looked on from behind the ornate iron railings in the fading light of mid evening. The man entering the building looked as if he had a meaningful physical presence; tall and well built with, as Hoare turned to look back across the square on the threshold of the house, cruel and callous eyes. Dietrich still had no idea of when the Minister was likely return to London; he had no inclination of the Minister's demise and wasn't likely to for a few days yet. He noted the lack of police presence around the house. 'Odd, the protection having been withdrawn so suddenly?' It struck him that all was not well. He watched intently as Hoare used the heavy brass door knocker to gain the attention of the occupants inside.

It was one of the Patterson's domestics that came to the door and answered it. The middle aged and slightly over weight maid in her traditional black with white outfit opened the door and looked mildly intimidated by the sight that greeted her; Hoare, tall imposing, menacing and slightly dishevelled.

"Can I help you, sir?" she asked politely.

"Yes. Major Hoare here to see Lady Patterson."

"I'll see if she'll see you, sir." A voice came from the generous Edwardian hallway with its ornate tiled floor behind her.

"Mary, thank you, I shall attend to our visitor." It was Lady Victoria Patterson.

"Very good, mam." Mary disappeared into a room leading from the hall as Victoria Patterson took over holding the door. She opened it wider to allow Hoare to enter and then closed it, leaving behind the prying eyes of Sepp Dietrich.

She turned and leant against the closed door with her hands behind her back looking him up and down. Victoria Patterson was mid to late forties; elegant, mildly greying blonde hair with classic high cheekbone structure. Slim but shapely, unusually green eyes, Hoare knew as he looked back at her that she still turned heads.

"Oh, Marcus!" She spoke cathartically as she pushed herself away from the door towards him. He took her in his arms. They kissed passionately for several seconds before she broke away from him. She looked into his eyes scanning them to ensure a truthful reaction as she continued to speak. "Is there any news of Cecil yet?"

"No. I was forced off the trip to the Peak District because of Ford. The police will be after me. We have to act fast, are you ready to go?"

"I don't care if he lives or dies. I'll go with you whenever you want and to wherever you want. Our love has been secret for so long. I just want to go overseas where no one will know us and where I can flaunt my affection for you." She pulled him towards her and they began to kiss again. Hoare then swept her off her feet and into his arms and carried her upstairs.

* * *

London, October 3rd

Ford had been given leave of absence following his return before attending a full governmental debrief at number 10 Downing Street. With the gravity of the situation, the murder of a serving minister, he was unsurprised and certainly not intimidated by the venue. No news had been broken to the press as yet as to the fate of Sir Cecil Patterson but Ford suspected that would occur later that day. It was 9.30.a.m when he kissed Karen on the steps of his Eaton Square house to begin a walk to the Prime Minister's home. He thought little of the nun he saw leaving an address in Hobart Place, as he had the back of Buckingham Palace in view, with a suitcase as if she was planning a long journey. Possibly, he pondered she may be commencing a pilgrimage to Rome.

What had become of Hoare? He was enraged by the news that he had been allowed to escape from the custody of the Northamptonshire officers. Hoare was dangerous and resourceful and Ford suspected that with or without Patterson the ex-Royal Marines major might push ahead with the industrial mission into Afghanistan. He was refreshed by the news that at least Hoare had not killed anyone in the process. Perhaps he did have a conscience after all. He reached the edge of Lower Grosvenor Place and Grosvenor Gardens. It was a busy road to cross with an almost constant stream of horse drawn traffic. 'God help us if this infernal internal combustion engine takes off' thought Ford. He managed to make a run in a gap in the traffic and reached the opposite pavement adjacent to the great perimeter wall of Buckingham Palace. He followed it round past the Royal Mews where a carriage was preparing to leave. It contained the Marshal of the Diplomatic Corps and was off to meet the newly appointed ambassador for some foreign country who would then be taken to see the King to present his 'letters of credence'. It was escorted by some household cavalry men front and rear to ensure its safety. Ford waited to let it pull out of the entrance of the mews and smiled as it continued along Buckingham Gate. He loved the ceremony of London; that's why there would always be a part of this great capital in his heart.

* * *

The previous evening

Victoria Patterson and Marcus Hoare were settling down in separate Chesterfield armchairs in the Patterson residence in Belgrave Square. Enjoying a large glass of vintage port after a fine dinner, there was a subdued atmosphere between them following the breaking of the news of Sir Cecil's murder to the newly widowed Lady Patterson a few days before. Although it left them free to do as they wished, an air of dutiful solemnity filled the house. The silence was frustrating Hoare so he left his seat and placed a record on the gramophone. The crackling sound of music from a warped vinyl disc, a legacy of the poor technology, began to echo through the house and room. It was some soothing Mozart played by the London Philharmonic orchestra.

It was an advantageous evening for Dietrich to strike. Hoare over the previous day had visited Patterson's official offices and, along with money from the safe at Belgrave Square, he had possession of all the bonds and cash that Patterson had amassed for the invasion and industrialisation of Afghanistan. He had heard nothing of Ford and there was no threat of arrest from any other quarter as yet. He would abscond with Lady Victoria first thing in the morning. The train tickets were booked as was their ferry sailing to France. The cab would collect them at 6.a.m sharp.

Dietrich's puppet masters would be very pleased that he was to accomplish the goal they had set for him in one evening. At 9.p.m it was dark and Belgrave Square was marginally lit by gas lamps. There was still no police protection assigned to the house and Hoare certainly only expected a threat from Ford or another interfering policeman. He decided to not keep any weaponry to hand for fear of adding credence to Ford's impending allegations against him. The port was rich and smooth and offset the taste of the Fine Stilton, this one from the town that gave the cheese its name, which they enjoyed on dry crackers; no need for butter to impede the cheese's sharp savoury flavour. Dietrich let himself in via the back door that typically for many London addresses at that time of the evening was not locked. He released the door soundlessly and moved with the stealth along the pantry to reach a maid who had her back to him. She was tending washing up in a large enamel butler sink when he placed a chloroform soaked rag over her nose and mouth and held it on to her tightly. There was a muffled cry. Some light, futile resistance, but in seconds she was unconscious. He laid her gently to the floor. He continued through the grand house following the sound of the music that he felt very at home with, and knew that would work to his advantage. It should dull the sounds of any squeaking floor boards. He pulled a heavy rubber cosh from his right hand inside jacket pocket. It would do to quickly quell any other staff he met if caught by surprise. The music got louder the further he moved through the ornate Edwardian House. Although a layman, he could see that it was furnished with expensive wooden furniture and wall adornments.

Hoare and Lady Victoria were oblivious to the impending doom that was stalking through the house to bring about their fate. The music continued; Hoare savoured the cheese and then drank another generous mouthful of the oak cask aged Tawny. Dietrich closed on the drawing room, now only feet away. The music faded and stopped. He came to a halt, was it a change of record, or the end of a track? The former would have Hoare, the man he only knew by sight and his imposing physical presence, on his feet. Seconds of silence seemed like minutes. The music began again. Dietrich put the cosh back in his pocket and drew a Bergman No. 5 self loading pistol. Its powerful 7.63mm calibre coupled with accurate marksmanship would ensure almost certain death. It held a magazine of five, a good number for him to allow two shots on each target, a classic 'double tap'. He had no silencer to dull the gunshot which could prove awkward. One shot on each would be best to draw a minimal amount of attention. A residence previously protected by police emitting the sound of gunfire would quickly attract attention.

Dietrich peered around the doorway. The man had his back to him; the woman he had observed greet him on the doorstep was not to be seen. He tried to increase his sight lines into the room; it was difficult without compromising himself too much. Then she came into view. She walked from right to left in front of him with her back almost turned to him and sat in a chair perpendicular to the man. He examined the room one last time before entering. On his route in was another arm chair with a cushion on its seat. He would enter swiftly, grab it, wrap it around the gun and rely on a single shot on each and then a coup de grace.

He moved with lightning efficiency borne out of his training prior to entering the Swiss Guard. He had hold of the cushion before he was in the woman's sight and the gun was obscured by it. Not seeing the gun she merely reacted to the impertinence of a 'ruffian' entering their house. She stood up.

"Who the hell are you?" He raised the gun and cushion up to chest height and took a shot. It struck Lady Victoria in the chest. The power of the round knocked her back into her chair. It would prove a fatal wound. Hoare was quick to react, but not brisk enough. He made it out of his chair to confront his killer. He had a split second to stare into Dietrich's eyes before the fatal shot struck him. They were only feet apart so Dietrich had the gun wrapped inside the cushion still levelled at Hoare's head. The single shot struck home in his forehead. Hoare stared blankly at him and then collapsed.

Dietrich was satisfied. Three shots left. He still possessed two more magazines if need be to aid his escape. The cushion had worked perfectly in silencing the sound of the two shots. He checked his victims before commencing his search. They were both dead. He looked around the room. As he did so he glanced back into the hall. There were a set of three leather suitcases and two large trunks in the hall just over from the drawing room door. He walked towards them. As his view opened up he noticed one more case, a suitcase still but one that would not hold many clothes. He assumed documents. He walked over and found it unsecured. He picked it up, laid it flat on one of the trunks and opened it. He had found his prize.

* * *

Midnight the same evening, Hobart Place

Dietrich lay on his bed. He felt a sense of elation and satisfaction knowing that he had achieved his end successfully. He had returned safely and undetected to his London bolt hole. He was enjoying a large glass of Bowmore single malt as he lay on his bed with a just a white cotton towel around his lean, muscular body. He felt thoroughly refreshed from a hot bath and he was enjoying the relaxing feeling that the alcohol was beginning to provide.

There was a knock on the door. He took another quick gulp.

"Come in." He put the glass on the cabinet next to him. Sister Amy entered the room. She was wearing just her simple robes with her hair flowing freely and she carried a tray. Upon it was a decanter of port, by the colour of the liquid, and some cheese and biscuits. 'How ironic' thought Dietrich. He had felt compelled to eat when he had seen the same at Patterson's house. The anticipation of further consumption of another alcoholic drink, the cheese and the almost certain sexual encounter with this gorgeous nun, whose beauty was wasted on the confines of the church, relaxed Dietrich further.

"Shall I pour?" She spoke with a luxuriant smile. He felt his face begin to warm with the flow of blood through a sense of excitement. He also felt himself begin to stiffen slightly under the towel.

"Yes, why not." She poured them both a generous glassful and brought his over to the bedside handing it to him. He took it and smiled. She sat down on the edge of the bed next to him and ran her hand under the towel. As she took hold of him he breathed in slightly with the sense of impending pleasure. She smiled. He took a large mouthful of port. Its taste was quite exquisite; a true vintage, rich and fruity. He took another large mouthful. As he swallowed he felt the pleasant head-spinning intoxicating effect of the thick burgundy coloured alcohol, it clung to the sides of the glass as its meniscus moved from side to side. Within a few seconds, however, he began to feel quite unwell.

The three cardinals had never intended to be good to their word. As far as Dietrich's commanding officer was concerned he had died of wounds whilst executing his duty. Sister Amy was one of the Cardinal's paid operatives. Never an ordained nun of any kind, Amy Scotney worked clandestinely for the church using sexuality to achieve her ends every time; and she was always rewarded handsomely for it. The cyanide laced port began to take its horrific effect. Dietrich dropped the glass onto his lap as he began chocking and gasping for breath. The port soaked into the white towel giving the effect that he had just been stabbed in the stomach. One hand reached for his own neck as he fought for breath, as the other took hold of her hand as he looked at her with desperation. He tried to pull her towards him but she simply squeezed his penis as hard as she could adding to his pain and anxiety. He let go of her hand and she stood up from the bed. He thrashed around violently on the bed for a few seconds and then began to foam at the mouth, his saliva stained red by the port. Then he became very still. She watched his breathing stop.

She looked around the room of the dead soldier. She spotted the case she had seen him return with. She picked it up and left the room. A few minutes later two Benedictine monks in their simplistic robes entered the room and removed the lifeless body. Within the hour there was no trace of Sepp Dietrich ever having been in London.

* * *

Ten o'clock. Ford arrived at the front of 10 Downing Street and showed his identity to a uniformed constable stood on the doorstep. The shiny, gloss black door was then opened by the custodian inside within a split second of Ford using the heavy brass doorknocker. He stepped inside. He looked around the reception room with familiarity; its curios scattered around the room. On one side was the grand fireplace; beyond it in the corner of the room was a leather hooded watchman's chair. It was one of a few survivors of a Chesterfield type chair built with an enclosing canopy and a drawer under the seat. Inside the drawer would be placed glowing hot lumps of coal which would in turn circulate heat inside the chair warming its occupant. Diagonally opposite next to the front door was a tall, narrow set of drawers that had been used by Wellington to contain his orders to various units prior to despatch on the field at Waterloo. Ford's attention was brought back into focus by a familiar voice calling him.

"This way, Inspector Ford. We're in the cabinet room upstairs." The voice should be familiar; it was the Commissioner Sir Edward Richard Henry. He had met Sir Edward the previous year after he had taken office when he had been awarded a Commissioner's commendation. They had spoken at length. Ford, however, immediately felt uncomfortable with his presence; by the manner of his handshake the previous year when congratulating him he suspected that Sir Edward was a freemason.

The Dressmaker Connection

Turning round to face Sir Edward, Ford looked him subtly up and down as they met each other. The Commissioner extended his hand to greet Ford. Ford was obliged to uncomfortably reciprocate. However, Sir Richard proffered him a conventional greeting.

"Hello, Sir."

"Ford, good to see you. You tried your best it seems, so no disgrace there."

"What's the purpose of the high level meeting, Sir?"

"Well, there are a few issues to straighten out. Like how the matter is reported. Need to make sure that there is nothing too sensitive leaking out. Leaving the government exposed; that sort of thing." Ford nodded his head.

Sir Edward led him through the finely decorated building and up the main stairs to reach the cabinet room. The Commissioner opened the oak wood panelled door when they arrived and gestured the now slightly nervous Ford into the room. He followed him in and shut the door. Ford became the entire focus of attention to those in the room. Sir Edward introduced him.

"Prime Minister and gathered gentlemen, this is Inspector Robert Ford." The Prime Minister, Arthur Balfour, was the first to speak.

"Please sit down and join us, Inspector Ford." Ford cautiously sat down and surveyed the rest of the gathered persons around the long, highly polished mahogany table. "Let me introduce you to everyone." Balfour continued. He pointed to the person each in turn as he spoke.

"The Home Secretary, Sir Matthew White, and The Commissioner you know, the two military chiefs of staff, Admiral Sir Digby Standage-Jones and Field Marshal Own Bowen-Long, Mr Alfred Baines the newspaper magnate and the Foreign Secretary Sir Edward Grey."

As the Commissioner finished Ford realised he was in awesome, intimidating company. This meeting had been convened for a very good reason. He started to shift uncomfortably in his seat already; the whole matter was going to be buried and he knew that he was going to be powerless to prevent it. His own personal sense of tenacity meant that he would not roll over to their suggestions or eventual demands without an uncomfortable fight. The Prime Minister opened the proceedings.

Immediately the address seemed to be directed to Ford alone; the others were already co-conspirators in the cover up.

"Now, the latest developments in this matter are as follows. Lady Victoria Patterson and a man by the name of Major Marcus Hoare were found murdered at the Patterson residence in Belgrave Square by staff late last night. The motive for the crimes is unclear; no theft or damage seems to have occurred at the property. It is believed that Hoare was an employee of the late Sir Cecil." Ford interrupted.

"I can confirm that, Sir. He was Patterson's enforcer and the leader of his new incursion into Afghanistan." There was an uncomfortable silence across the room. The Prime Minister broke it.

"What do you mean 'new incursion', Inspector?" Ford looked around the room. It would appear that the Prime Minister at least knew nothing of the SRP, the journal and Holden's twisted quest. Baines looked a little furtive in his seat. Ford stared at him; he knew that he had been instrumental in the murder of William Bates.

"Of course you know about that side of the story, don't you Mr Baines?" Baines tried to play the matter down.

"I know of petroleum interests in Afghanistan. Nothing else, no glimmer as to why this Holden chap went off the rails." Ford's analytical mind worked it all out very quickly. He knew from seeing Bates body that he had been murdered and the matter covered up.

"Oh, of course not. Was it not Bates that had gotten hold of the journal and brought it to you as an exclusive? With your major holding in Empire Petroleum you couldn't let that go public. The company would be ruined. And I suspect that I am here because as fellow masons you are all, more significantly, fellow investors in E.P. When this hits the street then you stand for the company's shares to collapse and all lose a substantial sum of money."

The Prime Minister cut in and spoke in an aggressive manner.

"Ford, shut up and listen. This is the situation. You are in no position to make demands having failed to prevent a madman from murdering a man under your protection. You have begun an affair with his mistress, sounds very scandalous with mind to Patterson not being here to suffer further disgrace and neither is his wife. This man Hoare I understand was under arrest by you for seditious acts and he escaped, not your fault but of course the press coverage won't read that way if you force our hands.

"And this incursion into Afghanistan. Baines was probably the only one to have knowledge of that with his closer affiliation to the company. Without a figurehead or funding it will just collapse. In fact, we'll make certain of that and buy off the mercenary soldiers who have chosen to become part of an illegal army. Where it was funded from I have no idea.

"And finally Holden and his men. They can be vilified or celebrated. You've read the journal, which do you believe? I can assure you, if you do anything other than support us, run with the press release over Patterson's death, or they will all be vilified as will you. Holden might deserve that but the others, I would suggest, probably don't." The Prime Minister fell silent. All eyes in the room were on Ford. He stood up to address them all.

"For a benevolent organisation you are very devious." He was interrupted by the Commissioner.

"We maybe Freemasons, but this isn't a matter regarding the Brotherhood. In fact far from it, that is purely co-incidental. This is pure and simple economics, we stand to lose a lot of money as shareholders in E.P."

"Ah, greed, one of the most natural human instincts. You can buy my silence with your blackmail perhaps, but the innocents in this scandal must be honoured and their dependants financially supported. Those soldiers used by Patterson died bravely but hideously. Have you ever read the SRP journal? Including Holden they must all be honoured. The crimes can be apportioned to the late Major Hoare; he killed a policeman in Belgravia, so he can be a scapegoat for this whole mess. Holden was a product of all your greed and especially the very man who sent him to his expected death; Patterson. Holden's family does not deserve the dishonour."

"And what about you, Ford? And why choose Major Hoare?" asked the Commissioner. Ford paused.

"Me? Why Hoare? I want peace in my life. I want an extended leave of absence to consider my future. I serve the Crown but the layers in-between are too corruptible and I don't know if I can do my job with that rotten layer above me. And why Hoare? Because he was a murderer. He quite obviously killed Will Bates, the two soldiers who died mysteriously in Dagenham. Then a policeman, and me if he had had his way. In a twisted way Holden's quest was about revenge through a sense of honour to his men. Hoare killed because he was paid to. That's fine in war but not in normal society. He was a state sponsored assassin."

The Prime Minister was the one to reply again.

"We respect those views. You have a history of being tenacious, but you seem to have come to the sensible view that you can't win the war against the system. The news regarding the Minister's demise is not intended to be scandalous, perhaps negative for a burgeoning invention. Your role in this affair could stand to be celebrated. Your suggestion regarding Major Hoare's involvement is noted. Take your leave, and if you return you'll return as a chief inspector. We do recognise the efforts you made over the last few months. Special Branch needs men like you to lead and mentor."

Ford looked around the fine wood panelled room and nodded his head slowly.

"Look, I don't need you throwing me empty compliments or patronising me. If I come back to take a leading role against forms of terrorism and other threats to national security it will be under my terms, and not any of yours." Without saying another word he left the room.

* * *

Paris, October 4th, evening

The overnight boat train pulled onto the platform at the Gare De Nord absolutely on time; a virtue of the efficiency of French railways. Amy Scotney stepped down from the first class carriage in which she had travelled no longer dressed in bland, monastic type dress. The corset that she wore enhanced her already enviable figure. She wore a stylish cream bonnet with a smart dark blue blouson jacket with a matching coloured long skirt. The heeled boots that she wore underneath accentuated the fine deportment with which she walked. A smartly dressed man in his mid twenties met her on the platform by the carriage and took her two cases. One was her own suitcase; the other was that she had removed from the custody of the late Sepp Dietrich during his last seduction. The smart young man now acting as her porter escorted her with her luggage along the platform. He took her past the ticket barrier through the station concourse and out onto the cobbled forecourt.

The grand triumphal design of the station façade, complete with its twenty-three statues representing the incoming services that the station served, framed Amy and her 'porter' as they walked out into the gas and moonlit street to the view of the waiting Cardinal de Vicompte. The porter directed her to the enclosed and very private looking carriage. The door was opened from the inside and using the step and an arm that extended to help her she boarded. Her own luggage was placed on the rear of the carriage by the porter, who placed the case of valuables inside with the occupants before joining the driver.

She sat down on the leather quilted seat in the carriage next to the cardinal and greeted him with a gentle kiss on the lips. He responded with equal subtle pressure and a squeeze of her thigh.

"No man can surely resist you, Amy." She smiled an arrogant, knowing smile; one you could associate with a temptress.

"Perhaps. But if they follow the alternative religion, your eminence…"

"Don't speak of such sodomites! It will spoil our glorious reunion. I have a very discreet chef coming to my residence to cook a special dinner. We have much to celebrate." He bent forward and moved his hand down to her calf. Reaching the hem of her skirt he then placed his hand underneath and ran it up along to her stocking-clad thigh. Her hand stopped him just short of her crotch on the flesh-exposed part of her upper leg.

"And my usual cut, your eminence?" She stared coldly into his eyes, the eyes that her hand had forced to look up from her lap. She felt the sexually excited tremble of his hand as he kept it held.

"Of course. Two percent of the outstanding total which, trust me, is a lot of money."

"I know it is. I have looked." He tried to force his hand up higher but she held him off.

"You are a naughty girl. That is with the proviso that there is no Swiss Guard to worry about?"

"Of course not. He has been taken care of. All the captain needs to know is that he met an unfortunate end from a mortal wound in completing his duty."

"All right. Three percent. Caravaggio and Sklinski will not allow me to offer you any more. You know that is still a considerable amount of money. You will not have to work for a long time, if ever."

She smiled and allowed the further passage of his hand. She slid down the seat very slightly as she allowed him to move his hand inside her silk French knickers and pretended to be aroused. The carriage rumbled on over the cobbles of the Avenue de L'Opera passing the ornate building made famous by Gaston Leroux's story, heading towards Notre Dame and the Ile de Cite.

* * *

The North West Frontier

For the men of the privately funded expeditionary force the days, for quite sometime, came and went with monotonous regularity. The regular supply lines had begun to falter and the essentials for life became scarce. Their numbers dwindled on a nightly basis along with stocks of ammunition that the 'deserters' took with them to aid their hazardous escape through the Khyber Pass. As the numbers of the Patterson-raised mercenary force diminished so did their morale and respect for discipline. Officers and non-commissioned officers lost control of the men within the camp and eventually deserted as regularly as the conscripted men. Within a fortnight all that was left was the remnants of the camp, a shell that was patrolled by wild dogs scavenging for food; their quest quickly became fruitless. The abandoned army had scoured the camp for supplies themselves leaving virtually nothing.

It would be many years before invading armies again breached the borders of Afghanistan and dared to subjugate the population within. Better equipped and supplied, those succeeding armies would fair no better; their soldiers captured and tortured in similar fashion to the men of the SRP as a clear message to the invading infidels. 'We will not stand by and be conquered without resistance and will be ruthless in our defence and counter attack'. The Baryalai caravan thrived as Mahmood's true heir, Ahmed, eventually took control. Generations of the family would become defenders of the nation on the North West Frontier. The names of Patterson, Holden or the Royal Geographical Survey would never pass through Ahmed's psyche again.

* * *

October 5th, London 8.a.m

Ford had been surprised by the missing coverage of the passing of Patterson in the previous day's editions of the national newspapers. His disappointment in the matter was quickly and dramatically resolved in today's editions as he picked them up from the black and white checked tiled floor of his hall by the front door. He really needed to read no further than The London Times. He sat down in the conservatory with Karen Wood to read the paper over a cup of Lapsang Souchong. Mrs Adkins had just made a fresh pot.

'Minister of War meets end with Wife in Hideous Automobile Accident hours after Killer is found

Sir Cecil and Lady Victoria Patterson met their deaths yesterday in the late hours of the evening in an automobile accident. The braking system seemed to have failed as they were near to home in Belgrave Square which caused the Minister to lose control and strike a tree. There were no other persons involved. Ironically this sad turn of fate occurred only hours after Scotland Yard detectives led by Detective Chief Inspector Robert Ford confirmed that they had discovered the body of a yet to be identified former military officer in nearby Wilton Crescent. After the sound of a single gunshot police attended the flat address to find the male dead from a single pistol shot with the gun clasped in his cold dead hand. An apparent suicide note was left in which he confessed to a campaign of terror against the Ministry of War. No reason has yet been confirmed for his prejudice to this government department. It was Chief Inspector Ford's tenacity in his role in protecting Sir Cecil and his investigative powers that had led to the discovery of the plot against the Minister. For another major development in this story go to the centre pages.'

Ford avidly thumbed through the paper to get to the centre pages to discover what the third fabricated story about the entire affair had been. He was even more aghast at the further lies that had been spun to put a non-scandalous closure on the events of the last three months.

'Truth about Missing Soldiers Discovered by Celebrated Protection Officer

Following the mystery discovery earlier in the year of a soldier presumed dead for six years washed up on the shores of the Thames in a wheelchair, the truth about his re-appearance can now be told. Following the discovery of lodgings used by the man identified as John Waldron. Police, led by Detective Chief Inspector Ford, have searched the premises and discovered a journal. Written by Waldron, it would appear that he was part of a seven-man unit who were scouting in Afghanistan in a bid to start to break the in-bred prejudice against the west. However, their efforts were in vain as one the Chieftains whose caravan frequents the area adjacent to the Khyber Pass that they had apparently befriended, turned on them.

The unit, led by the noted Captain William Holden, having assisted to bring medical care to the region and develop simple civil engineering projects was systematically executed or killed as they tried to flee. It is only now that the remit of their mission has been discovered. Waldron and Holden, according to the journal completed by

Waldron, escaped albeit Waldron having received crippling injuries. From that point on their fate is uncertain. After their successful escape from Afghanistan with superhuman efforts by Holden to ensure his subordinate's safety, their passage to London and life here is not documented. There is no record or indication as to the whereabouts of Holden at this time. His family are not prepared to comment on the story. A supposition is that he has returned to the North West Frontier unable to re-adjust to life back in England. How Waldron came to die in the cold murky waters of the Thames remains a mystery. The families of Captain Holden's six subordinates are at least now in a position to put closure on the fate of their loved ones. The Ministry of War has stated they will be recognising the men's bravery and efforts with posthumous awards and pensions for those they have left behind.'

Ford was stunned at the lies that had been published. They had taken the chance that he would not go to the press himself and had promoted him in the process. He felt cheated that he was unable to bring to public attention the corruption within government circles; it re-asserted his feeling towards those in public service who seemed to lead the vanguard in society's moral decline. He snapped the paper shut and rolled it up. He got up from his wicker chair at a table where Karen sat opposite and stormed over to the waste paper basket. He unceremoniously deposited the newspaper in it. She watched him and made eye contact with him as he headed back to the table. He avoided her stare as he realised she was watching him and picked up his teacup finishing its contents in two generous gulps.

"Are you all right, Robert?" She spoke with concern.

"Yeah. We're out of here for a while, it's time we had a break from London."

"Where are we going?" Ford pulled a small box from his trouser pocket and opened it up, going down on one knee and presenting it to her.

"Mrs Ford to be, I have a bought a coastal property in Dorset. It's been refurbished and ideal for a honeymoon by the sea. Will you consent to spend time there with me as my wife?"

Karen threw her arms around him and sobbed as she fell from her chair onto her knees with Ford on the quarry tiled floor.

"We must be brisk packing and shopping; the Poole registry office is booked for 10.a.m on the seventh."

"Who'll be our witnesses, Robert?"

"Mrs Adkins and Mark Vincent, if that's all right?" She nodded tearfully as he continued. "Now go and get ready. We need to go shopping in Knightsbridge and Saville Row." She left the room as Ford turned towards his bureau. He walked over to it and sat down pulling out the writing desk. He took two sheets of his notepaper and a sheet of carbon paper placing it in between them to compose a message.

ROBERT FORD ESQ.   14A EATON SQUARE
                                                                       BELGRAVIA
                                                                       SW2

                                                                       5th October 1904

Dear Mr Arthur Balfour, Prime Minister
Cc Sir Edward Richard Henry, Commissioner of the Metropolis

Gentlemen, I am writing to hereby inform you of my intention to resign on my return from leave of absence. I find my position somewhat untenable with the government's continued attitude to 'cloak and dagger' secrecy. As much as I have great affection and loyalty to my King and Country, at present I feel even with apparent promotion unable to serve its best interests. Please contact me via this address, my housekeeper will be forwarding mail to my out of London address.

Robert Ford, Detective Inspector.

Ford addressed two envelopes appropriately for Downing Street and Scotland Yard, and then folded the letters placing them inside. Mrs Adkins entered the room.

"Mrs Adkins, when you return from Poole later in the week would you be so kind as to pop this in the post?"

"Certainly, Robert. Is it urgent?" By this time Ford was stood by his antique globe drinks cabinet. It was very early in the day for hard liquor, but he felt compelled to have a small glass of Isle of Jura.

"No. Not at all. There is no rush at all." Ford stared out of the conservatory window of fifteen Eaton Square with a distant, glazed look as the sour, peaty taste of the single malt warmed his entire being.

Was his position on the moral high ground precarious? He visualised the corruption he had been witness to over the last three months. If it was typical of political manoeuvring throughout European governments he had no doubt that he and men like him would become relied upon to keep the peace. He took another sip from the glass. The Jura was a particularly good single malt.

BRYAN LIGHTBODY

Born in 1968, Bryan Lightbody is the son of a police officer and a teacher. He has served with the Metropolitan Police since 1988, the centenary year of the Jack the Ripper Murders. Inspired by coverage of this fact, he began avidly reading as much as he could on the subject and also watching relevant films and documentaries. This led to a good working knowledge of the crimes, and in 1993 he transferred to duties that brought him to work directly in the area in which the crimes were committed. This allowed the opportunity to observe the area regularly by night in its most atmospheric 'Ripper' sense. By the end of 1998 having left the area to move again to other duties he was inspired to consider writing a book. There are numerous reference books on the subject but few fictional period thrillers actually set during the events; inspired by Anthony Grey's 'Saigon' a historical novel, Bryan wrote his first book. Featuring the central character of Robert Ford, 'Whitechapel' tells the story of the murders of 1888 by placing Ford, a fictional Victorian constable, amidst the investigation.

With the success and acclaimed reviews that Robert Ford's first adventure received, Bryan decided to write a trilogy around his career which will culminate in Ford's final case 'Requiem in Sarajevo'.

Bryan has worked in the Borough of Redbridge, engaged in traffic duties around the East End of London, worked as a car and motorcycle instructor at the police driving school at Hendon and currently works within the Royalty Protection department.

Outside of work he is married with two dogs with interests in motorbikes, cars, theatre, Roman history and archaeology, travel, cinema and of course writing. A screenplay of 'Whitechapel' is currently in development as well the final book of the Robert Ford trilogy.

For more information about Bryan, his work, forthcoming events and book releases visit *www.bryanlightbody.co.uk*.

Printed in the United Kingdom
by Lightning Source UK Ltd.
135453UK00001B/69/P

9 781438 930060